Sept 2015

# WILDERNESS RISING

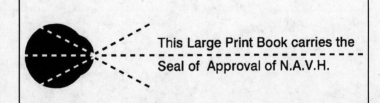

This Large Print Book carries the
Seal of  Approval of N.A.V.H.

# WILDERNESS RISING

## A. L. SHIELDS

**THORNDIKE PRESS**

*A part of Gale, Cengage Learning*

GALE
CENGAGE Learning·

Farmington Hills, Mich • San Francisco • New York • Waterville, Maine
Meriden, Conn • Mason, Ohio • Chicago

## GALE
### CENGAGE Learning

Thorndike Press® Large Print Christian Fiction
The text of this Large Print edition is unabridged.
Other aspects of the book may vary from the original edition.
Set in 16 pt. Plantin.

LIBRARY OF CONGRESS CATALOGING-IN-PUBLICATION DATA

Shields, A. L., 1954–
  Wilderness rising : a church builder novel / by A. L. Shields.
    pages cm. — (Thorndike Press large print Christian fiction)
    ISBN 978-1-4104-7973-0 (hardcover) — ISBN 1-4104-7973-0 (hardcover)
    1. Quests (Expeditions)—Fiction. 2. Secret societies—Fiction. 3.
  Relics—Fiction. 4. Large type books. I. Title.
  PS3619.H535W55 2015b
  813'.6—dc23                                                    2015010214

Published in 2015 by arrangement with The Zondervan Corporation, a subsidiary of HarperCollins Christian Publishing, Inc.

Printed in Mexico
1 2 3 4 5 6 7 19 18 17 16 15

*Once more, for my children*

"For thou hast hid their heart from understanding: therefore shalt thou not exalt them."

Job 17:4

# PROLOGUE

The passport worked. She hadn't really expected it to. The man in Baltimore had explained his scheme, and she had been impressed by its simplicity and its audacity. His plan made sense: so much sense that it seemed odd to her that the Homeland Security people hadn't gotten on to it. Yet she didn't really see how they could. The passport, although not in her name, was genuine, and there was every reason to suppose that it would survive scrutiny. Still, she worried. All the way across the Atlantic she assumed that when she arrived at Heathrow, she would be met by a brace of polite but very serious Britishers who would explain that she was under arrest for murder and heading back to the States on the next flight. When that didn't happen, she guessed that the problem would arise when the pink-cheeked immigration officer ran the passport through his scanner. When that didn't happen, she wondered whether they were waiting until she picked up her bag, just to be sure they had both their fugitive and whatever she was smuggling. When that didn't happen, she inferred that they would snatch her from the bus queue, tug a black hood over her head, and toss her into the back of a van that would carry her off to interrogation at some undisclosed location. But that didn't happen either.

Instead she bumped along unmolested into the city with the rest of the tourists, gawking at the same crumbling buildings they did and wishing she had a camera or at least a cell phone to join them in snapping photographs of everything and everyone. Lacking those basic accoutrements of contemporary life, she sat near the back of the bus, her face buried in a Daniel Silva paperback, even though she had already finished it on the plane.

The bus let her off at Hyde Park Barracks in Knightsbridge, where no Household Cavalry were processing out. Taxis were waiting but she preferred to take her chances on foot, dragging the overnight bag, stopping to peer with shielded eyes into store windows, hoping to catch the reflection of anyone across the street taking too close an interest in her movements. But five weeks living underground had taught her that you never really saw them until it was too late.

She had never imagined that it might be possible to be frightened every minute of every day.

But she was learning.

She left behind the fancy hotels and restaurants of Hyde Park. She hadn't been in this part of London in years, but familiar side streets slowly came back to her. The red brick buildings jammed hard one against the next, each topped with its turrets or gables or crenellations. An Oxford friend, the grandniece of some baronet, had maintained a flat in one of these brick buildings, there to carry on a second or third life beyond the scrutiny of her parents and their set.

A long time ago.

The sun dipped past the topmost towers. The shadows stretched across the street. She walked faster. She did not like being out among the crowds. She found her chosen lodging at the seedier end of a narrow mews. It bore the name and coat of arms of some forgotten knight, who had evidently left behind a considerable cache of weapons and shields fashioned from hard plastic, for they hung from every wall and

11

door. She paid for the room with cash, two nights in advance, and that, too, she imagined would set off all sorts of alarms. When it didn't, she supposed that the front desk must be under instructions not to alert her. But the furtive Russian couple behind her also paid cash, and she allowed herself to remember that she had chosen the place after reading on yelp.com that cash was gleefully accepted.

Her room was spacious but dowdy, the furnishings creaking without quite being old, the view unspectacular without quite being dull. There was no room service. There was no telephone. There was no Wi-Fi. But there was a shower and there was a bed, and these were the things she craved most. Tomorrow she would set off to pursue her true purpose.

A small voice in the back of her mind scolded her hourly for not turning herself in and telling her story. It was even possible that the authorities would believe what she had to say, and set her free rather than send her to death row. But she was skeptical. The evidence against her was too strong.

Besides, whether she liked it or not, there was too much at stake. More than her own freedom rode on the success of her mission.

Her name was Bethany Barclay, but the

name on the passport was different. Until five weeks ago, she had been an unknown lawyer who maintained a small practice in a quiet corner of rural Virginia. Now she was a fugitive sought by the Federal Bureau of Investigation, forced to London to track down a religious artifact that probably didn't exist. But she had to find it anyway. More than her own freedom was at stake. Lives hung in the balance — not all of them her own.

So Bethany showered and changed and lay down on the lumpy bed, praying for the peaceful sleep that had eluded her these past weeks on the run. Tomorrow she would head to Oxford to figure out how her best friend, Annabelle Seaver, could have had a conversation six months ago with a man who'd been dead for two years. Bethany would have asked Annabelle, but she was dead too.

■ ■ ■ ■

# PART ONE:
# BEGGARS AND
# CHOOSERS

■ ■ ■ ■

# ONE

"There's a bishop in São Paulo with his hand in the till," says Ralph Kelvin. "I've spoken to Elliott. His papers will give the story big play."

"Excellent," says Lillian Hartshorne.

Ralph eyes the old woman uneasily. Usually any bit of bad news touching a church will rouse her into an excited tirade about how the inherent contradictions of belief in God must lead inevitably to the final collapse of faith. But she will be eighty-six next month, he reminds himself, and it is possible that age is finally taking its toll.

He tries again. "That mess in Munich last week. Turns out one or two of the rioters were wearing crosses around their necks. If we're subtle and don't push the point too hard, by the end of the month the whole world will be describing it as a mob of fundamentalist Christians."

"Very fine work," says Lillian, her somber

gaze focused beyond the wide windows, out toward the rain-swept grounds of her vast Virginia estate.

Ralph toys with his short, bristly beard. His old friend's listlessness troubles him. They are sitting together in an octagonal conservatory attached to the family wing of her rambling house. The walls and ceiling are mostly glass. On a bright summer's day, sunlight would be streaming in, but as the stormy June dusk settles over the grounds, the room feels sad and gray.

"Is something on your mind?" he finally asks.

"Given my responsibilities, something is always on my mind."

But the effort at snappish derision comes off as merely querulous, and Ralph refuses to be deterred. He is a sometime philosophy professor who's published popular books on subjects ranging from the social culture of the anthill to the history of the Milky Way. At seventy-one, he remains in great demand on the talk show and lecture circuits. He never misses Davos or Sun Valley. He and Lillian have served together on the Council for decades. They have conspired together, kept secrets together, subverted government officials together, authorized the occasional killing together. Lillian is usually bursting

18

with a cynical energy, brilliant and cutting and full of ideas. Ralph has seen her toughness in times of crisis. He has seen her self-possession at moments of personal loss.

He has never seen her like this.

"Is there news of Bethany?" Ralph finally asks, because he cannot imagine another reason for Lillian's listlessness. "Is that why you asked me to come?"

"Apparently two FBI agents stopped her at Dulles." The old woman toys with a lock of the snowy hair she keeps clipped mannishly short. The aged eyes continue to gaze at the landscape. "They interviewed her, and then she boarded a flight to London."

Ralph selects his words with care. "I take it we were involved in the decision to release her."

"Then you take it incorrectly. We had nothing to do with the decision." She clenches a delicate fist on the arm of her chair. "We have assets over there. They've been activated, of course, but we can't tell them where to look. We found out too late to have her flight met."

"I don't understand. Why did the FBI let her go?"

"I have no idea, Ralph. All our people can find out so far is that the agent who let her board the plane is likely to lose his job."

"Maybe it was an accident. Incompetence."

"And maybe pigs have wings."

A brief interruption as Lillian's chief of staff steps inside. He is a slender, arrogant young man named Kenny Atwood, and Ralph secretly considers him slime. Kenny hands his boss a blue message slip and, smirking, leaves the room.

Lillian looks up from the paper. Ralph fancies he can hear her teeth grinding. "It seems they've given her a new code name. They're calling her WAKEFUL. Seems fitting, doesn't it? Our people were asleep on the job, so to speak, and so WAKEFUL got away."

"That's what the note says?"

"Never mind what the note says."

Ralph toys with his coffee cup. He would prefer something stronger, but Lillian, whose doctors no longer allow her to partake, has banned alcohol from the premises.

"What is it you'd like me to do?" he asks.

"I need you to go and see Findrake for me."

Rainstorm or no, Ralph knows that the sudden chill in the room is his imagination, but he fights a shiver all the same. Nobody on the Council mentions Simon Findrake. Ever. The very name conjures madness and mayhem, a past Ralph had thought well buried. And here is Lillian, digging it up again.

So Ralph says nothing and waits for the rest.

Lillian takes her time. She continues to watch the grim gray rain beyond the glass. "I also must ask that you refrain from informing anyone else on the Council where you are going or why."

"You want me to see Findrake without permission from the Council?"

"I alone am Lord Protector. Never forget that. It is for me to decide what the Council hears and doesn't hear."

Actually, Ralph Kelvin remembers no such rule, but this hardly seems the moment to argue the point.

"And why am I going to see . . . that man?"

Slowly, slowly, Lillian swivels toward him. Despite her faded vitality, the pale blue eyes are sharp, almost aglow.

"You are going to see Findrake because I trust you more than I do any other member of the Council. When I depart, you will be running things. Everyone understands that. No, no, spare me your reassurances. They are a waste of precious time. Listen carefully." Her small hands are like fine porcelain on the arms of her chair. "As far as the Council are aware, the reason Bethany Barclay is a threat to us is that she might find the Pilate Stone — if it exists — and turn it over to the adversary."

"You're saying there's another reason?"

"The Pilate Stone is important to us, Ralph. I won't pretend otherwise. But that isn't why you have to see Findrake." Lillian leans toward him now, her small oval face pained and imploring. "Findrake has to be on our side in this Bethany thing. He cannot sit on the sidelines. Only a personal emissary will make him see that."

"I don't understand. I thought the whole point was that Bethany Barclay would follow the breadcrumbs left by her friend Annabelle. And Annabelle was on the track of the Pilate Stone."

"That's not all she was on the track of."

Ralph declines the offer of a guest cottage for the night, so Kenny has a driver sent around to take him back to the city, where he has reserved his usual suite at the Mandarin Oriental with its splendid view of the Potomac River. Tomorrow he has media interviews and, in the evening, a lecture at American University. He hopes the protestors will be out in force. He might even invite a couple up onto the stage. He adores cutting their silly arguments to shreds.

The rain is worse. The town car is crawling cautiously along the narrow country lanes. Farmhouses and weekend McMansions mix uneasily out here, but tonight both are equally invisible in the storm. It is the middle of June and the trees are full and lush, but just now, heavy with water, they sag over the road, low branches brushing the windows like bones.

A photograph.

That is what has Lillian Hartshorne spooked.

A photograph of a silly love-struck girl, taken a long time ago, and stolen by Annabelle Seaver before she was killed.

Ralph leans back and shuts his eyes. He should call his wife to say good night, but he must first let his fury abate. A missing photograph — and so he has to see Findrake. Findrake!

This is not the sort of mistake their side is supposed to make. The Council is smooth and efficient. The fanatics on the other side blunder about constantly, hamstrung as they are by the confusion you'd expect from people who always have to stop and wonder whether they are offending their God.

But this time . . .

This time, a photograph that could bring down the Council is in the wild. Ralph asked the Lord Protector how she knew that the photograph was still hidden.

*Because we haven't been arrested,* she said cheerlessly. *Because we're still alive.*

A photograph.

A photograph for the sake of which Ralph will tomorrow call his agent and cancel the rest of his lecture tour, then board a plane the next day to head for Britain, to meet a man he has profoundly hoped never to see —

"Hang on!" cries the driver, and Ralph bolts upright, just in time to see the onrushing truck as it slams into the car, collapsing the front end and spinning it into a ditch. Upside down. Ralph is stunned, half-conscious, bleeding in the back seat. He can actually see, in the flickering light, a white sliver of bone protruding from his arm.

Odd that there is no pain.

He hears shouts in the darkness. Two men are crouching beside the car. One checks the driver's pulse and nods. The other studies Ralph's broken body, then reaches through the shattered window as if to give him a hand. Instead, he covers the injured man's mouth and pinches his nose shut. Ralph struggles feebly, but his assailant continues to squeeze until the philosopher and sage goes still. His final thought is that the adversary doesn't have the verve to kill in the interests of its mission. The puzzle of who might have orchestrated his murder chases Ralph Kelvin into darkness.

# TWO

Oxford had changed little but prided itself on precisely that. An aching Bethany Barclay alighted from the self-described luxury bus after two crushing hours from London. Had she known her new cryptonym she would have heartily endorsed it, because she had managed little sleep during the trip. The bus had spent most of the journey mired in traffic, and Bethany had felt claustrophobia creep up on her, surrounded as she was by noisy young people and their backpacks and their phones and their tablets and their music, all of them, to her twenty-nine-year-old eye, even more self-involved than she had been at that age. But she was a fugitive, and beggars can't be choosers.

The bus dropped its passengers on the south side of the High Street, just down the block from St. Edmund Hall. The morning was chilly. Wisps of fog clung to the landscape. Bethany stood on the pavement to get her bearings. All Souls was up the road, and she remembered how her moral philosophy tutor had urged her to put in an application for the Examination Fellowship, often described as the most difficult test in the world — and how, having grown up without money, she had decided to return to the States and attend law school instead.

"You probably wouldn't have passed anyway," was Annabelle's clumsy reassurance: but Annabelle was like that. And if Bethany had never set out to discover how her running buddy had died, she would not be on the run from the FBI, and certainly wouldn't be —

"Pardon me," said a young man from close beside her. "Are you in or out?"

At first Bethany thought he must belong to one side or the other — she thought of pretty much everyone that way now — and she began looking around for a place to flee to. Then she realized that he sought no more than entrance to the Queen's Lane Coffee House, and that she, in her moment of reminiscence, was blocking the door.

She walked through the morning haze, the tall Gothic buildings as mighty and intimidating as they were designed to be, even though Bethany had spent two postgraduate years here back in the days when nobody had heard of the iPad or *The Hunger Games,* MySpace was the chic social network, and the American economy was set to grow forever. Studying at Oxford after Barnard had thrilled her. She had grown up in rural Virginia and North Carolina, in a family where even a year of junior college was a rare thing. She had, for the most part, loved her time at Oxford and had always hoped to return.

She could never have imagined the circumstances.

They had taken Janice. It was that simple. Bethany was in Oxford because Janice Stafford, with whom she had spent the past few weeks on the run, was now a prisoner. Janice Stafford, veteran member of BLLNET, considered one of the most dangerous hacker groups in the world. Janice Stafford, about nine different kinds of genius. Janice Stafford, sixteen years old, fresh and excited and optimistic about the world.

And now a hostage to Bethany's performance.

She was worried sick, and worried sick was exactly what they wanted.

Unless Bethany delivered the Pilate Stone in the next two weeks, Janice would die.

The existence of the Pilate Stone had been

rumored for centuries: a limestone block on which Pontius Pilate had left a message relating to the life and works of Jesus Christ.

Annabelle had been on the trail of the Pilate Stone when a car ran her down in Washington three months ago. Bethany was her best friend. That was the reason for her enforced recruitment to Annabelle's mysterious cause. Bethany alone could follow the clues she had left behind, including cryptic notes saying that she had seen the Wise Man. When asked what this might mean, Bethany had professed mystification, but she knew — and Annabelle would have known that she knew. The moral philosophy professor who had tried to push Bethany toward All Souls had been a pompous little tyrant named Adrian Wisdom, and "Wise Man" had been her own secret nickname for him.

She had told no one but Annabelle.

In order to trace Annabelle's peregrinations, therefore, Bethany had no choice but to return to Oxford, to figure out what the Wise Man might have said to her. All in all a very sound plan, except for the minor detail that the Wise Man had died of congestive heart failure two years ago.

Whereas Annabelle's visit — when she

said she saw him — had been six months ago.

Her first thought had been that Annabelle must have been referring to his headstone, but a quick search at an Internet café in Baltimore had turned up the news that Wisdom had been cremated, his ashes scattered at sea, in accordance with his final wish to take up no space that could be put to better use.

And so Bethany was here, back in Oxford at last, tromping through the morning damp as the buildings receded into the thin blue mist. Oxford had to be the place. Whatever Annabelle meant by her claim to have spoken to Adrian Wisdom six months ago, it had to have happened here.

Bethany crossed Magdalen Bridge as students whizzed past on their bicycles and bemused dons sneaked glances at her, trying to remember who she was, because with her tall, strong body, intelligent eyes, and flowing, confident stride, she had to be somebody. Raymond Fuentes, during the single day he'd devoted to briefing her, had told her that two-thirds of fitting in is believing you fit in. Not acting. Believing.

And so Bethany believed. She made eye contact, she smiled, she belonged, anybody could see it, nobody challenged her, even when she joined a pair of early joggers and slipped through the gates into Magdalen College.

Memory hit her like a blow.

Bethany staggered. Suddenly there was no avoiding the harshest of truths: she had been happy here. And, for a bright instant — as she turned a corner on the wide staircase, and the sunlight prisming through the stained glass dazzled her with an infinitude of heavenly color — for that single shining moment, Bethany almost grasped it, the elusive vision of an entire life lived another way, not solitarily but in connection with others, a life in which the books she loved served as adjuncts to relationships rather than substitutes for them. She had fallen in love during her time at Oxford, with a dullard named Plunkett who was reading Modern Languages, poorly, and whose well-regarded family owned bits of land here, bits of water there, and bits of money no place at all. Plunkett, who in his spare time wrote bad love poems with which to court her, had talked eagerly about the two of them settling down on his uncle's Yorkshire estate, raising children, and farming — farming! — and Bethany had run as fast as she could, which was fast indeed, back to the security of her books. She

31

remembered the look of wounded confusion in his doe-like eyes, and how she had ached for him even as she refused his entreaties. Whatever the hole in her life, or in her soul, it would not be filled by the conventional, and when Annabelle asked her once what was so conventional about farming in Yorkshire, Bethany had snarled like a trapped animal.

Then the moment was past, and she was kicking herself for flirting with the temptation to sentimentality. This morning was neither a stroll down memory lane nor the occasion for romanticizing life. This morning was business, and life on the run had taught her that if you let your concentration slip for one second, you could be dead the next.

She found the familiar corner of the building without any trouble because her memory for places was nearly as perfect as her memory for people. She stood on the landing, looking down on the Fellows' Garden, and remembered walking on the cut stone path years ago, watching Plunkett and his new love giggling together a half dozen strides ahead, and leaning down and picking some delicate purple flower and, in a hidden rage, stripping its petals as cruelly as she could —

Bethany shoved the images away, hurried up the stairs, and found herself, as in the old days, before the simple wooden door to Gehringer's rooms.

Gehringer, who played the befuddled Mr. Chips he never quite was; Gehringer, whom all the students loved; Gehringer, who as far as she knew was the only Oxford professor other than the dead Wisdom whom Annabelle had actually met. And Annabelle had made an impression: Bethany remembered that too. Gehringer had told her later that Annabelle had "a most fantastic brain," and wondered aloud whether perhaps the wrong member of the duo had wound up at Oxford.

Surely Annabelle would have stopped here first.

Bethany drew a breath and said a prayer and knocked. Gehringer, by a miracle, was in, although now very old, as well as very fat. She told him her name was McMullen — which was, after all, the name on her passport — and explained that she had been his student a few years back, was in Oxford on business, and had come by to thank him for all of his help years ago. Reciting these lines, Bethany was conscious of not sounding remotely persuasive, but Gehringer said nothing to suggest that he doubted her.

"I remember," he announced, looking her up and down. "No. I'm mistaken. That was someone else. Who are you, exactly?"

She tried again, the same explanation, marveling that he could be so oblivious to her celebrity, or rather notoriety, but the donnish inability to cope with the world beyond academe had been a part of his act even in the old days, and the glint in his silvery eyes said he was putting her on. Perhaps he would be on the phone to the authorities the moment she was out the door, but Bethany doubted it. More likely he would store up this encounter as a good story to be sprung, at a dull moment, upon the High Table.

"McMullen, you say."

"Yes, sir."

"It's splendid to see you again."

Bethany was feeling conspicuous standing in the hallway. She needed to be out of sight, but for that she needed to gain the old man's trust.

"Yes, well —"

The fleshy lips curled into a pout. "But you did say McMullen? Not sure I've had a McMullen. There was a McMatthew, natu-rally — son of the banker, you know. You're not his sister, by any chance?"

"Um, no, sir."

"I'm afraid I'm not much good with names, and — oh, yes. Yes. Barclay. That's your name. Not McMullen. You're the one everybody's looking for. Murder or some nonsense. Terrorism. Dear me. I suppose you'd better come in before one of the students recognizes you and gets grand ideas."

# THREE

He seemed delighted. She was a fugitive from justice, but Gehringer gave her tea and a biscuit anyway. Bethany sat at the same wooden work table where he had tortured her with impossible translations of impenetrable German prose and called her one name after another until she got them right. It was odd, sitting there with the solemn yet haunting second movement of Beethoven's Seventh playing in the background, reminiscing as if she wasn't wanted for murder, and Bethany wondered whether the police might already be on the way. But Gehringer kept on talking, waving his chubby hands as he gossiped airily about classmates she remembered scarcely, if at all.

"Rather surprised you popped in, actually," said Gehringer as he poured the obligatory sherry. "You've been all over the news. Television, BBC, that webatron thing, the lot. 'Oxford-educated lawyer.' That's

what they're calling you. One rather sees the advantage. Man bites dog and so forth. Those we spew forth into the world usually only exploit its resources and its poor. Actual murder is rather rare, so I'm told. Some fool on the television the other night was talking about how lawyers are under all sorts of pressure these days, how they tend to snap and so forth."

Bethany accepted the glass. She said nothing. Her eyes roamed the long parlor, which was as bookish as she remembered: volumes jammed into shelves, stacked on the sills of the leaded windows, tossed in disorder across chairs and tables. They were mostly thick, and looked well read. She saw no television or computer.

"Still," said Gehringer, settling onto a dusty leather chair. "Don't suppose you popped in to tell me your life's story, did you? I hear there's a biggish reward for you. Dear me. Are you going to kill me after I tell you whatever it is you want to know?" Stroking his chin again. "Mmmm. Wonder whether they'd increase the reward if you did? How much do you suppose a professor's life is worth nowadays?"

"I didn't do any of the things they're saying —"

"Oh, no, my dear, no. Put your mind at

ease. There's no earthly reason to try to persuade me one way or the other. Makes no difference to me. I'm not interested in other people's affairs. You seem a sensible young woman. I see no signs of any psychopathology — not that I'm an expert. But I would say that you have your wits about you."

"Thank you, sir."

"What I'm saying is, whatever you did to those people, I have no doubt that they richly deserved it."

Bethany kept quiet. There was no point to further denial. His eyes were wide, but with fascination, not fear. Like Annabelle's sister a few weeks ago, and the FBI agent at the airport more recently, the old man thought that he was interviewing a killer. The difference was that Gehringer seemed absolutely delighted.

"Let me tell you why I'm here," she said.

"Please," said Gehringer, rising to pour himself more sherry. He offered the bottle, but Bethany had not taken a sip. He settled himself again, his expression open and eager. He was having fun.

"I'd like to ask you about a friend of mine. I believe she might have visited you recently. Annabelle Seaver."

"Seaver. Seaver." He cocked an eyebrow

and rolled the name around in his mouth. "Seaver. Never had a student of that name. Not that I recall. Seaver. No."

"She wasn't a student. She was a friend of mine. I introduced her when she visited me —"

"Oh. *Oh!* Annabelle! Why, yes." The flabby lips parted in a laugh that was halfway to being a groan. "Yes. Oh, dear. Oh, my dear girl, of course I remember. You brought her to Christmas cocktails."

"Yes, but that was some years ago. Then this past December I believe she —"

Some Oxford dons take unkindly to interruptions. Others ignore them entirely. Gehringer was of the second school. "Of course. The Bible, wasn't it? Oh, gracious. We fought about it, she and I, didn't we? Yes. Annabelle. Seaver, you say. Let me see. I'm better with ideas than with people. It was the provenance of the Gospels, wasn't it? Or the order of their authorship? Oh, dear." Stroking the chin, which bore the faintest fringes of a snowy beard. "Biblical studies is one's hobby, you understand, not one's profession. Still. One does follow the scholarship."

"Professor —"

"Wait. Ah. Was it the Q source for Luke and Matthew? It was, wasn't it? And you

39

were in the argument, too, weren't you? But, oh, dear. Were you for it or against it? I don't think I recall. You had some crazy notion or other. I remember that part."

"It was about the Farrer hypothesis," she began, but Gehringer did not care for her memories.

"Yes. I remember. You said that the church fathers never mentioned the Q source, and therefore there was no reason to believe it had ever existed. You thought Mark and the available documents were enough without the Q source. Annabelle said you'd need divine inspiration to make that model work, and you said you had no problem with that. I asked you for the evidence, and I seem to recall that things became rather mystical after that. But Annabelle stuck with the case, didn't she? Knew her Bible, even if she didn't believe a word of it." A smile of reminiscence softened the craggy face. "Yes. I remember Annabelle. And you, my dear. I admired your feistiness. I said as much to Matson, but he was a stupid toad. Matson. Wasn't he your tutor?"

"Yes, I —"

"He's something in the City now. Did you know that? Went after the money in the end. Well, they all do nowadays. Some lad comes along, takes a dazzling first in physics, but elementary particles don't pay well, so he's off to the hedge fund, using his brains for the benefit of his investors. Can't blame him, really. Nobody seems to respect scientists any more, except when they're useful to our politics. Dear me. You didn't read science, did you? I don't mean to offend, I'm sure. Matson was analytic philosophy, wasn't he?"

"Jurisprudence —"

"Same silliness. Ideas about ideas. Endless abstractions. No actual facts, you see. Angels on the head of a pin." He focused on her finally. "Barclay. Right. Comes back to me now. We tried to put you down for All Souls. But you went after the money, didn't you? Harvard Law, wasn't it? Never mind. We're not all cut out for the life of the mind. And look where you are now."

Bethany supposed she was being insulted, but with Gehringer you could never be sure.

"Professor, about Annabelle."

"Yes?"

"She — she died."

"Ah." A flicker in the wise old eyes. Perhaps he was wondering whether Bethany's body count stood higher than the newspapers reported. "I see."

"It was a hit-and-run accident, about three months ago." She hesitated. "That was

41

just after she made a trip to Oxford. I think she came here. I think she came to see you."

"Did she?"

"She wanted your help. I'm not sure with what, but given your interest — your hobby, as you put it — it presumably had something to do with the early Christians. I'm hoping that if you tell me what she wanted to know, I might be able to trace her work. To complete her final project, as it were."

Having explained at last what she wanted, Bethany waited. Gehringer frowned, stroked his chin, adjusted his cardigan. His eyes strayed to the grimy window, beyond which morning sunlight was mere rumor. He drummed his fingers, pondering.

"Those people they say you killed," he began. He was teasing his tufted hair. "I thought at first it had to be rather *currente calamo,* if you see what I mean. I believe I mentioned it in the common room to one or two souls, who wondered whether you might be some sort of psychopath." He caught her expression. "Oh, yes. Everyone is talking about you. Why, the other day I was chatting with a colleague who I suspect had never clapped eyes on you in his life but who immediately recalled yours as among the finest brains ever to pass through his hands."

"Sir —"

"Yes. Well. Where was I? Ah. Yes. You're not out of control at all, are you? Seeing you now, so practical and focused, well, it occurs to me that you must have some sort of plan. This isn't a lark, but neither is it an accident. You're looking for something, aren't you? Same as Annabelle was." Gehringer shifted his jaw like a man chewing on something sticky but not unpleasant. "Possibly the same something, hmmm?"

After which, to Bethany's immense relief, he didn't bother to fence, but told her straight off, with sufficient detail that she began to wonder whether everything up to this point had been playacting.

Harry Stean was in the main dining room of the Dorchester hotel, breakfasting on eggs and toast and reading the *Times*. He still preferred the print edition. People who caught up with the news on their phones and tablets reduced the world to a stream of data rather than a set of tangible sources, weighty material that took up space and was therefore worthy of being pondered. That, at least, was his view.

Harry was a large man, broad in size, and in gesture, and in personality. People made space for him and accepted his small oddities. He wouldn't have wanted it any other way. He was determined to remain a rock of his own generation. He had no interest in imposing his preferences on anyone else, and he wished fervently that fewer people were determined to impose their preferences on him.

In his overt life, Harry was an architect specializing in the design of grand cathedrals. He had built them around the world, a happy circumstance that supplied the official explanation for his presence in London. Later today a driver would take him down to Coventry to study the new St. Michael's Cathedral — "new" meaning, in this case, that it had been standing only for a bit more than half a century — because a client of his in Argentina wanted one just like it.

That was the official explanation.

Unofficially, he was in Britain because Bethany Barclay was. He wasn't sure just where in the country she might be found, but he was determined to track her down. It was Harry's plan that had put her in motion and led to the series of mishaps that nearly took her life. He hoped to persuade her to return to the United States, even though she would be arrested the moment she stepped off the plane. In the custody of the federal government, she would be worlds safer than she was here, on her quixotic journey to find the Pilate Stone. The authorities wouldn't harm a hair on Bethany Barclay's head. She would never go to trial. There was enough doubt about her guilt now at the highest levels of government: the Senator said so, and her sources were the best. Certainly Bethany would be placed in protective custody, and she'd be interrogated, probably for weeks. After that, the professionals would take over and clean up the mess that Harry and his colleagues had helped create.

He hoped.

In his other, covert life, Harry was known as the Church Builder, or, more often, simply the Builder. The organization he headed called itself the Garden. For hundreds of years, they had done battle against a cunning enemy they called the Wilderness. The Wilderness — or the Council, as it styled itself — had set itself a simple mission upon its founding in the late sixteenth century: the destruction of religious faith in all of its forms, but with a special emphasis on the elimination of Christianity.

The Garden formed a few decades later to work covertly to thwart the Council's designs. The battle had been raging ever since. But the Church Builder had begun to feel uneasy about his own side's methods.

Last year, the Garden sent off Annabelle Seaver to infiltrate the enemy. When she was killed, they manipulated an unknowing Bethany Barclay into following her trail. They had known, of course, that the mission would entail a degree of risk. They had never imagined that she would wind up —

The Builder let out a gasp, and his hand went to his abdomen.

A waiter was beside him at once, but Harry waved him away.

"I'm fine. I'm fine."

But he wasn't fine, and, as he climbed shakily to his feet and hobbled his way toward the lobby, everyone in the dining room could see. The pain was worse today. Worse than it had been in some while. He would go up to his suite and take a pill and rest until the car arrived.

They had warned him that this would happen if he refused the surgery. Before too many more months passed, the pain would be all there was. The Church Builder was willing to deal with that when it came.

As long as he had the chance to save Bethany first.

# FOUR

"Annabelle wanted to know about a manuscript," said Gehringer, leaning back in the
chair as the leather crackled agreeably. He
crossed one plump thigh over the other. "A
manuscript, maybe the notes and so forth
behind it sort of thing."

"What manuscript?" she asked too
quickly, but Gehringer was enjoying center
stage too much to allow himself to be
rushed.

"I'm surprised she didn't tell you. Didn't
I hear somewhere that you and she were
best friends?"

"We were. Yes."

"Mmmm. You'd have thought she'd trust
you. I don't suppose you have any evidence?
Proof that Annabelle trusted you?"

"No," said Bethany, very surprised. "What
kind of evidence did you have in mind?"

He shrugged. "A letter of introduction. A
token of some kind."

She shook her head. "I'm sorry, Professor. I don't have anything like that. You'll have to take my word for it."

Gehringer gave her a long, shrewd look, and for a moment she saw clearly the razor-sharp mind behind the flannel. Then he leaned back in the chair, steepled his long fingers, and looked at the ceiling. And it was odd how, in that instant, she sensed that whatever he was about to tell her had been edited from a larger truth; that Annabelle had sparked loyalty even here, in the strangest of corners.

"Well, well," he said to the light fixtures. "You want to know what Annabelle wanted."

"Yes. I do."

"Ah, well. You'll remember Adrian Wisdom, of course."

"Certainly I remember." She hid her relief that he had raised the name without her having to ask.

"He did the early Christians, poor fellow. Not much market for that knowledge in these degenerate days. Not that one is a God man, mind. But the Bible is the most influential book in the history of the West — maybe the world — and Christianity is the most influential movement — note that I do not say *religion* — in Western culture.

To the extent that our great universities, for the sake of being inoffensive, choose to turn away from teaching about Christianity and the Bible, they are hiding the great ideas on which Western civilization rests."

He paused, as if waiting for her to write this down, and this time Bethany was wise enough not to interrupt.

"Well. That was Adrian's field, you see. Seems to me he was your professor too, wasn't he? That's where you got those ideas you were spouting at us over Christmas cocktails, I suppose. From listening to Adrian and his pearls of . . . well, of wisdom, you know."

She smiled dutifully. Gehringer scarcely noticed. His gaze had settled on the middle distance, and she knew that in his head he was far away.

"Well. Yes. Mmmm. We were friends, Adrian and I, after a fashion. Not that he hadn't his share of mad ideas, but I suppose he must have thought the same about me. We both admired Heine, you know, and of course Goethe, even though Adrian's view of that Charlotte von Stein business was rather antediluvian. One had to set him straight now and then, and — never mind. You wanted to hear about Annabelle."

"Please."

"She dropped by with as little ceremony as you. Dear me. December, you said? I suppose it could have been. She asked if I remembered her, and of course I did — that whole business about Q — and then she wanted to know about Adrian. Funny, in a way. First, she wanted to know how he died."

"Surely she'd have looked that up online somewhere."

"Yes. Yes. These days, from what I can gather, young people hop on that webatron thing and have all the facts at their fingertips, including facts that aren't facts at all." He cocked his eyebrow the way he used to when preparing to zing you, but just now he was signaling only puzzlement. "I suppose she'd done that, hadn't she? She knew he was dead, after all."

"I understand he died of heart disease."

"Yes, well, your Annabelle didn't believe that. She kept asking me how Adrian really died. Said I was his closest friend, you see, so I'd be bound to know." He drummed his fingers. "Curious. In a way, I suppose I should have been flattered, shouldn't I? That she'd think I might know more than what she could find on the webatron, I mean. People think otherwise, you know. Young people especially, I'm sorry to say.

They see me doddering about in my gown and imagine I've gone gaga. But I have some years left, my dear. I have the book on Heine and Marx to finish. You'll know of course that they became acquainted in Paris. The traditional interpretation is that they were friends, or at least admiring colleagues, but I intend to show that if one parses the final correspondence, with proper attention to the German idiom of the period — never mind. Never mind. Um. Right. Where were we?"

"Annabelle asked you how Wisdom really died."

"Yes. Well, one can only respect the privacy of the departed for so long. So I told her the truth."

Bethany sat straighter. "Are you saying he didn't have heart disease?"

"Of course he did. Don't jump to conclusions. I remember that about you, come to think of it. Always leaping ahead. Wanting to know the answer. The journey, my dear. Remember? The journey is more important than the destination. That's the key to the life of the mind."

"Sir, about Adrian Wisdom —"

"There isn't much to tell. Adrian was sick. He'd had the surgery. Valves. Grafts. Stents. Something. I don't know the details. He was getting worse, and, to be frank, he hadn't long anyway. We managed to keep it out of the papers. That was the only blessing. Helped with the insurance, made it easier for the family. And of course it enabled him to be buried in consecrated ground."

"You mean —"

"I mean Adrian'd had enough of the pain and the fear. So one fine afternoon he walked up into the hills and blew his brains out. Goodness knows where he got the gun."

A silence as they both contemplated the tragedy: Gehringer mourning his friend, and Bethany too stunned to speak, as she began, dimly, to see what Annabelle must have seen.

"Well," said the old man suddenly. "Perhaps you've tarried long enough. I have no doubt that there are places you need to be. Or, perhaps, my dear, given your predicament, there are places you need *not* to be —"

"Professor, please. Just another couple of questions."

"Yes, well, one would love to chat all day, but, alas, one has one's duties —"

This time desperation made her bold, and she spoke right over him. "Please. Annabelle didn't just come here to ask about his cause of death. She must have wanted more than that."

Gehringer shrugged. "I'm not sure what you want me to say, my dear. She asked after his family, I suppose. How they were bearing up." He was studying his wristwatch. "That sort of thing."

The trained lawyer pounced. "But she also asked about a manuscript. That's what you said. Annabelle was looking for a manuscript."

"Yes. Yes. Indeed she did. I forgot for a moment is all. Yes. She wanted to know about Pilate."

"Pilate? Pontius Pilate?"

"Surely there's no other Pilate who might be the subject of academic conversation." A coughing laugh. "Yes. Well. Professor Wisdom worked on that Pilate biography for a decade. You remember, surely. Adrian had come into possession of some early sources, and he wanted to use them to present a new image of the man. Or was it to reinforce the old image? Oh, dear. I don't think I knew." A moment's distress. "Naturally, one argued with him. If he had new sources, he should be publishing in the journals, presenting them to the profession, not hoarding them in order to make a profit from some vulgar book. It wasn't to be an academic tome, mind. He intended it for a commercial press." He made *commercial* sound like the enemy army. "You knew, didn't you? About the biography? He adored you. Naturally he'd have told you about it?"

"No, sir. I never knew."

"And Annabelle never told you?"

"No, sir."

"A search of such importance, and she never confided in you? Well, well." He swiveled this way and that, clucking. "And no note from her either. Pity. Ah, well. Where was I?"

"The Pilate biography."

"Yes. Well. Curious. Um. He never finished. That's the point. He never published. I believe intervening work cast doubt on some of the sources he planned to use, and, just like that, ten years of research down the drain."

"He never finished," she repeated.

"No."

"But he had early sources. Sources nobody else had."

"I don't know who else had them. Adrian did tell me that nobody else had written what he was planning to write. He said it would blow the lid off things. Those were his very words, my dear. Blow the lid off."

"Did he ever show you the manuscript?"

"I'm afraid not. There were days, you

54

know, when I wondered whether he was actually making any progress. So often, you know, in the academy, people talk as though they're writing away, and then when you finally have a look, two years later, they have all of five pages."

"Do you have any idea what became of his research? His notes?"

"Annabelle asked the same. I told her I'd no idea. I suggested she check the archives at Merton, but she'd done that already, it seems. I'm afraid I hadn't any more ideas than that."

A Pilate biography. That was what Annabelle was after. Wisdom's biography, and, of course, his sources. The early sources that had come into his possession. And she'd approached Gehringer first, before speaking to the family, because she was wondering about that cause of death. Wondering if his passing was a little bit too convenient.

Two years ago. Adrian Wisdom had shot himself two years ago. Just about the time —

"And that was all she wanted? Nothing else?"

"Well, she did ask about poor Wisdom's family, naturally," said Gehringer in the same musing tone. "Said she hated to trouble them. Asked me how they were holding up and so forth."

It was beginning to come together. Annabelle's visit to Gehringer had not been altogether necessary. But it served a purpose after all.

"I seem to remember that he had two children," said Bethany.

"Yes, well, the son died, oh, three years ago. Four. Automobile accident, if I recall correctly. Daughter's the only one left. Dorothea." Gehringer was on his feet, moving to the desk. "I suppose you'll want to visit her next. Annabelle did."

"I suppose I might."

"Well, be careful. Dorothea's rather prickly. A hedgehog. She's a bit of an academic herself. Some kind of science, if I remember correctly, which I do. Ran as far from her father's field as she could."

"Where does she live?"

"Not far from here. I'll write it down." Scrounging in the hopeless desk for a clean piece of paper. "Funny."

"What's funny?"

"Adrian blows his brains out. Annabelle comes along and asks after him, and she goes under a car." He handed her the note. "Who knows, my dear? Maybe you're next."

# FIVE

In Manhattan it was the wee hours of the morning. Elliott St. John stood on the terrace of his triplex apartment high above Fifth Avenue. He loved the view. As he loved life itself. His family was secure. His fortune was secure. His media empire was secure. His life nevertheless was full of stress. Although he often slept poorly, he usually found, even in the midst of his worries, that the intricate patterns woven by the glittering lights of the city soothed him. But not just now. Just now one soft, trembling hand gripped the railing. The other held a mobile phone to his ear.

A special mobile phone, its transmissions secured by a proprietary chip that not even the National Security Agency was able to unscramble.

Supposedly.

"Morgan!" he cried, in fear as well as fury. "Why on earth would you send Morgan?"

"Because Morgan's the best we have by a mile. Far better than that grubby professor we set on her last time."

Elliott forced himself to calm down. He was speaking, after all, to Lillian Hartshorne, the Lord Protector: the leader of the group that called itself the Council, although its enemies called it the Wilderness.

"Morgan is retired. That's what you told us —"

"For a sufficient payment, most people will unretire."

"Yes, but even so, Morgan — Morgan is a killer."

The Lord Protector laughed rarely. When she did, the sound was like long icicles sliding off the roof: tinkling and pleasant, yet heavy at the same time, warning you to stay out of the way.

"Morgan is more than that, Elliott. Far more."

"Yes, but —"

"Yes, but. No, but. It isn't your call, it's mine. Don't worry. Morgan isn't tasked with doing away with her. For the moment, his only assignment is to observe and record."

"But why is it even necessary? It seems an unnecessary risk. You told the Council you'd taken out insurance. You said Bethany won't have any choice but to do what we want."

"I'm simply making assurance double sure. We have to know everything."

"Because of the Pilate Stone."

"Incorrect. To you, as I well know, everything is about the Pilate Stone. And the Stone does matter. But the Council has larger concerns, Elliott. At this moment, Bethany Barclay poses an enormous danger to us. Not to our plans — to us, to ourselves. To the members of the Council."

"I don't see how that's possible."

"You don't have to see. There are things you don't know. Things you cannot be permitted to know. For the moment, what matters is that we know where Bethany goes. Whom she sees. What side deals she's tempted to make. And who better than Morgan to watch her without being noticed?"

Elliott shut his eyes briefly. The night wind tousled his hair. Surely the Lord Protector didn't know about his own effort to make a side deal with WAKEFUL.

Lillian Hartshorne and the rest of the Council wanted the Pilate Stone in the hope of doing serious damage to the church. The fools over in the Garden wanted the Pilate Stone to keep it out of the hands of the

Council. Elliott St. John had no ideological agenda. He wanted the Stone for himself. For his private collection. Nobody else in the world but he and his curators need ever know that it even existed — much less that he possessed it. He supposed that this was what it meant to covet. Well, fine. He was a covetous fellow. Elliott had coveted wealth and power, and he had achieved both. A media empire spanning five continents didn't fall into one's lap by accident. To his mind, covetousness was a virtue, not a sin. Ambition was irrelevant unless you knew what you wanted.

Bethany had never said yes to Elliott's proposal, but she had never said no. The magnate had his hopes that she would still come around. But this time his covetousness could cause serious trouble. If the Council found out —

"I'm sure you know best," he finally said.

"Yes," said the Lord Protector. "I do." A dry pause. "But I always value your advice, dear Elliott. I hope your tenure on the Council is a long one."

"As do I, Protector."

A long pause. It was unlike Lillian Hartshorne to have trouble finding words. "There's something else, Elliott, dear. Some unfortunate news." Again the uncharacteristic hesitation. "Ralph Kelvin is dead."

"Poor Ralph. What was it? His heart finally?"

"No, you ninny. Not his heart. He was killed." A pause to let this sink in. "Not ten miles from my house. It was made to look like an accident, but it wasn't an accident."

Elliott's fingers were trying to dig into the concrete of the balustrade. Suddenly he was worried about his own heart.

"Do we know who?" he managed, faintly. "Do we know why?"

"There's really only one possibility."

"The Garden?"

"Don't be obtuse. You know who I'm talking about."

"Findrake? Are you saying it was Simon Findrake?"

"Of course it was Findrake." She drew in a breath. "I'd just asked Ralph to see him for me. I suppose Findrake couldn't have known that. Now I'll have to send somebody else."

"You — surely you don't expect —"

"Not you, you ninny." Affectionately this time. "Findrake despises you. With reason." The same chuckle, sliding ice. "Besides, I'm sure Findrake was just making a point. I doubt very much that you're in physical danger."

He knew there was no point in asking the obvious. "And what am I supposed to do in the meantime?"

"The same thing as the rest of us. Wait."

She hung up, as always, without a good-bye. Elliott stood looking out over the city he often felt he owned. It had seemed so simple, twelve, thirteen years ago, when the Council had approached him. They'd made it sound like a sort of discussion group, like-minded people with the resources to —

Never mind. Never mind. He had business to attend to. He switched phones, woke his executive assistant, and told her he wanted the bodyguards doubled for himself and every member of his family.

"Effective when?" asked his assistant, unfazed by either the request or the early hour.

"Immediately. This morning if you can, tomorrow if you must."

"We can do it this morning, Mr. St. John. Two hours at the outside."

*I've taken out insurance,* the Lord Protector had told the Council. She hadn't told the Council how, and nobody dared ask.

Insurance against Bethany, she meant. But against Findrake, Elliott preferred to have his own protection.

Still, he wondered what insurance Lillian could have taken out. What could she do, from her redoubt in Virginia, to keep Bethany Barclay on a leash? Especially if they didn't know precisely where Bethany was? She would have to be holding something Bethany valued very much.

Elliott wondered what it might be.

The same wee hour. Janice Stafford was trying to sleep. She had two pillows over her head, and the comforter over the pillows, but the house was still too noisy. The people assigned to watch her didn't seem to care that their loud and occasionally bawdy changing of the guard would wake their unwilling guest. At least she knew it was six in the morning. Shift change.

Janice had the guard shifts memorized — three women, three men, working in teams of two — and she had given them names, if only in her head, because no matter how polite or playful or wheedling she was, they refused to tell her very much. From the barred and triple-glazed windows of her bedroom she could see that she was being held in a residential neighborhood. Across the street was a white ranch-style house, and on the front lawn a pickup truck was mounted on blocks. She had no idea what town she was in, or even what state, but she was sure that if she had any way of reaching anybody, she could pass along these clues, and they could find her before —

Well, before whatever was going to happen happened.

A thirtyish man called Kenny, who had greeted her on her arrival at the house, had explained that Bethany Barclay was "doing a little job for us," and that they planned to release Janice just as soon as the job was done. Kenny was the only one of her captors who had offered a name, and she assumed it wasn't his true one. He had refused to answer any of her questions: to tell her, for example, who the "us" might be. Of course, Janice had her suspicions, but when she had asked him point-blank whether she was a guest of the Wilderness, Kenny had only smiled his condescending smile and suggested that she try to relax.

"You could be with us for a while," he'd said.

Still, they were taking good care of her. There was plenty of food, there was bottled water and juice, there were books to read, there were board games to distract her, there were yellow pads on which she could puzzle over the great unsolved mathematical theorems of the age. Yesterday they let her leave the room and took her down to the basement, where there was exercise equipment. The guards were polite, if not exactly friendly, and had even brought newspapers when she asked. But she had no access to anything digital. No computer, no phone, no television. In desperation she had managed to open the faceplate over one of the bedroom's electrical outlets, but even sticking her fingers in the walls, she could tell that she was nowhere near the cable that carried the Internet signal. And had she reached it, she had nothing to plug in.

She had been here three days now and could think of no way out.

But puzzles were Janice's best thing, and the bedroom in which she was imprisoned was just another. Janice Stafford was sixteen years old, a slight, short black girl with long braids and an inestimably brilliant mind. She'd begun taking college courses at age fourteen, and when she bothered to pay attention, she could solve the most challenging math and science problems with little more than a glance.

She was confident that she would solve this one too.

# Six

Bethany took her time, preferring a circuitous route to the neighborhood, the better to lose surveillance. She had learned in her weeks on the run that hurrying could be fatal. Nor could she outrun a phone call to the authorities. If Gehringer turned her in, she was lost anyway. Meanwhile, she had things to work out.

She used her illicit passport to rent a bicycle. She wasn't sure how much longer she could pass herself off as Elaine McMullen. The broker back in Baltimore had explained his simple system: he purchased passports from people not planning any international travel soon, who weeks or months later would declare them missing. Until then, the user was unlikely to be caught.

Until the day when the biometric revolution would sweep the broker's business aside.

Bethany rode the bicycle well up into the hills, the way she used to in her student days when a professor had embarrassed her, or Plunkett had wounded her. She chose the steepest road she could find, wanting the punishment, and her thighs burned with the effort. She found a promontory where she could sit on a boulder and look down at the university and lose herself in her thoughts. But sitting turned out to be too much of a burden, because all she could think about was how she'd lost Annabelle and probably Janice as well. She rode farther from campus and found meadows through which to hike, confident at last that no team of watchers could let her get this far ahead without showing themselves.

She forced herself to keep walking, because the more time she spent away from her goal, the harder it would be for anyone to predict where she might be going.

They had Janice. They were going to kill her if Bethany didn't deliver the Pilate Stone within two weeks. Probably they were going to kill her anyway.

Which was where Raymond Fuentes came in.

Fuentes was a strange man, formerly a seminary student and employee of the Central Intelligence Agency. Bethany didn't pretend to understand his motives for helping her, but without his assistance she wouldn't be in Britain. Probably she wouldn't be alive. He had helped Bethany escape a deadly trap in New Hampshire. He had outwitted the federal dragnet to spirit her to Dulles Airport, where he had seen her safely onto the plane bound for London.

And he had promised to find Janice.

Of course, Bethany had no sure knowledge that he would succeed. But if anyone could free Janice from whoever was keeping her, it was Raymond Fuentes.

Marching through the high grass, Bethany had found herself wondering, not for the first time, about her own motives. Yes, she needed to find the Pilate Stone to save Janice, and yes, she wanted to do it as a tribute to her late friend Annabelle. But if she was honest with herself, there was another reason.

She wanted the evidence that the Pilate Stone could provide.

That was the hard truth.

Bethany had been raised in North Carolina by a stern aunt for whom faith in God was as natural as breathing. John 20:29 had been Aunt Claudia's answer to every question: "Blessed are they that have not seen, and yet have believed." Bethany counted herself as a believer, but there were moments when she caught herself wondering —

Wanting evidence —

And today was one of them —

The Pilate Stone. Words about Jesus, carved in limestone by the prefect of Judea. From the moment Bethany had heard of the Pilate Stone, she had longed in her secret heart to lay eyes on it.

Just to look. Just once.

It was well into the afternoon before Bethany returned to Oxford, where she paid cash to reserve a room at a pretty bed-and-breakfast on the edge of town — just in case she needed options — before making her way to Dorothea Ziman's sad little semidetached house. It was nicely located, not two blocks from the shopping district where Bethany had stopped for a snack. But it was also small and low and old and painted a blinding white. It was shaded by thick, unruly trees, one of which bore gnarled, unhealthy looking fruit.

After a brief reconnaissance, she parked her rented bicycle inside the decorative iron fence. A sopping wet doll sat in a red wagon on the shared front walk, but Bethany suspected the toys belonged to the house next door, because even at this hour, and even out on the front walk, she could hear children inside screaming and a mother loudly shushing them with a multitude of threats that she would never carry out. Bethany stood on the creaking porch of Dorothea's home and rang the bell and waited. There was no answer, no footfall, no doused sound. The television was on; she could hear it from here. She rang again and waited again. She turned and studied the street, which was jammed with cars. She should have asked gossipy Gehringer what, if anything, Dorothea drove. She rang a third time and had decided to give up when the door of the other house popped open and a little head emerged. Wary juvenile eyes glared from a fat, grimy face. The head vanished. The door remained open. Bethany waited. The mother appeared, last night's hairnet shakily in place, her expression pinched and unhelpful, as though she had been awakened from a very short sleep after a very long drunk.

The woman muttered what sounded like a foreign language, but was more likely the hangover victim's equivalent of *Who are you and what do you want?*

Bethany smiled brightly and, she hoped, a

little vacuously. "I'm looking for Dorothea. I'm a friend of hers from the States. My name is Elaine. Elaine McMullen." She hoped there was no public alert for the name on her passport.

"Did you ring the bell?"

"Three times."

"Maybe she's not home. Sorry, dearie." The door was about to close.

"The television's on."

"She had a friend over."

"Someone you recognized?"

"I don't spy on my neighbors."

"Was this last night?" Bethany knew her tone was growing less cheery and more interrogatory but the lawyer inside her was suddenly wide awake.

The neighbor squinted, screwing up her entire face as she struggled to grab the facts from an aching head. "Could be. Maybe the night before."

"I don't think she'd leave the television on for two days. Do you?"

The woman opened her bleary eyes wider, looking the stranger up and down. "Well, I'm not giving you the key."

"You're the landlady?"

"Yes. And I'm only a drunk. I'm not a fool." The door slammed. Bethany's instinct now was flight. She was being both conspicuous and memorable — exactly what she was trying to avoid. With the neighbor alerted, the police might soon be on the way. She should go. Now.

The trouble was, she had no lead aside from Dorothea, and no way to conjure one. To turn back now was to turn back for good. She studied the door, estimating its strength, but knew that breaking in would only make matters worse. Bethany considered her options and had actually turned to go, retrieving her bicycle, when the neighbor's door opened a third time, and the landlady stepped out again, still in her robe but now with a light jacket over it, and the key in her hand.

"Well, come on," she said.

"What?"

"I might be willing to open the door for you, but I'm not going in there." A pause, then a dreary, sodden smile. "But you look like you really need to." *Tell me how much it's worth to you,* her drunken face invited.

# SEVEN

In Charlottesville, Virginia, it was late morning. Raymond Fuentes strolled across the sprawling Jeffersonian beauty of the University of Virginia. He was near the center of the campus, what those who loved the school liked to call the Academical Village. The students passing him were a considerably more diverse bunch than those who would have populated the Lawn a couple of generations ago. U Va, as it was known, was one of several colleges his sister, Megan, had tried. She had lasted a year and a half before being booted out over some disciplinary problem that she still refused to discuss. But given that she didn't do drugs and wasn't the type to cheat or steal, he suspected that it had to do with one of her political protests. Meg used to say that the Ten Commandments prohibited coveting and stealing but not the destruction of property. And given that she considered private property to be sin itself, she was able to persuade herself — in intellectual terms, anyway — that destroying it, if done peacefully, was justice. Their parents had reminded her that according to the book of Exodus, burning another man's crops was counted as stealing. But Meg remained unmoved.

Although he had spent time at a seminary, Fuentes never much cared for the academy. He was more comfortable lying motionless on a hilltop along the Helmand River in Afghanistan, clad in the *salwar kameez* and *chapan* of the Afghan tribesman, concealed by the underbrush as he called in a drone strike on a terror target. He was equally comfortable in Pico-Union, a neighborhood of Latino immigrants in Los Angeles, where he'd planted a storefront church beneath the belligerent glares of blue-clad members of Mara Salvatrucha, known popularly as MS-13, one of the most violent street gangs in the world. In his time Fuentes had played both roles, and although he would never say so, he had played them rather well.

A college campus, by contrast, he found to be a profoundly alienating place. He was not anti-intellectual. He admired the accomplishments of the mind and believed that a life that consisted of learning and teaching was a life well spent. The tragedy was the hauteur and hubris that so often accompanied collegiate life. It infected faculty and students alike. The denizens of the academy too often saw themselves as morally superior to their fellows, forgetting that their remarkable brains were God's gifts, to be used for God's purposes.

He hoped the professor he was about to visit wasn't in that mold.

Before putting Bethany Barclay safely on the plane to London, Fuentes had made her a promise. He was going to rescue Janice Stafford from wherever she was being hidden. His theory was simple. Whoever had taken Janice wanted to use her to pressure Bethany to locate and turn over the Pilate Stone. Ergo, whoever held Janice wanted the Pilate Stone. Ergo, if he could find out who wanted the Pilate Stone most, he just might have the vital clue he needed.

Fuentes was a man who kept his word. Today's visit was the next step.

"The Pilate Stone," said Professor Yu. He swiveled in his desk chair and steepled his hands. "Well, well. If I'd known the artifact you wanted to discuss was the Pilate Stone, Mr. Fallon, we could have done this over the telephone."

Fuentes smiled his best ingratiating smile. "Then I'm grateful I didn't tell you. Believe me, my interest is serious. And everybody says you're the man to see."

"Do they? Mmmm." Yu seemed disturbed at the notion. His chair rocked as well as swiveled and now he was moving forward and back. He was a beanpole of a man, a bundle of nervous energy, but Fuentes could sense the power of the brain pulsing behind the darting eyes. The office was pristine. There were several computer monitors and two laptops. A few books were scattered on the shelves. There was almost no paper. Most of the shelf space and both of the end tables held tasteful cubes of shaded glass, protecting tiny relics: the fruit of his archaeological digs. Jonathan Yu was among the foremost students of Near East relics in the world and easily the most prominent within an easy drive of the nation's capital.

"These artifacts are beautiful," said Fuentes, trying to make a connection.

His host was unimpressed. "Don't get the idea that they're mine. I don't believe in private ownership of the world's patrimony. These are all part of museum collections. They loan them to me for display here in my office. I like to look at them, but they turn over every six months. I don't want to become attached, you see."

"That makes perfect sense to me."

"People do that. They get attached to the artifacts. Collectors bid fortunes for them. Writers do fantastic and inaccurate stories about them. Religious cults are built around them."

"I don't do inaccurate stories, Professor Yu. That's why I'm here. They tell me you're the expert."

The archaeologist gave a little sigh that might have been disapproval or pride. The mouth never moved but one eyebrow went up. He looked, for an instant, exactly like Mr. Spock. "I googled you, Mr. Fallon. You don't look much like your pictures."

"You look exactly like yours," said Fuentes, who had chosen, with regret, to impersonate a journalist whom he roughly resembled. Then he pressed on at once, knowing that if he didn't take control of the interview he would never get it back. "So, the Pilate Stone. There's an artifact by that name in the Israel Museum. A limestone carving from the first century, inscribed by Pontius Pilate, apparently the dedication of some building. Apart from the New Testament and some later Roman sources, it's pretty much the only artifact supporting the existence of Pilate."

"You've done your homework, I see."

"The trouble is, there have always been rumors of a second stone, also known as the Pilate Stone. Back in the nineteenth century, I understand, there were expeditions to locate it. It's never been found. A lot of people think it never existed."

Professor Yu was nodding. His animation was taking on an intellectual focus. "It might well not exist, Mr. Fallon. But, logically, it should."

The archaeologist had settled into didactic mode, and didactic mode was what Raymond Fuentes, a natural listener, liked best.

"Let's take it as common ground that Pontius Pilate existed. He was a Roman prefect of Judea during the ministry of Jesus. Now, we have it attested by Philo of Alexandria, who was a contemporary, that Pilate was spiteful and weak. He offended the traditions of the Jews of Judea, possibly by intention but more likely through inadvertence, or even incompetence, because the Roman policy elsewhere was to leave their conquered subjects to their ways. Josephus argues that Pilate was perfectly competent but lacked good political instincts. He didn't know how to avoid offense. In any case, for whatever reason, Pilate offended the Jewish leaders. When they protested, says Philo, Pilate lacked the courage to admit his error. So they applied to the emperor Tiberius, who chastised Pilate harshly. Or so Philo says."

"Excuse me, Professor. I'm not sure I see the relevance."

"Then you're not thinking." There was no condemnation in his tone. "Consider. Philo might well have had reasons of his own for portraying Pilate as small-minded. But suppose his portrait is accurate. How would an incompetent like Pilate, a man already having trouble controlling the people of Judea, respond to the sudden appearance of a revolutionary miracle worker in the midst of his rebellious province? A miracle worker whose followers called him their king?"

"He'd want to be rid of him."

"He would indeed. He might incite the local leaders to do it for him, because he'd want to be able to say later that it wasn't his fault. Even back then, it was always convenient to blame the Jews. Again, you see Pilate's weakness at work. But consider. What would this spiteful weakling do after the miracle worker was dead?"

Fuentes found himself falling easily into the Socratic rhythm. Jonathan Yu was probably a wonderful classroom teacher.

"He'd deny that there were ever any miracles."

"Precisely. And that's one of the great mysteries of archaeological history. Why are there no contemporaneous letters or other works by Pilate denying the miracles?" The professor held his thin arms wide. "For a long time, various trendy historians have argued that either Pilate never existed to write the letters or Jesus never existed to work the miracles and have Pilate deny what He'd done. But archaeology and history, although related, aren't the same discipline. What archaeologists understand, and historians hate to admit, is that sometimes ancient records are simply lost. They are buried in a monastic archive or burned when one city-state conquers another, or they simply crumble to dust. It's always seemed to me most likely that Pilate would indeed have penned such denials — and that they're probably lost."

"So, the Pilate Stone —"

"The Pilate Stone, if it exists, and if it survives, would likely be a denial. You do see the point, don't you? Whether the miracles really happened or not, it would have been in Pilate's interest to deny them. So if there is indeed an extant carving somewhere that sets down Pilate's account of what happened, the carving will almost certainly deny the miracles. As a matter of fact, it would be odd indeed if Pilate hadn't left some sort of record of his side of the story."

"Why a carving? Why not a letter to Rome?"

"There might well have been a letter to Rome, because the tale of Jesus' miracles probably reached that far. Surely the emperor would want to know who was disturbing the peace of his realm. But the letters, if any, are long gone. Fortunately, the Romans believed in carving messages that would stand for the ages. Much of our history of the period is confirmed by plaques or headstones or — in the case of the Pilate Stone that's in the Israel Museum in Jerusalem — the cornerstone of a building expected to endure."

Fuentes consulted his notes because it was part of the role. Actually, he had everything memorized. "The stories I've read say that the second Pilate Stone is also likely a limestone carving."

"Makes sense. One theory is that there were multiple cornerstones of the building, most probably a theater. The Romans liked limestone. So do archaeologists, and for the same reason. It carves easily but it resists the elements. Limestone carvings can survive underground for a long time."

"But nobody's ever seen the Pilate Stone. Not since Roman times."

Again the eyebrow went up. "How do you know nobody's seen it? All you know is that there aren't any recent records of anyone having seen it. There are hints in some medieval scrolls —"

"Excuse me, Professor. My understanding is that a lot of people in your field think those scrolls are forgeries, maybe created in order to raise money for expeditions and crusades and the like."

"Most of them probably are. But even if every last one is a forgery, forgery on so grand a scale would be successful only if it built upon existing rumor." Yu glanced pointedly at his watch. "I'm afraid I have a luncheon in a few minutes, Mr. Fallon. May I ask you a question?"

"Please."

"Why this interest now? The rumors have been around for a very long time."

This was the key to the interview. The real reason Fuentes had come to see the expert rather than doing his research online and in the books. There was one fact that only a man in Yu's position would know.

"The story's interesting now because,

from what I hear, there's a new search being mounted for the Pilate Stone. A lot of feelers being put out. But I can't seem to find out who's doing the searching. That's what I think my readers would want to know."

Yu nodded, as if the answer had confirmed his worst fears about the press. "Of course. You're interested in the money angle."

"Is there a money angle?"

"With these artifacts, there always is. I could imagine certain private collectors paying ten, even twenty million for the Pilate Stone. More, maybe. I'm speaking not of museums, but of the kind of collector who bids anonymously on these works and then keeps them in his vault. Russian billionaires. That type."

Fuentes had his pen poised. "Any collectors in particular who might be interested?"

"Oh, I don't know. Scherbekov, of course. He's Russian oil. And Vaganian. Russian metals, I think. Copper, maybe. I'm not sure. An Indian who's in agribusiness — I forget his name. The Korean fellow who does those funny commercials for his company's cell phones. He's rumored to collect artifacts that nobody knows he has."

"Any Americans?"

"Ah. This is one of those parochial stories, then."

"Please. It's what would fascinate the readers." Meeting his host's eye. "It can be off the record, naturally."

"Naturally," said Yu, but dryly, as if confidentiality of sources was something else of which he disapproved. "A couple of software kings. Vannick, down in Texas. St. John, the media fellow. Two or three of the Hillimans, maybe. Nielsen, of course, with his hedge fund money. Oh, and the foundation."

"Excuse me, Professor. Which foundation is that?"

"The telecom woman. Mrs. Hartshorne. The one who's given most of her husband's billions away. Her foundation buys artifacts at auction, just to keep them out of the hands of the collectors. Buys them and gives them to museums for free. You might go see her. If there are rumors, she'll know about them. And she'll have somebody out there trying to find the Pilate Stone before Hugo Vannick or Elliott St. John or the Russians get their grubby hands on it." He was on his feet. "Now, if you'll excuse me, I have that lunch. Time to do some real academic work."

Walking back toward the parking lot, Fuentes considered his options. Janice's kidnappers wanted the Stone. From what Bethany had told him, he guessed that there might be a split in their ranks, but she refused to go into the details. She wouldn't say whom she'd spoken to. And Fuentes understood. If he were taken and forced to talk, he might wind up implicating Bethany's only potential friendly face inside the Wilderness.

But somebody inside the Wilderness had Janice.

So, where to start? He discounted the overseas buyers, not because it was impossible that they were involved but because pursuing them on his own was impractical. That left the Americans. Yu hadn't given him the names of the software kings, but Fuentes was sure he could find them if he had to. The Hartshorne Foundation seemed unlikely, if its practice was to give artifacts away rather than keep them.

Okay. He'd put them on the back burner. A quick check on his smartphone confirmed what he vaguely remembered, that the Texan, Vannick, was ill and not expected to live. Count him out. The Hilliman family had so many branches that he couldn't possibly investigate them all. That left Nielsen and St. John, both of them New Yorkers. New York was therefore where he would —

He stopped. Standing beside his car in the parking lot were two men, both of whom he knew all too well. One was black and one was white, and their surnames, unlikely though it seemed, were Allenby and Allenwood. They worked for the CIA's Office of Security, and their function was to monitor the activities of retired field officers.

People like Fuentes.

They were looking his way, and their expressions were grim.

# EIGHT

There was no body. Finding one had been Bethany's great fear, the reason for both her anxiety and her aggressiveness, the worry somehow that what had happened to Annabelle Seaver would have happened to Dorothea Ziman too. When she followed the sound of the television down the narrow hallway with its loose, creaky floorboards into a cozy room at the back of the house, with thick sofas and plenty of pillows, she even thought she saw Dorothea sprawled on the cushions, her throat an agony of last night's blood. But it was only a reddish-brown cat, sleek yet lazy, sitting atop a buff-colored throw pillow, its ears pricked at her intrusion, skeptical feline eyes demanding her business.

No body.

No body, but no Dorothea either. There is a vibration to an occupied house, even when everyone is quiet, the dust motes themselves dancing with an extra little kick, as if the life energy of human beings exerts a dynamic pull on the very air. This house was empty, and had probably been empty all night and all morning, because the atmosphere was so flat, and from what Gehringer had vouchsafed, Dorothea Ziman was nobody's morning person.

So why was the television on?

Obviously, Dorothea had left it on last night. That suggested that she had departed in a great hurry. Why? Had the friend Mrs. Harkle remembered come to warn her? To snatch her?

"You're missing something," she said to the air.

The cat gave her a puzzled glance, then flared its ears, stretched its fat body, and went back to doing nothing.

At first Bethany searched only with her eyes, disturbing nothing because she did not even know which instinct told her to look. Furnishings spare and student-looking, everything organized, history books here, science texts there, two computers, one a desktop, one a notebook. No sign that the owner of the house had ever picked up a book for the pleasure of reading. Everything was purposive. No art on the walls, except for a garish abstract print, straight lines made to look curved because of their smoothly flowing colors. It hung above the gas fireplace, directly in the line of sight of any guest who happened to be assigned the fold-out sofa. Bethany peeked into the kitchen, which was tiny and functional and a mess. Used dishes were heaped in the sink. Magnets pinned a list of local bylaws against the refrigerator. In the cabinets she found every kind of carbohydrate, but no secret messages.

Bethany climbed the stairs. The upstairs corridor was narrow. The walls were lined with photographs in cheap plastic frames. Dorothea, she saw, had grown stocky, and the evidence was in the pictures: Dorothea and her late mother, Dorothea and her late father, Dorothea and her late brother — a macabre gallery of loss. Farther along, Dorothea in a flowing academic gown, Dorothea behind a lectern, in a classroom writing on a whiteboard, Dorothea and friends —

*Dorothea and Annabelle.*

There it was, hanging on the wall, a glossy black-and-white print, eight-and-a-half by eleven, the two women smiling as they posed in hiking gear before a copse of bare trees, a distant gray cliff in the background.

From the way Annabelle's hair was done,

the women hadn't posed during her secret visit last December. The photo was a good three years old.

Three *years.*

Not possible.

Three years ago Bethany had been in her final year of law school, and Annabelle had been — well, she'd been around. Flighty. Disordered.

And she'd visited Oxford. Visited without ever telling her best friend in the world.

Annabelle and Dorothea. Bethany stared. How could the two of them possibly have known each other? Or, if they did, why on earth did Annabelle ever go to Gehringer in the first place? She had to know already where Adrian's daughter could be found.

Only one answer suggested itself.

Annabelle had visited Gehringer because she knew that if anything happened, Bethany would visit him too. Annabelle had wanted to know how the Wise Man died. She also wanted to leave more breadcrumbs for her running buddy to follow.

Just in case.

*I saw the Wise Man.* That was what Annabelle's note to Bethany said.

No, she hadn't. She'd seen the Wise Man's daughter. That was the whole point. When Annabelle traveled to Oxford in December,

90

she saw the Wise Man's daughter. The question was why.

Dorothea and Annabelle had somehow, improbably, been acquainted. And from the looks of things, Annabelle had visited her more than once.

Bethany leaned closer, studying the picture. A pink sweater, so incongruous: Annabelle was a woman for dark colors, always. Off to the side was a sliver of some sort of sandstone structure, but the building had been cropped out of the photo, and in Oxford there was sandstone everywhere. The trees, the peak — nothing looked familiar.

Hiking gear: perhaps the snapshot had been taken somewhere else.

Not sure what she was searching for, Bethany moved down the hall, scrutinizing the pictures.

Here was Annabelle again, this time leaning over a table with Wisdom himself.

The professor was pointing to a document, and Annabelle looked eager and interested. This, too, was three years ago; once more, Bethany recognized the hairstyle.

Again Bethany leaned close. The upstairs hallway was so narrow it was hardly passable, and she could hear the television next door. Probably the house had been built for a single family and then divided by the landlady, perhaps illegally, to earn an extra pound or two.

Bethany returned her attention to the photograph of Annabelle and Wisdom. The venue was familiar: heaps of books and papers everywhere, a mangy cat watching imperiously from atop the shelf. And beside the chessboard was a small crystal hummingbird, partly done up in wrapping paper.

They were in the grand house where Adrian Wisdom and his two children had lived back when Bethany was his student. It was a considerable comedown for Dorothea to have moved from her father's mansion on the edge of campus to this sad little space. Three years ago the photo of the trees was taken, two years ago Wisdom had committed suicide, and for whatever reason his daughter had not even been able to keep the old house.

A part of Bethany wondered what had happened. The rest of her wondered what document the Wise Man and Annabelle were studying. She needed a closer look. She took the small picture off its hook, then opened the back and slid it out of its grimy plastic frame.

A piece of paper slipped from behind it

and fluttered to the floor.

About to pick it up, she heard a creak from the hallway downstairs, but when she peeked she saw only the skeptical cat gazing implacably while cleaning its paws. She loved dogs but hated cats.

Bethany crouched once more.

The slip was not a paper, but another photograph, quite an old one, yellowing at the edges. The snapshot showed a bulky, confident man in his twenties or early thirties, standing in front of some sort of oddly shaped building or monument. And not all of the photo was there. A jagged strip had been scissored off, and half the photo with it.

The photograph had been sliced up, and the larger piece hidden in Dorothea Ziman's house. It took little guessing to understand that the other piece was somewhere else, probably with someone else.

Annabelle had visited Oxford. She'd seen the Wise Man. Indeed she had: right in the picture in the hallway. She'd wanted Bethany to follow her here and find this hidden photo. The logical next step was to figure out who had the rest of it.

Careful, careful. Don't jump to conclusions. The snapshot with its jagged cut could have been hidden for a hundred reasons. Her running buddy need not have had anything to do with it.

But Bethany was arguing against her own inclination. She knew. She couldn't say how she knew, but she knew. This photograph was what Annabelle had led her to Oxford to find.

She leaned closer, wishing for a magnifying glass. Draped around the man's shoulder was a slim arm. Judging from the bracelets and bangles, the arm belonged to a woman. Dorothea's late mother perhaps? But why cut her out of the picture?

Bethany could study the details later. She couldn't afford to linger. The landlady would grow suspicious. She slid the photo into the pocket of her Windbreaker and carefully hung the photograph of Annabelle and Wisdom back in its place. Just to be on the safe side, she pulled a few more random pictures off the wall, in case anything else had been squirreled away. She hit pay dirt with the picture of Annabelle and Dorothea in hiking gear. This time what tumbled out was not a photograph but a postcard.

She picked it up.

The postcard showed a very old church. The printed legend told her it was St. Mary's in Iffley, and that it had been built shortly after the Norman Conquest. The postcard wasn't scissored like the hidden photo. Nothing was written on the obverse side. No address, no postmark, no greetings of any kind.

So the message, if there was one, was in the image itself. Iffley, if she recalled rightly, was a small town a few kilometers from Oxford. Had Annabelle hidden something there? The church looked like sandstone. Was it possible that the other photo had been taken on its grounds?

Another sound from downstairs. Even if it was just the house settling, it was past time to get moving.

Unlike the old photo, the postcard was too big to fit in her pocket, and she didn't want to fold it. She put the card on the side table and was rehanging and straightening the photograph of Annabelle and Dorothea when she heard a genuine creak — more like a footstep. She rushed to the top of the stairs in time to take a kick in the stomach and a punch in the mouth from a man who looked, from her vantage point flat on her back in the narrow hallway, about eight feet wide and twelve feet tall.

# NINE

Morgan sat in a pub on the outskirts of Oxford, nursing a beer and studying the file sent via the Council's encrypted network. A finger touch flicked the iPad to the next page. He took in the photographs and other information. Another flick. Another.

A buzz interrupted the work. The killer delved in his bag, pulled out the secure phone. Probably the phone was less secure than the Council liked to believe, but nobody could listen to everything all the time, and decryption could take days or weeks or months.

"Yes?"

"She's definitely in the UK."

"That much I knew."

"We have the airport surveillance footage. She's changed her hair. The photos are on the way to your screen."

Morgan was impatient. "I'll know her when I see her. I don't need photos. I need to know where she is."

"We're working on that."

"So am I."

Morgan put the phone away and returned to a study of the screen. Flick. Flick. Bethany at the airport. Flick. Bethany in the bus queue. After that, they'd lost her.

But Morgan had a theory.

Flick. Bethany at law school graduation.

Flick. Bethany at Oxford.

Flick. Bethany's favorite professor. Adrian Wisdom.

Flick. The project Wisdom was working on when he died.

Flick. Wisdom's daughter, Dorothea. *Already approached,* said a superfluous note. Negative response.

The killer committed the photograph to memory, then signaled the waitress for the bill.

Bethany's father had made sure she knew how to use a gun, and back home in Virginia, a friend of hers named Sam De-Marco, now dead, had taken her to the range regularly the last three years, helping her hone her skills. She also took self-defense classes weekly, taught by Vivian, a grim ex-Marine who made sure they fell hard every session. *This isn't training to win some trophy in a tournament,* Vivian liked to say. *This is training to save your life.*

Vivian had taught them a lot of tricks. In Bethany's panic most of those tricks deserted her, but she remembered the part about ignoring what she saw in the movies — the chops to the neck, the knees to the groin — and going for the legs. *Take out his legs and he can't hit you.*

The man looming over her was broad shouldered and red bearded and silently angry. He drew his foot back for another kick, but by then the stars had stopped circling and Bethany was able to dodge the worst of it, curling into a ball and taking the strike on the shoulder. At that instant, while her assailant was off balance from the kick, she grabbed his ankle and yanked hard, toppling him to the floor.

His head hit the wall hard, cracking the particle board, and he let out a cry. Unfortunately, he sounded more annoyed than beaten.

Bethany scrambled to her feet, and her adversary leaped nimbly to his. Her plan to escape down the stairs was foiled by the fact that the stranger was in her way. She knew she had no chance in a fight. She had tripped him only because she had surprised him.

That wouldn't happen twice.

She braced for another punch. Instead, breathing hard, he demanded to know exactly who she was and what exactly she was doing.

And Bethany, relieved to discover that he had not been sent by the Wilderness or the Garden to kick her to death after all, said, "I'm a friend of Dorothea's."

He had small, pouchy eyes, and when he frowned they grew pouchier still. "And you ransack all your best friends' homes, do you? Or is this a performance you've laid on for Dorothea especially?"

Unable to muster a pertinent response, Bethany selected umbrage rather than embarrassment. "Who exactly are you? What are you doing here?"

He said, "I live here. The name's Bratt. A pair of Ts, not just the one." He was brushing off his dark sweater. "I'm Dorothea's husband."

They trooped downstairs, Bethany glum and apologetic, gigantic Bratt, no first name offered, consoling in his own way, for he himself, he said, had been caught a time or two in much the same situation. He was a private investigator by trade, he told her, offices in London, which meant that he was curious for a living. But Bratt's words failed to cheer her, because she was upset at having been caught so easily and wondered whether he was going to turn her in. She was also upset by the way the investigator kept one powerful arm locked around her shoulders, not sure whether he was trying to comfort her, control her, or come on to her. He held the postcard in his free hand, and he kept looking at it and shaking his head. His wife, he said, had not told him it was there, and he wanted to know what it meant.

"I don't have any idea," said Bethany.

"It says Iffley," Bratt pointed out. "I know this church."

"Then your guess is as good as mine."

Those eyes went tiny again, and for a moment, she worried that she was in for another fight. Instead he let her go and stuffed the postcard in a jacket pocket. Bethany knew she was unlikely to get it back. She hadn't told him about the jagged photograph and he hadn't asked. He had arrived at the top of the stairs too late, she realized. He'd seen her with the picture of his wife and Annabelle, but not the one of Annabelle with Professor Wisdom.

"Did you tell Dorothea you were coming?" he asked. "Because she didn't say

100

anything to me." *As usual,* his tone suggested.

"Ah, no." She wasn't ready to smile, but she didn't want to provoke him either. At some point he would just call his wife, and then Bethany's troubles would multiply. "I'm, um, just over here on business, and I thought I'd pop in."

"And search the house while you're about it?"

"I'm sorry. What can I say?"

"Elaine McMullen." Playing with the name. She wondered whether he'd heard it before. He picked up a book, leafed irritably through the pages, put it back. He tapped a key on the computer but the power was switched off. "She's never mentioned you," he complained, looking not at the unexpected visitor but at a photograph of a teen-aged Dorothea in a very short skirt, dancing vigorously with some other man.

"It's been a while since we've seen each other," she said. "Years, in fact."

"And that's why you searched the place?"

"I was worried. The landlady said the television had been on the whole night."

"This doesn't make any sense."

Another silence descended, Bratt prowling, openly impatient, yet determined to wait her out. Finally Bethany said to his back, "Where is Dorothea, anyway? At the lab?"

"Where else?"

"All night?"

"Some nights are like that." He sounded unhappy, and Bethany wondered how long the marriage was likely to last. For too many of her generation, marriage seemed to make no greater demands of fidelity or commitment than any other social arrangement. But Bethany, never married herself, was hardly in a position to criticize.

"I guess I'll go see her there," she said.

"Give me a minute to change. I'll run you over."

"Maybe it would be better if I —"

"I'll run you over. Nice surprise for Dorothea. Besides, it's the least I can do. Sorry about before. These days one worries." Bratt nodded toward the kitchen. "Get yourself something to drink if you like. Welcome to whatever's in the fridge."

He hurried up the stairs, running almost soundlessly. Bethany was impressed by his stealth and supposed he was good at his job. She remembered the days when she had been good at hers. She sat at the kitchen table, nursing an apple juice, and felt the cat snuggling warmly against her ankle and melancholy snuggling warmly against her brain. She kicked at the cat but could do nothing about the melancholy.

Why had Annabelle hidden the jagged photo? Who had the other half?

She thought of Janice, a prisoner until Bethany could turn up the Pilate Stone. She knew their patience would soon fray. But so far, all she had to show for sneaking into Britain and blundering around Oxford was half a photograph of a man she'd never seen before.

She heard the floorboards creak as Bratt moved around upstairs. She touched her lip and thought it might be swelling.

*Annabelle, what were you up to?*

Bethany sipped her juice and wiped her aching mouth. On the freshly painted walls of the minuscule kitchen hung more family snaps. She wondered what it must be like to value your parents and siblings so greatly that you want to be surrounded by reminders of them every hour of the day. She felt left out, as if everyone's life was correctly structured except hers. And Annabelle's. She glanced at the ceiling. It occurred to her that Bratt might be on the phone with Dorothea right now to verify her story. Bethany felt the raw edge of panic. She beat it down, but still had to act. She called his name — "Mr. Bratt?" — because it was all she knew. No answer. She moved to the bottom of the stairs and called again. She started up. Those photos that lined the stairwell and hallway were becoming positively oppressive.

She stopped.

Photos of friends and family.

No wedding photos.

No photos of a husband.

No photos of Mr. Bratt, who had told her not a single fact about Dorothea that she did not tell him first.

She took the stairs two at a time, but the window at the end of the hall was open, yellowed lacy curtains beckoning in the morning breeze. The stranger was gone, and the postcard with him.

# Ten

"You've been traveling a lot lately," said Allenby.

Fuentes said nothing.

"Those weeks in Chicago," Allenby continued, square brown jaw thrust forward in challenge. "Oregon. California. New Hampshire. Now Charlottesville."

They were well away from the Academical Village. The two men from the Office of Security had guided Fuentes several blocks to Lambeth Field, the old concrete stadium no longer in use by the university's football team. They were standing near the top of the bowl, within the colonnade. Sun dappled the columns. Down below, an intramural soccer team was practicing. The grass field was worn. Presumably both men from the Office of Security were wearing wires. By now his car was presumably bugged. Probably his apartment as well.

"Did you know the Bureau requested your

file after Chicago?" Allenby demanded. The mention of Chicago was a reference to the Village House, home of a religious cult Fuentes had infiltrated. That was where he first met both Bethany — who, like himself, merely pretended to join — and Janice, who was a member of the cult.

"I know," said Fuentes, but his tone gave no ground.

"Do you have any idea what kind of strings we had to pull to keep them away from you?"

"You're just lucky your apartment isn't under your real name," put in Allenwood. He was the more pleasant of the duo, and — as several disgraced former Agency employees could testify — the deadlier on account of it. "If they knew you lived right across the river from the District, I doubt we could have stopped them from hauling you in."

"What do you want exactly?" Fuentes asked. "I don't work for you any more. I can go where I want."

"And your postemployment agreement says we can question you whenever we want," growled Allenby. His receding hair was cut short and brushy. As always, he looked ready for a tussle. Fuentes had never seen him without his scowl. "And if you want to play the tough guy, my friend, don't forget, we can withdraw our protection and let the Bureau —"

"They think you were a part of the cult in Chicago," said Allenwood with his toothy smile. He had long, ungainly arms and a sleepy Southern accent. "What was it called? God's Planners. Well, our colleagues in the Bureau have it in their heads that you were a member of the group. A Planner. And the Planners made bombs. Let's not forget that part. They made bombs right in the basement of the Village House, and they set them off at laboratories that did research on human embryos."

"You're telling me what I already know."

A mollifying wink from Allenwood, the good cop. Down below, the soccer team had switched ends. "Well, this is the very point, Ray. You're a munitions expert. It's right there in the file. And, well, we know it's ridiculous, but the FBI seems to think you might have helped those crazies make their bombs. You didn't do that, did you? You'd tell us if you did, wouldn't you?"

"No."

"No, you wouldn't tell us?"

"No, I didn't make bombs for the Planners. Don't be ridiculous."

"Well, of course you didn't. We know that.

Still. Some of the Planners seem to have told the FBI that you were one of the leaders." He chuckled merrily to show that this was just a bit of joshing among buddies. "Now, all of us know none of that is true. We know you were at the Village House in the cause of justice. That's why we redacted the file we sent them."

"And I'm grateful," said Fuentes, but he knew they were a long way from the end of the interview.

"We're the good guys," Allenwood went on. They were walking again, circling the top row of concrete seats. "We're here to help you, Ray. We're on your side, okay? We know your sister lived in the Village House for a while. Maybe she was never officially a Planner, but she tried them out. And, well, you decided to join up — excuse me, pretend to join up — and take them down from inside. As a matter of fact, it seems that you used the very infiltration skills that we taught you. Okay. That's fine. Not the neat tidy way our Bureau friends like to do things, with arrests and indictments and so on, but it worked. Congratulations. Good job."

Fuentes refused to be snowed. The Office of Security didn't send their best people to tell you how proud you'd made them. "I asked what you want."

Allenby, the tough guy, took his turn. He stopped walking. He put a hand on Fuentes's forearm, signaling him to stop too. They were alongside a wall. Nobody was in eyeshot from the outside. The wall blocked the view from the field. Fuentes braced his feet against the concrete. If anything was going to happen, this was where it would happen.

"We want to know what you're up to," said Allenby in his familiar tone of confrontation. "Maybe you weren't a Planner. Maybe you were after revenge for your sister. We don't particularly care about that part. And let's say you had nothing to do with the bombings. What we want to know is why the Bureau has you on airport surveillance tapes at the same time that a woman who just might be their number-one suspect in those bombings is getting on a plane to London."

"I was catching a flight to Madrid."

"Exactly. You bought a ticket to give yourself an excuse for being behind security in the international terminal. That's consistent with your training. And you even flew to Madrid. You stayed two nights, you didn't see anybody, you didn't go anywhere. You had room service, you did your daily run, and you browsed the museums. Then you flew home."

Fuentes knew better than to be either annoyed or surprised. He had separated from the Agency less than a year ago, and he had been privy to very deep secrets indeed. Of course they would keep tabs on him.

"I didn't break any laws," he said.

Allenwood, the smiler, shook his head. "I'm sorry, Ray. If you assisted a fugitive in fleeing the country, well then yes, I'd say you did break a law or two. You're on the tape, she's on the tape, and, well, we like you just fine — we're your friends — but a lot of people over at the FBI would attach a lot of importance to a coincidence like that. Especially since they still think you were the bomb maker. You're the bomb maker, she's the bomber — you know the bureaucratic mentality. A child could connect the dots. They wouldn't worry about alternative explanations. Secret conspiracies. Any of that."

Now, at last, Fuentes understood where this was going. He looked at the two faces — Allenby's so dark and challenging; Allenwood's so pink and friendly. "Just tell me," he said.

"You have to be more careful," said Allenwood with his weatherproof Southern grin.

"You have to choose your friends and your situations in ways that won't raise suspicion."

"Can I have it in plain English, please?"

Allenby had no patience with fine words. "Meaning, if you want the Agency to keep protecting you, you stay away from Bethany Barclay. You stay away from WAKEFUL, you stay away from the whole conspiracy. It's all crazy anyway. There is no Garden. There is no Wilderness. Leave it alone, or the FBI gets the whole file. Everything, Fuentes. A précis of some of your missions. The PTSD after what happened with the Taliban. Everything they'll need to make a case against you. Is that clear enough? Because if it's not, there's also the matter of your sister. Megan. Meg, you call her, isn't that right?"

"What about her?"

"The FBI is still looking for former Planners. They know your sister was involved, but they don't know her name yet. How long do you think it will take them to find her if we step out of the picture? The sister of the chief bomb maker? A member of the same cult? The press will love a story like that. And if the FBI doesn't leak it, maybe somebody else will."

"You leave her out of this."

Allenby wasn't done. He was enjoying

himself. "Poor Meg. She'll need to hire lawyers, somebody to handle the reporters, the whole business. Weren't your parents some kind of itinerant preachers? And your sister lives on a commune in Oregon. I don't think your family has money for that kind of thing."

Fuentes looked from one unbothered face to the other. Everyone in the Agencies passed along stories about how the Office of Security liked to play hardball. But there was hardball and there was — this. "Who sent you?" he asked coldly.

"We just do what we're told," said Allenby.

Allenwood, the Southerner, had the grace to look apologetic. "We have to hear you say it, Ray."

He unclenched his fists. "It's clear, okay? You can tell them I got the message. Loud and clear."

"That's it, then," said Allenwood, and the two of them turned away and headed down the rows of seats toward the bottom of the bowl.

Fuentes stood there in the bright Virginia sunshine, watching them go. And wondering what had just happened.

None of his reports to the Agency or even to his counselors had mentioned the Garden or the Wilderness. Until this morning, he would have guessed that nobody at the Agency had ever heard of them.

It was no coincidence that Allenwood and Allenby had shown up today. Somebody had sent them. Somebody had learned what he was up to and made a couple of calls. The Fuentes problem had wound up on the Agency's desk, and the messengers had been dispatched.

Meaning that somebody was very frightened of what Ray Fuentes might uncover.

"Good," he said aloud, and headed down to his car.

# Eleven

Dorothea Ziman did not want to talk to Bethany, but she did not want to call the police either. Bethany waited out in the yard, watching the landlady's children pummel each other, because Dorothea, a rolling, rotund woman of considerable energy, would not have her in the house.

Summoned from her office by the landlady, Dorothea stalked frantically from room to room, assuring herself that the intruder had taken nothing she would miss. She did not tell her visitor to get lost, precisely, and Bethany even had the sense that she had been expected, because Dorothea kept emerging onto the front step and staring at her the way we do at addled relatives we cannot be rid of but keep expecting to do something crazy.

"So, it's really you," she said at one point. "You actually showed up. They were right. Amazing."

"Who was right?"

But Dorothea plunged inside once more.

Another time she said, "I could get arrested." Eyes fierce behind thick glasses. "Did that ever occur to you?"

"You haven't committed a crime."

"You don't know that. You don't have any idea what I might have done or not done."

Into the house once more.

Finally, Dorothea came back into the yard and stayed there, thick fists on her wide hips. She was wearing an expensive pantsuit and a hacked hairstyle.

"I suppose you're not going away, are you?"

"I'm sorry. I didn't mean to cause trouble. But we have to talk about Annabelle. And about the man who was in your house."

"Annabelle's dead." Dorothea paused, as if hoping that this intelligence would drive her unwanted guest away. When Bethany didn't budge, she tried another approach. "You owe me money, by the way. You broke the lamp in the upstairs hall."

"That wasn't me. That was the — the intruder."

Still Dorothea gave no ground: she didn't force Bethany to go, and she didn't invite her in. From the window, the landlady watched like a fan at a prizefight.

115

"The *other* intruder."

"That's right."

"Whom nobody saw but you."

"This is real." Bethany touched her swollen lip. "He said his name was Bratt. Bratt with two Ts."

Behind those thick lenses, the eyes narrowed. Recognition? Disbelief? Or just more of the same pulsing fear?

"Special Branch have been to see me," said Dorothea at length. "Just the other day. Had I seen you? Were you expected? When did I hear from you last? They gave me a card. A number to call." Waving toward the street. "They could be watching the house this very minute."

Bethany's life underground had taught her the answer to that one. "They can't watch everywhere all the time, Dorothea. Nobody's resources are unlimited."

"So *you* say."

"Dorothea, please. You have to tell me about Annabelle. I don't care how bad it is. I'm sure I've heard worse of her."

"Annabelle?" A tinny laugh. "Oh, Annabelle. She was all sweetness and syrup. Nobody has a word against her. Didn't you know?"

"Know what?"

"She was the daughter my father always

wanted. The one he loved best."

Lillian Hartshorne sits on the grand portico at the back of her Virginia estate. The grass is bright emerald in the morning sun. The hills roll on and on toward the blue mountains beyond. Her people automatically buy up any adjacent property that comes on the market. She no longer knows or cares exactly how many hundreds of acres she owns. In the winter of her life, what she craves is privacy.

Privacy — and a sense of having advanced her mission. People are such dunderheads. Therein lies the problem. People are dunderheads, and no matter how much progress is made in science, in the arts, in philosophy, in every field of endeavor where beauty might spring from the human mind, the dunderheads of the earth refuse to surrender their ridiculous faith in the love and protection of an all-powerful supernatural being.

As if any all-powerful being could possibly love such dunderheads —

"Ma'am?"

The Protector glances up. Her chief of staff is standing a few feet away.

"Come ahead, Kenny. I won't bite."

He moves closer. "Ma'am, there's confirmation from Morgan. She's definitely in Oxford. And she's met Dorothea Ziman."

"As we hoped."

"Yes, ma'am. Ma'am?"

"Yes, Kenny?"

"How did you know?"

"How did I know what?"

"That she'd make it out of the country. That she'd be able to follow Annabelle's clues."

There is a tray in front of her: shirred eggs and toast, her favorite. She takes a small bite, chews thoughtfully.

"It isn't knowledge, Kenny. It's hope. What the adversary is always going on about." Her chuckle is like winter rain. "That's why it's important to have more than one plan. A backup for the backup. If Bethany had gotten herself killed — or, worse, arrested — well, there were other ways."

"Yes, ma'am."

The Protector grows wistful. "It's a shame, really. I've met this Bethany Barclay a few times. Did you know that? I met her through dear Edna. The Judge. She lives right down the road. Edna Harrigan is her mentor. I suppose you know that. Bethany was her law clerk at the Virginia Supreme Court, and the two of them have long been close.

Like a mother and a daughter, perhaps. Grandmother." Almost a smile. "Well. Bethany didn't know who I was, obviously. As far as she knew, I was Judge Harrigan's best friend, the dotty heiress from up the road. Aunt Lillian, I asked her to call me. Aunt Lillian. I liked what I saw, Kenny. She's smart, disciplined, ambitious, conscientious — oh, all the things poor Annabelle never was. In a finer world, we might have recruited her."

"Ma'am, my understanding is that Bethany is some sort of believer."

"Oh, fluff," says the Protector, flapping a mottled hand. "That's a detail. We've turned the religious before. It can be done." She shoves the tray away. "Never mind. Water under the bridge. She's helping us now, whether she wants to or not."

"Yes, ma'am."

The Lord Protector lurches to her feet and almost topples, but neither Kenny nor the two stewards who stand just out of earshot dare offer to assist.

"Walk with me, Kenny."

"Yes, ma'am."

They enter the garden at what she thinks of as the tulip corner: all varieties, an entire acre devoted to nothing else, and arranged in neat, brightly colored rows — pink

Prinses Irene here, bright orange Unicum there, ivory and yellow Montreux next along.

"What's the word from Florida?" she asks.

"Ma'am, the sex scandal appears genuine. We won't have to take any action. The media will destroy that particular pastor for us."

"Elliott is on board?"

"Yes, ma'am."

"His people know not to mention that the rate of abuse among church leaders is lower than the rate of abuse among others who deal with young people?"

"Yes, ma'am."

"Very good, Kenny. Well done. Some of these preachers do make it very easy for us, don't they?"

"Yes, ma'am."

They continue their promenade. A steward trails them by fifteen yards. Kenny carries a walkie-talkie, in case his employer has a sudden yearning for — well, anything.

"That pastor in Michigan," she says after a bit. "The one with the mega-church. How is that going?"

"Ma'am, we have two people on his senior staff now. I'd say by this time next year we'll be ready to bring him down."

"Don't get too confident, boy. A few years

ago — before you were here — we tried the same trick in South Korea. Know what happened?"

"No, ma'am."

"Fool of a pastor converted our man on the inside. That's what happened." For a moment the pain of that particular defeat genuinely torments the Protector. One of the few times she has been bested by the Church Builder and his band of fanatics. Worse, she still isn't quite sure what went wrong. "Tell me about our guest," she barks.

If her aide is thrown by the sudden change of topic, it doesn't register in his tone. "Ma'am, she was doing well the last time I saw her."

"Go see her again."

"I was there the day before yesterday."

"Did I ask when you were there last?" Waving the cane before her like a flyswatter. "Go check. Make sure they're observing the precautions. Check on her mood and so forth. Make sure she's being well treated. And that she has everything she needs."

"Except a computer."

"Obviously, you silly boy."

"Of course, ma'am. Ma'am?"

"Yes, Kenny?"

"May I ask why we're taking such good care of her?"

Her face grows thundery. "Because we're moral people. We're not like the fanatics of the Garden. We do no needless harm. You know that." She softens. She almost smiles. "Think, boy. Sooner or later, Bethany Barclay is going to demand evidence that little Janice is alive. Eventually it'll come to talking to her. Let's make sure she's in shape to talk."

"Yes, ma'am."

"Oh, and Kenny."

"Yes, ma'am?"

"One last thing." Her voice remains grandmotherly and sweet. "Don't you ever question an order of mine again. Even when it's just the two of us. Is that clear?"

"Yes, ma'am," he says, and returns to the house.

Very fast.


"My father was a monster," said Dorothea. "You couldn't know what that is like. Well, maybe you do. You were his student. I'm sure he couldn't have treated you gently." She laughed in cold amusement. "The students he thought were capable he treated like dirt. The ones he didn't — well, he treated them worse."

"And you?" asked Bethany in sympathy. "He must have thought you very capable indeed."

Dorothea smiled. She had been smiling for some time, a strange, distant, superior look that never touched her eyes. They were walking back toward her laboratory, because she had students to see. Bethany had expressed reservations about accompanying her, but Dorothea had insisted that if they were going to talk, this was how they were going to do it. Then she'd parroted Bethany's own words: *They can't watch everywhere all the time.* And so they walked, Bethany pushing her rented bicycle.

"Annabelle was different," said Dorothea, answering the earlier question. "Dad liked her. She was so syrupy sweet to him. Don't give me that look. Not that kind of sweet. She was buttering him up. It was obvious to me that she wanted something from him. It would have been obvious to Dad too, if he wasn't such a . . ."

She trailed off, unable to come up with the word. Despite her heft, she stood very straight as she walked, hands linked donnishly behind her back. Dorothea's field was particle physics. From what Gehringer had said, she was competent but nowhere near the top of the pack. He'd also suggested that she'd chosen the specialty to remain as far from her father's work as she could get.

"I didn't mean Annabelle was my actual sister," she said. Dorothea grinned savagely. She evidently found most things funny, including the tale of an intruder stealing a postcard that fell out of a picture frame. She had already denied, with a thick trilling laugh, that she had hidden anything of any kind. When she liked a picture, she hung it on the wall, she said; when she didn't, she put it in a scrapbook or a drawer. So if, in fact, the postcard was there to begin with — Bethany was bewildered by Dorothea's willingness to announce her skepticism with such good humor — somebody else must have left it. Against this rock-ribbed agnosticism, Bethany had made no headway, so she decided to leave the truth of the matter in limbo, for the last thing she wanted was for Dorothea to call the police. Although Bethany hated abstraction and ambiguity with all her troubled soul, she hated the thought of incarceration and interrogation even more.

"I hope you didn't get the wrong idea," Dorothea continued. "I meant only that Adrian much preferred her to me. Oh, yes. To Adrian I was a lost cause. He liked acolytes. People whose attentive gazes told him every instant how brilliant he was. People like you," she said, without a trace of irony. "And like Annabelle, of course. Since I disagreed with him, I was *ipso facto* the enemy."

"You must have known her pretty well."

But Dorothea, like many lonely people, was determined to tell the story her own way.

"Adrian was a believer, no question. Church of England, of course. Very high church. Bells, incense, the works. And whenever his turn came round, he'd be lecturing the congregation about the need to maintain orthodoxy." She was wearing a necklace of glittering gold circlets and began to toy with the links. "No female clergy for the great Adrian Wisdom, thank you very much. He thought the American church had gone insane. I tried to get him to live and let live, but he wouldn't wear that. Whatever he believed, everybody had to believe. Otherwise there was something terribly wrong with everybody else. Never with him, you understand."

"I understand," said Bethany, marveling at the way we never seem to wonder whether the professors who mistreat their students also mistreat their families.

Then all at once Dorothea was arguing against her own thesis. "Well, fine. Lots of philosophers are like that. Adrian was still a genius. He wrote that wonderful book about Hume, and of course, his biography of Adam Smith is widely regarded as . . ." Again she seemed to lose the thread. "But then he went and got this bee in his bonnet about Pontius Pilate. I'd talk to him — scream at him, more like — 'What's the big deal? Who cares about Pontius Pilate these days?' — that kind of thing. But Adrian, well, you couldn't disagree with him. Least of all his own daughter. Worse since Mom died, of course, but still —"

Dorothea made herself stop. She was struggling visibly to maintain the chilly amusement with which she preferred to view the world. Bethany chose not to interrupt her reverie, not least because a dark blue Rover was passing them and she was busy wondering whether it was the same dark blue Rover she'd seen while she was arguing with Dorothea's landlady earlier. A trio of students passed, arguing loudly about terrorism.

"If only they knew who they just saw," said Dorothea gleefully, her gaze following the young people as they ambled down the street. "But I guess you don't look much like your photo on the news, do you? Dyed your hair, cut it — maybe you could add some fake glasses or something, but this whole outfit — the jeans, the ugly sweater — you fit right in around here." A snort. "I remember when you were Adrian's student, Bethany. You were just the same. Blue jeans. The whole look. I guess you haven't changed that much."

"Had Annabelle?"

Dorothea's smile was pasted back into place, but the merriment never reached the angry eyes. "Maybe I should call those men from Special Branch after all. Just to keep myself clear. My research subsists on government grants. I can't risk that."

"I wouldn't ask you to."

"If you ask me not to tell them we've talked, you'll be asking me to risk my livelihood then, that's for sure."

But Bethany had worked her out. This was Dorothea's way of teasing, keeping you constantly back on your heels. This was how she had her fun, showed you who was in control: by learning your weak spot and then tapping and tapping at it until you were ready to scream. As much as she claimed to hate her father, Dorothea was very much Adrian Wisdom's daughter.

"About Pilate —"

"Pilate. Pilate! Why is everybody so excited about Pontius Pilate? Until maybe half a century ago, there were plenty of Near East specialists who'd tell you there never *was* a Pontius Pilate!"

"But your father thought Pilate was important." Bethany spoke gently. They had left the residential area and entered a neighborhood of ugly modern office buildings, squat and low. "Your father was writing a book about him."

"Adrian was a fool. He was a genius, but he was also a fool. Well, that's not particularly unusual at a university, I suppose. It's just a bit painful to watch a man of his gifts go gaga. Poor old Adrian. He'd found some old documents or notes or something, and he was going to blow the lid off the whole thing, he said. I tried to argue with him. 'Blow the lid off what? What's there to blow the lid off of?' He'd just sneer at me, tell me to stick to my elementary particles and leave serious thinking to the philosophers. Like I said. A monster."

"But he told Annabelle, didn't he? She was all syrupy and sweet, you said. Like a second daughter to him. And so he told her all about the manuscript, the documents, the whole thing."

Dorothea's cell phone rang, and she snatched it up in relief. Bethany watched closely for any signal that she should bolt, but the physicist held up a restraining hand

128

and then sidestepped toward a fenced garden allotment, well out of earshot.

Whoever she was talking to, Dorothea didn't want Bethany to overhear.

"Where were we?" asked Dorothea brightly, returning three minutes later to Bethany's side.

"We were talking about Annabelle."

"Actually, we were talking about Adrian," Dorothea corrected. The practiced smile was back, even if Bethany knew by now that it hid a blazing anger. "I'm a scientist, Bethany. I work in a laboratory all day. We're studying the Yukawa interaction. We're close to a breakthrough in understanding the pion. This is work that matters. What my father was doing doesn't matter. It never did. We're unlocking the secrets of the universe. All he cared about was old documents written by a bunch of superstitious primitives."

They were walking again, the pace brisker. "I take it you're not a believer."

"I believe that if I jump off the roof of Buckingham Palace on December 25, the law of gravity means the earth will attract me and I'll attract the earth and the earth will have the better of the ensuing collision. I don't believe Father Christmas will swing by in his sleigh to catch me."

"What about after you die?"

"There's nothing after you die. That's the point." She was working herself into an even angrier state — probably at her father — and Bethany was beginning to worry that Dorothea might cause a scene. With every passing minute the smile was looking a little more strained and a little less sane. "I don't give a hoot about Pontius Pilate. And I don't actually think Annabelle did either. Oh, she pretended all right. From that first time you brought her by, six years ago, was it? Been back several times since then, but I'm not always here. She'd charm poor Adrian. Flirt with him, flatter him, talk to him about his work. And Adrian, well, he wouldn't crack a smile to save his life, but with Annabelle he was laughing and joking all the time. I'd never seen him that way. The truth is, it got on my nerves. I couldn't stand to be around him when she was here."

Dorothea's eyes were on the key card she'd pulled from her wallet. They had stopped in front of a featureless two-story building surrounded by a rusty link fence. The pain in her voice surprised them both.

"Well, fine. What do you want me to say? That he treated her like his real daughter? Fine. Did I hate it? I did. I'd been dutiful.

After Mom died, I took care of the house, did the cooking, *and* finished my studies as part of the bargain. And all he'd ever say was that it wasn't good enough. On top of the rest, I married twice, and Adrian — well, divorce was something else he'd never wear. Didn't help that my first husband was one of his students. Helped even less that husband number two wasn't of what Adrian considered 'our class.' Not educated, you see. Naturally, he drove Teddy away. Called himself a believer. Ha. What Adrian Wisdom believed in was the greatness and brilliance of Adrian Wisdom, and don't you forget it."

Morgan sat on a bench, for all the world reading the newspaper, but he was actually watching as the two women passed. The killer carefully catalogued Bethany Barclay's new hair color and style. She wasn't bad for an amateur. If the Council's sources were right, she'd had some excellent coaching. A man like Raymond Fuentes could teach you more about the clandestine life in twenty-four hours than most intelligence services could teach you in twenty-four days. Morgan had tangled with Fuentes before and, frankly, was grateful that there was an ocean between them just now.

But therein lay a conundrum. Fuentes was

a very loyal type. That was one of his great strengths — and one of his great weaknesses. It was most unlike him to send a young woman off on her own into certain danger. There should have been backups. Minders, as they're called in the trade. Morgan, however, was very thorough — and very certain that there was nobody.

Just Bethany, out on her own.

Strange. Fuentes must have a reason. Morgan wondered, not for the first time, exactly who might be employing Raymond Fuentes in this affair, and to what end.

The Council professed to have no idea.

Morgan turned a page. The two women had reached the gate. The killer settled down to wait.

They were at the laboratory. Dorothea led her past a guard who scarcely looked up, then down a flight of stairs to a narrow white corridor lighted garishly with banks of fluorescent bulbs. A couple of cheap sofas and matching chairs flanked a massive door.

"You'll have to wait out here. I have to see my team."

"Dorothea —"

"Relax. It won't be long. An hour at the outside." The cocky smile was back. "And I assume you want to hear the rest of the story, don't you? All about Annabelle and the manuscript?" She didn't wait for an answer. "So, wait here."

Bethany couldn't help herself. "You like being in control of things, don't you?"

Dorothea wasn't even interested. "Don't worry. I'm not going to call Special Branch. I have questions too, and if they arrest you, well, I won't get any answers, will I?"

She vanished through the heavy door. Bethany sat down to wait.

# TWELVE

Raymond Fuentes had been trained to flexibility. Out in the field, a stubborn refusal to appreciate how the odds had turned could kill a man. There was no longer any point in tracking down, one by one, the names on Professor Yu's list of those who might be interested in finding the Pilate Stone. By now Allenwood and Allenby would have the same list. Pursuing his original plan was exactly the way to keep his former employers on his back.

And that was the last thing he wanted.

So after leaving the University of Virginia, he drove his car to the train station, where he parked in the lot. He would never touch the car again. When he had the chance, he would donate it to a local church and send the key by mail. He grabbed a taxi to the far end of town, then went by city bus to a less agreeable corner of Charlottesville, where he had left his escape vehicle, a battered old gas-guzzler he had purchased with cash and rehabilitated. Despite the ugly exterior, the car ran smoothly and was street legal, even if the name on the registration was false. Fuentes hated lying, but this was war.

He drove around the countryside until satisfied that he was not under surveillance. It took a team of dozens or even hundreds to follow a trained operative without being caught, and nobody had that kind of manpower just now — not to follow a retired agent who was supposed to have been scared off.

Satisfied that he was clean, Fuentes found an electronics shop, where he bought a burner phone and a tablet computer, again paying cash. He went to a Barnes & Noble, where he sat for a while in the café, using the store's Wi-Fi to do research.

Then he got back into the car and headed north-northwest, toward the town of Flint Hill.

Bethany Barclay's mentor was a woman named Edna Harrigan, a retired justice of the Virginia Supreme Court. The two of them lived a few miles apart and, from what Bethany said, every time she had a problem, she went to see the friend she called only "the Judge."

Fuentes had been trained to be suspicious. He had spent a day and a half with Bethany Barclay before packing her off to London, but the more she'd told him, the more he'd been persuaded that Judge Harrigan was somehow a part of the group that had manipulated the young lawyer into following Annabelle's trail in the first place.

They called themselves the Garden, Bethany had told him, and now Allenwood and Allenby knew about the Garden too. But Fuentes had a shrewd notion that they knew the group only as a name. They had been sent to warn him away without ever quite being told what it was they were warning him away *from.*

Bethany didn't know much about the Garden, but she'd shared what she could: That it had been formed six hundred years ago. That it was dedicated to protecting the Christian church from the machinations of its enemy, known as the Wilderness. That it lived in the shadows. That one of its leaders was an architect named Harry Stean.

What Bethany didn't know, because it would never have occurred to her to check, was that Harry Stean was a close friend of Edna Harrigan.

Fuentes had no sympathy for the Garden.

They manipulated the innocent and sometimes sent them to their deaths. The church needed defenders, but not defenders who used the Devil's methods to obtain their goals. His mission was to find Janice Stafford, not to burn down the Garden. But he was more than willing to burn it down if that was what it took to find Janice.

And so he made a nuisance of himself. Flint Hill, where Judge Harrigan lived, was a small town, only a few hundred residents, and everybody knew everybody else. At the tiny post office, he waved a fake Drug Enforcement Administration identification and asked loud, blundering questions about Edna Harrigan. At a pub across the street, he worked his way through the bar, asking one drinker after another if they were aware of any suspicious activities on the old woman's part. At the town's sole bank he winkled out an assistant manager and assured her that he was not asking any questions about Judge Harrigan's finances, but wanted to know whether she had been acting furtively of late. Nobody had a bad word to say about the woman, but they would soon be talking to each other, and the word would get to Judge Harrigan's ear — and, if he was right about her, back to the rest of the Garden as well.

Because, at every stop, he asked whether anyone had heard Edna Harrigan mention someone called WAKEFUL.

Nobody had, but that wasn't the point.

Satisfied that he had done his job, he drove north along Route 522 for half an hour, stopping in the somewhat larger town of Front Royal to spread the same discord. Judge Harrigan would be less well known here, of course, but again, people would talk.

And at this point, talk was all he wanted.

Three hours later, he was in Washington, D.C., a city he hated. But Edna Harrigan had friends here, and lots of them. There was still much work to be done.

# THIRTEEN

Outside it was already evening, and Dorothea Ziman had remained closeted in the laboratory for over two hours while Bethany nearly climbed out of her skin. Three times she had been on the verge of leaving the building, and three times she worried that she would not have another chance to talk to Adrian Wisdom's daughter. If she was going to hear about Annabelle and the manuscript, this was the moment. And if that meant letting Dorothea play her power games, well then, so be it.

A nearby alcove had a small library, mostly periodicals related to physics but also a couple of battered Agatha Christie paperbacks. Nevertheless, Bethany felt nervous and unprotected. People kept passing by. A couple of students poked their heads in but ignored her. A dotty old man asked if she knew where the facilities were located. A severe middle-aged woman demanded to know what she was doing here, but came down a peg or two when Bethany mentioned Dr. Ziman.

"Well, I guess it's fine, then," she said, and withdrew.

Any of them or all of them could have a surveillance function. For all Bethany knew, she was sitting in the middle of a trap. So when Dorothea at last emerged, as perky and playful as if only minutes had passed, Bethany started at once to upbraid her, but Dorothea interrupted.

"Maybe you should stay the night."

"What?"

"With me. Your intruder might come back," she joked, but Bethany could tell that she was less scared than lonely. She was tempted to take Dorothea up on her offer, partly because she had nowhere else to stay, mostly because she was lonely herself. Yet she hesitated, and not just because instinct told her to keep moving. She also sensed behind Dorothea's invitation the same troublesome cold amusement that had undergirded their entire encounter, as if she knew an unpleasant surprise awaited. And it struck her as odd that a single woman living by herself would be relatively undisturbed at the thought of a man sneaking into her house, attacking the first woman he met there, stealing a hidden postcard, and leaving through the window.

They walked the streets of Oxford as the day drew in, and a fine mist, not quite rain, softened the street lamps to a rosy glow. The students were like students everywhere, but more excited about learning, and the ability of the British educational system to sustain that thrill had been the part of being here that Bethany liked best. They passed a tutor stooping to hear a young woman who looked less than five feet tall discoursing on the psychological forces that compelled Peter the Great to build the first Russian navy. They passed a couple of undergraduates who had found a point of major disagreement about Riemannian manifolds.

Dorothea seemed willing to talk forever. She answered everything Bethany asked: Yes, she often left the television on when she planned to be out all night. It provided company for her cat, Thoreau. He liked American game shows best.

She might have gone on all day, avoiding what she wanted least to discuss, had not Bethany brought her gently to heel: "Annabelle was a cat lover, wasn't she?"

Dorothea brightened. "You should have seen them together. They got along famously. She loved to tease poor Thoreau with a ball of string. She'd have him pawing the air for an hour, trying to grab it."

"And when was this exactly?"

"Oh, goodness. Annabelle came to see Adrian. This was — goodness me — I believe it was about two years after you were graduated. Maybe three."

Three or four years ago, then. Bethany's guess about the age of the photograph was correct.

"Came to see him about what?"

"I don't really know. She was in London on business. That's what she said. She came up to Oxford to say hello, and the next thing anybody knew she was with us for a week. Maybe ten days. There wasn't any urgency. She just stayed. Like a moocher."

Exactly, Bethany said, but only to herself. For all her many virtues, Annabelle Seaver had been a moocher. She dropped in on you without warning, she made herself at home, she hung around until you were half-crazy and had to throw her out to protect your sanity.

"And after that — well, after that, I don't think I saw Annabelle again until last year. November, it must have been. The middle of Michaelmas Term, anyway." Dorothea was walking faster. The night mist curled around their ankles. "Same as the other time. She just showed up. Only at my office this time, not my house. I'd moved by then, of course, with Adrian two years dead. I don't know that she knew where I lived. I was seeing students, and there was a knock on my door, and Annabelle was standing there. And I'll confess that for a moment, I wasn't sure who she was. Her hair was different. She'd lost weight. She looked a little wild, if you don't mind my saying so. A student, I thought. Maybe a late entrant, the sort who never showed up in the lecture hall. Then I remembered, of course. She said she was in London on business — just like last time — and that she came by to say hello and offer her condolences. But there was something off about her. She was frazzled. Furtive, I suppose."

November, Bethany registered. Not December. Annabelle had made two visits to Oxford last year, not just one.

"You didn't believe her," Bethany said, because every lawyer knows that with a reluctant witness you have to keep the conversation alive.

"That she was in London on business? That was possible. But that she'd just dropped by to say hello — no, that I didn't believe. And I had good reason."

They waited at the corner for the traffic to clear.

"She bought me dinner. She had a lot of cash; I could see it in her bag. And I thought that rather odd, because she hadn't struck me as the type."

"The type to carry a lot of cash?"

"The type to have any money at all, to be perfectly frank. Annabelle was more a borrower than a lender, if you see what I mean." A smirk. "On top of which, well, she always struck me as rather weakly tethered to the world."

"I suppose she was. Yes. Weakly tethered." They were passing a park. The night chill was sinking into Bethany's bones. "So, dinner?"

"Right. She waited for dessert and coffee, then came to the point. She said there was some research Adrian had been doing. They'd spoken about it when she was here the last time. She wanted to know whether she could go through his papers. I told her certainly not, and after that she got rather shirty."

"Did she tell you what she was looking for?"

"Not at first. As a matter of fact, that's probably why I was so adamant in my no. She was so secretive. She didn't seem to trust me. She thought I should let her have a go at my father's papers just because she wanted to. She told me there would be money in it for me, just to let her have a look. A lot of money. I was offended, and I said so. All right, Adrian didn't leave me particularly well off. He had a lot of debt, it turned out, and, well, my circumstances aren't what they were. Still, one isn't starving. Annabelle wouldn't take no for an answer. She even named a figure — a very high figure — and, yes, I admit I was surprised." For a moment, Bethany saw the neediness in the other woman's eyes. "Not that I believed she had the money, of course. She said she had plenty, and that I could have it in cash to avoid Revenue and Customs. Well, naturally, this got my back up. We went round and round a bit, and finally she told me what she was looking for. It seems that when she was here before — when she mooched for a week — she happened to come across Adrian working with some documents. I don't know the details. Anyway, they got to talking about it. She knew about the Pilate book from that first visit — the time she came with you — and this time, he told her that he was on the track of this Christian artifact."

Bethany couldn't help herself. "The Pilate

Stone," she murmured.

"Ah, so you know about it."

"I'd never heard of it until after Annabelle died. That's when I learned she'd been looking for it."

"Do you happen to know if she found it?"

"I don't think so. No."

"I'm not a bit surprised."

"Why is that?"

"Because the Pilate Stone is a myth. It doesn't exist. It never did. Adrian told me, not long before he blew his brains out."

They were back at the house. She expected Dorothea to be nervous, but the woman entered the house without hesitation, and Bethany followed her upstairs to look at the picture of Dorothea and Annabelle. She didn't ask about the Pilate Stone. There was no point. She had worked it out.

Annabelle knew about the Stone. Adrian Wisdom knew. And whatever Adrian knew, he wanted his daughter to have no part of it. Whether he shot himself in the head or somebody else did it for him, he sensed that the search for the Stone had carried him into dangerous territory. Dorothea might think her father had hated her, but at the end he protected her the only way he could: by lying to her.

"Oh, this," said Dorothea with the same forced brightness. She was holding the framed photograph up to the light. The cat, Thoreau, had crept up the stairs to see what the fuss was about. "That's me and Annabelle by the Thames. When she was here a few years ago. There's a walk I do when I'm blue, along the shore, sometimes as far as Abingdon. And I'm afraid I'm blue a lot. So I do my walk, and I wander a bit. Now and then up into the hills. I was unhappy — over some man, I should imagine — and, anyway, I took the walk. Annabelle attached herself to me. I didn't invite her. She just came along." A smaller laugh. "She called it a hike."

"And you stopped to get your picture taken?"

"In one of the towns. Yes." Scrunching her plump face. "I rather think it was Iffley. I like to sit in the old church and pray."

Iffley. St. Mary's. The postcard Bratt had stolen. "I thought you were an atheist," said Bethany, just for something to say.

"It calms me, I suppose. Sitting in an old church, surrounded by all that history. Besides, you never know. Somebody might be up there listening. And of course Adrian used to make me go to services when I was small. Old habits die hard, I suppose."

The physicist was really giving too many excuses, Bethany decided. Her determined atheism seemed flayed by doubt.

"I suppose," Bethany echoed.

Dorothea hung the photo back on the wall, brushed the dust from her hands. "You're saying Annabelle hid the postcard in the frame? And your intruder took it?"

"Yes."

"I don't see how that's possible." In the close upstairs hallway, her chubby figure stretching from one wall to the next, Dorothea exuded a scary monomania. "When would she have done that?"

"Probably when she was here in December."

"You mean November. And she never came to the house. We met at my office."

"She came back in December. Right around Christmas."

"Oh, I rather doubt that. I was in Asia all month. Are you hungry?" Closing the subject. "I can do us some sandwiches."

They trooped back downstairs, Bethany still trying to put the missing pieces together.

"About your father's papers —"

"Oh, no. Not you too. I'll tell you what I told Annabelle. What I've told everybody who's asked. I don't have the Pilate manuscript. I never even saw it. I have no idea what happened to it. I even went through Adrian's papers myself, looking for it. Nothing. I told Annabelle she knew more about it than I did."

*Everybody who's asked,* Bethany registered. Aloud, she said, "Did your father work with anybody else? On the Pilate biography, I mean?"

"He had some correspondents in Europe. Historians, I suppose. Italy, I think. Well, I don't really remember. Oh, and one of the tutors worked with him. Are you staying the night or not?"

Bethany was startled by the sudden shift in topic. Dorothea pressed her advantage.

"What if your intruder comes back? From what you say, I'm sure he didn't have time to do a full search. I can't believe that some postcard is all he expected to find."

"Dorothea, I —"

"And what I said before — I really meant it, Bethany. I can't imagine what it's like out there on the run. A safe place for one night — that's something you need, surely. And we can talk more about Annabelle."

"That's very sweet of you, but I really think I should keep moving."

Misreading her guest's freshened reluctance, Dorothea added, "Really, we'll be perfectly safe. You needn't worry about him. Truly."

For an instant Bethany was confused. Then she had it.

Oh, but she could be an idiot.

"That was his real name, wasn't it? Bratt. You know him."

"Yes, indeed. I know him." But behind the thick glasses the eyes said even more.

"Bratt was telling the truth, wasn't he? He does live here, and he's your second husband. The one your father never liked."

"Oh, no, he doesn't live here. Not any more. No. Teddy Bratt and I were married for a year and a half. As I said, Adrian drove him away." Dorothea had the grace to blush a bit, and looked, for an instant, surprisingly young, even girlish. "And Teddy — well, you know, since Adrian died, he still comes around now and then, the way men do. I changed the lock, naturally, but he managed to get a key. I changed it again and he came up with another key. Well, a private investigator, I should imagine he has the right contacts."

"But he can't just walk in whenever he wants. That's against the law in the States."

"Here too, I should imagine." Dorothea's expression was still amused, but it seemed to Bethany that her ability to sustain it was wearing thin.

"Then why don't you stop him?"

"Stop him? Stop him from what?"

"From entering your house without permission!"

"Who said he didn't have permission?" She shrugged her shoulders. "We live the lives we live, Bethany. Yes, Teddy was a bad husband. But — well, look at me." The aggressive good humor had finally drained away, replaced by a lonely helplessness, close cousin to despair. "I'm not like Adrian. I'm not charming. I'm not fun. I'm not anything, really." A shrug of defeat. "I'm afraid Teddy is the only friend I've got."

This was too much. Bethany raised her hands, as if to shove the idea physically away.

"You called him from the lab, didn't you? That's why you want me to stay. You called Teddy Bratt, and he's on the way back."

"He was in London. But he'll be here in another hour or so." Her eyes were luminous, desperate, enlarged by her glasses. "You can trust him, Bethany. I promise you can trust him. He'll help. Wait. Where are you going?"

At the door she had one last question. "You said one of the tutors worked with your father."

"Fellow by the name of Apple. Grant Apple. Adrian scared him to death. Kept asking me out. I suppose he thought it would make things easier with Adrian. Silly boy."

"Where can I find him?"

"Apple? Oh, he left, let's see, two years ago. Just around the time Adrian shot himself, come to think of it. Said he'd had enough of the academy. Runs a bookstore in the High Street. Sad sort of fellow these days. Outside-looking-in sort of thing."

"Dorothea, look —"

"Don't worry." She actually patted Bethany's cheek. "I've nobody to tell. I'd be in more trouble than you, believe me."

Outside, Bethany retrieved her bicycle and walked it to the curb, feeling the eyes of Adrian Wisdom's peculiar daughter burning into her back. She did not turn around. She slung a leg over the seat and began to pedal away, speeding through the rain to the bed-and-breakfast. Although the location was not entirely secure, she had to sleep somewhere, and anything was better than this madwoman's house.

It was so obvious, now that Bethany could look at the answers in the back of the book. Dorothea hadn't liked Annabelle any more than she'd liked her own father. She put up with her because she was lonely. And Annabelle, in her turn, wouldn't have trusted Dorothea with a shopping list. She'd never discussed the Pilate Stone with her. She'd tried to get into Adrian's papers in November, then returned and hidden the torn photograph and the postcard in December, when Dorothea was away.

And how had she gotten into the house?

With the help of Teddy Bratt, the ex-husband who still had a key. Teddy, not Dorothea, was Annabelle's connection. Teddy might not know what Annabelle had hidden — she wasn't fool enough to make him her confidante — but he had known there was something. Bethany wondered whether there was any point to searching the church in Iffley. If Annabelle had left anything there, there was a fair chance that Teddy had it by now. She would seek him out as soon as possible, but not while Dorothea was around.

Riding hard, she streaked off into the night.

Slipping in and out of the shadows, also on a bicycle, the killer called Morgan followed.

It was quite late when word reached the

Church Builder at his hotel. The call came from the Senator, to whom Edna Harrigan had poured out the story. The governing board of the Garden was small, and each member had a name linked vaguely with his or her pursuits in the overt world: the Senator, the Pastor, the Writer, the Mathematician. Edna was called the Judge. There had been another — the Critic — but the Critic was killed in an ambush a few weeks back. The Pastor had been seriously wounded in the same attack, and his recovery was up in the air. Harry Stean had ordered the others to lie low. Nobody was to take any action of any kind. He and he alone would bear the risk of contacting Bethany and trying to clean up the mess.

And now this.

"From the description, it had to be Fuentes," said the Senator. "I didn't mention that to Edna, but I don't see who else would have the motive."

"I don't follow, Gillian. What exactly is he up to?"

"He's trying to shake her up. Smoke her out. Force her to move."

"You mean he suspects her role, and he wants to find out who else is in on it with her?"

"That's essentially right." She paused.

"Harry, he tried to see me tonight."

"Fuentes?"

"He presented himself at my townhouse and claimed to have an appointment. He used another name, and the security people turned him away, but the surveillance image is clear as a bell."

Harry pinched the bridge of his nose. He was looking out over Hyde Park but not really seeing it.

"He wanted you to know it was him," the Builder finally said. "He thinks you're in it with Edna."

"He can't know for sure. I called three or four other people who are known to be friends of Edna's. Turned out he'd dropped in on a couple of them, asking the same questions. He's fishing, Harry."

"You said he's asking Edna's friends if they've heard her mention WAKEFUL. That's a message to us, not to Edna. I doubt that she's even heard of Bethany's cryptonym. He wants us to know how much he knows."

"I still say he's fishing."

"Maybe so, Gillian. But we can't take any chances." Harry straightened. "Before, it was a suggestion. Now it's an order. All of you are to stand down. Take no action of any kind. Don't even get in touch with each other unless it's an emergency."

"Harry —"

"Gillian, the only way this makes sense is that Fuentes is working with Bethany. Bethany might not know about Edna's connection to us, but he's figured it out. He's a trained operative who survived any number of dicey missions in Afghanistan. He's not turning back."

"I don't understand. What's his motive? Why is he after us?"

"I can't say for sure, but I suspect that he's trying to find Janice Stafford."

"The hacker girl? The one from BLLNET?"

"I haven't told you everything, Gillian. You know Janice and Bethany were on the run together. What you don't know is that Janice has been kidnapped. The opposition has her. I had confirmation just about the time Bethany left for London."

A prickly pause. "When were you planning to let me know?"

"I'm letting you know now. If Fuentes is searching for Janice, we should keep out of his way. But in the unlikely event that he asks you for assistance, it's your job to render it."

"That would mean admitting my role!"

"I know, Gillian, and I'm sorry about that. But Janice is a prisoner, and WAKEFUL is being blackmailed, and all of it is our fault."

"We didn't start this war, Harry."

"No, we didn't. You're right. But we chose the weapons."

# FOURTEEN

On the following morning the fugitive known as Wakeful rose early. Her sleep had been as troubled as her cryptonym might suggest. She had considered, quite seriously, fleeing Oxford entirely. But her weeks on the run had taught her to rest whenever possible, and Raymond Fuentes had counseled much the same.

Fuentes.

Bethany wondered whether he was keeping his promise. He was the sort of man who would, she decided arbitrarily. He said that he would find Janice, and she suspected that he wouldn't stop trying until he did. But another part of Bethany knew that she wanted him to be that kind of man. She didn't know him well enough to know whether he was, but she wanted him to be. She wanted to have reason to think well of him.

What might lie behind that, she didn't

want to guess.

Fifteen minutes after rising, she was downstairs in the dining room of the bed-and-breakfast, a rambling Victorian on the outskirts of Oxford. The only others breakfasting that morning were an elderly couple who barely spoke to each other as they chewed their careful little bites, and a pair of noisy children whose mother, coping inexpertly, kept glancing over at Bethany and shrugging in embarrassment.

"Custom is slim in the summer season," said the matron who ran the place, an academic widow named Cranch, when she came by with coffee. "Did you find your bookstore?" Mrs. Cranch was an engaging sort, and last night she and Bethany had sat in the parlor enjoying a friendly conversation about the local shops. And after her guest spun an unhappy tale about her laptop having been stolen, Mrs. Cranch was kind enough to let Elaine (as she called her) use her own computer in the back room to do a little quick online research.

"I did, thank you."

By nine, Bethany was out the door and on her bicycle once more. Yesterday she had left her rolling suitcase at her original lodgings. The bag held nothing she couldn't replace. What she needed was in the backpack that never left her side.

And in her head of course: there most of all.

The village of Iffley is a ten-minute bicycle ride from downtown Oxford, but again Bethany took a circuitous route because she was afraid of being followed. At a shop in Church Way, she bought a bun and coffee and sat for a time at the window, watching the traffic and the pedestrians alike. She was not entirely confident that she would spot any surveillance, but certainly she was better off trying. Satisfied at last, she walked her bicycle along the sidewalk, peering into storefronts and admiring the buildings, some of which had been standing for many hundreds of years.

St. Mary's church stood at the end of the road, set back a bit in its own bright field of summer grass. Bethany didn't know what she was looking for; she only knew that she owed it to Annabelle to see whether there was something to be found. Teddy Bratt had returned to London, Dorothea said. If that was so, perhaps he hadn't had time to do a full search of the church after all. Whatever Annabelle had hidden might still be here.

Inside, a handful of early morning tourists were gawking and snapping pictures. She took a leaflet from a rack and joined them. For a good twenty minutes she *oohed* and *ahhed* over the vaulted ceiling that had been painstakingly restored, and the high altar, which had been bricked up by the Puritans and then uncovered again. She marveled at the internecine wars believers fought with each other, as if they had no real common enemies.

Belief, as Aunt Claudia used to say, was hard work.

Now Bethany was moving from pew to pew, running her fingers beneath the rail here, glancing at the floor there, searching for she knew not what.

Then it occurred to her that she might have made a mistake.

The photograph of Annabelle and Dorothea wasn't taken inside the church. It was taken outside.

She stepped out into the sun, stood on the grass, and shut her eyes, trying to visualize the picture. The two women in hiking gear, each with an arm around the other's shoulder as they grinned for the camera. A sliver of the church in the background to the left. And, to the right, the copse of cherry trees — barren in November, but now in full bloom with their bright pink blossoms.

And Annabelle wearing that bright pink sweater, so odd a color for her.

Too obvious? Maybe. Maybe not.

Forcing herself to move slowly, for all the world a tourist still, Bethany made her way to the trees. She still wasn't sure what she was looking for. Suppose Annabelle had left a clue out here. It couldn't be buried. The ground was well tended, raked and mulched: anything beneath the soil would be lost. It couldn't be stuck between the branches. A storm, a bird, a squirrel, a climbing child — anything might dislodge it.

*Think. You're Annabelle. You're suspicious of the world. Here it is December and you're on your own, but you also think you might be followed. You don't have much time. Where do you spread your bread crumbs so that they'll survive the seasons, and the people, and the birds, and the animals?*

And then she had it. Obvious after all.

You do what Pilate did. You carve it.

She stepped into the middle of the stand of trees and began to study the bark. A pair of old women walking together asked if she'd lost something, and if she needed a hand. She thanked them, but could think of no sensible story for why she was studying the tree trunks so intensely, so she just said she was fine.

Then she watched them wander off, to be sure they didn't make another turn to keep her in sight.

Back to work.

This time, when she turned back to the trees, she saw the mark at once. Midway up the central cherry tree, just about eye height, as if to make sure Bethany wouldn't miss it.

Three letters and a number, carved inside a roughly hacked heart shape, as if by a pair of young lovers. Nobody who wasn't looking would give it a second thought:

A W + 7 T

Bethany ran wondering fingers over the bark.

"AW" for Adrian Wisdom. That part was obvious. As for "7T" — well, she would have to keep looking. But at least she had a clue in hand. She was not wrong.

Annabelle was still marking the trail. Bethany only wished she knew where the path led.

The Church Builder has never grown comfortable with the informality of what is nowadays known as networking. He is of an age to prefer to deal with men of his own generation, based on friendships of long standing, and an intricate mesh of favors, loyalties, and obligations. That is why he is sitting in an alcove at one of London's frostier clubs, beneath the alabaster eyes of peers long dead, sharing lunch with a man named Mark Satterwhite, very senior in the Foreign Office, whom he has known since they worked together on a series of projects in Africa a good thirty years ago. In the intervening decades they have carefully performed for each other what Mark calls "little kindnesses," as a way of knitting their loyalties more closely. And if over their long acquaintance Harry Stean has had the occasional inkling that Mark might perform certain less public functions on behalf of Her Majesty's Government — well, those suspicions, as much as anything, form the basis for today's meeting.

"Fancy the place?" asks Mark with a wink. He has thick silver hair and is wearing a vested charcoal suit that must have cost the gross domestic product of a small country.

"Nice enough, I suppose, if you don't mind all the statues looking over your shoulder." Harry leans closer. "I told you I wanted to meet confidentially."

"I remember."

"And this is what you call clandestine?"

"You mean, has anybody bugged the

steak-and-kidney pie? Is the waiter wearing a camera in his vest button?" Mark laughs. "Anything is possible, of course, but I'd think likely not. Nobody eavesdrops in a club, Harry. This club especially. Because there's too much risk of others doing it right back. And because, frankly, it just isn't the sort of thing that gentlemen do."

"The people I'm worried about aren't gentlemen."

The diplomat's face tautens. "This is going to be our only opportunity, Harry. If you want to talk, this is when we talk. If you want to talk in private, this is as private as it's likely to get."

Mark signals the waiter to refill their glasses, a gracious gesture allowing his guest the time to decide whether to tell his story. And Harry is grateful for the extra moments to think.

"I'm afraid I need your help," he says when they're alone once more. "And your word as an English gentleman not to share what I'm going to tell you with anyone else."

"Of course, Harry. What is it?"

"There's a woman in the U.K. who's being sought by the authorities back in the States for a string of bombings."

"She's actually here? Your Lab Bomber? I'd heard stories, of course, but I didn't know they were accurate."

"She didn't do it, Mark."

"Surely that's for your government to sort out."

"This is where the favor comes in. I know that you or people you're in touch with have the resources to find her, if I tell you where to start. What I need is for you to track her down and arrange for me to talk to her. After that — I need you to let her go."

The man from the Foreign Office grows somber. "That may be more than I can promise, Harry."

"I know."

"On the other hand, I suppose if I don't promise, you won't tell me where to start."

"That would be correct."

"You know your government's given her a code name? For use in dispatches? WAKEFUL. That's what we're supposed to call her."

"Then I need your word that if you find WAKEFUL, you'll arrange a meeting, and then let her go."

The diplomat shuts his eyes briefly and massages his temple like a man suffering a migraine. Then he looks at his old friend. "I owe you, Harry. I know that. So — fine. If my friends can track WAKEFUL down — a very big *if* — then I will see to it that you meet her, and that she's also allowed to depart. You have my word. Now, let's have the story."

"Have you ever heard of the Pilate Stone?"

"I'm afraid not."

"It's an early Christian artifact. It's not well known. It might not even exist. Nevertheless, there are people who would pay tens of millions for it, and other people who would kill to get it."

"And this is what WAKEFUL is after? This stone?"

"Yes and no, Mark. Yes, and no . . ."

Back in his cavernous rooms at the Foreign and Commonwealth Office in Whitehall, Mark Satterwhite took off his jacket — a thing he ordinarily would never consider during the workday — and carefully removed his vest, watched by two quiet men from what he liked to call the other side of the park. The wire ran from the button microphone to the digital recorder taped to his back.

One of the quiet men reached for the recorder.

Mark held it back.

"My friend isn't going to be molested in any way," he said. "I have your word."

"Nobody's going to touch Mr. Stean. He's

free to go about his business."

"But you will let me know? If you find her, I mean?"

"We're going to find her, sir. You needn't worry."

"Still," he persisted. "You will let me know?"

"You've done your job, Mr. Satterwhite. Now it's time for you to stand aside and allow us to do ours."

"He didn't tell me the whole story, you know. Not even close."

"We don't need the whole story. We just need WAKEFUL."

They took the recorder and left.

# FIFTEEN

The antiquarian bookstore was located in the High Street, squeezed uneasily between a pricey women's boutique and the sort of pub where an argument over Wittgenstein could start a riot. Bethany Barclay stepped through the door at half past nine precisely — the time was later established from a security camera at the bank across the street — and the place was pretty much empty, except for a stooped old man whose shaky fingers played idly over the spines of nineteenth century medical texts, and another man, perhaps five years older than Bethany herself, who stood behind the counter wrapping a parcel. He sported a dark unruly beard and a threadbare cardigan of the sort that not long ago had been almost a uniform for many a dowdy but brilliant British academic, and when he lifted his bespectacled eyes toward the new customer, she knew at once from the way that he stared that he knew who she was.

No way out but forward.

"May I help you?" he asked, and she supposed that the strange screechiness in his voice was natural to him rather than a sign of nervousness, because the customer, possibly a regular, never looked up. "Only the manager isn't here," he continued, as if expecting a complaint.

"I'm looking for Grant Apple," she said.

"And why would that be?" His tone was arch and probably meant as derisive. Seen up close, he was skinnier than she'd realized, his sweater and flannels ill fitting and loose.

"Are you Mr. Apple?"

"What if I am?"

"Is there someplace we can talk?"

Behind the heavy lenses his eyes blinked slowly, once, twice, then a third time, like the eyes of a character in a children's cartoon. He seemed to give her question genuine consideration, because he drummed his fingers on the counter for a bit, then went back to wrapping his parcel. "I'm rather busy," he said.

She leaned close. "It's about Annabelle."

"Who?"

"Annabelle Seaver."

"What about her?"

Bethany saw only one way to break down the belligerence. "She's dead," she said, not quite managing the harshness she was shooting for. "I was her friend."

The eyes came up. The old man was moving toward the door, but stopped and pulled a book of Renoir reproductions from a low shelf. He turned the pages, nodding and muttering.

"You're American," Apple said, quite loudly, as if he had solved the great puzzle.

"Yes."

"Then you'd be interested in Fitzgerald, I imagine. People like that. Not our greats. Only yours. That's what Americans are like."

"Actually —"

"Let me see what I have," he said, and vanished into the storeroom.

She wondered how long she should wait. The telephone system was old-fashioned, with lights to indicate that the line was in use. Fortunately, no light was illuminated. On the other hand, if Apple wanted to call the police, his cell phone was every bit as convenient.

The door chimed. Bethany glanced around. The old man wasn't leaving as she'd expected. Instead, a middle-aged woman had wandered in, gravitating at once to the display of maps along a far wall, and Bethany hoped desperately that she was a professor or a professor's wife, because the alternative was that she was the advance guard of somebody's surveillance team. A couple of teenaged girls giggled in, both of them around Janice's age. They didn't look at the displays but huddled in the front window, probably playing some elaborate hiding game. They were young, yes, but by now Bethany was ready to suspect just about anybody of just about —

"Here we are, miss."

Grant Apple was back. He slid a book across the counter.

"Take a look. This is *The Last Tycoon* — Fitzgerald's last, and unfinished, you'll recall. It's the 1941 Scribner's first edition. *Gatsby* is in here too, along with all of Fitzgerald's short stories."

"I — I think —"

"Do you fancy it, then?" The blinkered eyes were urgent and imploring.

"It's lovely."

"Two thousand pounds."

She blinked. "I beg your pardon."

"That's the best I can do, miss. Take it or leave it."

"I'm just here because —"

"This book is why you're here," he screeched. "This book is exactly what you asked for."

He was being intentionally awkward. Everybody was looking. He wanted them to notice; he wanted her to know how easily he could ruin everything.

"I only have dollars," she said.

"Then let's say four thousand."

"But the rate of exchange —"

"Take it or leave it." He nodded toward the queue. "I'm afraid I've other paying customers."

She calculated. Swallowed. This would take a big chunk of the money she'd brought with her.

"Is cash acceptable?" she asked.

He even wrapped it for her. She kept the parcel in a carrier bag as she walked swiftly along the street, nodding and smiling now and then but mostly keeping to herself. He was insane. Or she was. She had bought the next clue. Or she had bought only a book.

She would know in a few minutes.

She unlocked the rented bicycle and rode out of town to the bed-and-breakfast — a different one this time — where she had booked a room for the night. She waited until she was upstairs and alone before cautiously unwrapping the book. Sitting on the lumpy bed, she flipped through the pages.

Finding no note, not even a yellow sticky, she held the book upside down and swayed it from side to side. No secret message tumbled out.

Bethany was furious. And embarrassed. Grant Apple had known a mark when he saw one and took advantage. Maybe he had even called the police after all — once she was out of the store and he'd pocketed the money. Maybe she should get going.

She looked around the room for traces of her presence. She found the wrapping paper, balled it up to put in her backpack and carry to a trash can elsewhere, then sat back on the bed, hard, and unfolded it.

The message was on the inside of the wrapper.

ST. EDMUND'S CRYPT. TEN.

No specification of morning or evening, no date. But Bethany was no fool.

Her four thousand dollars had bought her a meeting. A meeting that would move her one step closer to Wisdom's manuscript, and thus, she hoped, one step closer to the Pilate Stone.

Ten o'clock.

Tonight.

# SIXTEEN

"It's some photograph," says Melody Sunderland. "That's what has Lillian so spooked."

Elliott St. John toys with his glass. "She told you?"

"Yes."

"Did she tell you what it's a photograph of?"

"Not exactly."

Elliott frowns. He hates indirection, especially in those who are beholden to him. As Melody has grown closer to the Lord Protector, her attitude toward the man who was once her mentor has inched toward disrespectful.

They are at a corner table in the private dining room on the sixty-sixth floor of the Central Park West building that is home to his media empire. The cavernous hall is otherwise empty. They have just finished a late lunch of steak and shrimp, and are now enjoying a rare port that leaves on the tongue an aftertaste of fruit and mocha. The floor-to-ceiling windows give a view of Central Park with the towers of Manhattan beyond glistening in the sunlight.

"What exactly did she say?" Elliott prompts.

Melody takes a careful sip, then brushes blond hair from her slim face. She is a political activist of some note. In her late thirties, she is by far the youngest member of the Council. She hosts a radio talk show wildly popular on the right and gives to animal-rights causes wildly popular on the left.

She is also, in Elliott St. John's view, entirely of his creation.

"She said it was a photo of a foolish girl taken a very long time ago. She said it could do a lot of harm to our cause." Melody has a smooth cable-ready voice that half the country hates and half the country loves. "She said it's in the wild, and that Bethany Barclay is our best chance to get it back."

"I see."

"Good. Because I don't."

His eyebrows arch. He is accustomed to this sort of snideness from Lillian. From Melody it is new and disturbing.

"What don't you see?" he asks, with exaggerated patience.

"I don't see how some old photograph can bring us down. We've been around for centuries, right? So what difference can one photo make?"

Elliott sighs, hoping his disappointment shows. Melody has been on the Council less than two years and is speaking as though they share a common history. He remembers the Melody Sunderland he first met a decade ago. She was a minor editor at an unimportant periodical in a distant corner of Elliott's realm, a twenty-something Princeton graduate with half a screenplay in a drawer and no other serious prospects. At one of his semiannual receptions for underlings, he overheard her ranting about politics to a circle of listeners. Although the actual content of her words struck him as nonsense, he observed the mesmerizing effect on her audience and wondered whether it might be possible to exploit her talent. He didn't speak to her that night — it was vital that she not doubt his motives — but he had her investigated, and observed, and promoted. This is how media stars are created these days: you pick the telegenic and build. One of his editors had her write a couple of silly polemics. One of his television shows brought her on as an occasional guest commentator. One of his companies gave her a book contract.

Melody Sunderland was launched.

Now she earns millions a year, and she was his discovery. His wife supposes that they are sleeping together, or that they did at some time, but Elliott is far too savvy to make that error. He knows Melody's value to his empire.

So does Melody.

Aloud he says, "You know there are things we can't discuss with you."

"I know."

"You're still fairly new to all this."

"I know," she says again, openly annoyed at being reminded. Or perhaps she recognizes that Elliott is only pretending not to be every bit in the dark as she is.

A hiatus while a white-jacketed waiter comes in to see who needs more coffee from the trolley, but they're both fine with the port. A tray of cookies appears, and Elliott goes into his act: the rich middle-aged buffoon the junior staff believes him to be.

"Melody. Say. Do you care for the port? It's Taylor's Scion. Family label. Canadian. Very rare. I don't believe there's a single bottle left on the market. They don't release them any more. My cellar has three, I believe. Why don't you take one with you?

Show off to your friends." To the waiter: "Have the steward bring a bottle of the Taylor's Scion for Miss Sunderland. Oh, and tell you what. Just to top it off — let's see — how about a bottle of the Domaine Faiveley Musigny Grand Cru 1959?" A dazzling smile for his guest. "You won't find that at the corner wine shop."

When they are alone again, the bonhomie vanishes. He leans toward his protégé. "What else did the Lord Protector tell you about the photograph? I want to hear every word."

Melody turns to gaze out at Manhattan, and he knows she is calculating: if this comes to a tussle between Elliott and Lillian, which side is the more likely to prevail? When she speaks, it is with an almost palpable reluctance.

"Annabelle somehow filched the photograph from Findrake. I don't know how, and I don't think Lillian does either. The point is, she wanted Ralph to go see Findrake to ask him to call off his dogs until after Bethany Barclay finds the photo for us."

"Which dogs are these?"

"The ones who killed Ralph and Annabelle and are trying to kill Bethany."

Elliott sees it then. He leaps ahead to the

connection that Melody has missed. Suddenly he knows exactly which photograph it must be, and at that moment — a rare instance — is ahead of them all, even the Lord Protector.

But of course he can say none of this to Melody, so he covers his excitement with another pertinent question:

"So Lord Findrake wants to kill Bethany. Why?"

"To keep the Pilate Stone hidden. He thinks we're taking a huge risk by bringing it into the open."

"Is he really that afraid of what the words might say?" But the question is rhetorical, and even this newer and cockier Melody has the wit not to interrupt her mentor in his reverie. "And I suppose that if Bethany does find the photo, Lillian thinks she'll turn it over to us for the same reason she'll turn the Pilate Stone over to us. Because of the insurance she's taken out."

"Exactly."

"The same insurance that keeps her on our leash as she searches for the Pilate Stone?"

"That would be the logical assumption," says Melody, her hauteur returning.

"And did she happen to mention what that insurance might consist of?"

"No," says Melody, too quickly, and the way her eyes dart away has Elliott suddenly worried.

The wine steward chooses that moment to bustle in. He is carrying a pair of wooden boxes, which he opens to display the bottles in their green wadding. Melody makes a great show of excitement, and as they rise, even kisses Elliott on both cheeks.

But as he summons his assistant to escort Miss Sunderland down to her car, Elliott wonders what the Lord Protector is sharing with Melody that she doesn't want him to know.

Janice Stafford looks up at the sound of the door being unlocked. It's the wrong day for her exercise and it's the wrong time for her food delivery. She's spent the afternoon working logic problems from an old Smullyan book the man called Kenny dropped off yesterday. So far, very few have presented her with any sort of challenge, but at least her agile mind has been occupied.

One of her guards is standing there, the one she's arbitrarily labeled Stettin, after a minor character in an Asimov novel.

"You're supposed to be some kind of genius, right?" he says.

This is the last thing she expects. "I'm sorry?"

"Some kind of computer genius. That's what they say."

"I know a little about computers. Sure."

His hand is on the knob. His gun is in its holster. He is taking her measure. "Good. My laptop keeps freezing. Can you fix it for me?"

Her heart leaps. "I can look at it."

"Fine. But I'll be watching your every move."

"I understand."

"I mean it, Janice. You hit a key I don't like — you go to a website I don't like — do anything I don't like — and you won't like what happens next. Are we clear?"

"We're clear."

"Then come on."

He leads her downstairs. The laptop is open on the counter beside the electric range. She has noticed it on her treks to the basement workout room.

Janice feels the old longing rise. It is like an addiction. She fights the urge to lick her lips. She has to be very careful. Already her thoughts are spinning away from escape and toward the simple joy of being linked to the world once more, to be able to lose herself in the smooth, loving contours of cyber-space.

Aloud she says, in the coolest voice she can manage, "Is it okay if I sit down?"

Two minutes later she is lost. In her own favorite world. She clicks more than she has to just to enjoy the feel of the touch pad beneath her fingers. She has the Task Manager and the Resource Monitor open, and she isn't thinking about escaping from the house or trying to send an encrypted message to her friends at BLLNET. She is trying to fix the computer.

"What's that?" a fresh voice says, and Janice realizes that it is her other afternoon guard, a woman she calls Noys — from another Asimov story — and that the woman is repeating a question she has asked two or three times already.

"What's what?"

"That little box at the bottom of the screen."

"It's for DOS commands." She doesn't look up. "It lets me communicate directly with the operating system."

Janice hears the two guards arguing softly. *You shouldn't have let her out of the room. It's fine. We could be in so much trouble.* Back and forth, back and forth, just like her well-to-do parents in the old days whisper-

183

ing angrily over whether to change her school. Janice doesn't care. She's much calmer now. She's diagnosed the problem. As she works on repairing it, she begins to think more clearly about . . . other opportunities.

"Your antivirus software is out of date," she says.

"Do I have a virus?"

"I'll know after I update."

After that Stettin leaves her alone with Noys for a while. Noys is a strapping forty-ish woman whom Janice is willing to bet has been a cop in her time. Behind Janice's back she is opening the refrigerator.

"I'm making a sandwich. Do you want anything?"

"Uh-uh," Janice says. Then she realizes that the woman is trying to make a bridge. She looks up, smiles sweetly. "No, thank you. I'd love some water, though."

Noys sets a Poland Spring bottle beside her. Stettin returns from his rounds. He peeks over her shoulder. "What are you doing now?"

She points to a line in the Resource Monitor. "Your computer is hanging because it's trying to execute too many read commands. That's usually either a memory leak or a problem with one of the drivers. More likely the latter."

"Meaning what?"

"I think it's your Wi-Fi."

"Can you fix it?"

"Depends. If it's the wireless card, there's nothing to do but yank it out and get a new one. Then you won't have Internet access. The driver is just software. If it's the driver, I might be able to come up with a work-around. Or we might be able to download a patch."

"From where?"

"Maybe the manufacturer's website. Maybe some other sites that specialize in this kind of thing."

"I can't let you go online."

"Then you can download the patch. I'll tell you how."

Stettin glances around, obviously wanting to make sure that they're alone. "Fine. You can do it. But I'll be right behind you."

"Okay."

"If you try to send a message, I'll see."

"I get it. I told you."

Again her fingers fly. She is in her element, her mind flowing along the Web as she searches, studies, puzzles. She finds and discards one solution after the other. Time begins to slip away. She finds a patch but it's the wrong one. She finds another but it doesn't work. She hunkers down. No computer has ever defeated her. She recalls the test pilots in *The Right Stuff* — the book, not the movie — who always assume there's a solution, even as the plane plummets toward earth: "I've tried *A*! I've tried *B*! What else can I try?" Janice tries *A*. She tries *B*. She goes on to *C* and *D* and *E* and *F* and . . .

She sits back.

"Done," she says.

The man she calls Stettin is practically dozing in his chair. Now he snaps awake. "Why did it take so long?"

"You want it to work, don't you?"

"Fine." He notices something on the screen. "What's that? In the corner?" He doesn't wait for her answer. "It's some kind of website."

Janice shrugs. She brushes her braids from her face. "I was testing the Wi-Fi. What did you want me to do?"

"Testing it on what?"

"It's just a Hollywood site, okay? See? Who's getting divorced. What the Kardashians are up to." She sees his expression, gives him a look. "What? Just because I'm good with computers doesn't mean I'm not still sixteen."

He doesn't like it. "How do I know you're

not playing some kind of trick on me?"

Janice is patient. "You were sitting right behind me the whole time. You saw what I did. I went to tech websites to read about the problem, I went to the manufacturer's website, and I downloaded the patch. I installed it. Then to test it I went to a couple of sports sites and a couple of Hollywood gossip sites. If you don't believe me, review the cache."

"What's a cache?"

"It's a record of the websites your computer's visited."

The guard's eyes go very wide. "All of them?"

"Usually for thirty days or whatever the default is. That is, unless you empty it."

"If you empty the cache, nobody knows where you've been?"

"Sometimes there are other ways. Depends on the operating system, the browser, and on lots of other variables. It's difficult, and it takes time, so most of the time even the experts won't bother. Not unless they have some reason to be suspicious."

Stettin gives a curt nod. "Can you empty the cache for me?"

"Sure."

"And you can teach me how? So I can do it myself?"

"Sure."

A hard swallow. "And can you . . . can you fix it so nobody can tell where I've been? I mean, if they're, um, smart enough not to just look in the cache?"

"Maybe. Probably. But what's in it for me?"

"What do you want?"

"Well, to start with, a Quarter Pounder with Cheese from Mickey D's would be nice."

"There's a McDonald's five minutes away," he says.

"Great." She turns back to the laptop. "Let me show you how to empty the cache."

Janice is back in her room. She eats the Quarter Pounder from her usual portable tray. She is eating very fast. Very sloppily. When she's in cyberspace she's never hungry, but as soon as she's done she's always ravenous. Burger, fries, shake: she'd live on this diet forever if she could.

When she's done, she follows the rules. She puts the tray on the floor, knocks twice, and moves to the far side of the room. The woman she calls Noys steps in, takes the tray, gives her a look.

"You know, Janice, we're not as stupid as you think we are."

"I don't know what you mean."

"I mean we're going to call Kenny and have an expert look at that computer to see what you did. I'm sure you did something."

Janice shrugs. "You won't find anything."

"Because there's nothing to find? Or because you covered your tracks?" She doesn't wait for an answer. She shuts the door and runs the bolt home.

The teen stares at the door, momentarily concerned. Then she turns back to her logic games. They won't find anything on the laptop. She's sure of it. They won't find anything because there's nothing to find.

With any luck, however, somebody else will.

# Seventeen

St. Edmund Crypt is, technically, the crypt of St. Peter-in-the-East, a church built in the eleventh century. The church is no longer a church. It's now the library of St. Edmund Hall. The crypt, which lies beneath the church, was built a century later. Bethany decided that it was best to reconnoiter the rendezvous by daylight. First, however, she checked out of her current bed-and-breakfast and found another at the opposite end of town. Then she spent an hour and a half riding or walking along the streets, hoping to spot any surveillance. When she finally arrived at St. Edmund Hall it was the middle of the afternoon.

In her chosen role of gawking tourist, she passed through the lodge and into the quadrangle surrounded by its mullioned windows. A steward smiled at her as he passed. He was wearing a Teddy bear tie, and she smiled at the irony. St. Edmund, she remembered, was known familiarly as Teddy Hall.

The path led her to the churchyard and meandered among the headstones. The old cemetery nowadays was got up as a lovely little park. On a bench along the inner wall, a statue of St. Edmund studied a book. An undergraduate lounged beside him, studying her iPhone with a ferocious intensity. Another young woman sitting on the grass nearby was watching Bethany.

It was too late to be inconspicuous, so she decided to be the opposite. She strolled boldly up to the pair of them to ask how she might get into the crypt.

"The crypt?" said one, smiling. "You can't get into the crypt. It's all closed up."

"Why?"

"Don't know," said the other, scarcely looking up. "Construction. Safety. Secret Masonic rites, for all I know."

In Bethany's own Oxford days, there hadn't been a single forbidden space whose secret weaknesses students didn't know. But she dared not press further. A tourist who makes a single inquiry is an idiot, and swiftly forgotten. A tourist who makes a pair is a nuisance, and remembered.

"Too bad," she said, allowing herself to look crestfallen — which in fact she was.

The students retreated to their own world. Bethany left the churchyard, wondering. But not before she noticed the padlocked gate and the stern warning sign at the south end of the church, bearing the tidings that the crypt was closed indefinitely due to unsafe conditions.

But she still had to get in.

The killer called Morgan didn't like it. The crypt was a terrible place for a meeting. There was only one entrance. There would be no light at night, meaning that Bethany would have to carry her own. That would mark her as a target.

Then there was the matter of this Grant Apple. Morgan had been in the man's flat and knew he owned a gun. He suspected that the bookstore owner would be carrying it.

Tight, shadowy quarters, a dozen or more squat pillars behind which anybody could be hiding. The crypt wasn't a meeting place. It was a killing ground.

But orders were orders.

When his cell phone rang, Harry Stean was walking in Hyde Park, struggling to shake off his sense of foreboding. He had spoken to the Mathematician and the Judge, the two leaders of the Garden to whom he was closest, and each had assured him that they were all keeping their heads down as promised. He had spoken to the Senator, who had told him that as far as she could tell — and her sources were very good indeed — the Bureau seemed to have slowed its search for Bethany. She didn't know why. He had spoken to the Writer, whose excellent contacts in Jerusalem had passed on the news that someone tried to break into the museum that held the publicly known Pilate Stone, a madman who, upon his arrest, explained to the police that he was actually looking for "the other Pilate Stone." He had spoken to the Pastor, who was home in South Carolina, and whose recovery from his wounds, it seemed, was slow.

The Builder hadn't really needed to get in touch with any of them. None had brought up anything of true importance. But he had felt the urgent need to hear their voices, to assure himself that things were not about to go as horribly wrong as his instincts told him.

He had called his friend Mark Satterwhite at the Foreign Office three times now and reached only voice mail. It was after the third try that Harry had taken himself off to the park, hoping to calm down. And now here was Mark, calling him back at last.

"Any word?" Harry demanded almost before the pleasantries were out of the way.

"Well, no, actually. It's a little confusing."

"What is?"

"You told us that WAKEFUL is in the U.K."

"She is."

A chuckle on the other end. "You mean, she was. I'm told that at this point, your own government seems to think that this was at best a staging point. WAKEFUL is somewhere on the Continent now."

"What do you mean somewhere? You don't know where? They don't know where?"

"Sorry, old boy. I've told you all I know. As far as our intelligence services are aware, WAKEFUL has left the country." A studied pause. "The thing is, Harry, if I were you? I'd consider doing the same."

Bethany Barclay stood on the Queen's Road, hands on her hips, pondering the challenges she faced in returning to the crypt this time of night. In the first place, it was raining, a dirty gray downpour like something you'd expect in a nineteenth-century coal town. And with so many um-brellas on the street it was impossible to tell whether anyone was watching her. Second, the college was locked. She could hardly go up to the door, ring for the porter in his Teddy bear tie, and ask if she could please go into the churchyard lugging her tools to force the entrance to the crypt.

On the Queen's Lane side she threw her bolt cutters over the wall, a feat that cost her three tries. Then she climbed. It wasn't easy, because the bricks were slippery, and she had to wait until she was sure there were no pedestrians about, but she made it.

And came down in a puddle, her backpack bouncing on her spine.

She was wearing sneakers, not boots, and the muddy water splashed her jeans and soaked her socks.

"Okay," she said, stamping her feet on the walkway. "Okay. Okay. You're fine."

Bethany didn't like cemeteries even in broad daylight, and sneaking past the head-stones as the storm pummeled the church gave her the creeps. She was wearing a dark rain slicker, and her backpack was slung over her shoulder. The bolt cutters were in her hand, and she supposed that if anybody should jump out at her, a la Teddy Bratt, she could always wield them as a weapon.

She reached the gate leading into the crypt and checked her watch. It was five minutes to ten. She stepped down, and discovered that the lock had already been cut.

She could have skipped the bolt cutters.

She turned on her flashlight and stepped through the gate.

# EIGHTEEN

The ceiling was higher than she'd expected. Bethany had been worried that she would have to crouch, but there were six or eight columns supporting vaulted arches, and although the stones beneath her feet felt loose and wet, the roof had stood for over nine centuries without caving in.

Of course there was always a first time.

She kept her flashlight beam low except when she was near a wall or a column, when she would run it up to the top. She saw nobody. There was the pounding of the rain, and the sluicing of water running down from the window above the *confessio.* There was also plenty of skittering in the darkness, and Bethany shivered. Next to cemeteries, rats were her least favorite thing by far.

"Grant?" she called, softly, expecting an echo. But her voice was swallowed by the storm. "Mr. Apple?" she tried, louder.

Nothing.

Something.

She heard a harder patter on the broken tiles, and what was almost certainly a human foot accidentally kicking a pebble loose. But when she swung her light toward the far end of the crypt, where the sounds had originated, she saw nothing but two tiny shining eyes at floor level before the rat scampered off into the shadows.

"Oh, great," she said aloud. "Perfect. All I need."

She wanted to sit but there were no chairs or benches, and the floor was sopping. She wanted to rush up the stairs and over the wall and back to her warm room, but she was fairly certain that if she muffed this chance Grant Apple was not about to give her another. She wanted to —

"Over here," came a hushed voice.

Bethany turned toward the *confessio.*

A beam of light momentarily blinded her.

"Turn yours off," Apple said. She did. "Walk toward me." She did that too, shielding her eyes. "Stop. That's close enough. Look down." She did. He was holding a gun.

"What is this?"

"I'm taking no chances, thank you very much."

"Chances with what? What's going on?"

198

"Chances that you're working with who-ever killed Adrian. Chances that they want to kill me too."

The light flicked off.

"I need to ask you a couple of questions," said Grant, his mouth quite close to her ear in the gray darkness. "To make sure you're who you say you are."

"Go ahead. But hurry."

As if in defiance, his voice grew slower. "You say you're a friend of Annabelle's."

"That's right."

"Then you'll know the name of her brother-in-law."

"David. He's dead."

"And the name of her dog."

"She didn't have one. She hated animals."

"She must have told you about that one dog, though. The one she really loved."

"There was never any dog, Grant. Can we please stop with the questions?"

Bethany felt him tense in the darkness, and for a moment she thought he was going to hit her. But he had heard something she'd missed, and was pointing his gun nervously toward the sound. He had no training, she sensed at once. Holding the gun the way he was, he would need ten kinds of luck just to hit the wall.

"Is somebody out there?" he whispered.

"Did you bring someone with you, Bethany?"

"No. I'm alone." She was exasperated. "Now, please. I need you to tell me."

"Tell you what?"

"Exactly what you told Annabelle. I need you to tell me too."

He was breathing very hard. "They'll kill you. You know that."

"So what else is new?"

And so he told her the story, straight out, like a witness in the courtroom. He stood there shivering in the crypt, the rain beating down, the gun now in his belt under his pullover.

"My field was Near East studies. The early civilizations. The dawn of the Christian era. That sort of thing. I wasn't the best student. I wasn't the worst. I wanted an academic appointment, but I knew that Oxbridge was beyond my grasp. I was hoping to at least get something in the Midlands."

Again he cocked his head, but this time he didn't stop talking.

"One day there was a note in my box from Adrian Wisdom. 'Come see me.' Like that. Of course I was flattered. I went to his office. We talked a bit — he had a way of talking around things — and he told me about the Pilate book. I have to admit, it didn't sound all that exciting. There just aren't early sources. Everything's from long after he died."

"But you worked with him anyway."

"I did. Yes. For a few months. He gave me mostly grunt work, and I hated it, but he was Adrian Wisdom. My ticket to opportunity, you might say. As it turned out later, he was testing me. Are you sure you're alone down here?"

"Grant. Be serious. Even if I wanted to bring someone along, I don't have anybody to bring."

"Dorothea, maybe. That awful ex of hers."

"He split my lip yesterday. I'm happy to stay away from them."

"He's an oaf," the bookseller agreed. After a further period of staring fruitlessly into the darkness, he turned her way again. "Fine. So. Adrian."

"At some point he told you what he really was after," she prompted. "He told you about the Pilate Stone."

He nodded. "I'd never heard of it. As I said, I dealt with documents from the time of Christ. Well, the Pilate Stone never gets mentioned anywhere until around 1000 A.D." He pointed upward. "About the time this church was built, as a matter of fact. That's why everybody in the field thinks it must be a forgery."

"But not Professor Wisdom."

"No. He believed it was real. He asked me to work with him, and of course I took it like a shot. Who wouldn't? He told me the project was to be kept very secret. I didn't care. I'm a burrower. I like old parchments. That's not exactly a skill that has the girls flocking. But now I was in the midst of this great search. Historic even."

Bethany heard the rising thrill in the screechy voice. She didn't have to see his eyes to know they were brimming with excitement.

"Adrian sent me to libraries across the Continent. I traveled for the better part of a year. I tracked down one rumor after another. Archives, monasteries, private collections. I was looking for anything. Scrolls. Old manuscripts. I kept coming up empty, and Adrian kept sending me back out." He grew reflective. "He seemed to have a lot of money to spend on the project, even though I never had to fill out paperwork the way you do when it's coming from a grant. And it's not as though Adrian had accumulated any wealth."

The storm intensified and their voices rose.

"Maybe he had a patron."

"Maybe so. Maybe you're right. That's the way it was done in the Middle Ages. A patron. Yes. That makes sense." He paused again, this time in memory. The rain was coming in sheets now, blowing in through uncovered windows, making muddy rivers between the tiles. "Well. I went where he told me, and then I went where other people told me. I tracked down rumors. One account, written around 1400, said the Stone had been part of a building and had been damaged in the Galilee earthquake of 363 A.D. Another story said it had been carried away and hidden before one of the sieges of the city in the seventh century. That could mean the Persians, or it could mean Umar the Great, because they both conquered Jerusalem within a few decades of each other. After the schism in 1054 A.D., the Eastern church supposedly spent a lot of time looking for the Stone, but that story doesn't show up until the sixteenth century, so I'm skeptical. The point is, there were rumors everywhere, and they all ran into brick walls."

"But you finally found something."

Shouting now to be heard over the storm.

Grant nodded, his enthusiasm at fever pitch. Lightning from without illuminated his rich beard. "It was about three years ago.

I came across a scroll in the biggest private collection in Berlin. It was in pretty bad shape. It was written around the year 1300 by a wandering friar. The Latin was quite poor, so he wasn't from one of the educated orders. As best I could make out, this friar claimed to have been in a *crypta* — the word can mean 'crypt,' of course, but also 'grotto,' or even 'passageway' or 'tunnel' — and, anyway, in this *crypta* he'd seen a carving by Pilate about a man named *Iesus*. He didn't say what form the carving took. He didn't say what message it contained. He described his ecstasy upon discovering it — that sort of thing."

"Did he say where the crypt was?"

"No. That's the point. As I said, the scroll was in bad shape. Big chunks were missing. There was a reference to the sea, but also to the mountains. He spoke of a monastery, but the surviving pieces don't give the name. What got Adrian excited was something else. In explaining where the Stone could be found, the friar wrote the words *Sed unus homo potest.* This appears to be part of a longer sentence, but the rest of the sentence is lost. Still, Adrian was excited. He said this was the vital clue."

"Did he tell you why?"

"No. He said he could combine it with

other information in his possession. He said he thought he knew where to go."

"What do the words mean?"

"They could have several meanings. There's an identical line in Aquinas's *Summa Theologica,* in his discussion of baptism. It's usually translated, 'But one man can baptize several at the same time.' However, that translation is based on context. It's not what the Latin words actually say. A literal translation would be, 'But one man can do it,' or, possibly, 'But only one man can do it.' "

"Maybe he meant that there was only one person who could find it."

"Maybe. I don't know. But Adrian said it was vital. He said it was the final clue."

"Did he figure out the correct translation?"

"He said he did." Again the wild glance around the crypt. For a moment his hand went to his gun, but whatever had spooked him seemed to dissipate. "He didn't tell me the answer, but he said it was in the manuscript."

And so she plunged. "Do you have the manuscript?"

"Me? Of course not. I never even got to read it."

"Where is it? Do you know?"

Bethany had bumped up against his reluctance. She could tell immediately.

"This is where things get dangerous," he said, voice slow again, and softer than before. "There are people out there looking for the Pilate Stone. That's what Adrian said. But there are also people who don't want it to be found. I'm not sure who they are. After Berlin, I started to get these odd messages. Untraceable e-mails, texts to my cell warning me to stop. And — well, call me a coward if you want, but I stopped. I even quit school. Just so they'd know that I really wasn't looking any more."

"And Adrian?"

"Adrian didn't stop, obviously. Somebody stopped him."

More skittering in the darkness. She pulled her arms closer to her body. "Grant, please. You have to tell me. You have to tell me what happened to the manuscript. Dorothea doesn't have it. But it has to be somewhere."

"Maybe whoever killed him took it."

"He'd have had another copy. With an obsession like his, he'd have had another. Where would it be? Think."

"I'm not sure. We parted on bad terms. The only person I can think of he might have trusted with it lives in Italy. She —"

The rest was drowned by a shout from the shadows: "Bethany! Get down!"

She didn't waste precious time being startled. She had no idea who was out there, but she hit the ground, fast. Grant Apple was in an awkward crouch, spinning around, gun in hand, but he was far too slow. Two spits from the darkness, and he was down. A louder gunshot echoed through the crypt. She crawled for safety behind a pillar, hugging the ground all the way, but not before she saw that the bullets had struck poor Grant center mass, just the way she was taught to shoot.

A hand grabbed her from the darkness.

She shook it off, swung the flashlight wildly, and struck the dotty old man who'd looked in on her at the laboratory when she was waiting for Dorothea.

"Get up!" he urged, tugging at her arm. "Run!"

"I — what —"

"I don't know how many of them are out there. Now, get out of here!"

"But who —"

Another spit from the other side of the crypt. The old man gave her a shove. "Go!"

She scrambled toward the broken exit door as the entire crypt erupted in gunfire.

■ ■ ■ ■

# PART TWO:
# NUTS AND BOLTS

■ ■ ■ ■

# Nineteen

Up to the last minute, Carl Carraway does everything exactly right. He has been effectively demoted. He is no longer involved in any way with the task force he formerly ran, a team of senior Bureau agents dedicated to capturing the woman known as the Lab Bomber, who until a few weeks ago terrorized the nation by blowing up thermite pipe bombs outside buildings, most of them on college campuses, where research is conducted on human embryos. The evidence quickly pointed the task force toward Bethany Barclay, an obscure lawyer wanted in Virginia for the murder of her ex-boyfriend. Carl began to have doubts that Bethany was guilty, but each time he shared them he was told by higher-ups that his only job was to catch her: let the Justice Department sort out who should be charged.

It was Carl who worked out that Bethany was being tracked in the United States by a killer for hire, and who arranged the sting that almost led to the man's arrest but instead left him dead. It was Carl who put together the theory that Bethany would try to get to Europe to trace the movements of her late friend Annabelle. It was Carl who studied her file closely enough to figure out which airport she would use and even intercepted her there, trying to leave the country under another identity.

And it was Carl who made the decision to let her go.

That was the big problem. He'd detained her at the airport, brushed aside her unpersuasive efforts to prove that her name was really Elaine McMullen, and, in the end — to the dismay of Jake Pulu, his partner — he'd let her go on her way.

A subsequent investigation concluded that Carl had ignored Bureau rules in the way he had used certain resources, and he had shared highly classified information with an outsider.

And so he had surrendered his gun and his badge. He was serving an administrative suspension, indefinite in length, salary paid until his hearing the month after next, at which time he would very likely be dismissed and might possibly face criminal charges.

Other men would have turned to drink or worse. Other men would have been bitter. Other men would have spent their days muttering about how badly life was treating them.

Carl had his moments of unhappiness, but he comforted himself with the certainty — and he was still certain — that he had done the right thing.

"It was that Lesofsky guy, wasn't it?" said his partner, Pulu, when they got together for a burger the other day. Carl was off limits, but Jake Pulu, a soft-spoken Samoan of formidable strength and intellect, had little patience for such bureaucratic niceties. "From the time you met Lesofsky and listened to his conspiracy theories, you got all weird."

Ted Lesofsky was a former Bureau agent and analyst whom Carl himself had helped dismiss a few years back because of his bizarre fantasies about the Garden and the Wilderness and their centuries of doing battle.

Now Jake Pulu was in effect accusing Carl of sounding just like him.

"You know I can't talk to you about it," Carl said.

"Because they're going to call me to testify against you."

"Because my lawyer told me not to."

Pulu laughed, crushed a French fry in his hand, made it disappear down his throat. "That's pretty funny. You listening to lawyers."

"I guess *funny* is one word for it."

"I'm just saying, though. This Lesofsky got fired from the Bureau, right? For all this stuff about these secret organizations fighting over the centuries? He wouldn't shut up; he wouldn't stop drawing his diagrams and his connections, all the photos and yarn, the whole business. He went a little nuts, and they threw him out."

"I was there when it happened, Jake. I testified against him. So, yes, I do remember."

Pulu's laugh could shake a house. "I'm just saying, Carl. This is why they're after you. Not because you let WAKEFUL go. They could put that down to a mistake — you'd say you didn't know it was her and you'd wind up with a reprimand for your file and two weeks without pay, and then you're back in the saddle. You're valuable. You figured out WAKEFUL's movements when nobody else could. They don't want to lose you is all."

Carl took a sip of water. "Then they're putting on a good show."

"That's my point. This isn't about missing her at the airport. This is about them being afraid you're turning into another Lesofsky."

"They think I'm crazy?"

"They want you to stop talking about the Garden and the Wilderness, all that nonsense. And they're right, Carl. Maybe you're not crazy, but if any of it is true — and I don't believe a word — then I figure it's way above our pay grade."

Carraway gave him a look. "They sent you, didn't they?"

"Not they. Her. The boss."

"Vanner? C'mon, Jake. She doesn't even like me."

"On a personal level? I'm sure she doesn't. I don't much care for you myself. That's why I want you back as my partner. I like the new guy too much." He hunched forward. "Carl, the Bureau values you. Even Vanner knows how talented you are. She says she'll fix everything. She'll even get you back on the task force. Just stop talking like you're headed around the bend."

"You're saying I shouldn't discuss what I believe to be true, even if it's relevant to the investigation."

"I'm saying it's time you started believing something else."

Carl pushed back from the table. "I don't think I can do that."

And that was the end of the negotiation.

All of that was a week ago. Since then Carl has begun to worry. About himself. About his perceptions. He finds himself memorizing the plate numbers of cars that passed, in case he sees them again. Or he stares at strangers in the supermarket until they look away: a time-tested technique for beating surveillance. And at home, he's started threading his door, the sort of thing they used to do in the field in the old days, placing tiny bits of string at two or three spots on the outside of the jamb, so that if they are missing when he returns to his apartment, he'll know somebody has been inside.

In all of this, he knows, he is behaving more and more like poor Ted Lesofsky.

And now he is having the same fantasies.

Except they aren't fantasies. They are truths, and he knows they are, and if he also knew where Ted had disappeared to, he'd gladly buy him a drink and apologize.

In all other respects, Carraway does exactly what he is supposed to. He stays away from the office. He resists the temptation to which suspended agents often yielded, the urge to call up Bureau friends to wheedle updates out of them. He doesn't write a book, or call a reporter, or sell his story to Hollywood. He obeys the rules. He does everything right.

Tonight, when Carl arrives home after a late dinner with friends and a late movie alone, he carefully checks the field threads. They are still in place. Satisfied, he steps into the apartment, and probably the first mistake he makes is to reach for the Glock 22 that would ordinarily be on his right hip. But he is suspended, so there is no gun, and it likely would make no difference anyway, because Carl has a hunch that the man sitting on the sofa without any visible weapon could quite easily kill him before his pistol is out of his holster.

"Why don't you sit down?" invites the stranger whose face Carl has seen a dozen times or more, back when he had access to the WAKEFUL case file. He sits as invited, selecting the leather recliner from which he watches basketball games. "I assume you know who I am."

"Raymond Fuentes, of the Central Intelligence Agency." A moment's pause as Carl considers. "Or is it formerly?"

"It's formerly, Agent Carraway. Yes." A ghostly chuckle. "Just as, from what I understand, you may soon be a former agent of the Federal Bureau of Investigation."

"What makes you say that?"

"You're on administrative leave. Don't do that."

Carl freezes. Pretending to scratch his leg, he was reaching for the personal weapon in the ankle holster he has lately taken to wearing.

"I don't want to hurt you, Agent Carraway. We're actually on the same side in this matter."

"I don't know what matter you're talking about."

"I was at the airport when Bethany Barclay left the country. I saw you detain her. I saw you release her. We both know that she was carrying someone else's passport. You let her go anyway."

Carl keeps his voice steady. "That never happened."

"It did happen, Agent Carraway. That's how I know we're on the same side. I don't know whether you let her go because you decided she was telling the truth, or because you'd developed an unscheduled emotional attachment. I don't actually care. What I want to know is whether you still want to help her."

"Without conceding any part of your

story, what exactly do you think I can help her with?"

Fuentes leans forward. He seems a good deal more relaxed than a moment ago. "When Bethany escaped from the Village House in Chicago, she was in the company of a young black woman named Janice Stafford."

"So?"

"So, as you might imagine, the two of them grew quite close during their two weeks underground. A sort of sisterly affection developed."

"That's what I assumed."

"And you assumed correctly. My question is, do you know where Janice is now?"

Carl takes a minute. The former Agency man is a prime suspect in the string of bombings that are still laid officially at the feet of Bethany Barclay. He is inviting Carl into his confidence. The why doesn't much matter. Suspension or not, training takes over: the key is to keep him talking.

And, when possible, to tell the truth.

"My working hypothesis," says Carl, "is that Janice has been kidnapped by these people — the Wilderness — the ones who are trying to get Bethany to do their bidding."

"That is precisely what happened, Agent

Carraway."

"How do you know? Did you kidnap her?"

"I know because Bethany told me. And before she left the country, she made me promise to find Janice if I can."

Carl shrugs. "I don't know where she is. And, just now, my, um, access to the Bureau's resources is limited."

"There's only one resource I need."

"What's that?"

"Do you know anyone in computer crimes?"

"Why?"

Fuentes explains what he has in mind. It takes several minutes. "I had originally planned to follow a very different path," he says. "I had intended to approach the potential buyers. But I'm afraid that the Agency has people trying to follow me. By now my source will have given them the same list he gave me. I can't take the chance of being intercepted. This is my backup plan."

"It's a pretty insane plan."

"I don't have a better one."

Carl stands up and stretches. "Would you care for something to drink?"

"No."

"Mind if I have a beer?"

"Help yourself."

Thirty seconds later, Carl is seated again. It is his turn to ask a question. "Why exactly are you so determined to help her?"

"Because I gave my word."

"You're a trained intelligence officer. You've probably broken your word in half the countries on earth."

"I never break my word if I can help it."

"Worried about your sterling reputation?"

"Not in this world, Agent Carraway. In the next."

Carl gets a little of his own back. Or tries to. "You can say that's your reason, Mr. Fuentes. And you might even believe it. But the way I figure, you seem to be the one who's developed an unscheduled emotional attachment toward Bethany Barclay."

The intruder's face is stone. "Will you help me or not? That's the only question that matters."

"You know I will. You knew before you broke in."

"You could get into trouble."

"I'm in trouble already. At least if I try to help, I'll know it's been worth it." Carl takes a long swallow. "But, please. Answer me one question."

"Yes?"

"I'm willing to believe that you were look-ing for field threads. But how did you manage to get them back on the door, in the right spot, from the inside?"

Fuentes smiles.

# TWENTY

It took Bethany Barclay a day and a half to calm down. She didn't go back to the bed-and-breakfast after the shooting. She pedaled straight to the bus station, locked up the bicycle, and caught the twelve-thirty coach back to London. Nearly all the seats were empty. She sat up front, near the driver, because she wanted to see who boarded, or who was watching, or whether they were approaching a roadblock.

Grant Apple wasn't the first person she'd seen killed during her odyssey underground. The whole mess began when she found her ex-boyfriend dead on the floor of her home, the scene staged to make the authorities think she'd done it.

And that was exactly what the authorities had thought.

People who tried to help her — in New Hampshire, her old friend Sam DeMarco — people who tried to hurt her — in

Chicago, Janice's uncle Daniel Stafford — she'd watched them die in front of her. But somehow she had imagined that by crossing the ocean she would leave the violence behind.

In one of her pockets was the slim New Testament pressed upon her by a friendly pastor in New Jersey during her flight. She opened it and read a bit, as Aunt Claudia used to urge on her at moments of stress.

She happened to come to Matthew 10: *I am sending you out like sheep among wolves. Therefore be as shrewd as snakes and as innocent as doves.*

Here she actually preferred the ISV translation: *as cunning as serpents.*

Yes. Exactly. Cunning.

Bethany put the New Testament away. If she was to finish this quest and win Janice's freedom, she had to be as cunning as her adversaries.

The bus made a rest stop at a town in the middle of nowhere. She took her bag and vanished into the night. She would find a motel that took cash, sleep until late morning, and then make a telephone call.

It was time to change the rules. Up until now Bethany had let those who were manipulating the situation push her around. Now she planned to see how they liked it

224

when she pushed back.

Elliott St. John doesn't recognize the number on his personal cell, a fact that makes him shiver with anticipation. Is it possible?

"Yes?"

"Do you recognize my voice?"

Ah! He admires her caution! But it's she. Bethany Barclay, calling from somewhere in Britain, presumably.

"I do," he says. It is seven in the morning in New York, and he is dressed for the office. Symington, his head bodyguard, is waiting near the front door. But Elliott waves him away and retreats into the apartment.

"Where did we meet last?" Bethany asks.

"Boston. The Public Garden."

An intake of breath at the other end, and he wonders how unsure of herself she must feel.

"I want to make sure that our deal still stands," she says after a moment.

Elliott frowns. The one time they met, at the carousel in the Public Garden, Bethany marched away without agreeing to anything. He made an offer, but they reached no deal. She never even replied: just turned and marched away. He wonders whether she might be trying to trick him, to get him into

225

some sort of trouble — but, no. If Bethany wants to hurt him with the Council, there are a dozen methods she might try without risking a telephone call that could betray her location. And this is precisely why he gave her the number of one of his private mobile phones: so that she could reach him when she was at last on the track of the Stone.

"Of course," he says. He hesitates. "Are you saying —"

"I don't have the merchandise yet, no. I want to make sure that I'm still entitled to my finder's fee."

"Of course."

"I'll need an advance. For expenses." She stated her sum.

Good. Money. Something he understands. True, she might merely be probing, but at least the test is in his native language.

"I can have it delivered wherever you wish."

"Good. Don't try to trace this phone. I'm on the highway, and it's a burner. I'm going to take out the battery and throw it away in about one minute."

"I understand. But how —"

"I'm adding a condition."

"Oh?"

"I want to speak to my friend."

This throws him entirely. "You should certainly seek advice from whomever you choose," he says carefully. "But of course, you should remember that our deal includes a requirement of confidentiality."

Her voice, although shaky, is as cold as he has ever heard it. "You know exactly what I'm talking about. And whom."

Elliott is standing outside his vault. A maid steps into the corridor carrying a pile of table linens, spots him, and hurries off in the opposite direction.

"I'm sorry," he says. "I don't know what you're —"

"I want her on the phone next time I call," she says, abandoning all pretense.

"Yes, well, that's going to be difficult to —"

"You have twenty-four hours," she says, and hangs up.

The billionaire stares at the phone. Janice Stafford. That has to be the one she means. Bethany is demanding to talk to Janice. The trouble is Elliott has no idea where she is. Until this instant, he had no idea she was even missing.

*I want her on the phone next time I call.*

Not only is Janice missing, then, but Bethany Barclay seems certain that the Council has her. Her certainty in turn suggests that

227

the Council does indeed have Janice and has told Bethany so. And that means there are things that the Council isn't telling him.

Correction.

Things the Lord Protector isn't telling him.

Elliott St. John heads for his apartment's internal stair. His mood is grim. Lillian told him that the Council had taken out insurance to make sure that Bethany does as she's told. Janice is obviously the insurance.

For a moment, his fury rises. How could they take Janice? Janice's uncle, now dead, had been a senior member of the Council and one of Elliott's own closest friends. He adores Janice and would never stand idly by were she in danger. More than once, at Daniel Stafford's urgent entreaty, he had used his connections to get Janice out of the messes in which her computer skills kept landing her.

Until she joined those BLLNET people: after that, there was no more that connections could do.

Janice Stafford. They'd kidnapped Janice Stafford, who actually called him Uncle Elliott. No wonder Melody was so nervous when he'd asked what threat Lillian was holding over Bethany's head.

And Elliott had no doubt that the threat

would be effective. Janice had a knack for inspiring affection and protectiveness in those around her, and Bethany struck him as the sort of person who is cursed by a sense of responsibility for others.

Yet Bethany called him rather than using whatever means of communication the Protector has forced upon her. That means she's guessed that there is a fissure between him and his colleagues. She even implied as much that one time they met. Well, Bethany's a smart girl, and perceptive. He admires her. He even catches himself hoping she survives.

But there is an immediate problem to be resolved. Smart or not, perceptive or not, admired or not, Bethany believes that Elliott can produce Janice. And he can't — not when he isn't even supposed to know that the Council has kidnapped her and stashed her somewhere.

He ponders. This is going to be tricky, but he is starting to see how it can be done. They say not to play both ends against the middle, but Elliott didn't rise from being a reporter on a forgotten newspaper to running his multibillion-dollar empire by avoiding risks.

And this risk is worth it.

His other cell rings. Trudy, his executive

assistant, lets him know that the car is downstairs. Elliott almost smiles. He has no doubt that to the outside world it must seem wasteful to have the driver call his assistant, who is at the office, who then calls Elliott to tell him that the car is in front of his building. Probably people think his ego drives the arrangement. Actually he works things this way because part of Trudy's job is to be sure that he is precisely where he is supposed to be precisely when he is supposed to be there. His reputation for punctuality, unusual for a figure of his prominence, is legendary, and among Trudy's principal responsibilities is ensuring that his reputation remains untarnished. Therefore she is as surprised as anyone when he asks her to tell the driver that he is running late.

"Running late?" she echoes, as if he has confessed to a heinous vice.

"That's right."

"May I say how long you'll be?" Hinting at his faux pas.

"Just tell him to wait," Elliott growls, and hangs up.

He knows Trudy. She'll call back in two minutes. He won't answer. He'll be busy.

The apartment is a triplex, and the third floor is his sanctuary. Not even his wife is permitted to intrude. At the top of the stairs is a heavy door, and behind the door is his home office, which occupies the entire floor.

Inside the office is another security man, just in case some clever burglar should manage to get this far. He rises to his feet as the boss passes. Elliott gestures toward the center of the room, where his vault is located. The office surrounds it on all four sides. The bottom is the second floor of the house. The top is the roof of the building, but in order to drill in from above, one would first have to move several tons of air-conditioning equipment just to get to the reinforced concrete that covers the thick steel shell that covers the cinder block that covers the lead.

Impossible to crack.

Only a card key and a code will open the vault. His wife has a card key. So do his two daughters. His assistant has the code. So does his curator. In an emergency, members of the group must track each other down and cooperate. Only Symington, his personal bodyguard, also possesses both the card and the code, and should Elliott ever be, say, blown to bits in the helicopter, Symington will be immolated right alongside him.

When the vault is finally opened, Elliott steps in alone. The main door remains open, but a glass panel snicks closed, to keep the air pressurized and free of dust and the temperature at twelve degrees Celsius. The lighting is subdued to avoid damage to his treasures.

Of course Elliott can keep only a small part of his collection here. Some is at his London flat. Some is at his estate in the Hamptons. Most is on loan to various museums around the world.

But this is the most secure of all his very secure locations. This is where no one else will ever trespass.

This is where he keeps items his very possession of which would cause international scandal — and, possibly, prosecution. His private collection. Things nobody knows he owns. A small piece of the Elgin Marbles, hacked off by an unscrupulous sea captain two hundred years ago during transport from Greece to Britain. A minor Raphael. A manuscript page from the *Commentarii,* the lost autobiography of Augustus, the first emperor of Rome. The jewel of the secret collection is Rembrandt's "The Storm on the Sea of Galilee," stolen years ago from the Isabella Stewart Gardner Museum and passed around from one underground collector to another.

In the center of the vault stands a pressurized display case, designed to preserve a slab of limestone two millennia old. At the moment it is empty, but his desperate hope is that one day it will hold the most valuable of all the world's relics.

For a moment Elliott bows his head, almost prayerfully, as if worshipping at the shrine of what he doesn't yet possess.

THE PILATE STONE, the plaque reads.

The Council can't have it. Nor can the Garden. Nor can whoever is trying to put a stop to the hunt.

The Stone *must* be his.

Two minutes later he is back in the outer office, as poised and self-possessed as ever. He nods to the guard, who swings the door shut. In the corridor, he calls his assistant.

"Please apologize for the delay, and tell the driver I'll be right down."

"Of course, Mr. Elliott."

"Oh, and Trudy. I'm going to need the jet this afternoon."

"Yes, sir. May I know where you're going? The pilot will need to file a flight plan."

"London," he says.

Bethany was in so great a panic that she nearly missed her bus. She had made her call from a café in High Wycombe, where she had spent a restless night at a small motel. Although it was just past seven in New York, the café was crowded with luncheon patrons, and crowded was what she wanted. Bethany's plan had been to make the call, sprint a block and a half to the terminal, and be on her way to London before anyone could track her down.

Instead, she moved in slow motion.

Elliott St. John was too nervous. That was what scared her. He was too nervous. When she met him in Boston two weeks ago, he was calm and confident, every inch the self-made mogul. But not today. Today, when she demanded to speak to Janice, he acted as if he had no idea what she was talking about.

All the way to London, she kept juggling the possibilities in her mind. Janice was dead. No. It wasn't that kind of panic. He was confused, not frightened. Meaning he didn't know. So someone else had Janice. But no. From the circumstances, it was obvious that the Wilderness had her. And Elliott St. John was a prominent leader. So maybe they had Janice but he didn't know. The girl's uncle, Daniel, second in command of the Village House, had been the billionaire's close friend: maybe the Wilderness didn't think Elliott could be trusted. But that was absurd. You couldn't hold any group together with its members taking each other's loved ones hostage. If they didn't trust him, they would surely just get rid of him, one way or another. So she was back to square one. Janice must be dead. Except he'd seemed more confused than frightened —

As the bus rolled on, the unanswerable questions chased her into sleep.

# TWENTY-ONE

"So, let me get this straight," says Carl Carraway. "You're saying these BLLNET people just hang out in chat rooms and talk about their plans? Right out in the open?"

He is in a diner in Alexandria, having coffee with Amy Santana, who used to work with him in the Washington field office and is now a supervisory agent at the National Cyber Investigative Joint Task Force. Amy owes him enough favors that she doesn't ask why he's asking. But she has told him from the start that she will share nothing that is classified.

"I wouldn't call it out in the open, but yes. They like to converse in real time. Most of the hacktivists do. They don't like e-mails or texts. They like the immediacy of conversation. Chat rooms, bulletin boards, private chats — and sometimes in password-protected forums. But still, the answer is yes. They're remarkably open about what they do."

Carraway considers. He thinks Ray Fuentes's idea is audacious and also slightly insane. But he doesn't have a better one. Janice Stafford was a part of BLLNET, one of the most formidable hacktivist groups on the planet. Getting in touch with them is the crazy part of the plan. But it just might work. And if anybody in Carl's circle knows how to reach them, it will be the woman sitting across from him.

"So, these message boards and chat rooms where the BLLNET folks hang out. Are they monitored in real time?"

"Not usually, no."

"Why not? Isn't BLLNET dangerous?"

Amy Santana grimaces. It is plain that she gets this question a lot. "They've been pretty quiet lately. A couple of their leaders are in custody. Of the others — the ones we know about — most of them are busy keeping their heads down. That Stafford girl who they think was involved in the bombings — well, she scared some of their members away."

"Surely they haven't disappeared."

She smiles at the evident concern in his tone, even though she can have no earthly idea what he's worried about. "Of course they haven't. It's just that a lot of other groups are more active now. We don't have enough techs to watch everything all the time. The National Security Agency does some recording of chats, and they flag things for our attention, but unless their AI detects signs of some sort of imminent attack, we have to wait for the humans to get around to screening the take, and that can be weeks."

"AI?"

"Come on, Carl. Join the century. Artificial intelligence? NSA has pattern-recognition software that scans the chats looking for certain key words and phrases. Different words set off different alarms. Even if an alarm does go off, the priority is usually low. Even then, it can be weeks before anyone gets around to looking at the chats. Sometimes months. In a couple of cases I've been involved with, more than a year."

Carraway does not trouble to conceal his astonishment. "Let me understand this. You're telling me that right now, at this very moment, a couple of BLLNET members could be meeting in a chat room — a chat room you know about — and plotting something dangerous, but as long as they avoid certain key words and word patterns — words they probably know to avoid —

238

you won't find out about it for weeks or months? Maybe a year?"

Amy goes prickly. "You double my budget, Carl, and I'll get you better intel."

"I'm not criticizing. I'm just . . . surprised."

"Me too. Funny budget priorities we've got sometimes. Every congressman gets a bridge named after him, and we don't have the people we need to — never mind." An elaborate shrug. "It's our job to make do with the resources they give us."

"Look. Tell me the names of the chat rooms."

"You're joking."

"I know my clearance has been revoked, but I assume the names of the chat rooms aren't a secret."

"Not exactly." She is pouring more sugar into her cup. "No, Carl. The problem is the Constitution of the United States. In particular, the Fourth Amendment."

Again he finds himself on his high horse. "Are you telling me that it would be against the law for an FBI agent to visit a chat room that's open to the public, just to listen in?"

"I'm not saying it. But a couple of federal judges have."

"Okay. Fair enough." Carl begins to calm as he sees his way to shore. "Still. I'm no longer a federal agent. I suppose I can hang out in any chat rooms I want."

"I suppose you can." Her face goes cautious. "Carl, look. You're a good guy. I don't want you in any more trouble. So I'm going to assume that you have a good reason for all this."

"I do. I told you." He pulls out a gold pen. "So, the names."

"The names of what?"

"The chat rooms."

Santana has recovered her good humor. "Names? Wow, are you behind the times."

"I don't understand."

"Carl. Come on. These are chat rooms, not city streets. They don't have names. Not the way you mean it."

"What do they have?"

"Pathways."

The Lord Protector was sitting once more on her portico, this time lunching with Melody Sunderland. The weather was gray, but outdoors was what the Protector liked.

"I've seen the report on the Oxford incident," Melody said. She was using the smooth yet crisp tone that endeared her to listeners. "It's still not clear exactly who the shooters were. The important thing is, Bethany Barclay is safe."

The old woman seemed not to hear. She was toying with a necklace of diamonds and emeralds that Melody's expert, envious eye valued in the six figures.

"Elliott is going to London," the Protector finally said. "Did you know?"

Melody nodded. "I heard."

"You heard."

"I did. Yes."

"And why do you think he would do that, dear?"

"I would assume he must have heard from Bethany."

The Protector sighed. Such children she was surrounded with. "Please don't waste time telling me what I can work out for myself." She enjoyed the stricken look on the young woman's telegenic face. People were already speaking of Melody as her possible successor. It was important, therefore, to keep her firmly in her place. "Of course he must have heard from Bethany. The question, my dear, isn't *whether* Elliott's heard from Bethany. It's *what* Elliott's heard from Bethany."

Melody shook her head. "I have no way to tell."

"You met Elliott two days ago. Surely you can hazard a guess."

"If what you're asking is whether she's

found the Stone, I would think she hasn't."

"Why not?"

"Because in that case she'd be getting in touch with you. She'd be worried about Janice, and —"

The Lord Protector sees the realization in her protégé's face. They sometimes think slowly, these children, but eventually they get caught up.

"He doesn't know," Melody said. "Elliott doesn't know that we have Janice, does he?"

"I haven't told him, dear. Have you?"

"No. But that means — that means Bethany must have told him." She works it through. "Indirectly. She probably called him to check on Janice, only to discover that he doesn't have Janice and didn't know she was missing."

The Lord Protector nods. She sips her coffee. "That would be my analysis, dear."

"But — but Janice is — she's close to him. That's why we didn't tell him." She puts her fork down with a snap. "He's going to turn against us. Is that what's happening?"

"I don't know what's happening, dear. That's why you're going to London too."

"Me? Why?"

"Because Elliott is sweet on you. Because he's a sentimental fool. Go to London. Find out what he's up to."

242

"Protector, I — this isn't the 1930s. I can't just bat my eyelashes or use my feminine wiles or something. And, frankly, I'm insulted that you'd even —"

"Did I ask your opinion?" The old woman's tone was silky. "You're to go tonight. I'm not asking you to do anything inappropriate. I just want to know exactly when and how Elliott is planning to betray us."

Melody was already shaking her head. "We can't touch him and he knows it. Those files of his, the ones that are so useful to us — he has information on me, on the other members of the Council — even on you, probably. We can't take the chance."

"He most certainly has information on me, my dear. More than enough to put me away for what's left of my life. But the files are *my* problem. From this moment until the operation is concluded, however, Elliott St. John is yours."

# TWENTY-TWO

Bethany arrived in London early in the afternoon. Her first visit was to a man named Nigel Tuck who had a shop off South Audley Street. He sold useless touristy gimcracks from the sunny front room and various legally questionable services in the dingy back. He closed for two hours at midday unless you knew the special number, and Bethany did, because she had it from Raymond Fuentes. He'd made her memorize three names, addresses, and contact procedures — and Tuck was one of them.

Tuck was used by everybody in the trade, said Fuentes, and was so far down the food chain that nobody was likely to have him wired. More important, Tuck was unlikely to turn her in, for it was his studied neutrality that kept him in business.

*What are the codes?* she had asked.

*Codes?*

*The password. So he'll know I'm official.*

244

Fuentes had laughed, and she'd been embarrassed. *No codes,* he'd said. *No password. Just mention my name and tell him what you need.*

*Then what?*

*Then Tuck will tell you how much it's going to cost and when to come back and get it.*

What she needed was an analysis of the jaggedly torn snapshot that Annabelle had hidden in Dorothea Ziman's house. And that was Tuck's specialty: all things related to the visual image. She felt as if she had aged a decade since finding the photo, but in fact, her encounter with Teddy Bratt in the upstairs hall had occurred just yesterday.

Tuck turned out to be a nervous little man with thin curly hair and two days' growth of beard, and his jeans looked as if he'd been wearing the same pair every day for about six years. Scarcely bothering to catch her name, he snatched the photo from her fingers with a careless, natural rudeness, chortled over the quality of the paper — "Kodak!" he beamed, delighted as an explorer in Tutankhamun's tomb — and dived into the back room as she followed, uninvited, in his wake. He slid the photo onto a clear pallet, which in turn he slipped into what looked for all the world like a DVD player. He studied the readouts, then pulled the picture out again and placed it under a lighted magnifier.

"VR-G 200 film," he announced. "Well, well. We *are* exploring the ancient world, aren't we? I'd say an Instamatic, probably the 804, although it's hard to say for sure. Ektar 2.8 lens. Clunky, beautiful old beast, with a flashcube on top. You don't know what that is. I can see it in your eyes. Too young. You think cameras either come in phones or cost five thousand dollars. But the Instamatic was popular and cheap. Kodak sold something like fifty million of them."

For the first time in a while, Bethany felt a genuine smile tugging at her lips. She admired people who loved their work.

"Actually, I was hoping you could tell me what it's a photo *of.*"

"It's not a photo. It's half a photo. Some man. The rest is missing." He ran a finger along the edges. "Not torn. Cut. A jagged cut. Ah. I see. This is one of those secret-identification things, isn't it? Ray Fuentes sent you, you said? So you find the fellow who has the other half and he gives you the stolen nuclear launch codes sort of thing?"

"Exactly."

"Huh," he said, and then, "Huh," again. He was looking at the magnifier once more.

"Come over here."

She did.

"Buildings in the background. People. Some sort of public park, maybe. Outside a museum. Possibly a university."

"That's what I was thinking," she said. She pointed at a blurry shape. "That looks like a Ferris wheel."

He took the photo between his gloved fingers, flicked at the paper. "I'd wager this is as old as it looks."

"How old does it look?"

"The 804 was introduced in 1965 or thereabouts. So it can't be any older than that."

"Can we enhance the background?"

He gave her a look of delighted condescension and led her to a laptop. "Already done. Took the imagery from the scanner. Ah. Here we are."

The new photo was crisper. The man in the foreground was clearer, his blond hair shining in the sun, his dark glasses and his frown suggesting that he took unkindly to having his picture taken. The slim hand resting on his shoulder wore a bracelet and almost certainly belonged to a woman.

"Look," said Tuck. Bethany did. The dark blur in the background had resolved itself.

"It looks like a tire," she said, mystified.

"A car tire."

Tuck tapped the screen. "It is. Read the lettering."

She did: "U.S. Royal." She looked at him. "Is that Uniroyal? The tire company?"

"It is now. It used to be called U.S. Royal. And I've seen that giant tire before." He slid onto a bench, used another laptop to search. Two minutes later he whistled with delight. "Ah. Here we are. I thought so. You were right. It's a Ferris wheel. It was part of the U.S. Royal Tire pavilion at the New York World's Fair." He looked up. "That was 1964 to 1965."

"So this photo —"

"Given when the camera was sold, it was taken in 1965. The man in the sunglasses looks to be in his mid-forties. If he's alive today, he's in his nineties."

"So he's probably not alive."

"Probably not," Tuck agreed.

Back in the front room, she turned the problem over in her mind. Annabelle had squirreled away half a photograph, the portrait of a man almost certainly dead. She wondered about the other half. Maybe that was the more significant part: the missing woman, not the visible man.

She wondered who had it, and why it mattered.

"About my fee," said Tuck, licking his lips.

"Please," she said.

"I was thinking that a thousand should do it."

"Dollars?"

"Sorry. Pounds."

She only had dollars, however, so they settled on fifteen hundred. The funds entrusted to her by Annabelle were dwindling.

Tuck made the bills disappear. "If this blows up," he said, "you never met me."

"I was going to say the same thing."

"I understand the rules."

Bethany was harder than she used to be: "Another thing. I'd delete that photo from my hard drive if I were you."

"Why's that?"

"Because I have a hunch that whoever that man is, if he does happen to be alive, he doesn't want this picture sitting around."

Tuck nodded. "I'd thought of that. That's why I'm going to fool around with some of my software, see if I can't get an image of what he'd look like today."

"When should I —"

"Tomorrow. Not here. Say, St. Paul's. Don't do the tour. You're there to pray. Choose a pew on the left. Same time." A smirk. "No additional charge."

Bethany had no idea where she would be

tomorrow; or who might have found her by then.

"If I don't make it —"

Tuck lifted a palm to forestall the warning. Plainly, he'd been down this road before. "If you fail to show, I'll delete everything, including my own memory of today's visit."

Out on the street again, Bethany once more did her sums. Annabelle had hidden the photograph, and not just for identification. This man was somebody, or had been; so was the woman in the other half of the picture. That was the point. This was about more than the Pilate Stone. Annabelle hadn't only thought about her running buddy following her tracks. She'd planned to make use of the photo. Maybe for protection, maybe for another purpose.

Maybe she was even blackmailing somebody.

Bethany knew that she was at risk and, like Annabelle, saw that she had to separate the photograph from her physical person as swiftly and efficiently as possible. She needed to stash it where nobody but her would be able to get at it, so that if she was caught — when! — there would be nothing to suggest that she'd ever possessed it.

She stepped into a sandwich shop and ordered a vegetarian panini and a bottled water. Instinct honed over the past five weeks prompted her to choose the table in a shadowed corner that nobody else wanted. By moving the chair to the far side, she obtained an excellent view of the street through the front window, and she would also notice at once anybody who came through the door. On top of those advantages, she now had an alternative exit, if necessary: the kitchen was just behind her.

In her head, she put the photograph to one side. Either she would find out who was in it or she wouldn't. She had a more immediate concern.

Oxford.

Not that somebody had taken a shot at her: this was the fifth or sixth time that had happened since she'd been forced underground.

What bothered her was the old man who'd saved her life. The old man she'd seen at Dorothea's lab, and now that she'd had the chance to think it over, at Grant Apple's bookstore as well. He'd been following her all over Oxford, and she'd barely noticed him.

An old man. Late sixties at least. Early seventies more likely.

With a steady gun hand and a grip like
steel.

He reminded her of Sam DeMarco, last
seen in his wheelchair in the living room of
the house where he was, supposedly, being
protected by federal marshals. Her dear
friend Sam, who had died protecting her.
But Bethany knew she could not afford to
get sentimental. If the old man had saved
her life, it could only mean that he was
working on behalf of her tormentors, who
wanted her to stay alive so that she could
find the Pilate Stone for them.

Speaking of which —

She glanced at her watch.

It was time to call Elliott St. John.

Bethany purchased a pair of new burner
phones at Waterloo Station. She was running very low on cash, but Elliott St. John
had indicated he would help with that
problem. She made her call from an alley
immediately behind a police station, on the
theory that if he was somehow able to
triangulate her position and send the thugs
after her, she could always throw herself on
the mercy of the law.

A silly plan, but it was getting scary out
here.

The billionaire had obviously been waiting for the call, because he picked up on the first ring.

"Hello?"

"Is she there?"

"We have to talk."

"After I talk to my friend."

A pause. "I don't have her. I can't get her. That's the truth."

Bethany looked up and down the street. Nobody was paying her any attention. "If you don't have her, who does?"

"I'll explain everything. But we have to talk. Can we meet?"

"You're not serious."

"I'm in London. I don't know where you are, but I assume you're still in the U.K." When she said nothing, he added, "I'll wait as long as necessary. Just tell me when and where." Still she kept silent. "It's the only way to get your friend back. Please. I want to help. I know you won't believe it, but it's true."

"Give me one reason to trust you."

"Because you can give me what I want." She said nothing. St. John rushed on. "Please. You can set any conditions you want. Name the place, the time, whatever makes you comfortable. I'll be there."

"With your goons."

"No goons. No staff. No aides. Just me."

"I'll call you back."

"When?"

She hung up. Got herself moving. This was wrong. All wrong. If Elliott St. John was in London, then Bethany herself should be somewhere else. The trouble was, her business here wasn't done.

She would think about his offer to meet. In the meanwhile, she had things to do.

She found a stationer and bought stamps and paper and several envelopes, then visited an Internet café to look up the address she needed. She dropped a blank envelope in a post box, then waited in the doorway of a shuttered clothing store across the street to see whether anybody showed any interest in it. Nobody did.

She waited another hour anyway, then walked to the Green Park station. She took the train several stops, got off in a neighborhood she didn't know, found a post box, and dropped the stamped, addressed envelope. Inside was another envelope, and inside that one was the jagged half photograph, along with a brief note, just in case.

If all went according to plan, she would be able to recover the photo in time. If things blew up — as Teddy Bratt put it — well, then it wouldn't much matter.

"Don't think that way," she warned herself, loudly enough that a couple of pass-ersby turned to look.

Bethany shook her head and smiled at them, then thrust her hands deeply into the side pockets of her dark Windbreaker, for the evening had gone chilly on her. She had more work to do. With steadily lengthening strides, she made for her next destination.

# TWENTY-THREE

Carl Carraway is sitting in a corner of the main room of the public library in one of the nicer neighborhoods of Washington, D.C. In his lap is an iPad that he purchased for cash and will never use for any purpose other than the one that occupies him at this moment. He is currently online, using the library's free wireless network, and has followed Amy Santana's painstaking instructions to click through a series of intermediaries to the chat room he wants. He has chosen a screen name — JFRIEND22 — and is now in the room, contributing nothing, just waiting. He doesn't have a warrant, but he isn't acting officially or looking for evidence. As far as he knows, he is breaking no laws; online loitering isn't yet a crime.

The waiting isn't exciting. The conversation is by turns esoteric and guarded, and either way beyond his understanding. Nevertheless, bit by bit, the characters emerge:

**CAPTHOWDY89**: i hear somebody tried to hack the post

**77NDR**: which post

**CAPTHOWDY89**: the newspaper

**NOT-ELLIEX**: nh

**77NDR**: there is no nh post

**SOLARIANDOG4**: not what she means

**77NDR**: what does she mean

**SOLARIANDOG4**: try to keep up

**NOT-ELLIEX**: flw rulez

**CAPTHOWDY89**: webmaster was really good

**JJ5SIM04**: in realtime?

**CAPTHOWDY89**: ye

**SOLARIANDOG4**: same somebody who did bitcoins last month i hear

**SOLARIANDOG4**: backdoor probably not spoof

**NOT-ELLIEX**: nh

**JJ5SIM04**: right come on

**SOLARIANDOG4**: sorry

[solariandog4 has left the chat]

At this point Carraway has his first glimmer of understanding. When not-elliex said *nh,* she didn't mean New Haven or New Hampshire. She meant "not here" — as in, "this isn't a safe place for that chat." That's why solariandog4 apologized after the bitcoin speculation, and that's why he (if it

257

was a he) left so fast. Carraway remembers the rash of thefts of bitcoins — online currency — over the past couple of years and makes a mental note to ask Santana whether BLLNET was thought to be involved.

Carraway wonders why he is so certain that not-elliex is a female. Maybe because he envisions a young woman named "Ellen" or "Eleanor" who is fighting fiercely against the diminutive nickname.

**JJ5SIM04**: idiot
**JJ5SIM04**: theyre always watching
**CAPTHOWDY89**: not physically possible
**77NDR**: whos always watching
**NOT-ELLIEX**: nh
**JJ5SIM04**: @ellie, whos jfriend22
**CAPTHOWDY89**: some nerd
**77NDR**: npc
**NOT-ELLIEX**: ??
**NOT-ELLIEX**: 404

So not-elliex isn't just an officious enforcer of the rules. She is someone the others respect: otherwise, why ask her who the unknown visitor is? One participant guesses he is a nerd, another a non-playing character, as the gamers say — that is, a bystander. But not-elliex, whoever she is, professes not to know.

Time to climb down off the fence. Carl checks the notes of his conversation with Santana, who has given him several of Janice's screen names.

**JFRIEND22**: i am a friend of kranjan97
**77NDR**: who is that
**JFRIEND22**: trying to find her
[not-elliex has left the chat]
[jj5sim04 has left the chat]
**77NDR**: who is kranjan
[capthowdy89 has left the chat]

Well, that conveys information too. Just by mentioning Janice's screen name, Carl Carraway has spooked the three chat participants who seem to know what they are talking about. He has been left alone with 77ndr, the one least likely to be a BLLNET member. More likely he — or she — is a BLLNET groupie.

Carraway hesitates. Poor 77ndr is so naïve and so desperate to belong that Carl might save a lot of time just by engaging him in conversation. But if, as he suspects, those who have marched out are BLLNET members, Carraway knows instinctively that in order to be taken seriously — to be regarded as, just possibly, the friend of Janice's he claims to be — he has to follow.

So he exits the chat.

Tomorrow night he will try one of the other rooms on Santana's list.

Bethany chose a hostel on East India Dock Road, not far from Canary Wharf, obeying another of Raymond Fuentes's dictums: sometimes the first place they'll think to look is the best place to hide. The building was eight stories high, relatively new and relatively clean, and offered a discount for cash. It was midweek, so she was able to get a room on the top floor. She wasn't sure why this was so important. Surely escape would be easier lower down. But she wanted a view.

Maybe my last ever, she told herself. Depending, of course, on which prison they sent her to.

From her window she could see the brightly lighted towers of HSBC and Barclays and the rest — proud symbols of a city determined to refute every sad tale of British decline. Somewhere out there people were scouring London for her.

She had to stay ahead of them a few more days.

Bethany lay in the narrow bed, too agitated to sleep. The lights of passing cars traced bright intricate patterns on the ceiling. The circles reminded her of the giant tire, and the New York World's Fair. She wondered how the man in the photo was related to the Stone and to the woman whose image had been scissored out. If the man by some chance was still alive, did he know the relic's hiding place? Did the invisible woman?

Tomorrow. Those questions were for tomorrow.

She shut her eyes and, finally, slept.

Only to wake two hours later to the sound of approaching sirens.

She leaped from the bed and pressed her face against the window. Down below, two police cars converged on the front entrance. By now Bethany knew the drill. Her bag was packed at all times. She didn't pause to brush her teeth. She tugged on jeans and a sweater and headed for the stairs.

But the police were already in the stairwell, a man and a woman, climbing fast. One of them pointed upward.

Bethany darted back onto her floor, looked up and down the hallway. The elevator was a trap. Maybe she could sidle out the window of her room and reach the slightly lower roof of the building next door. She wouldn't be out on the ledge for more than a few —

The police were in the corridor with her. She was caught.

Except she wasn't. The officers, guns drawn, brushed past her with scarcely a glance. Two more emerged from the elevator, and they banged on the door of another room farther down the hall as other guests peered out to see what all the commotion was.

Bethany sagged in relief. They were after somebody else.

Except they weren't.

A young woman answered the door, and the officers asked, quite loudly, whether she was Bethany Barclay. She denied it and demanded to know what was going on, and two seconds later she was on the floor with a knee in her back and her hands cuffed as the police swarmed into her room. A couple of plainclothes detectives showed up, followed by two older men who looked as if they had stepped out of a different movie. One of the newcomers held up a wallet, flashed identification, and ordered everyone back into their rooms.

"Special Branch," he said.

Bethany, mystified, slipped into the stairwell. Two minutes later she was on the street, heading for the river. She had no idea what had just happened but, in the midst of her bewildered relief, took a moment to be sorry that it had happened to somebody else.

# TWENTY-FOUR

Elliott St. John's London residence was at One Hyde Park, a modern building on the south side of the eponymous park. The development, as many an awed reporter had noted, was so exclusive that press interest was actively discouraged. The billionaire's purchase of a four-bedroom apartment for well north of twenty million pounds cash had made the tabloids. There were multiple entrance halls and sitting areas, and a treetop view across Hyde Park. He used the apartment rarely but kept as permanent staff a live-in maid, a cook who arrived at dawn even on days when "Mr. Elliott" wasn't expected — just in case — and a quartet of hard-faced men who worked six-hour shifts and whose deliberately vague job description involved security.

For this visit, his assistant arranged for two extra security men to accompany the boss whenever he went out. Symington, his full-time bodyguard, went with him everywhere in the world. When they were in London, as now, Symington simply moved into one of the spare bedrooms.

Also in Elliott's entourage were two quietly efficient assistants, one male and one female, each of whom had a room at the Dorchester on the east side of the park, a crisp four-minute walk away.

Elliott's wife thought he was in London to have an affair with the female aide.

This was false.

His staff assumed that he was in London in connection with his concerns about the declining growth rate of his British operations.

This was also false.

His rivals suspected that he was in London to press his negotiation to buy into the thriving British satellite market.

This too was false, but the suspicion alone triggered swift movements in the shares of his company and those of his competitors.

No, Elliott St. John was in London for one purpose only. To meet Bethany Barclay.

In so doing, he hoped to save both of their lives and Janice's as well: he owed that much to her late uncle, Daniel Stafford, a dear friend. And if he were able to pick up the

Pilate Stone along the way, well, that was bonus.

There were only two challenges to his plan at this point.

The first challenge was getting Bethany to trust him enough to meet. Without a meeting, they could not possibly coordinate a plan.

The other challenge was sitting on his pricey modern furniture in the palatial living room, sipping a glass of wine as he stood in the window, hands linked behind his back, looking out at the trees.

"She'll call," said Melody Sunderland. "She doesn't have a choice."

He didn't turn around. He didn't much like Melody, but that didn't matter, because she made a lot of money for his networks. The problem was that he didn't trust her.

"She has a thousand choices," he said.

"She won't call the number the Protector gave her. The psychology is all wrong. She's fixated on you. She won't want to deal with us as an abstraction. She'll want to deal with real people."

Elliott turned and crossed his arms. He leaned against the glass. "What kind of New Age text did you get that from?"

Melody colored, but pressed on. "And that's not all. We don't think she has any actual contacts in the Garden, so they can't help."

"What about her friend Judge Harrigan? We know she's one of the leaders."

"But Bethany doesn't. That's the point. She loves that old woman. She'll never risk involving her." She swirls the wine in her glass. "There's Annabelle's brother-in-law. The Russian mobster. We have somebody keeping an eye on him. She'll guess that. And that just leaves us Raymond Fuentes."

"I was wondering if you'd forgotten him." Elliott's sarcasm could be awe-inspiring. "I'd say he's her likeliest call. And he's also the scariest from our point of view."

"The Agency is sitting on him. No way can he get out of the country. And I'm sure they're into his phones and e-mail by now. She can't contact him undetected. If she so much as tries, we'll know within hours." Melody gets to her feet. She pads to the window, puts her nose against the glass, wondering, maybe, how many books full of partisan invective she'd have to sell to afford a place like this. "No, Elliott. In the end, she'll come to you, because she won't have a choice."

"And then your plan goes into effect."

"It's the Protector's plan."

"I wasn't aware that there was a difference."

Melody touches his cheek. "Oh, there's a big difference. Believe me."

It had to happen sooner or later.

She was upstairs at Harrods, killing time before her meeting with Tuck, browsing fashions she couldn't afford and didn't really want but still found fascinating, when she heard her name being called.

"Bethany? Bethany Barclay? Is that really you?"

Caught by surprise, she swung around, quite stupidly, and found herself staring into the gray-green eyes of a law school classmate, Wendy Eisenman.

"It *is* you," Wendy cried and drew her into an unwanted hug before she could answer. Then they were at arm's length, Wendy holding tightly to her shoulders. "But what are you doing here? All that trouble in the States — is that all over with?" She reached up, familiarly, the way old friends can. The two of them had nearly won the first-year moot court competition, but they'd lost touch after that as Wendy climbed the law school ladder of law review and postgraduation clerkship with a federal judge. "Your hair's all different. I like it this way." Her smile faltered. "Are you going to say anything? Oh, goodness. You're still on the run, aren't you?"

"I'm sorry," said Bethany, voice shaking. They were drawing attention. "I have to go."

"Do you need help? A lawyer? I practice in London now."

"Wendy, I —"

"Look. Why don't you come back to the office?" A warm motherly tone that nearly had Bethany in tears. "We'll talk. Confidentially. Whatever's going on, I'll help. Okay?"

She was tempted. Achingly tempted. As she had been when Dorothea invited her to stay, except now the need was more intense, because Wendy was an old friend and her concern was real. But Bethany couldn't accept. For one thing, Wendy would counsel her to turn herself in, and would probably be bound not to help her if she refused. For another, the people who'd gone out of their way for her had a habit lately of winding up dead. Or kidnapped.

"Sorry," Bethany repeated. She turned and plunged into the thronging shoppers.

*Calm down. Calm down.*

By now someone would have raised the hue and cry. If not Wendy, then one of the onlookers. Pretty soon the story would be

269

all over the tabloids: MAD YANK BOMBER SPOTTED AT HARRODS!

Bethany kept moving, did her best to check her back, and at half past four exactly was climbing the steps of St. Paul's Cathedral, once upon a time her favorite spot in all London for prayer and meditation. Tuck had told her to select a pew on the left, but after her encounter with Wendy Eisenman, Bethany was feeling conspicuous, so she joined a group of tourists gawking at one of the massive crypts. She slipped away and chose a quiet alcove where a kneeler invited visitors to pray for their favorite saint, then she doubled back toward the entrance and browsed a bit in the gift shop. Satisfied at last that she was clean, she slipped into a pew along the far side of the nave and knelt on the rich burgundy cushion, bowing her head and folding her hands.

"I almost didn't come," said a familiar voice. Tuck, whom she had already spotted, was kneeling behind her.

"Me, too." She matched his whisper.

"You're suddenly very hot. The word is out, Bethany. Everybody's looking for you."

"Everybody as in whom?"

He lowered his voice further still. "Some official, some unofficial. Various rewards for information leading to you, et cetera. And some of the unofficial types aren't particularly choosy about what kind of condition you're in when they find you."

"I'm sorry," she said. "I didn't mean to put you at any risk —"

"Don't look at me. And don't worry. I have my plans. I'll be out of the country tonight. If you have any sense, so will you." An envelope tumbled from his fingers onto the smooth wood of the pew. "Don't open it. Not until I'm gone."

"What is it?"

"The enhanced photo."

"Just one?"

"One is all you need. There's no question. The man in the photo is Simon Findrake."

"Who?"

"Lord Findrake. Ninth Earl of Clougham." He pronounced it *cluff-um*. "I guess what they say about you Yanks is true. Until you have the chance to check Google, you don't know a thing, do you?"

"If you're through making fun —"

"Hush. Just listen. Lord Findrake was foreign secretary years ago for one prime minister, and before that, something in the shadows. He negotiated with leaders all over the world. An Empire man still, but a liberal for all that. And he's still alive. That's the point, Bethany. He's in his nineties, but he's still alive."

"Where is he?"

"No idea. I think Clougham Hall was sold a few years back. That's it. I have to go." But he remained behind her. "Bethany, look. Come with me. I can get you papers. Get you out of the country."

"I can't. That's very generous, but I can't."

"Don't go looking for Findrake. I'm begging you. Maybe he's just an old man, and you'll be wasting your time. But maybe he's mixed up in whatever is going on, and you'll be putting yourself in danger. Either way, you have to get out of Britain."

She sensed in his tone both desperation and protectiveness. "What is it?" she asked. "What aren't you telling me?"

"It's just that I had word this morning. About our mutual friend."

Fuentes. The only mutual friend they had was Raymond Fuentes.

"What about him?"

"He's disappeared."

The last thing she expected. She swallowed, hard. "Maybe it's intentional."

Hoping it was true.

"Maybe. Maybe not. My offer still stands."

"Thank you. I mean that. But I can't go. I have to see this through."

"You're making a mistake, Bethany. I wish

you'd listen to reason." Pausing to let this sink in. Then he touched her shoulder from behind. "Well, anyway, good luck."

Then he was rising, then he was moving, then he was gone.

Bethany remained in the pew, half thinking, half praying. Lord Findrake. Whoever he was, his photograph from 1965 was valuable enough for Annabelle to hide it.

And Bethany suspected she knew why.

In the notes she'd left behind, Annabelle had talked not only of the Pilate Stone and the Wise Man. She'd also written about the Wilderness itself. She thought she'd identified some of the leaders.

That had to be it. This Findrake was — or once had been — one of the top people at the Wilderness. Bethany was willing to bet that the woman cropped out of the photograph was another. She didn't know exactly how a fifty-year-old photograph could prove anything about the Wilderness today, but that was the only conclusion that made sense.

*Oh, Annabelle. What did you do? Why did you do it?*

The tears were close again, and again she wrestled them down.

On the way out, hoping she was not committing a blasphemy, Bethany put a dollar in the slot and lit a votive candle. She did not know what urge had taken her, except that it seemed like the right thing to do. Deep inside Bethany's head, Aunt Claudia had a word or two to say, but Bethany ignored her.

There was work left to do.

Out on the steps again, she placed her call. "It's me. I'll meet. Do exactly as I say."

# TWENTY-FIVE

Elliott slowly strolled the river walk that bordered the Thames along the Victoria Embankment. As promised, he was without aides or bodyguards, despite Symington's furious protests. He would play this one straight. He only hoped that Bethany would understand their mutual self-interest and risk breaking cover to talk to him. He walked as far as the Middle Temple Gardens, where he lingered by the fountain for several minutes before turning and retracing his steps. He was becoming winded. He was no longer in his first or second youth, and his weight was nowhere near what his doctors ordered. He had made this walk, back and forth, five times now. And he was beginning to see Bethany's plan. The nearer he came to collapse, the greater the pressure on any guard who'd been told to stay out of sight to break cover and save the boss.

Finally, after an hour, Elliott could take

no more. He dropped onto a bench near the tour boat docks, and waited.

If she wanted to come, she'd come. If she didn't trust him, there was nothing else he could do.

"Hi," said a friendly female voice, but when he looked, it wasn't Bethany. It was what his mother used to call a lady of the evening.

Elliott looked away.

"Didn't you hear me?" the woman said.

She sat next to him.

"Go away. I'm not interested."

"I have a message for you."

This got his attention. "From whom?"

"Are you Mr. S. J.?"

"I suppose I am."

"Then follow me."

She hopped nimbly to her feet, balancing on absurdly high heels, and marched away. Elliott forced himself to stand and, unsteadily, to walk. There was more to the plan, it seemed. No doubt Bethany would be recording this scene: the media mogul letting himself be picked up by a prostitute in the middle of London and following her into the park.

A very cunning young woman.

The stranger stopped near a large boulder. "She said you'd pay me."

"I'm sure she did." He coughed. "How much?"

"Since you're being so rude, let's say five hundred."

Elliott didn't hesitate. If he was caught on camera, then he was caught on camera. He peeled off the bills from his bankroll and handed them over.

"Wait here," she said.

A moment later she was gone.

He sat on the boulder and put his head down, trying to catch his breath.

Bethany stood just beyond the trees, her dark outfit camouflaging her in the shadows. She waited, watching the three paths that converged on this spot. Nobody stirred. If it was a trap, it was too good a trap for her to avoid.

Besides, there was no way forward without risk.

She stepped into his line of sight. "Are you all right?" she asked, surprised at the genuine sympathy in her own voice.

Indeed, Elliott St. John looked terrible, his cheeks sunken and red, his breath coming in a series of hitches. For a terrible moment she was afraid that her clever plan had given him a heart attack. But he managed to lift his head, and even, more or less, to smile.

"Thank you for meeting me, Miss Barclay."

Caution to the winds. She walked up to him, took his wrist, checked his pulse. She put a hand on his chest.

"Deep breaths," she said, remembering her father's final illness. "Try to relax."

"So now you're my nursemaid?"

"I need you alive."

He coughed. Straightened. And by an apparent effort of will, slowed his breathing.

"I'm fine," he said. Another long breath. "Ah. Now. Again. Thank you for meeting me."

"Tell me about Janice."

"I don't have her."

"I don't believe you. I saw the note in New Hampshire. I know the rules your side plays by."

"Now, wait. I didn't say my . . . my side doesn't have her. I just said that *I* don't. I'm willing to believe that, ah, that *we* have her." Another cough. "I'm just saying I had nothing to do with it, and I would never have allowed it. Her uncle was a dear friend."

"So she told me."

"I would never harm a hair on Janice's

head. If my side has her, that's why they didn't tell me."

"If you don't have Janice and don't have access to her, why are you here?"

"We don't have much time, Miss Barclay." He tried to stand, obviously thought better of it. "I'm afraid we're going to have to work together now."

"I'm not interested in working with you."

"And yet you're here."

"Because there are things you know that I need you to tell me." A half smile. "And because I need money."

He nodded and patted the package in his jacket. "I brought ten thousand. Well, less the five hundred I just gave your new friend." He half-smiled back. "If you need any more, I can get it for you on an hour's notice." He didn't stand this time, but he managed to lean rather than sit. "So then, Miss Barclay, ask away. Tell me what you need to know, and I'll help you if I can."

"Tell me about Lord Findrake."

For the first time in their brief acquaintance, she had managed to surprise him completely. His soft face was, for a moment, undefended. A hand came up and nearly covered his mouth, until he realized what he was doing and balled the fingers into a fist, forcing it to his side.

"You obviously know the name," said Bethany, pressing her advantage as she would in a deposition. "Who is he, Mr. St. John? What is Lord Findrake to the Wilderness?"

"Well," he said. Then: "Um." And finally: "I suppose there wouldn't be much point in claiming not to have a clue who you're talking about."

"I'm glad you retain your sense of humor."

"Are you sure you want to go down this road, Miss Barclay? It has nothing to do with the Pilate Stone, I assure you."

"Maybe not. But I have a hunch that however little Lord Findrake may have to do with the Pilate Stone, he has a great deal to do with the Wilderness."

He shook his head, but only in astonishment. "This is Annabelle's doing, isn't it? She's in the grave, but she's still up to the same mischief."

"What mischief is that?"

"You may think we have different agendas, Miss Barclay, but we don't. Not really. The Council — that's what we call ourselves — the Wilderness is an insulting name dreamed up by our adversaries — the Council doesn't trust me any more. So we're in this together." He was growing stronger by the second. "You don't have to trust me. But at

280

least accept that I would brook no harm to Janice."

"Fine."

"Good." His eyes roamed the hedgerow, but he evidently saw nothing to disturb him. "Now. There's a woman here in London — a member of the Council — who wants to meet you."

"Not a chance."

"The only way you get to speak to Janice is if you talk to her first."

Bethany was already backing away. "Why? What does she want?"

"I believe that she wants to offer you a deal."

"Like your deal?"

"No. Better. It's going to be something like this: She'll tell you to pretend to go along with me, to find the Stone, and then to tip her off. Tell her what arrangements you've made to deliver it. Usually I'm well protected, but they know I'd break cover to get the Stone if you were to insist. At the handover, you get Janice, they get the Stone, and I disappear. For good."

"I'd have thought all three of us would disappear." Bethany had selected an ironic tone to cloak the hot worm of fear slithering through her.

"Promises are easily made."

"She'll know I'd never agree to those terms."

"You might, if you thought it was the only way to save Janice."

It was Bethany's turn to clench her fists. "Then why are you telling me this? Obviously I won't have a choice."

"But you will, Miss Barclay." This time he did manage to stand. He walked in small circles. "You see, Miss Barclay, while it's true that your friend Annabelle was searching for the Pilate Stone, she was also searching for the Council. For a long time, we've known some or most of the leaders of the Garden. But today, for the first time in history, the leaders of the Garden aren't aware of a single one of us."

"And Annabelle —"

"And Annabelle, in addition to whatever financial stake she had in finding the Pilate Stone, was also hoping to smoke out our leadership."

"Why would she do that?"

"Because she was working for the Garden from the start. She was, for lack of a better term, their agent. They sent her out with her big talk about the Pilate Stone, but that was just a cover story to attract our attention. The search for the Pilate Stone has occupied the Council for centuries. Naturally the Garden was aware of this. They were hoping that we would, in our greed, expose ourselves." He nodded in approval of the plan. "It worked, too. She learned my name, anyway. What the incompetents over at the Garden didn't anticipate — what anybody on our side of the fence, the reality-based side, would have seen at once — was that the financial rewards of finding the Stone might prove too great for your friend Annabelle to resist. She wound up reversing the priority of her missions. Yes, she'd still try to smoke us out. Mostly, however, she wanted the rewards."

"The two-million-dollar finder's fee you promised."

"And which can still be yours. Yes."

"So, Lord Findrake —"

"It isn't a good idea to talk about Lord Findrake, Miss Barclay. You should forget him. Let's talk about how we might help each other."

"Why isn't it a good idea to talk about him?"

"Because fanatics are better left alone."

"Who's the fanatic? Findrake? The people around him? Who?"

The color had returned to Elliott St. John's face, and a hint of the old strength to his voice. He lifted his watch, pointed to the time. "I should get back. She'll be wanting your answer."

"Your fellow Council member."

"That's right."

"Does she have a name?"

"She does."

Irritated by his flippancy, Bethany grows curt. "Let's get back to Findrake."

"Lord Findrake presents a considerable problem. For us and for you. In his day, he was formidable, and he's still dangerous. He still has the old contacts. He calls in very grimy favors from very grimy people. We can't control him. He won't even meet with us. He served on the Council for decades. He was the Lord Protector for more than twenty years. That's what we call our, ah, our CEO. Goes back to the time of Cromwell —"

"I get the reference. Tell me about Findrake."

"I told you. He's a fanatic for the cause. Not just a believer. A fanatic. We've all done things — we on the Council, the fools over in the Garden — all of us have occasionally made decisions that would be difficult to defend in the light of day. Findrake was worse. He was violent. Irrationally so. Blowing up churches in the 1960s, not to scare black people away from the civil rights

284

struggle but to scare them away from going to church. That kind of thing."

Bethany digested this. On another occasion she would like to learn more about him. For now, however —

"And how does this relate to Annabelle?"

"I thought you'd have worked it out. Findrake knew Adrian Wisdom — was up at Merton with his uncle, I believe — and, well, the short of it is, when Findrake heard about Annabelle and her search for the Stone, he insisted on meeting her in person. Now, he's not active on the Council any more, so he could hardly compromise any current projects, but it was still bad security. Somebody should have stopped the meeting, but somebody didn't. This was Findrake, after all. The legend. One of the great men of England. He never said Britain, always England. Nobody commanded him. He did as he liked. Still does, for all I know. He sold the old estate long ago. He has a small place in Bath now. Private nurses, the works. He never goes out, but he has people in. He had Annabelle out for lunch, and well, from what we learned later, he wound up talking her out of school. He told her a great deal, I'm afraid. Because he's senile. Because she was a charmer." He licked his lips, deciding whether to tell the rest. "I don't know all the details. From what I understand, she became interested in some of his old photo albums, and that's what started the stories flowing. When our people checked later, they found a couple of empty spots on the pages. Clever girl. She'd taken the photos with her. One in particular caused a bit of a furor."

"Why?" Hoping he couldn't sense the quickening of her attention. "What was the problem?"

His shoulders slumped. "I won't tell you the name. That's asking too much. I'm sorry."

"Whose name? What are you talking about?"

"I can't say for sure. But I suspect that it would be a photo of Findrake and a woman he recruited to the Council. Taken at the World's Fair in New York back in the sixties."

"Why is that a problem?"

"Several years back, when Findrake was still active in the British government, there was some kind of investigation. A minor scandal. Missing funds, something of that order. Findrake was cleared, but both of his careers were ended. His work for Britain and his work for us. He's always been bitter about that, always wanted to pretend he's still in the game. Both games."

"But if he was cleared —"

"The charges were true, Ms. Barclay. Funds had gone missing. They were funneled to the Council's work. The Brits didn't know that, but they did trace the funds to the United States. That's where they ran into the brick wall. They looked at every known Findrake acquaintance in the States. Turned them inside out I believe is the jargon. Everyone came up clean. Nobody had fiddled any funds."

"But the woman in the photograph —"

"Exactly. The woman in the photo was the intermediary. The British authorities never knew she existed, you see. She's still alive, Miss Barclay. If her role is discovered, even now, the case would be reopened. The statute of limitations has passed, but we're not talking criminal prosecution here. The point is that the funds would be tracked, and the Council and its secrets would be laid bare. That's how big a deal it is."

"And Annabelle had the photo."

St. John nodded. A fresh bout of coughing doubled him over, and when he straightened his face was gray and sweaty.

"So it would appear. Annabelle had the photo. Exactly. And now that she's gone, it's in the wild. That's what we call it. In the wild, waiting to be found."

"And you think I'm going to find it?"

"I think Annabelle would have directed you to it. Sure, she'd give you the clues about the Pilate Stone. But somehow she knew that the photo was the true prize."

"Why are you telling me this?"

"Because the woman in the picture is now the Lord Protector. There is nothing she wouldn't do to get that photo back."

She told Elliott to stay next to the rock for ten minutes, and he saw no reason not to comply. He didn't bother to watch her go. Whatever path she took, he knew, would be chosen to cast false light. He liked Bethany Barclay, but she remained an adversary.

To be on the safe side, he allowed fifteen minutes before climbing the stairs to the street level. Pedestrians everywhere. Naturally, no sign of Bethany. He hadn't expected to spot her, but a part of him had hoped she might linger. Jostling his way to the taxi stand, he felt the odd sensation that they had unresolved issues to discuss, that he should have tried harder to entice her into a partnership. No doubt Melody would give him a hard time later.

Riding toward One Hyde Park, Elliott saw that his hands were trembling, a fact that annoyed him quite unreasonably. He prided himself on his calm in all situations. His ability to keep his head had helped make his fortune. He stared at his hands, willing the shiver to stop, and when that didn't work, the billionaire decided on a walk. He told the driver to let him out at the next corner. Or tried to. His mouth wasn't working. His throat was closing. His heart was pounding. As his body screamed for air and the shadows closed in, he remembered, vaguely, a pinch in the neck on the crowded sidewalk, like an insect bite.

Dying in the back of the cab, Elliott St. John wished he could tell Symington, his bodyguard, that he'd been right all along: Elliott should never have left without him. Had he the energy he would have laughed.

# TWENTY-SIX

On London's foggier days the dark falls suddenly, as though the sun, having failed all afternoon to burn through the clouds, just decides to give up and get some rest. Bethany slipped out the rear entrance of her Kensington hotel at half past seven, stepping into the inky shadows of the sleazier world. The hotel was the last one on her list, a seedy cash-only backwater that catered to what her aunt Claudia used to call women of easy virtue. Probably the management assumed Bethany was one of them.

For now, that was just fine.

She walked, because walking would give her time to think, to plan, to work out the practicality, if not the morality, of her next step toward recovering Janice. She was playing in the big leagues now, just as Ray Fuentes had warned her. Playing in the big leagues, but playing alone.

Bethany walked.

She had two strikes against her: she was still a fugitive, and the Wilderness still had Janice. Elliott St. John had tossed her a curve, and she had managed to foul it off.

Now Elliott was dead — the news was everywhere — and she had no illusion that he had been killed for any reason other than the indiscretions he had shared with her about the Council and Findrake. Yet whoever had managed to follow Elliott St. John and eavesdrop on their conversation had left her alive. The Pilate Stone was the reason she was still in the game.

She had only one swing left, and she was pretty sure there was only one pitch she could hit. She could still track Annabelle. She could still follow her running buddy's path toward the Pilate Stone. And somewhere along the way, she was confident she would find the other half of the photograph. If she knew who the woman was, she could buy Janice's freedom.

"That's going to have to be enough," she said to the air.

And so she walked, watching her back, even though it was likely pointless. Nigel Tuck had said everybody was looking for her, and she had no reason to doubt it.

She had called Dorothea twice, from two

different call boxes, and reached her neither time. That worried her.

Tuck said Ray Fuentes had disappeared. That worried her more. Elliott St. John had been a friend of Janice's father and would not have allowed the girl to come to harm. With the billionaire out of the picture, Fuentes was the only person actively searching for Janice. If he'd been taken — or killed — well, then she was truly on her own.

Or was she?

She thought again about the package she'd mailed. A final protection against the worst.

She hoped.


"Are you certain it wasn't our people?" asked the Protector.

"Morgan's sure, ma'am," said Kenny.

"Did he witness the attack?"

"No, ma'am. He was following Bethany. He reports nobody else observing their meeting. Any surveillance must have been from long distance."

The Lord Protector rubbed her eyes. Exhaustion, she knew, was corrupting her judgment. They were in her capacious study once more, seated in the alcove with its splendid leaded windows. Her lunch of scrambled eggs and soup sat all but untouched on the tray. She had spent half the afternoon on the telephone with her fifty-five-year-old daughter whose marriage was collapsing, and whom she fervently hoped would not feel the need to rush home to Mommy, bringing along her several dreadful children to disrupt the house. She'd had tea with Edna Harrigan, who was taking poorly to the stress of Bethany's flight.

And now this.

"It was Findrake," she said at last. "It had to be Findrake."

"I would think so, ma'am."

"This is absurd. He can't go around eliminating members of the Council."

Kenny had the wit to say nothing.

"How is Melody Sunderland taking it?"

"Badly, I'm afraid."

"I would think so. She hasn't been on the Council long enough. I suppose this has been something of a game for her. Now she has her baptism by fire, as it were." She picked up her teacup, touched it to her papery lips, changed her mind and put it back. "And I can't touch him. Findrake. He knows I can't. The old fool. Didn't he realize that Elliott would have files to protect him from this sort of thing?"

Again Kenny recognizes the question as rhetorical.

293

"Melody. Where is she staying?"

"Ma'am, she has a suite at the Savoy."

"Good. Tell her to stay put while we work this out. And have somebody call her producer. I don't want her going on the air in her current state."

"Yes, ma'am."

"We'll have to do something about Elliott's files, of course. I'll give that some thought. Kenny?"

"Ma'am?"

"Who else do we know over there? Somebody who can keep an eye on Findrake for us."

"Ma'am, the best we have there is Morgan."

"Yes, well, Morgan has another job. As a matter of fact, this means that he'll have to keep tighter watch. He's smart enough to know that without being told, but let's be sure to remind him. We don't know what Elliott told Bethany before he died, because we don't know how much he knew. But Findrake will assume the worst. She's now twice as important a target for him." The old sardonic smile. "I never imagined it would be in our interest to protect that girl. But we still need the photograph."

"And the Stone, ma'am."

Her eyes flickered. Was that a hint of

impudence?

"Of course we need the Stone, my boy. A man like Findrake could never understand. He's worried about what will happen if Pilate wrote that Jesus really did the things the Bible says. And Findrake is a fool for worrying about that. Would you like to tell me why, Kenny?"

"Because we know those things never happened. Given that they never happened, there would be no reason for Pilate to claim they had."

"Exactly. The only function the Stone can serve is to damage the claims of Christianity. Perhaps irreparably. It can't stay buried, Kenny. Our Bethany has to be protected until she finds it."

"And after that?"

"After that, Findrake is welcome to her."

Bethany walked. The instructions were clear. If she wanted the meeting she had to go on foot and take her chances. She walked all the way back to Harrods, notwithstanding having been spotted there only this afternoon. She stood across the street in front of a teller machine, remembering an afternoon spent wandering the massive store's precincts with Annabelle, who had needed an outfit — "a slimming gown," she said, although, unlike Bethany, she had always been a toothpick — for a formal event she would be attending with a boyfriend who was, in her words, made of money. Annabelle had liked rich men, she had liked poor men, she had liked smart men, she had liked stupid men, she had just liked men, and she chased them down with a ferocity that would have put some of the ladies of easy virtue in Bethany's hotel to shame. Annabelle never minded if the men were married. She told Bethany once that she preferred it. Affairs with married men were problems, Annabelle had declared, only if you believed they would leave their wives. Once you understood that all men were babies, and that a baby, forced to choose, would stick with the woman who had taken care of him all these years, no matter how much he might chafe in her familial embrace; once you faced these "home truths," as Annabelle called them, you could be perfectly happy in the arms of a married man. Bethany thought this philosophy both nihilistic and destructive, but preaching to Annabelle never did any good.

Time.

A burgundy Mercedes-Benz, well cared for but not new, had slowed in front of her, the hard-eyed men in the front seat staring at her so openly and obviously that either they were not watchers, or they were very good ones. The car drove off, and Bethany felt a little sick, exposed to public view when her every instinct told her to hide, but she had been in no position to set the ground rules. Either the car was after her, in which case it was too late to run, or the car was a coincidence, in which case she had no reason to worry. Either way she should stay where she was, as she had been instructed.

But she could not. The nervous energy pulsing through her veins was suddenly too much for Bethany to withstand. She had to move if only to regain a measure of control, for if she stood in front of the teller machine much longer, she would begin to tremble, and then might go to pieces. She walked a dozen paces away, joining a crowd of West Indians waiting for a bus. Feeling oddly comfortable, Bethany turned and looked toward her previous spot, watching to see who slowed down to look for her. A pair of sullen teen girls stopped in front of the machine to light a joint, then shuffled on. A police car drifted along the street, but the men inside looked bored. A tall man in a cheap coat stopped directly in front of the machine, and Bethany stiffened, but he patted his pockets, found a wad of bills, then smiled and walked on, perhaps having decided that he had enough cash after all. Then one of the chattering people waiting for the bus put his mouth close to her ear and whispered an order. The small gun pressing against her side provided reason enough to do as she was told.

They snared a waiting cab at the stand outside the department store, and he opened the door as though out of politeness, then stepped past her and rolled down the window and got in first, the gun pointing to make her follow, the open window his reminder that he could shoot her easily if she tried to slam the door on him and flee. She might have tried anyway. *Never get in a car at gunpoint* seemed like a sensible rule, because whatever is waiting at the end of the ride is probably worse than getting shot in the street. But she knew that Teddy Bratt, private investigator and ex-husband of Dorothea Ziman, was only taking the ordinary and necessary precautions.

He had to know, ever since she called him earlier today, that Bethany had guessed most of the story. What would surely worry him now was what she planned to do about it.

The cab crossed the bridge and dropped

them at a low seedy building in the shadow of the Globe Theatre, where Bratt forced her to precede him up the narrow stairs to the two musty rooms that served as his office. There, his gun hand resting on the desk between them as Bethany sat on the other side with her fingers interlaced atop her head, the ungentle giant spoke his first words.

"Annabelle warned me about you," he said. "She told me if anything happened to her, sooner or later you'd be on my doorstep."

"And here I am," Bethany said evenly. A pair of handcuffs lay on the blotter, and Bratt obviously meant her to notice, but she would make him shoot before she allowed him to put them on her.

"You're the one who called me," he said. "Why don't you tell me exactly what you want?"

Bethany knew she would have to choose her words with care. She had seen what Teddy Bratt could do when angered. She knew by now that he wasn't all there. But he was huge, and he was strong, and he was armed. Unless she could work things around to her advantage, she'd get no information from him.

He'd kill her instead.

# TWENTY-SEVEN

"May I take my hands down, please?"

The red-bearded giant gave this careful consideration. She waited while his mind worked through the possible scenarios. "Fine," he said. "But keep them on the desk. Palms down."

She did exactly that.

"Now. Tell me why you're here."

"I'm interested in what happened between you and Annabelle."

Bratt frowned. The gun rested on his hip, but was still pointed her way. Probably he didn't know that Bethany was as familiar with guns as he was. Between her mad father and Sam DeMarco, she'd spent more time at the shooting range than the shopping mall.

"It wasn't like that," he said. "We were friends. That's all."

"Of course you were." Bethany smiled encouragingly. "Trusted friends. That's why she asked you to help with her project."

"What project is this?" He shook his large head. "I have no idea what you mean. What project?"

Bethany wondered whether Bratt was often called upon to lie in the course of his work as a private investigator. If that last speech was any indication, he wasn't very good at it.

"At the house the day before yesterday. You pretended to be surprised that I'd found something hidden behind a picture in the hallway, but when you went out the window you took it with you. That means you knew it had value. My guess is that you were perfectly aware that Annabelle had hidden that postcard. That's why you left so fast. You drove all the way up from London to get it, only to discover that I'd already found it. That's how I know you and she were working together. She obviously trusted you, Teddy. She would have told you all about her project."

"Some project." Despite his size, his voice had a raspy quality that belonged to a sicklier fellow. "She didn't even know what she had."

"No? Why not?"

"She was too limited in her vision." He laughed, rolling his chair around on its casters. Bethany's was stationary. "This is potentially some very valuable stuff. I just need a little help fitting all the clues together."

Sometimes Bethany's intuition was like a sixth sense. "Clues like the research she hired you to do."

"What do you know about that?" he demanded, eyes glinting. Bethany, gaze fixed on the gun, tried to hide her jubilation at his confirmation of a part of her theory.

"I know enough that I almost got killed the night before last."

"That shooting in Oxford. I wondered."

"I wondered too. Like, maybe, if you were there."

"I was in London. Missed the party." The giant laughed, his gun hand remaining rock steady. Outside, a police car rushed past, siren wailing, but it was not meant for them. "But I'll tell you something. That shooting? It just confirms my theory. If people are willing to kill to get the information, I'm sure they'll pay for it too."

"Maybe they were shooting to hide the information. Did you ever think about that?"

But Teddy was in fantasy land, and not amenable to argument. "I mean, the way Annabelle talked, this could be worth millions. All we have to do is put the clues together, and we can auction it off and retire."

"So, you have other clues too? Not just the postcard?"

"Maybe."

"That's right. She trusted you. She'd have left something with you, in case things went wrong. Left it, given you instructions." She hesitated, not wanting to set him off. "That's why she told you I'd turn up on your doorstep, Teddy. You were to hand something over to me, if anything happened to Annabelle. What was it? What did she leave for me?"

"Nothing," he snapped.

She kept her eyes on his. "So, you're saying Annabelle didn't trust you after all?"

"She trusted me."

Aunt Claudia had raised Bethany to the virtue of patience. It came in handy now. "Annabelle told you about the hidden postcard. She didn't tell you what it meant. And she didn't give you anything else. That doesn't sound like trust to me." She shook her head. "I'm sorry, Teddy. Annabelle had no right to involve you. But the only way to get you out of this is to give me whatever she gave you to hold. Try to forget that the rest of this ever happened."

"Give it. For free."

"That's right."

He squinted as if the idea of charity was new to him. His chair rolled back and forth. "It's valuable. That's what Annabelle said. It's really, really valuable."

"The thing she was looking for?"

"The piece of paper she gave me to —" He brought his fist down on the desk. The room rocked. "Stop doing that!"

"Doing what?"

"You're trying to trick me, and it's not going to work. I'm not telling you anything else!"

*Careful, careful.* "Teddy, listen to me. If Annabelle gave you this valuable piece of paper, don't you think the people who were after her — the people who are after me — don't you think they might come after you next?"

"Or maybe they'll pay me. Maybe they'll pay me big."

"These people aren't in the habit of paying for things they can take."

The gun wavered: bewilderment more than fear. Teddy, despite his threats, was a small-timer, and she was introducing complications beyond his experience. "I can take care of myself."

"You don't know these people."

304

"Then I can hardly wait to meet them."

But the braggadocio was forced. Teddy Bratt was starting to understand that he was out of his depth. And that made him more dangerous than ever.

Morgan huddled on a bench across the way, shivering for effect, to all the world just another of London's homeless. Passersby gave him a wide berth, and that was just how the killer liked it. If interviewed by the police, witnesses wouldn't even remember that anyone had been sitting there. Who remembered the detritus they kicked aside when walking?

The perch gave Morgan a clear line of sight to the second-floor windows of the office. Bratt was a loose cannon with a history of violence. Morgan couldn't decide how long to leave the two of them up there alone. Bethany was brave but at times foolhardy and could easily provoke the man into —

Morgan sat up straight. Someone else was watching. One of the people who'd avoided his bench had taken up a post beneath the awning of a darkened store. Nobody would notice from up in Bratt's office, and a passerby would have to peer into the gloom to pick out the small, slim figure. But Morgan was paid to miss nothing.

Mathematical induction: a single watcher doesn't imply a second, but two might imply a third.

The night had just turned interesting.

Bethany's hands were still on the blotter, fingers spread wide. Bratt's decision to place the desk between them was clever, because it rendered useless most of the tricks the guys in the movies used to disarm the bad guys. Not that the few techniques Bethany had learned from Vivian did much good the last time she tangled with this man.

"So, let's see if I have this straight," she said. "Annabelle gave you a piece of paper with a clue on it. When was this, Teddy? When she was here three years ago? Or was it more recent? Say, in December, when she went up to Oxford while Dorothea was in Asia. That's when she hid the postcard. She would've needed a key to get in. A key she could have borrowed from you, for example."

Bratt said nothing. It was like taking a deposition. Sometimes you have to walk and let the witness follow. Lead a little, and even if you're walking wrong paths, you'll learn from his denials.

She selected a brisk tone. "Annabelle had

you do some research for her. She also gave you a paper to hold for me. She told you there was another clue hidden in Dorothea's house. She told you the clues were valuable. She'd have warned you that there were risks involved. And that was smart of her, because a man like you would want to impress her. So the more dangerous she made it sound, the more eager you'd be to help out."

"I'm not that easy to manipulate."

Was he referring to Bethany's supposition or Annabelle's scheming? Either way, she could hardly stop now.

"And now you're stuck, aren't you? You know you have something valuable, but you don't know who to sell it to."

"That's where you come in."

"You think I'm going to tell you?"

"You're the one who called me. You're the one who's sitting here under the gun. Yes. Unless you want to get hurt, I think you'll introduce me to your friends." His childish lips protruded with a fullness that made him appear arrogant, but all he really was, was bossy.

"I'm a fugitive, Teddy. A mad bomber. People like me don't have friends."

"I'm warning you!" Hammering the desk again. He didn't like the word *no,* especially from women. "I'm out of options here. And so are you!"

He was nervous. And growing wilder. This was the moment. The only moment.

"I see your problem now," she said archly. "Annabelle led you on. That's why you're so angry, isn't it? She took advantage of you."

"No girl takes advantage of me!"

"I bet she didn't even pay you for whatever she got you to do. She was always good at getting her way with people. Men especially. You were just another one, Teddy."

"What kind of a thing is that to say?" His gun hand was jerking now, emphasizing his words. "None of that is true!"

"What did she promise you? Did you really think the two of you were going to stroll off into the sunset together? She used you. She led you around by the nose —"

"Don't say that! You can't talk to me like that —"

She had worked out Teddy's pattern. He squeezed tightly each time the weapon went up, then released the pressure on the trigger when it came down. On *me* Teddy brought it down again, and both of Bethany's hands flew up from the desk, one knocking his arm aside so he wouldn't shoot her in surprise, the other grabbing for the gun.

# TWENTY-EIGHT

It almost worked. It should have worked. Bethany actually got a knee onto the desk, one hand twisting the gun, the other bending the wrist, and Teddy, big man though he was, was caught by surprise, his knees stuck beneath the desk in his rolling chair, unable to use his greater leverage. The trouble was the gun came free too suddenly, too unexpectedly, before she had the chance to break his wrist for him, which was what she wanted. When he dropped the gun she made a grab for it, and that was her mistake, because Bratt at once brought his empty gun hand up in a fist, which took her on the chin. As she flailed, still kneeling on the desk, he smacked her across the neck. Her head smashed into the wall, and she hit the floor, the gun trapped beneath her body as he got to his feet and managed another kick. He did a lot of kicking. She curled up instinctively, a bad move because his kicks could reach her thighs now, and that hurt like the dickens. But when she tried to prop herself up sufficiently to slide a hand under her body and grab the gun, he leaped on top of her and grabbed her hair and smacked her head once more into the wall. Then he did it again, grunting, and blood trickled into her eyes. A third smash would have put her out of commission, perhaps permanently. But Bethany — whirling stars, bloody gash, and all — managed to remember a technique Vivian had taught in the self-defense course. When Bratt banged her face into the wall, his own head jerked forward to add momentum. She pressed the flat of one hand against the wall that was his weapon, bent the other at the elbow, palm upmost, knuckles rigid, and as his head snapped toward her for the final bang, drove two fingers hard into his eye.

Bethany had never tried it before but, to her astonishment, got it right.

Her forehead still hit the wall, but weakly, because he was howling and rolling off of her, hands clapped to his wounded eye. Bethany, still woozy, knew she could not tangle with him a third time. She scooped up the gun and stumbled to her feet. Weaving, she barked for his attention, then tossed him the handcuffs from the desk and ordered him to shackle his wrist to the radiator pipe.

"No."

"Yes," she said, and a bullet plowed into the floor between his thighs. The gun was a Beretta 9, a close cousin to the one the police had seized from her in Virginia. The magazine held fifteen rounds but the weight told her it wasn't close to full. Only Bratt knew how many were left.

"You're crazy," he snarled, but he didn't move.

Bethany was reluctant to fire again. He had screwed a suppressor onto his gun and it looked carefully machined. It would keep the gunshots from deafening them, and neighbors from summoning the police, but the device was ruinous to accuracy. Even if she wasn't dizzy she might kill him by mistake.

"Do it," she said, steadying the gun with both hands.

Bratt complied, his baleful gaze promising a reckoning.

Then she sat back on her haunches, exhausted, bleary, aching, and sick to her stomach. She didn't know how much time she had. She didn't care. She had to rest. And so, ignoring Bratt's unoriginal, unending vituperation, Bethany allowed her eyes

311

to close.

The braying of the telephone woke her a few minutes later, but Teddy Bratt's loud struggles would have done so in any case. The answering machine took the call and they listened together to a woman explaining that she would need a few more days to pay his fee, so he shouldn't call her again.

"I told you," he said, eyes half-defiant and half-defeated. "I can't afford to give anything away for free."

"Why don't you tell me what's going on?"

"You're tougher than I thought. I was pulling my punches."

She believed him.

"Tell me," she repeated, the gun pointed at the floor.

Tamed, Teddy remained angry but told her most of the story anyway. His life had been a hard one, he began. He had always been a big, clumsy lug, and back in school, the other boys made relentless fun of him until he punched their lights out. Bethany nodded, letting him run as she mopped the blood from her forehead with a paper towel moistened with bottled water she found in his refrigerator. Teddy rambled on. He had been tossed from one school to another, he said, because the headmasters, runty little jerks, never understood what it was like to be big and strong and tough and not get any respect from your teachers because you can't do the maths as well as the other boys. He might have continued on in this self-pitying vein for the next hour had not Bethany, menacing him with his own gun, called him at last to heel.

None of this interested her, she said, dabbing at her bloody forehead and rubbing the small of her back where he had yanked her body around. She felt an unfamiliar coldness toward this man. She just wanted information.

"I need to know about you and Annabelle."

His answer was a stream of invective.

"You're going to tell me, Teddy. You don't have a choice."

Actually, it had taken most of her psychological resources to best him in their fight. She would never hurt him to make him talk, but she hoped he didn't know that.

"No matter how many times you shoot me, I can't tell you what I don't know." He struggled to find a comfortable position. Bratt's eye was swollen half-shut, but his confidence was growing. Maybe he had finally guessed that she would never shoot except in self-defense. "I told you. I did

313

some research for her, and she gave me a piece of paper to hold. That's all. She didn't tell me what she was doing. Not really. I knew it had to do with that manuscript Doro's pop was fiddling around with. I knew Annabelle was looking for some ancient relic. She said it was worth millions, okay? Millions."

And the dollar signs had blinded him to everything else.

She perched on the edge of the desk, swinging a denim-clad leg. She had been through his files and his closets and his drawers and found unpaid bills, both from him and to him, along with reports on the activities of faithless spouses and reports on how to improve security at the neighborhood grocer. "Where's the paper?" she asked.

"What paper?"

"The one she asked you to hold for her."

His reply was a stream of earnest if not particularly clever curses.

"Come on, Teddy." She struggled to keep her voice steady as exhaustion once more tugged at her. "Let's stay focused. You did research for her, and you held papers for her. I need the research. I need the papers. When I've got what I need, I'll give you the handcuff keys and leave."

"Forget it."

"And I need to know one more thing."

"I'm not telling you anything," he said, still fighting the cuffs he'd intended for her. "All that blood you've lost, all I have to do is wait, and you'll collapse. Then I'll get loose, and then we'll see who winds up on top."

Bethany pretended to ignore his words, although she knew he was probably right.

"The other thing I need to know is why you went back to Oxford the day before yesterday. Why you went to the house."

"To look behind the picture."

"That's not what I mean. You returned to Dorothea's house at the very moment that I was there. That can only mean somebody told you I was there."

"It was coincidence. I saw you on the news. Read about you in the papers. You were on the run." He shrugged those mighty shoulders. "I figured you'd head for Oxford."

Yes, she was right: Teddy was a poor liar. Either that, or he didn't think she was worth a smart lie.

"I'm old news, Teddy. You'd have heard about my alleged crimes five weeks ago. If that was what sent you to Oxford, you'd have gone then. But you didn't. You waited until I was in Britain. I'm willing to accept that it's a coincidence you got there the same time as I did. What I'm not willing to accept is that it's a coincidence you got there the day after I arrived in the country. Somebody told you I was here. I want to know who that was."

He glared toward the window. Outside, a building under construction blocked most of the view. Bobbing distant lights were boats on what could be seen of the river. "Maybe I'm just lucky. Right place at the right time."

"Come on. Somebody told you to go to Oxford. I need to know who."

He shrugged, but she could see his attention was on the cuffs, trying to work out an escape. "I told you. It was a coincidence."

Bethany fired the gun, startling them both. She was careful to point it away from him, toward the other end of the cluttered room. Her bullet shattered the small mirror above the basin, a shot she couldn't have made once in five tries had she been aiming for it.

Morgan wasn't sure. That might have been a gunshot. A silenced gunshot from a worn suppressor. Maybe. Maybe not. Bethany was sitting in plain view, her back to the window. It was impossible to see anyone

316

else, but she was talking and seemed in control and unharmed.

The other watcher, equally hesitant, had slipped from concealment and slowly, slowly, testing each step, was crossing the street.

And Morgan had a decision to make.

"You're out of your mind," said Teddy Bratt, baring his teeth.

"I want to know who sent you to Oxford."

"And I want the winner in the next sweepstakes." His voice was a sneer, but she could tell from a fresh wariness in his eyes that he thought she'd hit the mirror on purpose. "You don't look so good, Bethany. Your head is still bleeding."

"Tell me who it was."

"What I'm telling you is that you need to go to hospital. Look. There's a clinic a couple of blocks away."

"I'm fine."

He guffawed. "You can hardly keep your eyes open."

"Don't press me, Teddy."

But he wasn't pressing. He was only watching. Closely. So closely that Bethany grew uneasy. He continued struggling in the cuffs, and she should have told him to sit still, but the dizzying shadows at the fringes of her mind kept trying to claim her. He was right. The wound on her head was bleeding profusely, but if she walked into a clinic she was finished.

She shrugged off her doubts. "Okay. Let's do it this way. Annabelle told you she was looking for an ancient relic. What did she say about it?"

He shrugged, his gaze locked on the gun. "An old tablet. Something Pilate supposedly wrote about Jesus. A load of rubbish if you ask me."

"Sure, you thought that at first." She felt a fresh wave of dizziness but fought it down. "But somewhere along the line you mentioned it to somebody, and that's when they came to you and asked you to keep your eyes open. Maybe report on her progress."

"Maybe."

"Then you didn't hear anything for a while, until they got in touch and told you that I was in the country. That I might try to contact you and you . . . you should . . ." She sat up straight. "You should let them know if I got in touch." More wooziness. "Did you contact them, Teddy? Are they on the way?"

"Maybe." His wariness was gone. He looked predatory.

"No. You didn't. You wanted to check first,

see if we could make a deal. That's what the cuffs were for. If I refused to work with you, you were going to turn me over to them."

"You're bleeding all over yourself, Bethany."

"You haven't called them yet. There's still time. Just tell me, Teddy." She pinched her wounded wrist to stay awake. "I don't care who your contact is. I just want the research you did for Annabelle and the papers she left with you."

She watched his eyes as he calculated. He plainly thought she was about to collapse. Probably he was right.

"The research was to turn somebody inside out," he finally said. "Let's say, a certain guy. Annabelle wanted to know everything about him."

"Who was it?"

"Let me go and I'll tell you."

"Was it Findrake?"

"Who?"

His bewilderment seemed genuine but left her confused. Who else might Annabelle have been researching? But Bratt was talking again. To fill the time, she realized. He knew she had little left. He would chatter until she fainted from loss of blood.

"As for the paper, it was something she got from Doro's pop. Nothing much on it.

Just three letters."

"What three letters?"

"Will you take the cuffs off?"

"We're out of time, Teddy. I have to know."

"Listen —"

"Tell me!"

"Wait!" he cried, surprising her.

She realized that the gun was pointing at his chest. Hastily she lowered it. Then she put it on the desk, not wanting to make a mistake in her weariness.

"The name," she said.

"A man named Hagopian. Earl Hagopian."

"What did you find out?"

"It's all in the file."

"What file?"

He nodded toward the cabinets. "Second drawer. A thick blue folder."

Bethany eased herself to her feet. She found the file on Hagopian right where he'd said it was. Still near the cabinet, she began to page through, so she was a good four feet away from the desk, and therefore from the gun, when Teddy, with a roar, yanked the cuffs so hard that the radiator pipe burst, then leaped toward her as hot steam spewed everywhere. The loss of blood slowed her. Before she could fully turn, the giant had her in a lock from behind, his knee in the small of her back, his other arm like an iron bar across the front of her neck, squeezing. Bethany did her best to twist, to struggle, to kick, but he was ready for all her tricks and refused to lessen the pressure. She couldn't let it end this way, she kept telling herself, but his rigid grip informed her that it might. She pressed a hand to his face but he bent it contemptuously away and she heard the snap of bone before she felt the nauseous rising pain. She would have cried out but had no room to draw a breath. Her struggles weakened as the shadows rose round her. In the far, far distance, the broken radiator hissed and spewed. Her eyes grew hot and misty and full and the patterned wallpaper lost its vividness and began to blur. The iron bar pressed and pressed on her throat, and Bethany could draw no air. In all the universe there was no oxygen to breathe. An invisible rushing dark matter had replaced it. Her arms went limp and fluttery at her sides. She heard a shot and guessed that was the end. She heard a cry. Voices. But they likely were imagined. She was done. The pains shooting through different corners of her body morphed into a single desperate ache, a chill spreading outward from her dying lungs. Her eyes glazed, her

mind switched off, and the shadows claimed
her.

# TWENTY-NINE

Night.

Carl Carraway is back online. Based on what happened last time, Fuentes thinks they're getting close. Something is about to break. Ray has abandoned his apartment. Carl has no idea where he is living now; he knows only that the CIA man seems to watch his back with regularity.

Carl smiles to himself. He might be the first FBI agent in history to have an Agency minder. On the other hand, Fuentes is no longer Agency, and Carl is no longer Bureau. So they're not making history after all.

Carl is typing, working his way through the labyrinth until, once more, he is in one of the chat rooms frequented by BLLNET members. He waits. He offers no comment. He ignores all queries and watches as, one by one, the others depart. Soon he is alone.

And still he waits.

Other members pop in and out. A few chat in a desultory manner. They are aware of their visitor, and they don't much like it.

After twenty minutes, not-elliex arrives. She doesn't greet him. She requests a private chat, and then, when it's just the two of them, sends him a link.

**JFRIEND22**: you expect me to click
**NOT-ELLIEX**: y
**JFRIEND22**: where does it go?
**NOT-ELLIEX**: just click
**JFRIEND22**: why would i trust you
**NOT-ELLIEX**: ??
**NOT-ELLIEX**: you will need a password
**JFRIEND22**: what is it?
**NOT-ELLIEX**: you already know
**NOT-ELLIEX**: only chance
[not-elliex has left the chat]

Carraway is at a Starbucks in Georgetown, once more hiding in a crowd. Again he glances around, wondering whether BLL-NET has made him yet. They will be cautious, because they are worried, but sooner or later they are bound to start tracking his movements, first on the Web, finally in the real world. He is reasonably certain, however, that they are not watching him yet.

Not in the real world, anyway.

Click or not? She did say this was his only chance.

He clicks the link.

His browser goes dark, then green. A cursor appears, and nothing else. No bells, no whistles, no fancy design. He is about to move deeply into the dark net, where Amy Santana said that the most experienced of hacktivists often hang out.

He already knows the password, not-elliex said.

He types his user name: JFRIEND22.

Another cursor appears. They have created an account for him.

He types KRANJAN97 and hits enter. The cursor reappears, along with a warning that he has two tries left.

He already knows, she said.

Carl frowns. There can't be much time before they give up on him. Maybe they've identified him after all. There is a password he uses for nearly everything — Gmail, Amazon, Netflix, even his bank. It's said to be poor security, but like most people he can stomach the security regulations only up to a point.

He types his regular password.

The cursor returns, and with it a warning that he has one try left.

The only other password he can think of

is the one that he uses to log on to the closed system at FBI headquarters, and he is not about to give them that one —

*Give them?*

Idiot!

He closes the browser, clears the cache, clears all cookies, and restarts the tablet. He waits, fists clenched, for it to boot up. He prefers enemies he can fight in this world, not enemies who wreak havoc online.

When he is up and running again, he immediately opens the Web page of his bank. He scrolls through his accounts. Not a penny has been touched, but they have already been here. He knows because the log-on information tells him that he was on the site three minutes ago, even though he knows he wasn't.

He changes his bank password, then logs onto Gmail.

His entire e-mail inbox has been deleted.

Carl groans. Several heads turn. He has been snookered. It is as simple as that. He thought he was being smart, but the BLL-NET team outsmarted him. With ease. He still knows nothing about not-elliex and the rest of her crew, but they suddenly know everything about him.

A ping as a new e-mail arrives.

He glances at the screen.

A dark blue Explorer is waiting for you outside. Go right now. The car will be gone in ninety seconds.

He goes.
Right now.
The Explorer is idling at the curb. Carraway looks around the parking lot but sees nobody paying obvious attention. No sign of Fuentes. The back door is open, right behind the driver. Carl climbs in, and the car streaks off almost before he can get the door closed.

There is only the driver. Carraway puts him in his middle to late forties. He has a disordered red beard flecked with gray and is wearing a dark slouch cap. He is smoking a pipe, and the fumes seem to emanate from every corner of the car at once, so Carl supposes that he must be the owner.

"Where are we going?"

In the mirror, the driver's dark pouchy eyes flick toward his, then back at the road. Carl is not handcuffed or blindfolded. He hasn't been searched for a weapon. He could take command at any moment, but of course that would take him no nearer to his goal.

"You can get out any time you want," the driver finally says.

"What should I call you?"

"Mackerel."

"Like the fish?"

"It's my real name. Dennis Mackerel. You can look me up later. The FBI already has me in its files. They didn't have enough to prosecute me, but they sure had enough to make sure I lost my job."

"What job?"

A moment's hesitation. In the rearview mirror Carl can see the play of primitive emotion over the bland face.

"I was a high school math teacher," Mackerel finally says. "You people made them fire me."

"And what do you do now, Dennis?"

"This and that."

"I see."

"You don't. But you will."

Dennis is driving at a leisurely pace. They pass the Washington National Cathedral with its grand scaffolding. The car turns right onto the straight but often narrow side streets of Cleveland Park, one of the city's ritzier neighborhoods. In the darkness nobody seems to be following. Two abrupt lefts leave them pointed back the way they came.

The Explorer glides to a stop.

In the distance a light flashes.

"Walk toward the light. Hands in front of you at all times. There's another car. Get in the back and don't say a word." Again their eyes meet in the mirror. "I'm sure this is very old hat and low-tech for you, Mr. Carraway, but we don't have your expertise. However, we do know how to protect ourselves."

"This is where you tell me that you know where my mother lives."

"We're not like that. We're not violent people. That's why we didn't search you. What's the point? I'm sure you could take us all out without any weapons. All I meant was that we're being as careful as we know how. We have to take precautions." The light flashes again. "No more time. Go now."

There are two more cars, and two more drivers, and so many sudden turns that nobody could possibly follow. They wind up in College Park, where they lead him to a townhouse not far from the campus. They park him in the tiny dining room with a man and a woman for company. The man is black and handsome, perhaps twenty. The woman, thickset and openly suspicious of Carl, is white and in her thirties.

"Not-elliex, I presume?"

The next thing he knows, she has launched

into a speech. About how they oppose censorship and online copyrights, and how they believe in freedom and helped connect the protesters during the Arab Spring. They have been persecuted by the FBI, she says, and by plenty of governments abroad, but they aren't going to stop. Not ever.

"Do you know why?"

"Why?"

"Because technology is supposed to make us free. But people like you — you use it to keep us down. To control us. And that's just wrong."

Carl lets all of this flow past him. Still nobody has displayed a weapon, and it dawns on him that they very likely are every bit as nonviolent as they claim.

"I just want to talk about Janice Stafford," he says.

"I bet you do," she says.

The younger man is very smooth. He smiles sadly as he lays out the simple facts of life.

"Carl, look. May I call you Carl? Look. It's like this. We can get into your files any time we want. We've planted all kinds of little apps in parts of the Web you use. Okay? We can do a lot of damage. We can frame you for serious crimes. Whatever. And, yes, you'd beat it in the end, but we

330

can cause you all kinds of trouble. Okay?"

"Okay."

"I assume you don't want that kind of trouble."

"I don't want any trouble at all." He spreads his hands. "If you've looked me up, you know I've been suspended from duty. I'm not here in any official capacity. I don't have any powers of arrest."

"That could all be a ploy," says not-elliex. "You could be trying to get us off our guard."

Carl sighs, remembering his Schiller: *Against stupidity* . . . and all the rest. But, no. That's too pat. Hers is a practical caution, learned from years of trying not to be noticed. The dining room has a table and chairs and a low credenza, everything extremely cheap. There isn't a single digital device. They don't want him to see what's on their screens.

"I'm here for one reason only. I want to find Janice. She's being held against her will."

"Hey, you're FBI," the woman says. "Isn't that what you do? Find kidnappers? Stuff like that?"

"I told you. This isn't official. And — well, we can't make it official. The truth is, I don't know whom to trust over there." He

331

sees their wary eyes. They've been down this road before. "If you didn't think there's a chance I'm telling the truth, you wouldn't have brought me here. You would have ignored me. But you're as worried about Janice as I am. Please. Let me help get her back."

The two exchange a look. The woman is talking again, and her somber tone tells him that what went before was playacting.

"Fine. Let's be serious. Let's assume you're telling the truth. Why do you come to us? Why do you think we can help?"

"I don't know if you can help. This is desperation. But from what I'm told, Janice Stafford knows as much about the Internet as any five professors. If there's been the smallest opportunity, she'll have found a way to send you a message."

They react to this. Definitely.

This time the man speaks up. "Maybe you're right. Maybe we do know where she is. More or less."

"Do you know or not?"

"I told you. More or less."

"Where is she?"

"In a minute." Not-elliex again — or Ellie, as Carl now thinks of her, even though it probably isn't her name. "But don't you want to know *how* we know?"

Actually, Carl does wonder. And his genuine curiosity is at this instant a good thing, because Ellie clearly wants to show off.

"As a matter of fact," he says, "I'd love to know."

"Because she sent us a message." Positively gleeful now. Carl realizes that he was wrong about Ellie. He can see it in her eyes. She's not proud of herself. She's proud of Janice. "Just like you said. She's been kidnapped, she's a hostage or something, but she still sent us a message. She's so brilliant."

"Surely they wouldn't let her anywhere near a computer."

"Of course not. But our kranjan97 is a genius."

"I know that."

"No, you don't. You think you know, but you don't. I don't mean like a 170 IQ. I mean like there aren't tests for people like her. She can just *do* stuff. She sees patterns. She sees flaws. When she was with us she used to say that every system has to have a hole, because of the incompleteness theorem. If it's an algorithm, it can be beaten. And the thing is, even a prison — I mean, she's not in a prison, but that's not the point — the point is, a prison, anyplace where you can lock somebody up, it's just an algorithm for her to solve. It can be beaten. She got us a message. Right now that's all you need to know."

Carl stares. "I didn't come all the way out here to hear that." His gaze flicks from one pair of watchful eyes to the other. "Listen. I'm not going to turn you in. Not if you give me what I want. But remember. I know you too. If you don't think I can track you down, then you're not thinking."

"It's time for you to go."

He can't believe it. This isn't happening. But it is. Two or three of them escort him down the hall. When they open the door, Raymond Fuentes steps inside, craggy face like thunder.

"I guess it's time to give the bad cop a chance," he says.

No dining room for Fuentes. He has everybody gathered in the basement, where there are multiple monitors and desktops and laptops, even a couple of servers. Somebody upstairs actually tried to pull a semi-automatic pistol, a very old Ruger, poorly cared for. He turned out to be a hanger-on who deals drugs, not a member of the group at all. Fuentes emptied the clip before handing the gun back. Cradling his wounded wrist, the young man shook his head. "You keep it," he said.

So now they're sitting sullenly, half a dozen of them, and Carl realizes, even if Fuentes doesn't, that these tactics might produce desirable answers now, but they might also produce problems later on, once the hackers get their second wind.

But when Fuentes speaks, his voice is gentle and compelling.

"I know you don't believe me, but we're in this together. There's a clock, and it's ticking. Janice isn't just being held hostage. She's being held hostage to make someone else do what these people want. And there's a deadline. If we come to the deadline, and this other person hasn't performed, Janice is dead. If this other person goes under a bus, Janice is dead. Do you get that? This isn't the kind of situation where she winds up in federal prison, and you get to visit while she waits for the appeal. The kind of people who have her, there won't even be a grave. Is that plain enough?"

A stir in the room. The combination of the soft tone and the hard reality is getting through.

"You don't trust us. We can't make you. All I can say is, you have to have some faith. Can you do that? Faith the size of a mustard seed can move mountains." Their blank faces testify that they are missing the allusion. Kids today. "Listen. You want to rescue Janice. Fine. You're all very good at what you do, but in the end your considerable skills won't be enough. You might know all there is to know about how to break into some corporate or government server, but if you want Janice free, then you need actual people who can act in the world. Actual people.

"You have a tradition in BLLNET. You don't tell each other's secrets. Where I used to work, we had a tradition like that too. And you know what? Sometimes you don't have a choice. That's the reality."

He is actually smiling now, and a couple of the kids are smiling back. "Sure, you can follow your traditions. You can keep the secret of where she's hiding. But that won't help you get her loose. Ever since you heard from her, you've been wondering how to rescue her. The only way is people like us. So unless you know other people who can do what Carl and I can do, then you have two choices. Either tell us where she is, or go back to your current plan of doing nothing."

The hackers exchange a long look, conferring without speaking. Then Ellie nods, and even smiles a bit. "She's in Virginia. A town called Warrenton."

Carl is stunned. "You're joking."

"Warrenton is only about an hour and a half from Langley. That's why we figured the feds have her."

"They don't," says Fuentes. Even Carl looks startled by the certainty in his tone. "I'd know," he says, without explanation.

"Where in Warrenton?" Carl asks.

"We don't know. We have the IP address she sent the message from, that's all."

Carraway is all business now. Once the witness decides to cooperate, nobody is better than Carl at ferreting out the facts. And Fuentes, seeming to sense this, blends into the background.

"What form did the communication take?"

Uneasiness. Discussing secrets with an outsider is plainly a new experience for not-elliex.

"A posting on a comment thread," somebody says.

"Online?"

"Of course."

"A comment thread she knew you'd visit?"

"It's a method we use sometimes to get around surveillance." Again that pained tone: Ellie hates to give up so much. "We use some of the wilder Hollywood gossip blogs. We all have unique screen names for the comment threads, so when something's posted, even if it seems to be about one of the Kardashians or something, it's really for us. For BLLNET. And that's how we know it's really from her. If they made her tell them how we get in touch? Well, there's lots of other methods we use that she could tell them about to get them to stop . . . well, to stop whatever they might be doing. And they'd all be true. They could check."

"Don't worry," says Carl. "I'm sure they're taking good care of her."

"You can't know that for sure."

"She's their insurance policy. They won't hurt her."

"Until the deadline," says someone else.

"That's why we have to find her fast. Did she tell you anything else?"

Ellie nods, defeated but obviously relieved. "She has a window. She can see a white house across the street. There's a truck in the front yard. I don't know what she means. Maybe in the driveway. Maybe up on blocks. Oh, and one other thing." She's grinning now. "There's a McDonald's less than five minutes away."

Upstairs, Fuentes is already gone. Carl lingers. He takes Ellie aside.

"We'll get her back."

Her eyes are wide now. "I'm sure that guy will," she says.

"Well, we sort of work together."

"Okay."

At the door. "Mr. Carraway? Carl?"

"Yes, Ellie?"

"If you have the chance, will you do one thing for me?"

"What's that?"

"Hurt them. Hurt them a lot."

# THIRTY

The house stood on a nameless road outside an unpronounceable town in Wales. It was old and grand and surrounded by what looked from her casement window to be hundreds of poorly tended acres. There were turrets and detailed stone carvings and windows of leaded glass with little stained panels to show the triumphs of the family ancestors. There was a building for the cars and a building for the servants and a lot of other buildings besides. Even over nearly empty roads the drive had been close to four hours, and an unsteady Bethany, having decided escape was impossible, caught up on her rest instead. Whatever they had given her for the pain before setting her wrist helped a lot, and she was too canny, or too sleepy, to resist it. As they pulled into the graveled forecourt, the woman sitting next to her stayed put, but a polite young man in a tight suit walked up to the car and opened her door and, the soul of courtesy, extended a hand and helped her out of the car. Everybody was being very nice to her. Nobody had flashed a weapon or, for that matter, a badge. The massive doors were oak with forged iron decorations. Another man closed them when the group was inside. It was late, she was injured and heavily sedated, and they appreciated the degree of her exhaustion. As for Bethany, she had never realized that the simple act of putting one foot in front of the other could be so difficult, or so hilarious. During her freshman year at Barnard she'd had a guitar-playing roommate who'd sung "The Mandolin Man and His Secret" over and over, but until this moment she'd never understood what the song was about. In the softly whirring currents of her drugged-up mind, the words suddenly, if briefly, made perfect sense.

Supporting her gingerly by the elbows, they led her to a claustrophobic, shuddering elevator, then to a spacious room on the second floor, where two women helped her change into fresh pajamas, just her size, for she could not possibly have managed it herself. Bethany did not try to struggle. She could not even form the intention, and she supposed the sedative must be an amytal or fentanyl, but the knowledge provided no energy. The two women tucked her into bed. Before closing her eyes, she just had time to note that one sat herself in an armchair near the door, as though they expected her, groggy though she was, to make a break for it. Chuckling merrily at this foolishness, she passed happily into dreaming.

In the morning two other women were at her bedside, or perhaps it was the same pair. Certainly they possessed the same somber English prettiness and the same dedicated, crinkly eyes. Bethany shooed them out, assuring them that she could dress herself. To her relief, they went.

The broad windows were neither barred nor locked. She cranked them open. A lone guard stood in the forecourt, scuffing the gravel with his heel. Morning sunshine struggled in a lowering gray sky. She guessed four hundred yards of winding driveway to the road. Her wrist ached in its cast. Her knee ached on general principles. She did not bother to turn on the burner cell that stood immaculate on the desk. Her backpack was slung on the chair. As far as she could tell, all of her belongings were intact. Searching further, she found no sign of the tracking devices they had no doubt hidden inside, but technology was not her thing. She was glad she hadn't been carrying the photograph.

She went to the window again, wondering who had her and what would happen were she to make a break for it.

"Don't think about it," she commanded herself aloud, although she had no doubt that her captors were listening. "You're here. You're alive."

And that was the point: they had saved her life, whoever they were. Maybe they were even the good guys. But so far, her questions had yielded nothing but polite smiles.

Breakfast was in the vast dining room, Bethany sitting alone over underdone steak and runny eggs, served by a silent, muscular fellow, as her two female guards kept watch near the door. There was nothing to read, so Bethany looked out on the lonely stone terrace at the back of the house, and over wide, brumous gardens beyond. In the distance she sensed more than saw the furtive imprint of shadowed green hills, but perhaps her imagination was working overtime. She drank a lot of orange juice and studied the cast on her sprained wrist.

Nobody had signed it yet.

When she was done the women asked if

she was ready and Bethany asked if she had any choice. They told her that the doctor had ordered rest if she needed it, so she was free to go back to bed, but she should be aware that they had very little time.

"For what?" she asked the four somber eyes.

"You sound ready to me," the younger of the women answered.

A thick carpet runner, its colors faded, guided them along the marble corridor. They walked past chilly marble busts and old oils. Dead empire builders gazed down unhappily on its inheritors. Two men joined the group. Everybody kept on the rug, so Bethany did too. Probably nothing would happen if she missed a step, but why take chances? She studied the layout of the house as they marched but suspected that any escape attempt would be hopeless. Her so-polite escorts seemed to know what they were doing, even though none was display-ing a firearm. Besides, the several pas-sageways intersecting the hall likely led to rooms full of guards who would come run-ning in the event of a commotion.

It occurred to Bethany that whoever had rescued her from Teddy Bratt possessed an awful lot of resources. She thought of Elliott St. John's ravings on the Embankment and suppressed a shudder.

Bethany steeled herself but was unable to keep her one good fist from clenching and unclenching. This was only the second time she'd been caught since dropping out of sight last month, and she hated it just as much as the first.

She wondered what had happened to Bratt.

At last they reached another set of solid wood doors, not as large as those in the entry hall but impressive nevertheless. One of the escorts rapped solidly, a voice inside answered, "Come," and one of the men shoved the door open and then stood aside.

Bethany walked in alone.

The door snapped closed behind her.

The room was long and narrow, a library. The bookshelves were two stories high and a ladder ran on rails all around the walls. Hunting prints hung on the few patches of bare walls, except above the fireplace, where a lion's stuffed head looked down on her. It had seen better days, and probably had once smelled better too, but right now her imagination was working overtime. It occurred to her that a manse of this quality should have a better brand of art hanging on the walls. A fire blazed but it was far too small for the massive hearth, more a special effect than a source of warmth. The plaster ceiling, ornately painted, wanted repair. The whole house had the feel of a showpiece, shuttered and empty most of the time, not kept up too well but dusted off every now and then for special guests. The floor was wood. Old furniture stood in two separate arrangements: near the center of the room, a set of sofas and aged but comfortable high-back chairs for reading or chatting with a table in the middle for drinks, and at the far end of the room, near the windows that also stood two stories, was a huge and uncluttered desk. Until she had completed her reconnaissance of the room, Bethany ignored the sandy-haired man who stood behind the desk, waiting without any visible sign of impatience for her to acknowledge him. The two of them were alone, except for the cameras and the microphones that she assumed were around somewhere.

She finally turned toward her host. He was perhaps sixty, a tall man with skin so pale it was almost translucent. His narrow, somber face, drawn in a bit at the cheeks, gave him the look of a man trying hard to whistle and not getting it out. His suit, neither old nor new, had the classic dowdiness affected by a certain segment of the British upper class. His accent when he spoke was Eton and

Harrow.

"Well, you've certainly had a time of it, Miss Barclay. Welcome. Is everything to your liking? Your room and so on? No complaints, I trust?"

He smiled as he spoke, but the smile never touched the pale eyes, which flicked constantly from her face to her hands, as if he expected her to be bearing a package, or planning an attack.

"My name is Elaine McMullen —"

"Really, can we skip all of that? We know exactly who you are, and we've expended considerable effort to bring you here. You're not under arrest. We're not sending you back home, or you'd already be on your way. But let's not have any lies between us, shall we?"

Bethany looked around the ornate room once more. "What is this place?" she asked, as calmly as she could manage, which wasn't very. "Who are you people?"

"You're at what we call a transit house. One of our nicer ones, I might add. We maintain it as temporary housing for defectors and so on. A lovely sojourn in the countryside while they're debriefed and we make decisions about resettlement." All of this in a confiding tone meant to imply that they were now good friends. "And as to us,

347

we're just exactly who you think. My name is Paramay. We're Her Majesty's Secret Intelligence Service, Miss Barclay, and I'm afraid we need your rather urgent help."

# THIRTY-ONE

The Lord Protector is furious.

"Gone? What do you mean she's gone?"

"We're not entirely sure." Kenny is nervous. He hates being the bearer of bad news. "We have reports from Morgan, but they're incomplete. WAKEFUL never met with Miss Sunderland, as you know, and we don't have a recording of her meeting with the late Mr. St. John. She seems to be safe. We know that much."

They are in her office. Lillian is seated behind her wide, shining desk. Three computer monitors are ranked to the side, angled so as not to block the alcove of windows.

"How can someone seem to be safe, Kenny?" That silky tone: by far her most dangerous. "Either she's safe or she isn't."

"Yes, ma'am. There was some kind of altercation at the office of that fool of a private investigator we bribed last year." He is speaking, unthinkingly, in his boss's cadences. "Before Morgan could get there, someone else intervened. We're not precisely sure who, but Morgan is of the opinion that it's the British government."

"The Brits? What in the world would they want with her?" A frightening thought. "She's not under arrest, is she? They're not sending her home?"

"Ma'am, our sources don't indicate any Washington awareness. Morgan thinks they've likely taken her to one of their safe houses."

"To interrogate her?"

"No, ma'am. To recruit her."

"Recruit her for what? No, never mind." All at once the Protector sees the whole clever plan. She wastes half a moment raging inwardly at herself for not detecting it sooner. She purses her lips. "You know this must be Findrake's doing."

"That's a possibility, ma'am. But there's another."

"Don't keep me in suspense, boy."

"Ma'am, Harry Stean is in London."

"And why am I just learning of this now?"

"We — we thought he was there on business —"

"And didn't remark on the coincidence. Oh, you are a dunderhead, Kenny. You truly are." She gives him a look. Her agile mind is already leaping ahead by several stages. "I want you to double the guards on the Stafford girl."

"How is that —" He stops, remembering last time. "Yes, ma'am."

"Good boy. You're learning."

"Thank you, ma'am."

"Oh, and there's one thing more."

"Yes, ma'am."

"I have fresh instructions for Morgan."

She spoke for five minutes.

They sat catercorner in one of the several seating arrangements, and Bethany declined his offer of coffee or tea. Paramay dismissed the steward she hadn't heard enter, then prepared his own cup and beamed like a clever schoolboy.

"Nobody knows you're with us just now, Miss Barclay. Please set your mind at ease. We haven't told your government. We haven't told those wretched people who sent you here and think they own you. As I said, we need your help. Unfortunately, what we have in mind is not exactly kosher. Will you hear me out?"

"Do I have a choice?"

"Of course you do. You're not a prisoner. If you are tired, you are welcome to return to your room. Or, at any moment of your choosing, the young people who brought you here will drop you at the hotel in Kensington and leave you to make your own way. It's entirely up to you."

"Where's Teddy Bratt?" she asked, because she had to keep punching or she was going to go down.

"Alas, he has, for the moment, escaped our clutches. I can't say more than that, I'm afraid. Not unless you're ready to listen to my proposal."

"How did you find me?" she persisted. "Who turned me in?" Thinking of Gehringer, of Dorothea, of that immigration officer. And of the old man with the gun in the crypt. It occurred to her that perhaps they'd been watching her all along.

Paramay — if indeed his name was Paramay — never dropped his gaze. "Are you ready to listen?"

Bethany took her time. Lawyer's instinct told her to make him wait. Paramay might be in charge, and he might have a dozen minions at his call, but she, not he, was the supplicant.

"I've heard a lot of proposals the past few weeks," she finally said. "Every one of them has been a lie."

"All you have to do is listen. You're not

committing yourself to anything." He stirred his tea. "Even just for listening to us, we'll reward you with a fresh passport. A British passport that won't raise any alarms at any border you cross."

"Except that you'll be able to follow me every step."

"Oh, I'm afraid that's going to happen anyway, Miss Barclay. Water under the bridge. No more anonymity where you're concerned. So why don't we try to be adults, you and I? Listen to our proposal. You can always say no."

She agreed to listen. And added that on second thought maybe she'd have that coffee after all. The steward returned and offered digestive biscuits, although even back at Oxford she'd had to suppress a giggle every time someone used the fancy name for sugary cookies.

Two minutes later they were alone again: just Bethany, Paramay, and the microphones.

Paramay launched at once into his explanation, and she listened hard for the half truths she knew he would tell.

"First of all, let me say again that although you remain a fugitive wanted by your government, they are unaware that you're with us. They know you're in the U.K., of course.

But they don't know you're here. Part of the decision to get you to Wales rather than leave you to blunder about London and Oxford calling attention to yourself was to keep you from their clutches. So if you're worried that we're going to send you home, let me put your mind at ease. That's not why we've gone to all of this trouble."

He paused, and sipped, awaiting her questions, but she had the wit to stay silent.

"We know you're innocent, Miss Barclay. We know you didn't bomb those laboratories or murder that silly boy in Virginia. We know you were framed, and we have a reasonable idea who did the framing. And your government has worked it out too, if they've half a brain in their head — not always a given, I grant you. You were framed by people who want you on the move. They want to narrow your options until you have no choice but to do what they want of you. And, thus far, their plan seems to have worked to perfection."

*If you don't count how close I came to getting killed two nights ago,* Bethany thought. But she said, "I could have done all the things they're accusing me of. What makes you so sure I'm innocent?"

"Let's just say we're good at what we do, and leave it at that, shall we?"

354

But her stubbornness would not allow him so easy an out. "No matter what you believe, you should be sending me back anyway. Aren't you bound by treaty?"

Paramay's smile widened into near sincerity. "I believe that's what you lawyers call an argument against interest, isn't it? But what you say is true. We've made the calculation that the reward is worth whatever small risk we take. But shouldn't you be considering the risk to yourself? We can take care of ourselves, I assure you."

Bethany tried a second biscuit, but they were losing their taste.

"So can I," she said.

"True. You can. They had you in Chicago, but you got away. You were cornered in New Hampshire, but you got away. You should have died in Oxford, but you got away. Yesterday Mr. Bratt had you captive in London, but you got away. True, you proved unable to best him in hand-to-hand fighting, but that has nothing to do with your cleverness. Only your physical skills."

Not sure what to make of this — whether, for instance, she was being fulsomely complimented or subtly insulted — Bethany decided to change the subject.

"What exactly is it that you want of me?"

"We want you to keep doing what you're

355

doing. Only with our assistance now."

"And what is it that you think I'm doing?"

"Let me turn your question around a bit, Miss Barclay. Let me tell you more about who exactly we are. Then we can discuss the particulars of your mission."

"I thought you said you were British intelligence."

"So I did. And so we are. But that's not all we are." He gestured toward the walls. "There are microphones in this room, but they aren't functioning right now. What I'm about to tell you shouldn't be overheard."

"Not even by your own people?"

"I'm afraid not. Very few are cleared for this information, you see."

Bethany rubbed her bandaged forehead. The sutures itched. And something about the presentation seemed off. Maybe she was still loopy from the drug.

"There are a lot of people in the house," she pointed out. "You needed even more to follow me around the country, find me in London, and bring me here."

"All true," Paramay conceded, the smile tighter than ever. "What I'm going to tell you, however, is above their grade. You aren't to discuss it with them. Should you try, I suspect they will do their best not to listen."

"I see." Meaning she didn't.

"What we are, Miss Barclay, is a group of independent-minded individuals who have a common interest in battling fanaticism of every stripe. We've members from different nations — some of which would surprise you, I suspect — but we're united in this particular effort."

"What effort is that exactly?"

"We know that you are searching for the Pilate Stone."

She didn't blink. "What's the Pilate Stone?"

"Come, Miss Barclay. No games. I told you. We're good at what we do. We know what you're looking for. We also know that powerful pressures have likely been brought to bear to persuade you to take up the task. We would like to help you."

"Help me do what?"

"Why, help you find what you're looking for, my dear. Of course."

# THIRTY-TWO

Behind the study was a walled garden, and beyond the wall were high hedgerows. She didn't know what was beyond the hedgerows because Paramay had warned her not to venture any farther. Bethany supposed the young woman who kept quiet at her side was there to see that she didn't.

The garden had once been beautiful, but now the beds were overgrown and clumps of grass had forced their way between the heavy bricks that made up the plaza. The hedges needed trimming, or perhaps they were eight feet high for the sake of privacy. Bethany sat on a cracked stone bench with her face in her hands, trying to work out exactly what was happening.

*We would like to help you.*

She didn't really believe him — the offer was entirely too convenient and ingenuous — but she could not deny the lure of not having to do everything alone. All she had to do was say yes, and she would suddenly be working with British intelligence. Or she could say no, and return to her hotel in London, after which they would leave her alone.

Bethany didn't really believe that either.

What she did believe was that Paramay wanted the Pilate Stone. What she couldn't work out was what he wanted it for.

Beside the stone bench, a few scrawny flowers had made their way through the unturned soil. Bethany supposed that this house had been grand in its day, with a staff of gardeners to keep everything fresh and bright. The poorly tended beds made her yearn for the view of rural Virginia from the window of the bedroom she might never see again.

She tried to snatch a bit of wisdom from Aunt Claudia, but nothing came to mind.

Bethany sprang to her feet. She had no interest in Paramay's rules. She stepped through a gap in the hedgerow, and found herself in a grassy meadow. If they wanted her, they would take her on her own terms. She began to march. Nobody stopped her, not even the petite woman strolling easily beside her. A lone guard followed them at a respectful distance.

The crisper afternoon sun lent sharp

definition to the distant hills. In the years since Oxford she had forgotten that Wales was so splendidly green and, for the most part, unspoiled. Even the cattle who watched indifferently from endless soft meadows beyond the fence seemed to hail from a rustic dream of bovine perfection.

Bethany glanced at her companion, but beneath the jet black hair her face was inscrutable. From the hue of her skin, Bethany guessed that she was biracial, part Caucasian, part Indian or Pakistani. Paramay had told Bethany that this was the woman who had followed her to Bratt's office, driven him off, and summoned help. Bethany supposed that bit might be true. The woman had given her name as Felicia, and that, too, Bethany regarded as likely an untruth.

Bethany finally spoke. "I'm told I owe you my life."

"It's possible." Felicia's voice was flat and passionless. "I have no way of knowing whether Mr. Bratt was trying to kill you or not."

"Mr. Paramay says you shot him."

"If I was going to shoot him, I should have caught him. He got away. And it's just Paramay."

"I'm sorry?"

"Not Mr. Paramay. Just Paramay."

"Well, I want to thank you. For saving my life."

"Oh, you're very welcome. From what I'm told, I might be called upon to do it again a time or two."

"I haven't committed to anything."

Felicia ignored this. "Did he tell you our cover story?"

"No."

"We're young Englishwomen on the prowl." Her voice remained flat. "Heading to the Continent looking for men."

"I see," said Bethany stiffly.

"This offends you. It's out of character. But that's exactly right, you see. Even if the papers you've been carrying were still good, this Elaine McMullen has no life. No backstory. She's like you. A loner. If you intend to slip the net, we're going to have to turn you into someone else. Gregarious. Less serious. And not traveling alone. That's important. They'll be expecting you to be by yourself. That's the expectation that you and I are going to confound."

"You're going to be my minder."

"I prefer the term companion."

"I don't have a British accent."

"You didn't have a Scottish accent either. And I shouldn't worry about that part of it.

361

The British accent, as you call it, is fading anyway. The relentless march of American English — fueled by your movies, your music, and your television — is changing the way we speak. It's tragic, of course, to be an unwilling observer of linguistic collapse, but there we are."

"I see."

"I know this is going to be difficult for you. But you have to try to get used to it. Cover is life and death, Bethany." From the dryness of her tone she might have been reciting the weather report. "You and I are best friends. You have to get that through your head. You're going to have to live it, every day."

"I don't know that I can do that."

"Why not?"

*Because people I travel with don't fare well. And because I don't trust you, or even like you very much. Most of all, because I don't want you looking over my shoulder, and I'm going to lose you the first chance I get.*

"Never mind," said Bethany. Her wrist was throbbing again, but she wanted no more medication. "I'll do my best." Another thought struck her, a question she'd been hesitant to ask Paramay. "Who was down in the crypt in Oxford? Who were the shooters?"

"Forensics tells us there were three. Two at the far end, and one nearer the entrance."

"I asked who."

"We don't know."

"The one near the door was an older man. I'd guess seventy."

Felicia stopped. Turned toward her. When she spoke, there was finally animation in her voice. "Seventy?"

"Is that important?"

"Forensics says he wounded one of the other shooters before he escaped. To make that sort of shot in the darkness, especially at his age, one has to be very lucky — or very good." She sank in thought. "This changes things."

"How?"

"We have to get back inside."

In the hallway it was Bethany's turn to stop. She put a hand on her minder's arm. One of the portraits hanging on the wall had caught her attention — a very familiar face.

"Felicia."

"Yes, Bethany?"

"Do you happen to know who that is? The painting?"

The minder put her hands on her hips and tilted her head back, studying the painting. "No idea. I could try to find out if you like."

363

"That won't be necessary," said Bethany, deep in her thoughts.

"It's confirmed, I'm afraid," said Mark Satterwhite. "The spies have her."

The Church Builder stood once more at the window of his suite, gazing down at Hyde Park. His shoulders sagged. His spirit was weighted down by the twin burdens of searching for Bethany and fighting his illness.

"What can you do about that?" he asked.

"Nothing. One doesn't mess with those people."

"I don't accept that."

"Accept it, Harry. It's out of my hands. I'm in the Foreign Office, and I'm not without clout. But the SIS is a world unto itself. We don't interfere. Not without leaving a trail that would lead back to you in five minutes."

"So, what are you telling me, Mark? That I should go home?"

"That's exactly what I'm telling you. There's nothing else you can do. They'll have her under tight surveillance and protection from here on in. You'll never get close."

"And the Pilate Stone?"

"I assume that the intelligence people have

their own plans for it."

"Again. I can't accept that."

"Accept it. You have no choice."

"I'll have to think this over."

"I wouldn't think too long. My information is that they're on to you."

"I beg your pardon."

"That's the other reason I called. If you don't get out of the country soon, you might be here a while. They think you're involved with some sort of group of religious fanatics."

"That's the most asinine —"

"Makes no difference to me either way, Harry. We've known each other a long time, and I know that I owe you. That's why I'm giving you this warning. Get out of the country. Go back to the States while you still can."

"And the search for the Stone?"

"I'm afraid you're going to have to search for something else."

The Church Builder hung up the phone, perplexed, and worried, and not seeing any choice.

Some two hundred miles away, in a sprawling house just outside a small town in Wales, Mark Satterwhite hung up the phone too.

"Now that should do it," he said.

Paramay nodded. "I should rather think so."

Bethany stepped back into the library. Paramay stood beside one of the shelves, an aging book in his hands.

"Ah. There you are." He gazed at her over those half glasses. He hefted the book as if to offer it to her, his tone donnish and vague. "Do you by any chance know the work of Thomas Reid? Adam Smith's successor as professor of moral philosophy at Glasgow? No?"

"I'm afraid not."

"More's the pity. This is an original copy of his finest work, *An Inquiry into the Human Mind on the Principles of Common Sense.* You should give it a study. Reid argues that the Creator has endowed us with two faculties, which he calls principles. There is the principle of veracity, which makes us natural truth tellers. Even the liar, says Reid, would rather tell the truth. All of the liar's senses militate against the lie, you see. Lying is a struggle against our nature."

"Not in my experience."

The thin smile again. "Opposite this is the principle of credulity. We are designed to believe, not to doubt. Doubt comes hard to us. We are more comfortable when we believe. That's why we often have such a hard time detecting the liars among us. Even though they must struggle and strain to tell us their untruths, we often miss the signs of that struggle, because we so desperately need to believe that whatever anyone says to us is true."

Bethany's hand rested on a delicately embroidered antimacassar along the back of the sofa. Everything about Paramay seemed to involve misdirection.

"Why are you telling me this?" she asked.

"Because I know that you doubt me." He shut the book, slid it lovingly back onto the shelf. "And no assurance I can give will cause you to believe me."

"I suppose that's true."

"Good. Cards on the table, then."

"Please."

"This Bratt fellow. The one who got away. How much does he know?"

"I have no idea."

"I suspect you have a very good idea. You just don't trust me." He didn't wait for her to answer. "Look here then. We found this in his safe." From a folder he drew a piece of paper covered in clear plastic. The paper was torn along both edges, and in the space that was left were three block capitals:

E S S

"Any idea what this means?"

"No," she said truthfully.

"But we both know it means something. An abbreviation, perhaps. Electronic Switching System. Earth and Space Sciences. Or part of a word. Chess. Essence. Largess. Stress. Essential. Messy. Our people say that there are literally thousands of possibilities." He slid the paper back into the folder. "I have a theory, Miss Barclay. May I share it?"

"Please."

"Adrian Wisdom was searching for the Pilate Stone. Someone evidently believes that he found it. This paper" — tapping the folder — "might well be the crucial clue. My thought is that Adrian tore it into several pieces and distributed them to different parties. You'd need all three to make sense of the thing. This one belonged to your friend Miss Seaver and found its way into the possession of the unfortunate Bratt. The question is what became of the other two."

"Even if your theory is right, I would have no idea." She realized that she was rubbing her injured wrist. She made herself stop.

"I think you would. I think Bratt might know. You met Felicia. Your rescuer, as it were. It's her testimony that after she shot

Bratt, he managed to punch her in the jaw
— this with a bullet in his side — then grab
a folder from the floor and escape. Why
would the folder be so important that he'd
risk an extra second to grab it? My thought
is that the folder either contains a second
piece of Adrian Wisdom's clue or will lead
him to it. But I suppose you're going to say
you don't know what's in the folder."

"I really can't be of any help," she said,
wondering if he meant to force the information from her.

But Paramay only nodded as if to say it
didn't matter. "Well, then, let's talk about
the Pilate Stone itself. Suppose you succeed. Once you've got the Stone, what
precisely are your plans for it?"

"I hadn't really thought that far ahead."

"Well, believe this, Miss Barclay. Those
who have manipulated you into this quest
have most assuredly thought that far ahead.
And I have no doubt that each side has its
own plans. Therefore I should make our
position clear." He raised a finger as if to
begin a declamation. "Her Majesty's Government is determined that the Pilate Stone
shall not fall into the hands of fanatics, of
either the religious or the antireligious
stripe. Period."

"So my minder won't be there to look

369

after my well-being. Her job will be to make sure that I don't decide to turn over the Stone to the wrong people."

"She will serve both functions, Miss Barclay. She will protect you in your search, and she will see to it that the Stone winds up in the right hands."

"Why do you care?"

This caught him up short. "I beg your pardon."

"What difference does it make? To you? To British intelligence, to Her Majesty's Government, to your group of like-minded thinkers — to anybody? I thought this was the secular age. Who cares what happens to an ancient relic that might not even exist?"

For the first time, he seemed disappointed in her. The smile disappeared. "Come, Miss Barclay. You cannot possibly be so naïve."

"Oh, I'm not. These days, I'm the opposite of naïve."

"You are speaking from the reservoir of cynicism you have developed as a result of your experiences during your flight. That's understandable. But you know that isn't what I mean." He was walking toward her. "I am speaking of the Stone, Miss Barclay. And don't go thinking that the age in which we live is entirely secular. On the contrary. Systems of belief are, if anything, more entrenched. The world has become a dangerous place. This is not the moment for the West to be divided against itself. If the Pilate Stone exists, it will cause conflict where we need unity. And, believe me, the battles that will ensue are not something any sensible person wants."

"So the British government wants to gain custody of the Stone to keep it away from the public."

"We'll study it. The finest minds will work out its significance. Of course the Stone belongs ultimately to history, and therefore to the public domain. We'll release it. We'll even display it. But only after we've had a chance to prepare the way, so to speak."

The biblical allusion did not escape her notice; nor, she suspected, was it meant to. "If I'm to help you, I'll need you to help me too."

"Please, Miss Barclay. Tell me how we can sweeten our offer."

"It's not money that I want. It's information."

"If it's within my gift."

"First, I'd like to know about the old man in the crypt. The one who saved my life."

"His name is Morgan, and it's very unlikely that he was there to save your life." He spoke matter-of-factly. "He's an independent contractor with a shadowy list of clients. Probably he's tasked with following you."

"Does he know I'm here?"

"Not remotely possible."

Bethany disrupted this. "Second, I'd like to know why there's a portrait of Lord Findrake, ninth Earl of Clougham, hanging on the wall out there."

She had managed to surprise him. She could tell. But his answer was swift and probably truthful. "Because this is Clougham Hall. Until the family fell on hard times, this was their ancestral home."

She left Britain three days later, traveling by commercial plane, economy class, with her new identity in her pocket and Felicia beside her on the aisle. The minder was chattering madly about the men they would meet in Europe. The excitement was a pose, Bethany knew, but Felicia was very good at it.

"There won't be anybody else covering you," Paramay had warned. "We're not in a position to requisition the resources needed. Most of the time, it will be just you and Felicia."

Felicia, as it turned out, could be charming and fascinating and fun. Yet as the miles ticked by, Bethany tuned her out. All the way to Berlin she thought only of Janice.

"I'll keep you safe," she whispered, face against the cold window. "I promise."

■ ■ ■ ■

# PART THREE:
# LATIN AND GREEK

■ ■ ■ ■

# THIRTY-THREE

Edna Harrigan is running errands. She has a sick friend to visit at hospice and a minor transaction to conduct with her bank manager and a birthday present to mail to a grandniece who lives in Florida. She has saved the gift shopping for last because she wants to savor it, to use the joy of a ninth birthday to help her forget other worries. The dying friend, for instance. Or the plight of Bethany Barclay. She visits a toy shop in the nearby town of Little Washington, where they wrap the parcel in brown paper. The post office is barely a stone's throw from her house, just up Route 522, Flint Hill's main thoroughfare, which is perhaps a one-minute drive from her home.

"Hi, Judge," says Sandy. She is the only clerk on duty. "What can I do for you today?"

Edna hands over the package for Sandy to weigh.

"Anything going on?" the Judge asks, wondering whether Raymond Fuentes has been back.

"Not really," says Sandy, busy on her computer. She is a sweet child who might never have earned her GED if not for Edna's patient tutoring. The town is full of people who owe Judge Harrigan tiny favors. She lives alone, but the townspeople are her early warning system. So when Sandy says, "Not really," Edna is reassured, because if strangers were in town asking questions, the child would have heard and passed it on.

"Can I help you with anything else today?" Sandy asks brightly once the package is paid for and labeled.

"No. Thank you, dear."

Edna has actually turned away when Sandy says, "Oh, Judge, wait. Sorry. I almost forgot. There's a letter for you."

"It's not in my lockbox? Do I have to sign for it or something?"

The clerk looks embarrassed. "It's weird. It was addressed to old Ben Coates — you remember, he used to go hunting with Sam DeMarco and Bethany? — and Ben brought it in because there's a letter inside asking him to deliver it to you, and, well, I didn't think you'd necessarily want it in your box."

*Where whoever's watching could break in*

*and find it,* she meant.

Edna looks at the small package. The sender's name and address are written so sloppily that they could be anything at all, but the postmark is London.

Edna's blood runs cold.

She is sitting at the butcher-block table in her kitchen, sipping her third cup of Darjeeling, studying Bethany's unsigned note for the third time. Sending a letter and a photograph was a risk, but Edna decides that her protégé has calculated well. Everybody monitors phone calls and e-mails and Internet usage these days. Mail is low-tech, and watching it is labor intensive. Steaming open letters, as they did in the old days, is no longer worth the investment of resources.

Edna looks again at the jaggedly cut photograph, the severe face of the man in the sunglasses, the arm of the absent woman possessively around his shoulder. Then she turns back to the accompanying note:

Sorry I've been out of touch so long. I'll drop by when I'm next in town. Meanwhile, please hold the enclosed for me. Or if I don't manage to drop by in the next few weeks, can you give it to my friend Carl?

Thanks. See you soon, I hope.

P.S. — Please don't tell your friends.

No salutation. No signature. But she knows Bethany's handwriting as well as she knows her own. And she knows who Carl is too: Carl Carraway, the FBI agent who formerly led the task force assigned to catch the Lab Bomber, and who interviewed Edna herself a number of times. From what the Senator says, Carl has been suspended from duty and is likely to lose his job. Until this moment, Edna was unaware that Bethany and Carl had ever met. But the Senator's story about the agent's current circumstances, combined with the words "my friend," suggest not only that they met, but parted on good terms.

*If I don't manage to drop by in the next few weeks . . .*

A gentle way of saying, *If I die out here.*

And that postscript. *Please don't tell your friends.* Bethany isn't referring to locals like Sandy and Lillian: she knows that Edna, no gossip, would never share secrets that way. The message within the message is surely that Bethany knows or at least suspects that Judge Edna Harrigan has acted all along on behalf of the Garden.

It's the Garden she doesn't want knowing.

Edna isn't sure what Bethany's reasons are, but she intends to respect them. She locks the package away in the safe in her bedroom closet. She makes a mental note to try to find out, very quietly, how to get in touch with Agent Carraway.

Just in case.

Agent Carraway, as it happens, is also thinking of Bethany, albeit for quite different reasons.

"We should go together," he is saying to Fuentes.

"No."

"It's likely going to take both of us to pry Janice out of the house. Maybe even a bigger operation, depending on what sort of setup they have."

Fuentes shakes his head. They are sitting in his car on an upper level of the White Flint shopping mall. "Janice knows me. I'm a familiar face. The last time she saw me, we were in the basement of the Village House, the night your team took it down. I was making sure that she and Bethany escaped, unharmed, before the assault. So she'll trust me. That's number one. Number two, you're FBI, and the FBI has been hounding her for a year and a half. She might decide to run if she thinks you'll put her in prison."

"That's ridiculous —"

"Number three. You have an administrative hearing coming up. I have no official connection. If things go wrong, I'm completely deniable. You cause problems. If the people running the Wilderness realize that you're on to them, they might decide to put a bullet in Janice's head to avoid future complications."

Carraway's pride won't let this lecture go unanswered. "You can't keep me away."

"Of course I can." Fuentes is perfectly calm. "Let's not play some macho one-upmanship game."

Carl tries another tack. "Suppose you do go alone. Suppose you reconnoiter the house and decide it's doable and go in and get her out. What do you plan to do next?"

"I'd rather not say."

"Meaning you have no idea."

"And you do?"

"As a matter of fact, yes."

Then Carl tips his head back against the headrest and waits for Fuentes to ask.

# THIRTY-FOUR

The largest private collection of Christian artifacts in Berlin belongs to the brothers Kupfenberg, estate investors whose in-town residence is an elegant old mansion in Charlottenburg that miraculously survived the Allied bombings. It was constructed in the baroque style popular in the early eighteenth century and stands not far from the famous palace. Between the two are several ritzy shopping streets and a pricey subdivision for upwardly mobile professionals.

Felicia and Bethany present themselves at the gatehouse at five minutes before nine on a dreadfully foggy Monday morning. As the uniformed guard studies his appointment sheet, Felicia flirts with him in reasonably fluent German.

He doesn't flirt back.

"Sometimes it works, sometimes it doesn't," she explains as she parks in the forecourt under the direction of a liveried footman, whose gloved hands beckon and point. She glances at Bethany. "You could help out a little more."

"With what?"

"Flirting. We're supposed to be —"

"Englishwomen on the prowl," she grumbles. "I remember."

Felicia frowns. "Maybe I should start introducing you as my dowdy cousin."

The footman leads them inside. The ceilings are very high and, mostly, frescoed. The furniture is contemporary but elegant, with a bias toward the Scandinavian look that Bethany thought went out of style before she started college. They are told to wait in a long room with surrealist artwork lining the walls, including an early Miró that features a cacophony of disembodied heads.

"Charming," says Bethany.

"One must cultivate the taste," says Felicia drily.

The massive doors open. The man who enters is fiftyish, with a silvery pompadour and a serviceable paunch well disguised by his hand-tailored suit.

"Miss Farraday," he says, shaking Felicia's hand and calling her by the name on her fake passport. "Miss Beale." Another shake. His English is only lightly accented. "So good of you to come," he says, as if the idea

was his to begin with. "I am Ernst Kupfenberg." A round, prematurely balding fellow
hovers in the great man's shadow. "This is
my curator, Mr. Wallace."

"I'm American," the curator explains, also
extending his hand. "Doctorate from North-
western."

"They don't care about your pedigree,"
says Ernst, sharply, and Wallace shuts up at
once. The German addresses his visitors
once more: "You are from Oxford University. You are interested in my scrolls."

"That's right," says Felicia with her
bouncy smile. "Our project involves —"

"My assistant explained. I require no
details." He is shaking their hands again,
giving a small bow. "I have duties. I am
afraid I shall have to leave you with Mr.
Wallace."

"He's really a very nice man," says the
curator as he leads them along the hall.
"Once you get to know him."

Bethany cannot help being mischievous.
"Have you gotten to know him?"

A sheepish grin. "Not yet."

Felicia winks at her. *That's the spirit,* she
mouths.

The collection was housed in a long library
built behind the main building. There were

locked doors but no guards. Inside, the light was muted. There were no windows, but panels of thin marble high in the walls allowed one to discern daylight from darkness. Below the panels were racks and shelves of polished wood. The main floor was lined with pressurized glass cases.

"How did you wind up here?" said Bethany to Wallace's bald pink scalp as he led them down a circular stair. "An American curating a private collection of Christian artifacts in Berlin?"

"I was at the *Pergamonmuseum* before this. The Kupfenbergs pay more."

"But how did you wind up in Germany at all?"

"Oh, I see." They were walking among the display cases now, the thick carpet whispering beneath their shoes. "These early artifacts and scrolls are my passion. There aren't many serious American collectors."

"There was Elliott St. John," she blurted before she could stop herself.

"And a few others." A wistful smile. "He was here a couple of times. Executed a couple of transactions with the brothers. Ah. Good. Here we are."

They spent the next forty minutes studying a variety of scrolls, some of them long and ornately decorated, others barely ribbons. Two intact pages supposedly from Geoffrey of Monmouth's *Historia Regum Britanniae.* A palimpsest dated to the thirteenth century by an inscription visible under x-ray fluorescence. A rare, nearly intact copy of the *Compendium historiae in genealogia Christi* by Peter of Poitiers. A fragment of a sermon from about 1450 on the *lachrimae Christi,* complete with pin marks to tell the speaker when to pause. According to their prearrangement, Felicia did most of the talking while Bethany took copious notes in a leather-bound journal. They were careful not to indicate that they had come to examine any particular scroll. Their cover story was a possible exhibition at the Ashmolean. They were visiting several private collections on the Continent, as proved by a series of almost-genuine e-mails and phone calls and letters of introduction.

"Now, you wouldn't want this one," said Mr. Wallace as at last they reached the scroll that had excited the attention of Grant Apple and Adrian Wisdom. "It's in poor condition. I'm not sure the brothers would allow it to travel, to be honest."

Poor condition was an understatement. The scroll was really no more than fragments cautiously reconstructed, and Wallace, rubbing his hands together nervously, was already explaining that there was a degree of guesswork involved.

Bethany nodded distractedly. She had spotted the Latin sentence that had drawn Adrian Wisdom's attention. The words were faded but perfectly legible: *Sed unus homo potest,* the initial *S* grandly illuminated, its head and tail drawn as a serpent. "But one man can do it," Grant had translated. Or, "But only one man can do it."

Seeing the words inked on the ancient parchment, a physical confirmation of poor Grant's tale, momentarily took her breath away. Objectively, however, she was no further forward. She still had no clue what the phrase meant. But now it was Felicia, the minder, who surprised her.

"As I understand it, Mr. Wallace, you have recently obtained what you believe is another piece of the scroll."

Bethany looked at her. Felicia winked again, as if to say, *I have my secrets too.*

"Where did you hear that?" asked Wallace, astonished.

"It's true, then?"

"Oh, indeed, yes, we have acquired another portion. That is, the brothers have. From a religious order in Kurdistan, selling off their patrimony to survive, I'm afraid. It's not yet on display — it's being cleaned and pressed, as a matter of fact, and we won't have it in the library for several months — but you can see a transparency if you like."

On his desk in the corner was an oversize computer monitor. It took him only seconds to bring up the image. "In the old days, scholars spent years arguing about which pieces go with which. Nowadays, we use facial recognition software. Same as at the airport. It doesn't always give the right answer, but it saves us from going down a lot of wrong turns."

"This is so fascinating," Felicia enthused.

The curator smiled at her. "Here," he said, and touched the screen. The lettering leaped and grew. "We believe this sentence follows the one you were looking at in the other fragment."

*Et impium judicabit ceciderit,* Bethany read.

"What does that —" she started to ask, but Felicia was glancing at her watch and exclaiming that they were late for their next appointment and begging Mr. Wallace's pardon and hoping that he would stop in when next in the U.K. and let her buy him lunch, and through all of this perturbation somehow moving them back to the stairs, so that by the time she was done, they were in the main hall once more.

"Please thank Mr. Kupfenberg for us," she said.

They all shook hands.

They are in the car and through the gate before Bethany, from the passenger seat, erupts. "What was that about back there? Why didn't you let him translate it for us?"

"Because we don't want to draw his attention to it. We can't have him thinking that particular scroll held any special importance for us."

Bethany glances at her notes. *Et impium judicabit ceciderit.* "So, what do we do now?" she asks tartly. "Pick up a Latin dictionary?"

"That won't be necessary," says Felicia, gliding through the late morning traffic. The fog is worse than when they arrived. Faintly twinkling headlights of oncoming cars are invisible until too close to avoid, but Germans, it seems, do not slow down for anything. "My Latin is a little rusty, but I think it means, 'And the wicked shall fall.' Or 'the unholy' or 'the Godless' or 'the sinful.' *Impium* can take all those meanings."

Bethany looks at her. "You don't sound like your Latin is rusty at all," she says.

"Maybe not."

"And maybe that's why Paramay picked you."

"Well, he did say I was here to help."

"I thought he meant to protect me." But her questing mind has leaped ahead. "So, if Wallace is right that the sentences are consecutive, then we have 'Only one man can do it, and the wicked shall fall.' Does that seem right?" Felicia says nothing. "Maybe it's a description. A physical description, maybe, of what kind of place we're looking for. Narrow. You can fall off. A bridge, say." She drums her fingers on the dashboard. "Or it's a spiritual caution of some kind. Maybe the reference is to some particular man. But I guess he'd be long dead now, and —"

"Hush," says Felicia.

"I'm joking —"

"I mean it. Hush." She is slowing the car. "We might have trouble."

Bethany peers into the mist. She sees a waving light. "It's a broken-down car blocking the road. That's all."

Felicia lifts her chin toward the rearview mirror. "That's not all."

Behind them a truck is roaring up, very fast.

As the *Landespolizei* and the *Bundeskrimi-*

*nalamt* later reconstruct the events, both from forensics and from interviews with bystanders, what seems to have happened is this: not far from the Brandenburg Gate, the two Englishwomen driving the rented Nissan Versa were waved down by a man pretending that he was having car trouble. As soon as they slowed, a large truck hit the Versa in the offside rear, forcing it up onto the sidewalk. Two armed men approached the car, one on either side. The driver of the car reached through her window and struggled with one of the men. The other attacker was shot from behind, his assailant still unknown. The man on the driver's side then fled the scene on foot. Although it was difficult to tell in the fog, witnesses said his face was bloody. The dead man has not been identified. Both the decoy car and the truck were stolen, and neither yielded any prints. The attack is presumed to be the work of a local criminal gang, likely intent on either robbery or kidnapping. Two inspectors who argued that the setup was too elaborate for so simple a motive have been transferred to other duties. The women in question have left the country. The investigation is continuing . . .

# THIRTY-FIVE

When the report comes in, the Lord Protector is studying a recommendation that the Council double its support of a controversial foundation that distributes to churches in the Third World pamphlets purporting to prove that HIV in humans is not the cause of AIDS. All it takes is a handful of unlettered pastors to proclaim this nonsense as truth, and the cause of Christianity is further damaged. An important emphasis of Lillian's reign as Protector has been to nudge the Council's awareness away from the West, where religion seems to be in retreat anyway, and toward the developing world, where the eerie resiliency of belief often needs a push in the other direction. Getting non-Western elites to adopt the reflexive secularism of the educated classes in Europe and North America seems to her an excellent place to start —

The buzzer sounds and Kenny steps in.

His portfolio allows him to interrupt her. She pushes the report aside and lifts her chin expectantly. She says nothing. She does not believe in wasting time on pleasantries.

"Ma'am, an hour ago there was an attempt on Bethany Barclay's life. She survived. Morgan reports killing one of the assailants. It appears that Bethany's traveling companion injured the other, who fled the scene."

"This was in Berlin?"

"Yes, ma'am."

"She was at that hideous Kupfenberg mansion?"

"Yes, ma'am."

"Do we know why?"

"Not yet. We will."

The Protector nods. "Very well. Tell Morgan good work. Where are they now?"

"As of ten minutes ago they were checked out of their hotel, on the way to the airport."

"It has to be Findrake," she muses. "He doesn't seem to want us to get anywhere near the Pilate Stone."

"No, ma'am."

"This bodyguard or driver or whoever she was. What do we know about her?"

"Probably British intelligence."

"That part I could work out for myself."

Kenny colors. "Ma'am, Morgan suggests

that they don't dare put on a full team, for fear of attracting the attention of the locals. And given that they probably don't know whom to trust — who wants the Stone for themselves, who's in league with us — well, Morgan thinks this one bodyguard may be all there is."

"And?"

"Ma'am, it could be good for us. It could be bad for us."

"Kenny, my dear, you must escape the habit of stating the obvious. It rather makes me wonder whether you're a dullard, or whether perhaps you think that I am." She waves away his sputtering reply, then hands him the paper she had been reading. "This project is approved. See to it."

"Yes, ma'am."

"Also, I want our guest moved someplace more secure."

"I don't understand. I thought the idea was to hide her where nobody would think to look. You said nothing could be safer than that."

Her face hardens. "Call it woman's intuition if you like. Call it an abundance of caution. I don't believe that Bethany Barclay would be blundering around Europe with a British intelligence operative unless her deal includes an effort to locate our guest. So get it done, Kenny. Find a more secure location. Maybe the Adirondack facility. Mexico is even better. You figure it out. But I want her moved as soon as possible."

"Yes, ma'am."

"Oh, and Melody Sunderland. She's still in the U.K.?"

"Still at the Savoy. Yes, ma'am."

"We've arranged protection and so forth?"

"Yes, ma'am." He hesitates. "Ma'am, our people say she's having a difficult time."

"Tell her to stay exactly where she is. I'll send separate instructions via courier."

"I believe she wants to come home."

The Protector gives him a look.

"Yes, ma'am. I'll see to it."

In the Builder's world, news travels more slowly. He distrusts the modern means of communication and would rather avoid entanglement with e-mail and mobile phones and the Internet. So it takes several tries before the Senator can get him to answer his cell.

"It was Bethany," she says as soon as Harry picks up. "The Bureau is sure."

"I beg your pardon. What's Bethany? Where?"

"In Berlin. The shooting."

Harry rubs his eyes. "I've been napping.

What shooting?"

She explains, briefly and succinctly.

"I suppose I should get over there. I'm still at the Dorchester. I can get the evening flight."

"No, Harry. You shouldn't get over there. There's nothing to do. She's left the country. This isn't your problem, and you'll never catch up to her. You need to come home. We need you here."

"You don't understand —"

"Do you really think you're the only one who's had to watch other people suffer because of a mistake? I'm a member of the United States Senate, Harry. However confident I might appear in public, I go to bed with that fear every night. My bad decisions — bad votes — can be the cause of untold suffering."

"I have to tell her —"

"You don't have to tell her anything. If she finds what she's looking for, you'll be free to apologize at your leisure. If things go wrong, there's nothing you can do to help."

"Gillian." He pauses. It's an open line. But this has to be said. "Gillian, she's working with the British now."

"Good. They can protect her."

"Somehow I doubt that. This is why I need to find her."

"Why?"

"Because the senior staff of the Secret Intelligence Service is full of disciples of its legendary chief from the 1970s. Lord Findrake."

# THIRTY-SIX

Warrenton, Virginia, is home to two Mc-
Donald's restaurants, one on the Lee Highway, one on the James Madison Highway.
Raymond Fuentes spends time in each, nib-
bling a burger, nursing a Coke, watching
who comes and goes. He doesn't expect his
targets to saunter in wearing *I kidnapped
Janice Stafford!* T-shirts. He is trying to get
a feel for the pace of the town, the better,
later, to recognize anything out of the ordinary.

Both locations are on busy divided roads.
Both are crowded. The whole town feels
crowded. Warrenton is really two or even
three towns combined: the central shopping
strip, the homes and low-rise offices nearby,
and the older houses and working farms
farther off. Given Janice's description,
Fuentes is betting that they are holding her
near one of the main drags.

A white house, then, with a neighbor

across the street whose front lawn features a pickup truck for sale.

He has to search carefully, without giving signs that might signal to a passing sheriff's deputy that he is casing the neighborhood — which, in point of fact, he is. Because when he finds the house, his plan is to break in and take Janice by force.

Carraway still wants to be a part of the operation. But Fuentes hasn't told him about tonight's trip. He hasn't made up his mind about the FBI man. Yes, he's trustworthy, but trustworthy isn't the same as reliable.

Fuentes is driving now. It's half past five, and everybody is getting back from work, and a crowd of cars is what he wants. He is following a random pattern rather than traveling up one street and down the next. The last thing he wants is to be noticed. Regularity is noticed.

Finding the location takes less time than expected. In just over an hour he has the house, a raised ranch on Sycamore Street, half a block from East Shirley Avenue. The house is old but the aluminum siding is freshly painted. The house across the way does indeed feature a rusty pickup on cinder blocks with a FOR SALE, BEST OFFER sign beside it. He wonders whether Janice is still inside. If they suspect she's left any online traces, they will certainly have moved her.

Fuentes decides to be bold.

He pulls over and climbs out, pretending to have a look at the pickup when out of the corner of his eye he is studying his target a few hundred feet away. An older man emerges from the house, wiping his hands on a napkin, and Fuentes guesses that he's disturbed him at dinner. They shake hands and chat a bit, and two minutes later they are laughing together, because Fuentes's great talent is getting people to like him. Nor is his goodwill feigned. Nearly always, he likes the people he meets right back.

"No, I don't think I want to drive it or restore it," Fuentes is saying. "I'd more likely break it down and resell it for parts. Maybe use a few myself."

The owner smiles approvingly of this strategy, adding that were he a few years younger, he might do the same. He offers Fuentes a beer, and a sky blue Volvo sedan pulls into the driveway across the street. A slim, thirtyish man in a nice suit hops out and hurries to the door, and Fuentes is sure he is no guard, but somebody's aide.

The old man follows his gaze.

"I don't know what they're up to over there," he says, mouth turning down. "Men

401

and women coming and going all times of night."

Fuentes agrees that he doesn't know what the world is coming to. They laugh again, and Ray says he's in a little bit of a hurry just now, but he's hoping to come back later tonight, maybe with a friend, and have another look. The old man gets suspicious, so Fuentes gives him a hundred dollars to hold as security.

"I'll make you a fair offer," he says, and he intends to do just that. "I'm just saying, if you see me out here later, maybe with a friend, I don't want you to wonder who it is."

"I'm guessing you're a bit of a night owl."

"I suppose I must be."

Janice sees the man called Kenny climb out of his car. The buzz-beep-buzz tells her the front door is opening. She spent half of yesterday considering whether there might be a way to create a feedback loop in the alarm sensors on her window and trip the circuit breakers, but eventually gave up, because tripping the breakers won't help her get through the bars. Today she has spent with a couple of old chess books the guard she calls Stettin dug up somewhere. He also sneaked her another Quarter

Pounder with Cheese. She is still enjoying this delicacy when she hears feet on the stairs.

Only one visitor. Kenny must have told the guards to stay away. In other words, this is one of those moments when they are going to talk business.

The door opens and Kenny steps in. She smiles, but only because she has sensed the second-in-command bearing in him. He will likely be briefing whoever is running this thing.

"Before you ask," she says, "I'm being treated fine, I have enough to eat, and I'd really like somebody to call my parents and tell them I'm okay."

Janice is seated at the desk. Kenny is standing by the door, twirling the key on its big metal ring.

"You contacted somebody," he says, voice flat.

"How did I do that?"

"When that idiot downstairs let you mess around with his computer. You left a message out there."

"Prove it."

"This isn't a court of law. I know what you did. You know what you did. Do you have any idea how much trouble you've caused?"

Janice brushes a stray braid from her face. "I need to get my hair done," she says. "It's been weeks. I'm a mess."

"Who did you contact, Janice?"

"Whom. It's the object of the sentence."

"You think you're smart, don't you?"

She shrugs. She's acting a lot braver than she feels. She suspects he knows that. "I wish I could cause you trouble," she says. "I would if I could. But I didn't leave a message for anybody."

"Well, it doesn't matter. I have some news for you."

"What is it?"

"The good news is, your friend Bethany is still alive. Somebody tried to take her out, twice, but she survived both times."

Relief floods the teen, who hasn't wanted to admit to herself just how sick with worry she is. "Where? Where is she?"

"I'm not allowed to tell you that. Sorry."

"Do you even know where she is?"

"I'm not allowed to say." His eyes are cold and unsympathetic. Janice realizes that he isn't trying to reassure her after all. He's playing with her emotions. And she has a shrewd insight that Kenny isn't really supposed to be talking to her: that these business meetings are his own invention, because he likes to see people squirm.

"So, if that's the good news, what's the bad news?"

"We're moving you."

"You mean, I get out of this house? About time."

"I don't suppose you have much packing to do."

"I have four outfits, as you well know. I'd appreciate a suitcase to put them in."

"I'll have someone bring up a garbage bag."

"Thanks a lot." She is half-annoyed and half-frightened. "When is this big move taking place?"

"Maybe tonight. At latest tomorrow. I'm afraid your new digs won't be quite as comfortable." About to depart, he changes his mind, looks her way. "And the guards are a whole lot smarter."

He goes out and locks the door behind him.

Ray Fuentes is in the backyard, lying in the grass twenty feet from the house. He doesn't like the amount of activity — the car that came and went earlier, the way the guards are scurrying around. Something is up, and it's time to move.

He senses more than hears the presence

behind him, and rolls over and scissors his legs.

The man tumbles to the ground, and Fuentes is atop him, an arm against the throat, his gun against the temple.

"I thought you might need some help," says Carl Carraway. "What, you think you're the only one who knows how to follow somebody?"

The guard she calls Stettin is closing up for the night.

"Need anything?" he asks.

"No, thank you."

At this point he would usually lock the door. The night staff would come on, the faces she almost never saw, and Stettin and Noys would return in the morning. But he lingers.

"Janice, you know they're moving you."

"They told me."

"I'm sorry. I just want you to know that. You seem like a nice kid."

She gives him a look. "This is the part where I say, 'Please, mister, don't let them take me,' and you say it's your job and slam the door."

This brings a smile, as it's meant to. "I just meant I'm sorry you're mixed up in whatever's going on." Like Kenny earlier, he takes a step closer. "I just want you to know —"

That's as far as he gets. She has been rigging her trap for days now, and finally has a chance to use it. The guard is standing on the rectangular throw rug. Janice is leaning against the back of her chair. With a sudden motion, she knocks the chair over. The twine she has made by patiently unraveling the bottom of the rug is attached to the legs. The chair goes down, the rug goes out from under him, and he topples. He doesn't fall all the way down but he doesn't have to. His free hand flails instinctively, grabbing onto the dresser. Janice pulls another hidden cord, and the heavy dresser mirror whose bolts she has been loosening slams down on his fingers.

Stettin howls and yanks his hand free.

He isn't unconscious and his hand probably isn't seriously wounded, but in his surprise he has gone down on one knee, rubbing his hand, and Janice leaps nimbly past him, scooping up the fallen key on its big ring, and is out the door before he can turn.

She slams the bolt home, closes the padlock, and runs for the stairs.

Carraway and Fuentes are moving toward

the back door, keeping a ninety-degree angle between them with the door at the fulcrum. Both have drawn weapons that they possess illegally.

Fuentes moves to the side of the step. Carraway reaches for the knob. Fuentes nods.

Before Carraway can try the door, it jerks open.

Janice Stafford comes stumbling out. She collapses on the grass and lies still.

Carl bends over her. He gestures to Fuentes, points at the house. "Go!"

Fuentes rushes into the kitchen. A woman is standing there, eyes wide, holding a syringe.

"She was trying to escape," she explains, obviously mistaking which side he is on. "I know we were supposed to give it to her later, but —"

By that time Fuentes has an arm around her and a gun at her back. He has removed her firearm from inside her jacket.

"Who else is in the house?"

"One man. He's — I don't know where he is. He was upstairs with her, but she came down alone."

He sits her on the floor and cuffs her to the refrigerator. Then he rushes up the stairs.

■ ■ ■ ■

Although Janice calls him Stettin, the guard's real name is Steven Willoughby. He washed out of both the army and the police force but finally caught on at the lower end of the private security business. He did adequate work, but his record made it impossible for him to advance very far. He soon moved to the illegal side, where the money was a lot better anyway. He has guarded drug shipments and drug dealers and even the prisoners of drug dealers. He is pretty good at this sort of work, if he does say so himself. He has never before guarded a child, however, and certainly has never been bested by one.

When he finds himself locked in the room, he shoots the door up around the bolt. The fourth shot does the trick, although it also overheats his silencer. He kicks his way out of the room and hears the commotion in the kitchen.

"Who else is in the house?"

"One man."

That's enough for Steven. He doubts that they're feds — there would be battering rams and SWAT — but he knows they aren't friendlies either. He darts into another bedroom just before the stranger charges up the stairs. This room has a window opening onto the roof of the back porch. He climbs out onto the roof and lowers himself over the side. He is standing on the grass when he sees the second man, just rising from Janice's prone body, raising his gun.

Both fire.

Fuentes hears the gunshots and realizes that he has been had. He rushes back down the stairs. The woman struggling with the cuffs is not a factor for the moment. Outside he sees Janice still on the ground, and another man racing across the lawn.

He lifts his gun, then thinks better of it. If he misses, the slug could injure a neighbor.

He doesn't see Carl.

Odd.

Crouching, he lifts Janice's wrist. The pulse is strong and steady. Whatever they gave her, it seems they were careful about the dose: just enough to make her sleep for a bit.

"Carraway?" he whispers.

Then he sees the bloody mess a few feet away in the grass.

"Carl!"

# THIRTY-SEVEN

It is a night FBI Special Agent Jake Pulu will remember for the rest of his life. Both children have contracted some sort of virus, and between the fevers and the cold sweats, getting them to sleep was a chore. Now Jake and his wife, Joey, are trying to unwind. They're snuggling on the sofa, eating popcorn while they watch one of her beloved romantic comedies and chat, lightly, about the latest minor scandal to hit Capitol Hill. They have just reached Joey's favorite part of the movie — the ex-boyfriend, realizing his mistake, hops on a plane to try to stop the wedding — when the doorbell rings.

"It's eleven o'clock," says Joey.

"Eleven-thirty," says her husband, on his feet. He considers taking his gun, but they live in Falls Church, one of the safest communities in the United Sates. Besides, Jake Pulu can't imagine too many would-be home invaders who wouldn't be intimidated by his size and glare.

When he opens the door he immediately sees his mistake. Standing on the front step is Raymond Fuentes, the most senior member of the Village House leadership still at large — and the most dangerous by far. Pulu would have slammed the door and grabbed both gun and cell phone, except for one thing.

Fuentes is cradling a barely conscious Carl Carraway. The agent's sweater is stained with blood.

"He took two in the abdomen," says Fuentes woodenly. "I did what I could to stop the bleeding."

"Stand right there," says Pulu. "Don't move."

"He needs a hospital."

"I told you not to move."

But the command comes too late. Fuentes is moving, and Pulu is cooperating, because what the fugitive does is transfer Carl from his own arms to Jake's.

"He's a brave man," says Fuentes, backing away. "When he's out of surgery, tell him we got her. She's safe."

"Got who?" Pulu demands. "Who's safe?"

"Just take care of him," says Fuentes, and rushes off toward a waiting car.

■ ■ ■ ■

Edna Harrigan's night is equally unforgettable. She is reading Shakespeare aloud when she hears a car in the forecourt. It is well past midnight, but she is known throughout the county as a night owl. People come to her at all hours with their problems. Nevertheless, she takes down the shotgun from above the fireplace before padding barefoot to the door.

There is a car, but no driver.

Odd.

"Put the gun down," says a voice from behind. "Turn around slowly."

She does both, and finds herself confronting a tall, broad-shouldered man who looks terribly tired and terribly sad. There is blood on his jacket, a lot of it. She does not see a weapon.

"Who are you?"

"Judge Harrigan, Carl Carraway vouches for you absolutely. He says you can be trusted. Can you?"

At last the name and the picture and the file line up. "You're Fuentes. You're Raymond Fuentes."

"Bethany's friend Janice is in the car. She's been sedated."

413

"I — Carl — Agent Carraway said —"

"She'd been kidnapped. Yes. We rescued her, Carl and I, and now I need a place to leave her for a while."

He picks up the shotgun and hands it back to her, then goes out to the car. He returns a moment later with the groggy teenager in his arms. He sits her on the sofa. She is blinking owlishly. Fuentes sits beside her, whispering, while Edna puts a kettle on for no reason she can later recall. Janice begins to nod. Yawns. Nods again.

Fuentes crosses to Edna. He draws her to the side.

"Judge, listen to me a minute. Listen. You have to take care of her yourself."

"I beg your pardon."

"Her kidnappers were about to move her when we got there. She was already trying to escape, but one of them grabbed her and managed to give her some kind of injection. Now, it's wearing off, and I don't think she'll need medical care. But if anything goes wrong — if you decide she needs a doctor, the hospital — you have to take care of it yourself. Do you understand what I'm saying, Judge? You can't turn her over to your friends."

"What friends?"

"I believe you know exactly what friends I

mean. And I'm sure Agent Carraway knows too."

"I don't know what you mean."

"Fine. So if Bethany Barclay isn't in Europe on a mission that you maneuvered her into, if she hasn't been risking her life for your cause, then I'm probably making a mistake by leaving Janice in your care instead of taking her to the police. This girl was kidnapped, after all. That counts as a police matter, doesn't it?" His rocky stare is too much, and she turns away. But Fuentes is relentless. "Is that what you want me to do, Judge? Should I take her to the police? Or the Bureau?"

"No, no. You should leave her with me."

"Then you'll have to protect her."

"I wouldn't do anything else, Mr. Fuentes."

"Including from your own friends."

"I understand the rules," says the old woman coldly. "And now I have a question for you."

"Oh?"

"All that trouble you caused for me out here and in the city. Asking questions. Raising suspicions. What was the point?"

Fuentes gives her a long, measuring look. "I had to immobilize you. I would have gone after other leaders of the Garden as well, but I didn't know who they were. I only knew you. Bethany's friend and mentor. The one who got her involved in this mess to begin with. The one who betrayed her."

"I regret that decision every day, Mr. Fuentes."

He is unrelenting. "With respect, Judge Harrigan, you and your friends are amateurs. Every time you get involved, you make matters worse for Bethany. You have to stay out of the way." His tone turns reflective. "I've spent most of my life in the secret world, and if there's one lesson I've learned, it's that those who act behind the scenes have to be subject to the strictest checks and balances from those who answer to a larger public. You and your friends are answerable to nobody but yourselves. That makes you dangerous."

Fuentes seems about to say something else. Instead he nods his long head, then crosses the room to where Janice sits on the sofa, still wrapped in the blanket. He sits beside her. He whispers again. After a moment she whispers back. He asks her a question. She seems to hesitate, then shrugs. He asks again. She whispers back.

He hops to his feet, returns to Edna.

"I'll call tomorrow," he says.

"When?"

"When I call." His expression softens. "Sorry, Judge. I don't mean to sound rude. But you can understand why I'd rather not say."

"I can. But you need to understand that when you call, we may be asleep. We may be out walking the property. It all depends on how well the girl holds up."

"And I suppose cell phones don't work out here."

"Not really. No."

He smiles. "Fine. If you don't answer, I'll call back. And I'll do my best not to disturb your sleep."

"I'd appreciate that, Mr. Fuentes."

A moment later he is gone.

The two women stare at each other, neither quite sure how to proceed. At last Edna breaks the awkward silence.

"I'm Edna Harrigan. I'm a friend of Bethany's. You're safe."

Janice rubs her eyes. The sedative is wearing off. She doesn't say anything.

"Do you need anything, my dear? A cup of cocoa? Some nice soup? Or would you just like to go to bed? It's rather late, and my understanding is that you need your rest."

Janice yawns. "Do you have a computer?"

"Of course, dear."

"Do you have Internet?"

"I don't really know."

The teenager grins. "Can we find out?"

Eventually Janice sleeps and Edna has time to think. If Janice needs protection, she needs more than the Judge alone can give her. The authorities are out of the question. Fuentes said not to call her group of friends. Obviously he knows that Edna is part of the Garden. Presumably Carl Carraway told him. She wonders if Carl also told Bethany, a prospect that fills Edna with regret.

Still, Edna needs assistance. And if she can't call the Senator or the Mathematician, she could at least call her neighbor. And so despite the hour she tries Lillian Hartshorne.

The phone is answered on one ring, as always.

"This is Edna Harrigan. I need to talk to Mrs. Hartshorne. I'm afraid it's urgent."

"I'm sorry, Judge Harrigan," says the butler. "I'm afraid it's quite impossible."

"I know she's asleep, Mr. Fellows. But this is an emergency."

"She's not asleep, ma'am. She's not here."

"Where is she?"

"Ma'am, the helicopter left not ten minutes ago to take Mrs. Hartshorne to the

418

airfield. I believe she's on her way to Europe."

# Thirty-Eight

"Now you know why we carry three passports apiece," said Felicia.

Bethany, sitting at the dressing table, gave her a look. They had a suite at a small and rather baroque hotel overlooking the Villa Borghese. The terrace doors were open, admitting the angry sounds of the endless Roman traffic along with the night breeze.

"Actually you carry all the passports," Bethany said. "You seem to think I can't be trusted with my own."

"I was speaking figuratively."

"I'm not."

Felicia was, in her own curiously dated parlance, dolled up. She was waiting for Bethany to finish dressing so that they could go down to the club across the street. Felicia explained the outing as a matter of establishing cover — they were supposed to be, as she kept saying, on the prowl — but Bethany suspected that what her minder really wanted was to dance.

"I still don't think going out tonight is a good idea."

Felicia was peering up at the sky, checking for rain. "Why not?"

"Because we almost got killed this morning."

"Number one, we did not almost get killed. Number two, anyone who's looking for us will figure we'll hunker down tonight. Two girls out on the town — who'll ever suspect us?"

Bethany was having trouble deciding on her earrings: this one, that one.

"Can we at least go over our plans for tomorrow?"

"At ten we're going to see Professor Fabiana Cialdini at the Sapienza. At noon we'll see Giuseppe Amendola at his loft. Happy now?"

"Not particularly." Now Bethany was fussing with her makeup, acutely aware that during her weeks on the run she hadn't given her appearance much thought, except to make herself as uninteresting as possible. "I'd rather see them alone."

"I know."

"They were Professor Wisdom's correspondents here, and the chances are bet-

ter that they'll talk to me if I'm by myself
—"

"It's not happening, Bethany. Forget it."

Felicia was selecting shoes. They had arrived to find the suite already well stocked
with clothing in their sizes. Felicia had
explained to her that two women planted
by the SIS, matching their descriptions and
carrying identical passports, had been staying here for two days, shopping merrily.
Anybody who might trace the two women
who had fled Berlin to Rome would look
only for those arriving today.

"You still won't tell me who the old man
is? The one who shot the man who did
indeed almost kill me?"

"Paramay says you have no need to know."

"I have to know who to thank the next
time you let somebody get that close."

The minder turned, her brown face serious. "Bethany, listen to me. That old man
— he's not your friend. I don't know what
he's up to, but he isn't out there to protect
you from harm. He has an agenda. Most
likely he's going to follow you until you have
the Pilate Stone. At that point he'll take it
from you any way he can."

"So his job is roughly the same as yours."

Felicia folded her arms and leaned against
the jamb. "You don't much like me, do you,

Bethany?"

"I don't like being a prisoner." She frowned. The new shoes pinched. "I like being free to make my own decisions. Go where I want to, when I want to."

"You're accustomed to being on your own is all."

"Actually, I had a traveling companion for a couple of weeks."

"Your friend Janice. The hacker. I know all about her." Felicia inspected Bethany's outfit. "You look wonderful. The guys will be all over you."

"That's not why we're here."

"It's just cover, Bethany. Lighten up."

"I'll lighten up when Janice is safe."

"Oh, right. I almost forgot to tell you."

"Tell me what?"

A look of sly triumph. "It seems she's been rescued."

Melody Sunderland wasn't accustomed to fear. Anxiety, sure. The anxiety, say, of lecturing at a college campus where she knew the auditorium would be full of boo birds. And simple nervousness, like when she was waiting to hear about her mom's test results. But terror was a new experience.

And this was her second round with it in

three days.

The first was when she got the word about Elliott St. John and finally accepted, as somehow she had not when Ralph Kelvin was murdered, that her corporeal life might be at stake, that she might not live to see her fortieth birthday.

And the second time tonight.

Tonight she was seated in the Grill Room of the Savoy, in accordance with the Lord Protector's instructions. Melody kept checking her watch, but she was early. She had been ordered to arrive early.

At a quarter past nine, the emissary from Findrake would arrive.

Lord Findrake, late head of Her Majesty's Secret Intelligence Service.

Lord Findrake, former Lord Protector.

Lord Findrake, who, from the comfort of his retirement in Bath, had reached out and casually swatted two of the most influential members of the Council.

It was Melody's job to find out why.

By twenty past nine she was on her third glass of wine and had nibbled nothing more than a handful of nuts. Nobody had showed. She sagged in relief. The two bodyguards who were supposed to look out for her shared a separate table and evidently had noticed nothing amiss.

Half past nine. Another glass. She had no instructions on what to do should the emissary not arrive.

At a quarter of ten, Melody asked for her check. As she left the dining room, one of the guards preceded her while the other trailed behind. Her room was on the third floor. One of her guards took the elevator, while the other escorted Melody up the stairs. It was in the stairwell that a pair of efficient young men met them, guns already drawn, ordered the guard onto the floor, bound his hands behind him, and had Melody out through the side entrance inside of thirty seconds. A clapped-out van was waiting, the sliding door open, and the men tossed her inside and scrambled up after.

At a stoplight a few blocks away, they trundled her out of the old vehicle and into a waiting limousine. The van streaked away, running the light, and as Melody watched in dismay, a car driven by a man who looked much like her bodyguard gave chase.

"We're not going to hurt you," said one of her captors. She didn't believe a word. "We're just taking you to your meeting."

They drove past Buckingham Palace and ended up at a white stucco house in Belgravia, where a respectful butler opened the door and showed her to the drawing room. Melody was bewildered. Maybe they weren't going to kill her after all.

The door opened, and a sixtyish man with thinning sandy hair stepped inside.

"Ms. Sunderland. A pleasure. My name is Paramay. I apologize for the theatrics, but I'm afraid we need your rather urgent help."

"Who's we?"

He smiled.

The women are back in the suite. Felicia is at the desk, working with her tablet, writing texts or e-mails or official reports. Bethany isn't sure, because every time she approaches, the minder blanks the screen.

"You seemed to enjoy yourself," says Felicia, not looking up.

"I still think it was a terrible thing, going out tonight."

"We have to keep up our cover."

"I know, but —"

"And I had to observe."

"Observe what?"

Felicia finished with her iPad. She folded it away and slipped it into her briefcase, which she locked. Then she withdrew the secure phone from her purse and began scrolling through the texts.

"The men who came up to you," she said,

426

tapping the keys. "The ones who didn't. The ones who danced with you. The ones who watched other men dance with you. It's hard to hide surveillance in a club, Bethany. I know that seems counterintuitive, but when a crowd is engaged in a joint activity — ah! Here we are!"

Bethany was on the sofa with her shoes off, trying to figure out the remote control.

"Here we are what?"

"The file on this Amendola character."

"The art dealer we'll see tomorrow."

"That's right. Well, well. Not his real name. We knew that. He stole — or adopted — the name of the famous composer. No relation, but the familiarity no doubt helps his business. Mmmm. A lot of the art he sells is fake. At least that's what the Italian government suspects. They haven't been able to catch him at it yet. He seems to know when they're going to do a surprise inspection or put in an undercover buyer, but that's par for the course over here. Mmmm. Possible organized crime connection. The narcotics heroes took a look at him a couple of years ago in connection with counterfeit statues of Buddha filled with heroin. Your Adrian Wisdom had some peculiar bedfellows."

"He was mission driven."

"I'll say."

Bethany stood up. "I'm going to bed."

Felicia nodded. "Your room is clean. I checked it twice."

"Can I ask you something?"

"Sure."

"Are you mission driven too?"

Felicia grew solemn. "You're asking what I'd do if I had to choose between saving the mission or saving you?"

"I guess so," said Bethany, surprised. Felicia had articulated her fear better than she could herself.

The minder shrugged. "I'm good at what I do, Bethany. There are people who are better, but I'm pretty good. I've been trained to put the mission first. The mission, then the Service, then the country."

"I see," said Bethany, feeling her courage shrink.

"On the other hand," Felicia continued, "I'm still a human being."

"Meaning what?"

"Meaning, let's hope we don't face that choice. Sleep well," she added, already back at her messages.

It was past eleven when a chastened Melody Sunderland returned to the Savoy. One of her bodyguards was waiting in the lobby and seemed quite unsurprised to see her. He asked if she was all right, and she answered testily that she was, but preferred this time to take the elevator. Upstairs, a pair of security people she'd never seen before were standing outside her suite. A third opened the door.

From the inside.

Lillian Hartshorne was seated at a low table near the window. Kenny, her factotum, lounged on the sofa, doing something on his tablet.

"Back at last, my dear," said the Lord Protector, not rising. She seemed entirely exhausted. "How did things go with Findrake?"

Melody looked around the room. The guard who had admitted her had stepped into the hall.

"I didn't see Findrake."

"His man, then."

"Can we talk privately?"

A glance from Lillian had Kenny hopping to his feet and gliding from the suite without a word. The old woman had some notes in front of her on the table. Melody, unbidden, took the chair opposite.

"Well?" said Lillian, coldly.

"His name is Paramay. About sixty. We met in Belgravia. He said he's with British intelligence."

"And?"

"And I'm not sure whether he's with Findrake or not."

"Explain."

Melody took a long breath. She was still coming down from the adrenaline high of fear and relief. She hadn't expected this oddly chilly interrogation.

"He said he's sorry for the trouble Findrake has caused. He says he thinks he has him under control now. Then he laughed and said he'd thought that before."

"To what trouble was he referring?"

"He seemed to know everything, Lillian. The Garden. The Council. He called us the Wilderness. The Pilate Stone. He said he's taken measures. He said we're to stay away. That was his message. That he's taken measures to secure the Stone, and we're to stay away."

Lillian was writing a note to herself. "You confirmed none of his suppositions, of course."

Melody swallowed. Hard. "Of course not."

"You didn't admit you are part of the Council. Or mention any other names."

"No. I wouldn't do that."

"Then why did he let you go?"

The younger woman sat very straight.

"What?"

"He went to enormous trouble to drag you from the hotel and take you to Belgravia. He made startling accusations of what amounts to a criminal conspiracy. And you expect me to believe that when you denied everything, he just let you walk out the door?"

Melody looked at her hands: the perfect untruthful witness. "He told me I didn't have to say anything. He said I should just carry the message. And he said — he said he needed my help."

"With what, my dear?"

"I don't know. He said he would contact me in a day or two. He said he would always know where to find me."

Lillian's expression turned rueful. "Ah. I see. How very clever of him."

"Clever how?"

"He's setting you up, my dear. He wants us to think that you've been turned. That you're working for British intelligence now. Are you? This is as good a time as any to say."

"No. Of course not."

"You were away from the hotel for an hour."

"I walked back. I got lost."

Lillian chuckled. "Oh, my dear. My poor

dear. You don't see, do you? Such a dunder-head."

"I don't see what?"

"This Paramay of yours. He expects us to kill you." She smiled at the younger woman's distress. "Don't worry, my dear. We'll do nothing of the kind. That's his test, you see. If something happens to you, he'll know he was right in his suppositions. He'll start investigating your acquaintances, and he'll find — us."

"Lillian, I didn't tell him anything. I didn't."

The old woman patted her hand. "Calm yourself, dear. We have work to do, you and I."

"I didn't say a word. I swear I didn't."

"It doesn't matter, Melody, dear. Paramay is just being clever. Assuming he's telling the truth — that he isn't somehow Findrake's man — then he's not interested in the Pilate Stone at all. He wants that photograph."

"He — he didn't mention —"

"Relax, my dear. Paramay's presence simply adds a layer of complexity. We can handle it. It's time you learned about the hard end of the business anyway."

"I don't know what you mean."

"What I mean, my dear, is that you and I

are going to go and find Bethany Barclay and her friends, then take possession of the Pilate Stone and the photograph both. After that, you will be bound to us absolutely. For life. Would you like to know why?"

For the third time, Melody was terrified. No words would come. She shook her head.

The Lord Protector gripped her hand with surprising strength, squeezing until the bones ached. In that instant, her gaze turned feral.

"Because, my dear, after Bethany has secured our trophies for us, it will be your job to kill her."

# Thirty-Nine

It had been years since her last trip to Rome. Just before the start of her third and final year of law school, Bethany and a couple of girlfriends had used savings from their summer internships to spend a week at one of the cheaper hotels, supposedly to pick up culture. Bethany was hoping to show off the knowledge she'd gleaned during her Oxford days — but her classmates preferred to study the city's fashionable night spots, hoping for romance, preferably with someone titled. That style of life had never appealed to Bethany, so she had wound up mostly on her own, especially in the mornings, when her girlfriends slept in, and she topped up her culture in this most historically fascinating of Western cities.

This time she didn't expect to spend much time visiting museums and churches and ruins. She was here for one reason only — a reason that would require her to find a way to leave the ubiquitous Felicia behind.

On the morning after their night at the club, an exhausted Bethany slept late, and only woke because her minder pounded on her door at nine-thirty, warning that they were going to miss their appointment with Professor Cialdini.

"You planned this, didn't you?" Bethany asked as they descended the sweeping stair a half hour later.

"Planned what?"

"The dancing. Wear me out so I'd get my sleep. You were worried about me after Berlin."

"I don't know what you're talking about. I told you why we went out."

"You're a trained liar, Felicia, but you're also a very sweet one."

They stopped at a kiosk where Bethany bought a new burner phone. Felicia neither inquired nor interfered. This was their modus vivendi: Bethany was free to conduct the search her own way, as long as Felicia remained by her side.

Their visit to the sprawling *Città Universitaria* campus of the vast Sapienza empire was quick and efficient. The blocky structures were grimmer and more functional than those of Oxford, but in their own way no less imposing. Professor Fabiana Cialdini had an office with a view toward the train station and the classically styled buildings beyond.

Today Felicia and Bethany were students again, but this time they were assisting a don they were not permitted to name in research for his biography of the great Adrian Wisdom.

"Adrian was a strange man," said Cialdini.

"Did you know him well?" asked an ingenuous Felicia.

"Well? No, no, not at all. We were mainly correspondents. He was working on a biography of Pontius Pilate. I have written several articles on Pilate, particularly on the rhetorical themes of the account of Pilate in Josephus. He was not a popular man."

Whether she was speaking of Pilate or Wisdom, she didn't make clear.

He had sent her portions of his manuscript, Professor Cialdini explained, but never all. She found little that was new. She tried, she said, to limit his use of anything written after about 1000 A.D. "Around then, there was a great surge of interest in the early Christians, and every monk who could read and write was busy forging documents said to date back to the first century."

But Adrian was adamant, she said. He

kept insisting that his sources were unusual. Specially reliable. And so forth.

"Toward the end, he told me that he thought he had discovered the Pilate Stone. The second one, you understand. The one that supposedly mentions Jesus. It was in a monastery, he claimed. He had found — what else? — several ancient scrolls that marked the way. I told him that there was only one Pilate Stone, and it was in the museum in Jerusalem. The other one was a myth. He wouldn't listen to me."

Bethany could contain herself no longer. Ignoring Felicia's warning glance, she interrupted with a question. "Did he tell you where this monastery might be located?"

The professor's eyes crinkled. "Ah. I take it you have heard the same rumors. About how the Stone would be worth tens of millions of dollars. How churches and governments would kill for it. You see, then, how the stories are exaggerated over time. A medieval bishop wants to raise an army to invade Constantinople, so he tells his wealthy patron about this fabulous relic, and the tales of its value grow and grow and grow." The energy went out of her face. "But there is no reason to think it is real. There are so many stories of ancient artifacts, especially artifacts from the time of

Jesus. But apart from the Gospels, no contemporaneous writing about Jesus has survived."

Still Bethany could not help herself. "That doesn't mean that there are no writings."

"Of course not. But we must be scientific, mustn't we? We cannot infer from a lack of evidence that a thing exists."

"You said you had Wisdom's manuscript," said Felicia.

"Parts of it only. They may still be around." She buzzed for her assistant, spoke to him in rapid Italian. A moment later, a skinny young man glided in holding a folder.

The professor flipped through it, pulled out two pages. "This is the part you want."

"We'd like to look at the whole document," Felicia began.

"Oh, I doubt that somehow. This one" — lifting her chin toward Bethany — "is obviously interested in a narrower goal." She was still holding the pages. "As I told you, Adrian was a strange man. He was, very likely, not sane. He wrote me a note and said that his research was putting his life at risk. He was therefore adopting the style of the monks whose work inspired him. He was not very good at this style. He asked me to help him to improve his text. I told him that it will not work in English. If he wanted to write like the monks he must write in Latin." A final shrug, elaborate and Mediterranean. "And, of course, it would help were he to write truth rather than fantasy."

Two minutes later they were out the door, pages in hand.

Waiting for their appointment with Amendola, the crooked antiquities dealer, the women sat in a café and studied what they had.

Much of Wisdom's story tracked what Grant Apple had told her in St. Edmunds Crypt: that the Stone was carried away before the sack of Jerusalem in the seventh century, that it made its way from one monastery to another, that massive and expensive expeditions were launched to try to track it down. Then there was something new:

According to a scroll held by a collector in New York, the custodians of the Stone decided in the eleventh or twelfth century to hide it among relatively valueless relics, in the hope that those who sought it would be fooled. It took me a great deal of time, but I found it nevertheless. I have seen the Pilate Stone. I know what Pilate wrote.

But that secret is not mine to divulge.

And therefore, my gentle reader, in the manner of the medieval scribe, I shall set out the steps to be followed if you wish to reach your goal. But only through thorough study and reflection will you be able to follow them. They are not to be pursued except by faith.

**The Stone lies in a crypta.**

**Sed unus homo potest.**

**You must descend according to Tertullian.**

And remember always the wisdom of Deuteronomy 29:29, which I here render in the Authorized Version: "The secret things belong unto the Lord our God: but those things which are revealed belong unto us and to our children for ever, that we may do all the words of this law."

"Not much to go on," said Bethany.

Felicia was studying the biblical quotation. "The secret things."

"Implying that he hasn't told us all that he knows?"

"I'm sure he hasn't. That's what the papers are for."

"Which papers?"

"Teddy Bratt had one. The E S S. I suspect that a second is held by some person whom you know but are refusing to identify. Which isn't too smart, by the way." A beat. "Anyway, as Paramay told you, given the size of the fragment from Bratt's safe, and the kind of paper used, we believe that Wisdom tore the note into three pieces."

"And you think Giuseppe Amendola has the third?"

"Let's go find out."

Giuseppe Amendola's studio was on the third floor of a newly converted building on the Via Diamiano Chiesa. The neighborhood was a mixture of commercial buildings, old low-rise flats, and modern new apartments. They took the bus and got off several blocks from their destination, to give Felicia time, as she put it, to sniff the air a bit. When she decided that they were clean, they headed toward the building. The minder's gaze swept over doorways and windows and pedestrians and passing cars. Something had made her nervous, so Bethany was nervous too.

"What is it?" she asked.

"Just stay behind me."

"Why?"

"I'm not sure. Call it bad vibrations."

They reached the building without incident. There was no doorman. Several dozen

441

buzzers were set in an exterior panel.

Felicia pressed Amendola's button. An Italian howl emerged from the static. She gave their cover names, speaking in English.

"Come on up," he said, his accent heavy.

And that was when the building exploded.

Not the whole building. As investigators would later determine, the bomb was actually in the dealer's loft, in a credenza beneath the alarm panel, set to go off when he buzzed someone in. Although Bethany had been shot at and had helped to disarm a bomb in the basement of the Village House during her odyssey underground, she had never been so close to an explosion. For her the sound was like the entire world being smashed to pieces. Her brain shook, and her thoughts with it. Her limbs didn't seem to work right. She couldn't hear. She was surprised to find herself flat on the sidewalk. Felicia was lying on top of her, blood trickling from her ear.

"Lie still!"

"What happened?"

"You can see what happened." Felicia slowly got up. People were screaming, running everywhere.

Bethany sat up.

"No," said Felicia. "We don't know who's

out there."

"We should get out of here."

"Wait," the minder said, now on her feet. "Get behind those cars. Stay down."

"Where are you going?"

"To see what's left."

"There's nothing left."

But Felicia was already joining the throng, racing toward the burning building, talking on the secure phone.

Bethany lifted her head. Her body ached. The wrist she had injured was no longer in a cast, but it was still sore, and now it was worse. It occurred to her that without Felicia, she was suddenly quite vulnerable. The explosion could have been a planned distraction, a way of separating her from her bodyguard.

Then she remembered that Giuseppe Amendola had been inside the loft. And here she was, thinking about herself. Acting like Annabelle, who at any given moment seemed to worry about nothing other than her own needs or wants —

Oh!

Bethany saw that this was her opportunity. By coincidence or not, she was away from Felicia's constant scrutiny.

Bethany stepped back from the car and let the stream of panicky pedestrians carry her down the street. She darted into an alley and was gone.

# FORTY

"The explosion was meant for them," says Melody Sunderland. "It had to be."

They are having lunch in Lillian's grand suite overlooking the Thames. "For that to be true, they would have to be in Rome. And Findrake would have to know it."

Melody cuts into her underdone steak. "I don't understand. Paramay said he has Findrake under control."

"Perhaps he was lying. Perhaps he was mistaken. Perhaps the plan was already in motion and there was no way to call it back." She catches the expression on the younger woman's face. "I told you, my dear. The hard end of the business. We shouldn't be cavalier about death, but we have to accept that it happens. And there are times when a sacrifice is called for. Where Lord Findrake and I have always differed is over how often to use that particular — tool."

"Killing isn't a tool!"

"Of course it is, dear. The police kill criminals. Soldiers kill the enemy. And don't lecture me about how criminals and the enemy have chosen their fates. Every war has civilian casualties. In some wars, more civilians than soldiers die." She pushes her plate away. "And don't you go thinking the adversary is more moral than we. Why, that Bible of theirs is full of the most awful killings. As instruments, my dear. God sends his own Son to die horribly on the cross. An instrument! Abraham is ordered to sacrifice his little boy. An instrument!"

"That little boy survived, Lillian. That's why Jews call the story the binding of Isaac rather than the sacrifice of Isaac."

"And what about the Old Testament and its endless wars? All the slaughter?" The Lord Protector shakes her head. "No, Melody. There will be no escape from fate. Not for you. Not for Bethany. You will take her life, and her sacrifice will be the instrument of your deliverance."

Once more Melody cannot meet the old woman's glare. She wants no part of this. She wants to turn back the clock and reject the initial overtures from Elliott St. John, who made her a media darling, and who made the Council sound like a low-key group of like-minded atheists who get together from time to time to complain about the state of the world. Failing that, she wants to escape from this madwoman who expects her to kill Bethany Barclay. She wants to run to the police, to her embassy, anywhere that Lillian Hartshorne isn't. But she has discovered, to her dismay, that the guards who protect her are also her jailers. She isn't even allowed to use her phone unobserved.

"Are we going to Rome, then?" she finally asks.

Lillian is eating her eggs again. "No, my dear."

"But Bethany's in Rome."

"I don't care where she is now, Melody. And neither should you. She doesn't yet have the Stone, I assure you. What matters now is where she goes next."

"Do we know where that will be?"

"As a matter of fact, my dear, we have an excellent idea."

Janice Stafford, too, was wondering about that explosion in Rome. She sat beside Edna Harrigan watching CNN. A dealer in early Christian artifacts and medieval scrolls had died in the blast. It couldn't be a coincidence.

"We have to help her," the teen said.

"I can't see any way that we can."

"I need to be with her."

Edna patted her hand. "I know. I'm sorry."

"You don't understand. I need to be there. She's like my big sister. She took care of me. Now I want to take care of her."

The Judge looked at the clock. She had little experience of children, mercurial teen-aged geniuses in particular, but she had already learned better than to argue. "Mr. Fuentes will be here in an hour. Why don't you discuss it with him?"

"Fine. But I'm going. I just have to figure out how."

"That's very thoughtful of you, Janice, but how will you even find her? Because if you're right — if Bethany was the target — well, I'm sure she's long gone. She wouldn't stay in Rome after that."

# FORTY-ONE

Bethany took the train north to Lombardy. A puzzled overnight in Milan provided ample opportunity for her to decide what to do next. She could still walk into the consulate, waive extradition, and head for home.

Where the prison door would gape wide for her.

Or she could return to Rome, where, she was sure, the hotel was being watched. Poor Felicia might be in trouble, and Bethany genuinely felt bad about that, but maybe if British intelligence got her back, the punishment would be light.

No matter. These were fantasies. There was no possibility that Bethany could turn back. Not with her objective so close.

In Milan, Bethany found an all-night car rental agency that seemed to have nothing but wrecks yet appeared prosperous. She stepped inside and had her instinct confirmed. The office was a dump but the man behind the desk was expensively dressed. Her request did not so much as slow him down. Lost your credit cards? We take cash. Misplaced your driving license? We take cash. Don't want any records kept of the rental? Did I mention that we take cash?

The villa stood on a grassy rise in the village of Pescallo on Lake Como above the Po Valley. Flowers paraded in neat boxes. Small boats bobbed at anchor in unusually straight rows. The setting sun did its fiery dance across the lapping waves. Spring was brilliant green in the country air. Olive trees clustered in groves except for a few iconoclasts who set out on their own. Every street seemed to lead to the water. Cars were unpretentious and old because it was not yet high season. The roads sloped gently upward from the lake, then steeply toward hazy mountains. Buildings rose with the slope, in colorful disarray.

Villagers stood here and there in insolent trios and quartets, first watching Bethany's BMW climb the hill, then watching her climb out. The sight of a foreigner consternated them, for tourists tended to cluster elsewhere on the lake. Bethany stood their scrutiny. It had been many years since her last visit, but she remembered how, in the off season, there was little for the men to do but fish in the morning and, in the evening, wait around for the invasion that always arrived at holiday times. So Bethany made no effort to conceal herself. Besides, to try sneaking up on the house would be pointless, not only because of the townspeople, and not only because she doubted her own skill at stealth. There was another reason.

Earl Hagopian was expecting her.

Her, or somebody.

All the lights were blazing, though it was only afternoon. A hefty dog started barking the moment the wheels of the rental touched the cobbled drive. How the animal knew the sound of a car stopping from the sound of a car passing was a neat question, but Bethany was here not to speculate.

An old woman opened the door and coughed out a sentence in Italian, then repeated the message in something much like English. She stood aside, then led Bethany to the library. The house had once been beautiful but was showing its age. Floor tiles were cracked. Pale spaces on the wall suggested that Earl was selling paintings for upkeep. Crucifixes held places of honor but wanted polishing. Walls were covered in a fabric once expensive but now slushy with water damage. Even the buttresses seemed to sag. Bethany studied the ceiling, wondering when it would tumble down, hoping not today. The old woman muttered, and Bethany finally worked out that she was offering refreshment. She declined and then, alone again, studied the books jammed haphazardly onto intricately carved wooden shelves in desperate need of cleaning, sanding, polishing, or, better yet, just replacement. She remembered how Earl used to say that living over here was cheaper. But living anywhere was cheap if you let the house fall apart.

She should have thought of Earl long ago, well before Teddy Bratt uttered the name. Back in New York, he'd been one of Bethany's few friends not connected with school. For a while they'd stayed in touch, and they still exchanged Christmas cards, but Bethany hadn't clapped eyes on him since leaving Oxford.

A clever choice on Annabelle's part.

Bethany waited. She was nervous in the library. *Don't startle,* she warned herself. More advice from Ray Fuentes. *Don't jump, even when they sneak up on you.* She reminded herself that although her various pursuers had likely never heard of Earl Hagopian, Teddy knew all about him. He had, in his own words, turned the man inside out for Annabelle. Bethany's running buddy had wanted to be sure of her ground before trusting Earl with . . . well, with whatever she'd entrusted to him.

To distract herself from these worries, she studied Earl's shelves. They were thick with books. To stand among them was already an act of refreshment. She ran long fingers along the spines. Leather-bound editions of Milton, Proust, Goethe. First editions of trivial poets. Untouched hardcover novels in several languages, squeaking agreeably when Bethany opened them. A multivolume set of Shakespeare made up to look like an early folio. A sprinkling of nonfiction titles showing signs of age and disuse. It was as though Earl had told the decorator that he wanted to display the right books to make him look like an educated man, which he was; except that in all the years that Bethany had known him she had never known him to pick up a work of literature for the sheer pleasure of reading.

"Hello, Bethany," Earl said.

Bethany neither startled nor jumped but carefully replaced William Dean Howells on the shelf. The book, full of marginal notations not remotely like Earl's hand, screamed flea market. Then, slowly, she turned and smiled.

Earl was about fifty-five, pale and soft, with wavy hair like dark spun sugar; a prim, uneasy mouth; and weak, watery eyes, although everyone's eyes look stronger when their owner happens to be pointing a gun at you.

"Hello, Earl." Bethany did her best to keep smiling. She tried not to stare at the gun. She reminded herself that all he knew about her lately was what he'd seen on the news. His next words confirmed this judgment.

"Did you come here to kill me?"

"Of course not."

"Then why?"

Bethany took care to make no sudden moves. She remembered the first time they'd met, volunteering at a soup kitchen a few blocks from the Barnard campus, nine or ten years ago. Earl in those days was doing something clever on Wall Street, and they struck up a distant, careful friendship. Earl had been to law school and enjoyed giving advice. When Annabelle met him, she'd speculated that he was after Bethany, but Annabelle said this of every man, particularly the ones she herself was after.

By the time Bethany was a senior, Earl had retired with his millions and moved to Italy, and he made Bethany promise to visit during her time at Oxford.

She promised, but when she finally made the trip, between terms her first year, she was careful not to go alone. She took along her running buddy.

"Would you mind putting down the gun?" said Bethany. She gestured toward the muted television screen. "I'm not who they say I am."

He lowered the muzzle only slightly. "I asked why you're here, Bethany."

"Because I need your help."

"I'm not going to hide you. I'm not going to drive you to some secret meeting where you pick up a false passport or whatever you people do."

"What people are those, Earl?"

"I don't know. Spies. Terrorists. Whatever you've turned into."

All at once she understood. "The Italian police have been to see you, haven't they? Asking about me?"

"*Polizia di Stato* and *Carabinieri* were both on my doorstep the day after you left the States."

"Whatever they told you, it isn't true." She took a small step in his direction. "Come on, Earl. This is me. This is Bethany Barclay. I'm not some crazy killer. You know that. I'm here to pick up whatever Annabelle gave you to hold for me. That's all."

The gun was pointing at the floor now. "I'm retired, Bethany. That's the big advantage of working on Wall Street. If you can keep from getting indicted, you can retire early. Well, that's what I did. I'm retired, and I haven't been to America in probably six years. When on earth would I have seen Annabelle?"

"This past December." She tried a smile but he didn't return it. "In November she hired a private investigator to look into your affairs. In December she traveled all over Europe, including Italy. On her sister's passport, by the way. Anyway, she came to see you and she entrusted some document or manuscript or something to you. And now I'm here. You can give it to me."

He glanced at her backpack. "Do you have something for me?"

Bethany frowned. "I can't believe you need money."

"Everybody needs money. But that's not what I'm talking about."

"I don't understand."

"A message. A note. Something of that nature."

"You mean the photograph."

His voice was bland. "Photograph?"

"I don't have it with me, Earl. I sent it

somewhere else. For safekeeping."

The gun came up again. "In that case, I think you should go."

"You're saying it's not for me?" Kicking herself mentally for her prideful assumption. "It's for whoever has the other half of the photograph?"

"All I'm saying is that it's time for you to go."

The library door burst open. "Maybe not just yet," said Teddy Bratt.

Teddy seemed hardly the worse for wear. The pouchy eyes were wilder, perhaps, and a stiffness on his left side was no doubt the result of Felicia's bullet, but it still took him no time at all to disarm Earl Hagopian, whose gun turned out not to be loaded. And it took him scarcely more to get Earl to talk, once he was safely tied to a chair — Bethany's enforced contribution — with Teddy's gun prodding at his neck.

Yes, yes, yes, Earl admitted. It was all much as Bethany had said. Yes, Annabelle came up in December. She didn't stay long. She asked him to hold something for her, until she or somebody else came with the other half of the photograph of the World's Fair. She paid him money, he said, and implied that a lot was involved. And then —

"Let's get to the good part," said Teddy, the gun now pointed at Earl's knee.

"I don't know what you mean."

"What did she give you? What did Annabelle give you to hold, and where is it?"

Earl looked from Teddy to Bethany and back again. Despite his terror his face bore an expression of puzzlement. "But don't you already know?"

"Of course I don't know. That's why I'm asking you."

"But you said it already." Tilting his head toward Bethany. "She said it, anyway."

"Said what?"

Bethany covered her mouth, not sure whether she was about to laugh or gasp. "Teddy, all he has is the other half of the photo."

In the false bottom of a drawer in his pitted Chippendale secretary, an envelope held the missing piece. At Teddy's direction, Bethany took it out, examined it briefly, then passed it to him.

"Who is it, Earl?" Bratt was waving the photo in front of the terrified eyes. "Tell me. Tell me her name."

"I don't have any idea. I was just holding it for Annabelle."

"Why? What did she tell you?"

"To give it to the person who had the other half!"

"I don't believe you. That doesn't make any sense."

Bethany was on the sofa. Teddy had commanded her not to move. "It does make sense," she said quietly.

The giant swung her way. "How so?"

"The photograph is valuable. The woman is important."

"This thing is fifty years old! Whoever she was then, she's surely dead now!"

"You still don't get it, Teddy." She was sitting very still. She knew what he could do if provoked. "I tried to tell you in London. These are dangerous people. And for some of them — well, this is what this whole search has been about. Not Adrian Wisdom's manuscript. And not the Pilate Stone. This photograph. Nothing else."

The investigator was staring now. Not at her. Not at Earl. At the half-century-old snapshot. "Why, then?" His words were addressed to the woman in the picture. "Why is it so valuable?"

"Because of what it proves."

"Which is what?"

"Teddy, listen to me." Gently. Gently. "You can still get out of this alive. Put the photograph down and leave. Just go, and never tell anyone you got this far. If you do — maybe they'll let you live."

He extended the gun. Toward her. His arm was rock steady. "If you tell me, maybe I'll let you live."

"Teddy —"

The first shot shattered the glass. Even before Teddy could finish turning, the second caught him in the chest. The old man from Oxford and Berlin leaned over the sill and shot him twice more to be certain.

Working in silence, he checked for a pulse, then collected his shell casings and put them into his pocket. He took Teddy's gun and put it in another pocket. Then he picked up the photograph, studied it, nodded, and slipped it somewhere else.

Bethany had yet to budge from her perch on the sofa. Hagopian's eyes were comically wide as he struggled to process the events of the past few minutes.

"You're the one they call Morgan," she said.

The killer made no response. He was on his knees, methodically searching the late Teddy Bratt's pockets.

"What happens now?" she asked.

"That's complicated," he said without looking up.

"This is what you were after the whole time. Not the Pilate Stone. The photograph. You were protecting me until I led you to it."

Morgan took something out of Bratt's wallet. When he spoke his voice was tinged with amusement. "I apologize if I gave the wrong impression. But we had to have this back." He lifted his gaze her way. Faint crinkles around the eyes marked the age of his watchful face. "I take it the other half is somewhere safe. If the British had taken it off you, I'd have known."

He didn't say how. Bethany didn't ask. She'd seen Findrake's portrait at Clougham Hall, and that was enough.

"The other half is safe," she said.

"It's not life insurance for you, you know. It's useless without this half."

"I believe you."

"Good." He hopped to his feet. "Then my work here is done."

"You're letting us go?"

"You, yes. Him, no." Scarcely turning, he shot Earl in the forehead with Teddy Bratt's gun. Bethany cried out and covered her mouth. The killer ignored her. He was on his knees again, curling Bratt's fingers around the gun.

"You're insane," she gasped.

461

"Just careful." Now he was going through Earl's desk, pulling out a handful of banknotes. "Your testimony is that Teddy Bratt shot him, then was shot through the window. An assailant whose name you don't know and whose description you don't remember climbed in, stole money from both men, and let you be. The rest of the story is as it was."

"You know I can't tell anybody what happened here."

"That choice is in your hands."

"Why are you letting me go?"

"Because you cannot do me any harm. You don't know my real name or where to find me. Nor can you harm the woman in the photograph, even though we both know you recognized her face. Talk about her and you're deluded, and a fugitive, and will likely wind up shot resisting arrest." He was finished. He stepped toward the window. "In the meanwhile, if I were you, I'd keep searching for the Pilate Stone. It's the only insurance you're going to get. Just try not to get killed on the way."

"But —"

"Perhaps you should return to Rome. The lovely lady from British intelligence hasn't budged from your hotel suite. No doubt she is hoping you'll come to your senses and return. Oh, yes. I almost forgot."

"I'm quite certain that you're not the kind of man who forgets."

The assassin ignored this remark. He had a small piece of paper in his hand. "Mr. Hagopian would seem to have lied. A gun at his head and he lied. This was in his desk all along. I'd guess he was supposed to give it to whoever brought him the other half of the photograph."

He climbed over the sill, and she was alone with the cherished paper and the two dead men.

# FORTY-TWO

"You're sure they're in Rome," said Ray Fuentes.

Edna nodded. They were having coffee in the kitchen. Janice was down in the basement, playing with the laptop. The jagged photograph was on the table between them, along with Bethany's note.

"I'm sure," she said.

"You must have excellent sources."

"I do."

"I meant, you, plural. Somebody's feeding you regular and detailed information."

The Judge stirred in more sugar. And changed the subject. "Janice wants to go to Rome."

"That's a very bad idea."

"She assumes you'll be going. She wants to join you."

"I haven't decided what I'm doing." He pushed his cup aside. "My movements are somewhat restricted just now. Crossing borders would present some difficulty."

She tapped the photograph. "We should discuss this."

"There isn't much to discuss. It's obvious Bethany entrusted it to you because she didn't want it on her person. The circuitous route by which she sent it suggests she knows there's a chance your mail is being watched. Whoever has the other half doubtless is holding something of great value."

"Something like what?"

"I have no idea, Judge Harrigan. I assume that Bethany knows."

Edna sensed the determination in his tone. "You're going, aren't you? Borders or no borders?"

"I haven't made up my mind. There are things I have to do here." He pointed toward the basement stair. "If I do go, Janice can't know. You'll have to look out for her a little longer."

"Of course."

"There's still the problem of getting out of the country undetected."

"I might be able to help. Via a friend."

"You'd help me."

The Judge shrugged.

Fuentes finally smiled. "You, plural?"

In the end Bethany went back to Rome. She

had no choice. It was all very well to bribe a rental clerk with cash to loan her a car, as it were, under the counter. It was something else again to work out how to cross the sea with no passport.

And that was what she needed to do: to cross the sea.

In particular, the Ionian Sea.

She sat on the train, trying not to think about the carnage she had left behind, or the fingerprints she had left in the carnage. Instead, she studied the piece of paper Morgan had handed her before vanishing.

Two letters only:

T H

Nothing more.

Added to the paper Paramay's people had found in Teddy Bratt's safe, that made not *chess* or *mess* but *Thess*.

No doubt the rest of the word had been lost in the explosion at Amendola's loft, and as Bethany puzzled over the many possible continuations, she began to perceive, albeit dimly, the challenges facing those who spent their lives reconstructing ancient documents.

The partial word "Thess" would have to be enough.

Paul's Epistle to the Thessalonians, perhaps. Or the modern city of Thessaloníki.

Either way, pending the receipt of contrary evidence, she would assume that the answer lay in Greece.

And then there was Annabelle's cryptic message carved in the tree in Iffley. A seven, then the letter T.

She scribbled on a note pad.

T H E S S

7 T

Together they meant something. But still she couldn't puzzle out what.

Bethany put the paper away in her backpack. She turned to the window and watched the night, letting the smooth blackness soothe her roiling fears until, finally, she slept.

She arrived just before midday. She had grabbed a snack on the train but was famished. The Roma Termini was as sprawling and complicated as an international airport. She found a fast-food outlet but later could not have said what she ate. She wolfed it down on her way to the taxi rank. As far as she could tell she was not being followed. She didn't know whether Morgan really intended to leave her alone from here on, and a part of her almost hoped he wouldn't. He had saved her life three times, all to recover the photograph of the Lord Protector.

Bethany had the taxi drop her three blocks below the hotel, on the Villa Borghese side. She hurried through the gardens, watching to see if anyone else was hurrying in the same direction. She entered the hotel through the back door and chose the stairs rather than the elevator.

The suite was on the third floor, but Bethany climbed all the way to the fourth. She had to be cautious. It had been two days. There was no earthly reason to think that Felicia was still in the suite. Not on Morgan's say-so alone. Most likely the minder had been recalled. By now the room might be occupied by another guest. Or — happy thought! — staked out by someone she didn't want to meet. The Italian national police, the Wilderness, anybody.

After a search, she found the floor maid she had effusively tipped the other day against just such an eventuality.

"Oh, yes," said the maid when Bethany explained. "Your friend is still there."

Making her way along the hall, Bethany wondered whether the maid might have been paid to say that. Whether the maid herself was a plant now whispering into a radio to spring the trap. But if everybody in

468

the world was in on the conspiracy, then it wasn't a conspiracy, and she was the crazy one.

She decided she was too tired to care.

She slid her card key into the door, and the light flashed green. She stepped inside and stopped dead. She was dreaming. She had lost her mind after all. She was in a hospital hallucinating.

Curled on the sofa, watching television and eating a burger, was Janice Stafford.

Felicia heard the shriek and raced in from the other room. Her eyes widened. By now Bethany and Janice were in each other's arms, and from the look of things would never let go.

"Well, this is a pleasant surprise," said the minder, sounding like she meant it. She came over and, to Bethany's surprise, hugged her too. "I was so worried about you."

Bethany was wiping her eyes. "What are you doing here?" she said to Janice. Then, to Felicia: "What's she doing here? What's going on?"

"Mr. Fuentes brought me," said Janice.

"Ray Fuentes is here?"

"He's out looking for you." Felicia was

still smiling. "I was worried sick, but he was worse."

Bethany still had trouble taking it in. "But how did they know where to find us? To find you?" To Janice again, her beloved proxy sister: "Are you okay? Did they hurt you?"

"They didn't hurt me. They shot Mr. Carraway, but Mr. Fuentes says he's going to be fine."

She would go into that later. "And how did the two of you get here?"

"A private plane. It was so cool. I've never been in one before."

"Whose plane? Who sent it?"

"I don't know. I guess you'll have to ask Mr. Fuentes."

Evening. She sat with Fuentes on the terrace. Felicia had taken Janice for a walk.

"We're a little bit at risk," he said, all professional. "On the flight manifest we were carried as crew. Usually the government scrutinizes the passenger lists on charters."

"Whose plane was it?"

"A corporation. Your friend Judge Harrigan arranged it through another friend of hers. A United States senator, apparently." He had a glass of mineral water and was taking small sips. She resisted an insane

470

urge to grab his hand. "Judge Harrigan is also the one who told us where to find you. Right down to the hotel, Bethany. She wouldn't say how she knew. Obviously, somebody was tracking you and in touch with her, but she wouldn't give us any details."

"The whole world can't be following me." Bethany had slipped off her shoes and tucked her feet beneath her on the chaise lounge. She was terribly tired.

"Well, somebody told her. She claims her information comes from the good guys, but, to tell you the truth, I'm not persuaded that there are any good guys in this thing."

"You're a good guy," she said.

"Not really. You don't know me particularly well, Bethany."

"Maybe when this is over, we can —"

"Yes, about that." Briskly. Dismissing her clumsy efforts. For a moment she thought she would die from embarrassment. "Tell me why we're going to Greece."

She explained about the paper. "Can you make that happen?"

"I think so. Do you know where to go?"

"Not exactly. But I know where to start."

"I'll need a day to make the arrangements." He hesitated. "You do understand, Bethany, that Felicia can't go with us."

"What? Why not?"

His tone was unexpectedly harsh. "Don't be naïve. If she goes, British intelligence goes. We have to drop off everyone's radar, Bethany. Felicia and I have already discussed it. She understands."

"Does she?"

"She's on your side, Bethany. This isn't just a job for her. It was at first, but now — she'll let us go. Don't worry."

She leaned back, let her head drop to the cushion. She stared up at the stars, white and brilliant in the velvet dark.

"And Janice?"

"I know what you're wondering. The answer is, she refused to stay behind. It's as simple as that. Once she knew where you were, she insisted on coming along. She wants to help, Bethany."

"She's a child."

"She helped you immeasurably when you were on the run. She saved your life." He let the rebuke sink in. "You're right, of course. I'd have left her if she hadn't been through so much. You're an anchor for that girl, Bethany. Part mother, part sister. She's fragile. I think being left behind would have been . . . destructive for her."

Bethany's eyes were shut. "You're thinking of your sister."

She was sure he wouldn't answer, and when he spoke, she thought at first that he was evading her question.

"I told you when we first met at the Village House that I'm an army of one. That's who I am, Bethany. I'm a loner. I go after my targets, I fulfill my missions, and I do it alone. I'm very good at operating alone. Not everyone possesses that particular character flaw. Most people need other people. Janice needs to be near you just now. And, to tell you the truth, I think you need to be near her too."

Bethany felt the old embarrassment creeping up on her. Still she could not restrain a final question: "What about Ray Fuentes? What does he need?"

To her surprise, he stood up. Very fast. She opened her eyes. In her confusion, she half expected him to take a step in her direction. But when she looked at his face she saw only the same unbothered stare. "Get your rest," he said. "I'll be back in the morning."

The Church Builder sat in a café across from the hotel, sipping a very bad cappuccino. He reminded himself that the traditional beverage's origin was in Austria, not Italy. He watched as Raymond Fuentes

473

stepped out onto the pavement, turned his collar against the night breeze, and headed down toward the gardens. Harry waited to make sure that the former CIA man wasn't just making a circuit, guarding the premises. But no. He didn't come back. Perhaps he had some other mission tonight. In any case, he had left Bethany under the care of the woman from British intelligence.

Finally, they could talk.

Harry put some bills on the table and, not without difficulty, climbed to his feet. He had waited weeks for this opportunity. Even so, it was not too late. He would apologize and, with Janice safe, persuade Bethany to turn from her mission and go home. The Senator assured him that Bethany wouldn't be prosecuted. And the Pilate Stone, wherever it was, would stay hidden.

Harry left the café. He was moving slowly. The pain was intense, but he welcomed it. He had sinned, especially in his hubris, and the thorn in his flesh was exactly what he needed. He no longer possessed the agility to dart across a busy Roman street, so he headed for the corner, and it was at the corner that Raymond Fuentes grabbed him by the arm and frog-marched him into a car.

"What are you doing?" gasped the Builder,

struggling in the mighty grip. "Let me go."

"Be quiet and listen."

"People saw you grab me —"

"I said to be quiet." Fuentes drove with one hand and easily kept his hold on his guest with the other. He didn't quite shake Harry like a doll, but the bunching of the smooth muscles in his neck warned that he was capable of doing just that. "Listen carefully. I don't like having to repeat myself. You are not going into that hotel. You are not going to speak to her. You are getting on the next plane home. End of message."

Harry had recovered a bit of his gravitas. "This may surprise you, Mr. Fuentes, but I'm not actually subject to your orders."

"No. You're not. So let's talk to your conscience. You've put that young woman through enough. She's brave and she's tough and she's smart, but you've put her through one misery after another. And her friend Annabelle before her. You have a lot of blood on your hands, you and your friends from the Garden. You have a lot to answer for." His anger, Harry saw, was entirely unfeigned. He was driving very fast, the snarled Italian traffic no sort of obstacle. "And for what? All the schemes, all these machinations, because you're protecting the faith? From what? From the Wilderness?

You can't possibly think they can win. Not when the gates of hell itself cannot prevail against the church that God has built."

But the Builder, too, was tough and smart, and he had a way with anger himself. "Those are fancy words, coming from a man who used to make his living calling in drone strikes on terror targets. How many innocents died in those attacks, Mr. Fuentes?"

"We're not here to argue about our relative merits. We're equally sinful. What I'm doing is seeing to it that you don't compound your original error."

"I'm trying to help her! I've followed her all over Europe!"

The car whipped around a traffic circle. "She doesn't need your help. Frankly, every time you do get involved, you make things worse."

"You don't have the slightest idea of the responsibilities I —"

Fuentes was not even interested. "A few hours ago, I tracked a pair of gunmen who were planning to kill her at the hotel. All because of the seeds you and your people planted. All right, I stopped them. But what would have happened if I hadn't been there? This is the life Bethany Barclay lives now.

The life you and your people bequeathed her."

"That's why I want to talk to her. To get her to stop. To come back to the States."

"If you want to help her, Mr. Stean, just stay away from her. That goes for your whole group. Senator Manning. Even Judge Harrigan. That was the ultimate betrayal. You used her mentor against her, you got her best friend killed, and you nearly lost Janice Stafford too. Stay away. You don't have the right to wound Bethany Barclay further for the sake of unburdening your conscience."

The car slammed to a halt, directly in front of the Hassler, where Harry was staying.

"Go home, Mr. Stean. I'll know if you don't."

Again Harry climbed up onto his dignity. "Are you threatening me, Mr. Fuentes?"

The stony face never flickered. "You're a decent man, Mr. Stean. You'll do the right thing."

The doorman helped him from the car. The Builder watched the red taillights disappear in the traffic. Then he went in to speak to the concierge about changing his ticket.

■ ■ ■ ■

Raymond Fuentes and Bethany Barclay left Italy the following afternoon, traveling by private yacht. There were no passport controls any longer within the European Union, but a train ride would have crossed the borders of jurisdictions not members or not fully in compliance. There were fast ferries between Italy and Greece, but they required passport checks. As it happened, they were carrying false passports — courtesy of people Fuentes knew — but a border scan would have triggered alarms somewhere in the vast security bureaucracy. On the yacht they were once again crew, meaning that their identity cards would receive only token scrutiny.

"You'll have to clean the bathrooms, though," said Felicia, teasing as she saw them off.

They were on the street a few blocks from the wharf. "How much trouble are you going to be in?" asked Bethany.

"I was in trouble already."

"Won't this make it worse?"

"Probably."

"Then why are you helping me?"

"We'll cover that another time."

The yacht moved off. Felicia stood on the pier waving, like the classmates you say good-bye to at graduation, "best friends forever" whom you know you'll never see again.

As they stowed their gear in the crew bunks at the stern, Bethany asked Fuentes if he was sure they could trust Felicia.

He spoke without hesitation. "No."

"Then why are we doing this?"

He seemed startled. "I think you should ask your mirror that question."

"What's that supposed to mean?"

"Janice is safe. From what I understand, the feds are nearly ready to drop the charges against you. Nobody has any hooks in you, Bethany. You can abandon the search for the Pilate Stone."

She opened her mouth. Closed it. Tried again. "I can't," she said. "If there's any chance that it's real — well, I have to see for myself."

"I know." The gentleness in his tone surprised her. "I'm just glad to see that you know too." About to exit the tiny compartment, he turned her way once more and withdrew an envelope from his jacket pocket. "Edna wanted to make sure I gave you this. Just in case."

479

When he was gone, Bethany looked inside.

And pulled out the jagged photograph she'd sent via a circuitous route to Edna Harrigan for safekeeping: Simon Findrake, fifty years ago at the New York World's Fair. She didn't see what possible good it could do, given that the other half was back in the hands of the Wilderness, but she slipped it into her pocket all the same.

Just in case.

# FORTY-THREE

"We may have a problem," says Kenny.

The morning sun sketches intricate patterns on the carpet, but the Lord Protector is examining her toast. Her mouth shifts into a moue of distaste. Somehow in Britain the bread is always either cooked to a crisp or soft and wet. But the marmalade is wonderful, and she supposes that one balances the other.

"I don't care for indirection," she says, adding a bit of pepper to the shirred eggs. "Just tell me, please, without the drama."

Her aide-de-camp swallows. And swallows again. "Ma'am, there's a priority message from Morgan. The photograph that he recovered in Italy is not the original."

Lillian puts her sterling fork down. Hard. The room seems to shake before righting itself. All at once she feels her age. "Not the original," she echoes, seeing the work of a lifetime turn to dust, as, soon, her body will.

"No, ma'am. Morgan says it's definitely a forgery. It's well done. It's not a scan. Somebody went to the trouble to make it look real, he says. Whoever did it took a photograph of the original and printed it from the negative onto a backing that feels like the 1960s to the touch but is actually a lot newer. The forger even went to the trouble of reproducing the date marked on the edge, and the serrations fall into exactly the same pattern as —"

She waved him silent. "I see the point, boy. I see the point."

And she did see the point. She had been tricked. It was as simple as that. Annabelle Seaver had reached out from the grave and fooled her. It was pride, Lillian told herself sternly. The photo fell into their hands far too easily. Why on earth would Annabelle entrust it to a man she'd asked that fool Teddy Bratt to investigate? Anybody could have followed that trail. And Lillian should have seen that. Annabelle had been remarkably clever for a girl who, by the end, was back on the drugs. She had hidden a copy with Earl Hagopian while preserving the original . . . well, somewhere else.

The photo was still in the wild, meaning that the attention of British intelligence could still be directed to Lillian.

She had no illusions that her cover could survive that sort of scrutiny.

Kenny was speaking again, and it took her a moment to catch up with the words. "Ma'am, Morgan would like to know if we'd like him to follow WAKEFUL to Greece."

The Lord Protector glared up at her aide. Was it her imagination, or was his posture a tad less deferential than yesterday? When had his voice developed this timbre of mild condescension?

"On no account," she said. "He's to do nothing. Absolutely nothing. Is that clear?"

"Yes, ma'am" — although his tone said *No, ma'am.*

Lillian felt an unaccustomed urge to explain her thinking. "He failed us, dear boy. He let himself be snookered by a dead woman. He's not what we need."

Kenny processed this. She didn't like the way he was suddenly processing everything. "What would you like me to do?"

"I want you to call Stavros and tell him I need his house for . . . oh, let's say two weeks. Then tell Ms. Sunderland to start packing. Call my pilot. We leave today. And have Vassily send some of his people to meet us. The bodyguards aren't enough this time. We need some people who are willing to be a little violent."

"How many people should I ask him for?"

"Kenny."

"Yes, ma'am?"

"You're so smart. You decide."

The man known as Parmay is seated in his office on an upper floor of the hideous modern building housing the Secret Intelligence Service, a birthday-cake structure situated on the Albert Embankment at Vauxhall Cross, known to its neighbors as Legoland. He has a view of the Thames, but just now his back is to the view. He is perched on the edge of his desk. His arms are folded and his face is thundery.

"You lost her twice, Agent Latif," he says. "Not once, but twice."

Felicia is seated primly on the other side of his desk. "Yes, sir."

"You let her go to Lake Como, and then you let her depart on a yacht."

"Yes, sir."

"With Fuentes and that hacker girl."

"Yes, sir."

"And you don't know where the yacht is headed."

"Not for certain, sir."

"No point in lying to me. You know we can track the yacht."

"I imagine that will take some time, sir. Unless you want to go to the trouble of asking the Americans for satellite imagery — a request you'd have to justify in writing — all you can do is send people to nose around the docks until you can work out which yacht it was."

Paramay nods. "I see. You think you're rather clever, don't you, Agent Latif?"

"It's been said of me, sir."

"You seem confident that I won't discharge you or have you thrown in prison."

"Not for misconduct in an unsanctioned operation. No, sir."

"Then why are you bothering to file a report at all? Ah." He smiles faintly. "You want something."

"Yes, sir."

"Explain yourself."

"Sir, Fuentes will notice surveillance. There is no way we can keep Bethany under observation any longer anyway. There is no possibility that he would have let me accompany them in any case."

"Go on."

"My advice is to wait. Sooner or later, Bethany will surface, and the Pilate Stone with her. Meanwhile, we have a bigger problem here at home."

"Findrake, you mean."

"Nobody else would have blown up Amendola to stop us from meeting him."

Paramay sighs. "I'm doing what I can, Agent Latif. I have people watching him. Listening to his telephone. It's harder now for him to call in all the favors he's owed. He's essentially in prison."

"Except that you can't move against him."

"Not formally. Not unless that photograph turns up." A sidelong glance. "I don't suppose, Agent Latif, that you'd happen to know its whereabouts."

"No, sir. From the little Bethany told me about her trip to Como, however, I think that Morgan may have it."

"In which case Findrake remains immune."

"Sir, my advice is still to wait. It may yet fall into our hands."

"And do you have any basis for that . . . prediction?"

"Only faith, sir. Only faith."

# FORTY-FOUR

A crypt likely meant a church or a monastery, and Thessaloníki was populated by hundreds, some more than a millennium old. On their first morning, as an exhausted Janice slumbered in the bedroom of the hotel suite, Bethany and Fuentes sat in the parlor working out a plan. To visit each in turn was impossible. They had to narrow it down.

The manuscript pages Fabiana Cialdini had provided were before them. So was the word THESSA, which Bethany had scribbled on a separate bit of card, and the 7 T, which nobody could place.

"I still don't know what it means to descend according to Tertullian," she said. "I've looked all over the Web."

"Maybe you're being too literal. Tertullian is credited with developing the doctrine of the Trinity. He wasn't the first of the church fathers to comprehend the Trinity — credit for that usually goes to Theophilus — but Tertullian was the most unequivocal."

Bethany looked at him in surprise.

"We read him in seminary," he explained, and if a man like Fuentes could look embarrassed, he would have. "Tertullian also argued that we are always at war with ourselves. The seeds of the good are planted in each of us at creation. Satan tries to obscure them, but baptism grants us sight. The battle is over our ability to see what God has planted within us."

Bethany smiled a bit. "That's all very interesting, but I don't see how it's helpful."

Fuentes moved hastily on. "Let's assume that the reference to falling is literal," he said. "Not a spiritual fall, but a physical fall. This suggests that the crypt is elevated. Built into a hill, a mountain, something like that."

"It can't be a gradual slope," said Bethany. "The fall wouldn't kill you. So it has to be a cliff."

They were breakfasting from a tray of cold cuts, buns, yogurt, and a warm dish of cracked wheat known as frumenty.

"There are no cliffs in Thessaloníki," said Janice from the doorway. "The highest elevation is a couple of hundred feet." She saw their facial expressions. "What? I read an article about it once."

While the women hugged, Fuentes studied a map. "So the cliffs have to be outside the city."

"How far away?" asked Bethany, leaning close to look. "How many monasteries are we talking about, then?"

Janice's mouth was stuffed with pastry, but she still managed to laugh. "You guys are cute together."

Bethany hastily moved over. "Very funny."

"Anyway, see this?" She had the manuscript pages in her hand. "Why didn't you show me this before? I could have told you."

She was pointing at the line that read 7 T.

"We looked at that already," said Bethany gently. "There's no chapter seven in Thessalonians, so it's not that. And there's no road of that name —"

"That's because we're not supposed to be in Thessaloníki. We're supposed to be in Thessaly."

"What?" said Fuentes and Bethany at the same time.

"I told you, you guys are cute together."

"Come on, Janice," said Bethany. "What's Thessaly?"

"It's one of the old Greek states. Don't you guys know *anything*?"

"But why do you think we're supposed to be there?"

"Because Meteora is in Thessaly." She saw their blank stares. "Oh, guys, come on. Meteora? The seven monasteries at Meteora? Hello?"

Fuentes was growing impatient. "Okay, so there are seven monasteries. So?"

"So, 7 T — seven for the seven monasteries, and T for Thessaly again."

"There are probably lots of places with —"

Bethany put a hand on his arm. "Let her finish. This is how her mind works. Tell us, honey. How do you know?"

"The Meteora monasteries are famous. They're all on these jagged peaks. They built them around the tenth or eleventh centuries, and they're on these peaks for security against the hordes. You have to climb these winding stairways to get there. They go on forever, all the way up the cliffs. And they say, if you take a wrong step? You can fall and kill yourself."

They rented a car. Fuentes wanted to go alone, but Bethany wasn't having that. She wanted him to stay and look after Janice, but he said that was out of the question, and Janice threw a fit. So in the end they all three piled in. The drive would be between two and a half and three hours, depending on traffic and weather. They would be climbing a lot of winding roads, said the concierge, and storms could appear out of nowhere. All three recognized the other risk, the reason that Fuentes and Bethany had each tried to go alone: a high winding road would be the perfect spot for an ambush.

There were moments when they wondered whether they were being followed, and Fuentes several times noticed a helicopter he seemed not to like, but nobody attacked them.

"We made it," said Bethany as they descended the final pass. She hadn't realized how tightly her fingers were gripping the console. "We're safe."

"Possibly," said Fuentes. He saw her stricken look. "Probably."

A broad gray valley opened before them. Traffic was suddenly heavy. They were stuck behind an old Dodge panel truck. A helmeted man on a red Vespa weaved between cars but never glanced their way.

"They didn't ambush us," Bethany pointed out.

"Maybe they're waiting for us in Meteora," piped Janice from the back seat. She sounded more excited than worried.

"Maybe they know where we're heading."

"We can still turn back," said Fuentes. "We can give what we have to the authorities and let them worry about the Pilate Stone."

Bethany thought about Annabelle's sacrifice and the trail of bread crumbs she'd left; and about the lives the search for the Stone had claimed; and about her own desperate need to *see*. "No. We go on."

"Janice could be right." He studied the sky uneasily. "The Wilderness might very easily be waiting at the other end."

"We've gone too far. If we give up now, we'll always be worried about where they're waiting."

Ray nodded. "On to Meteora, then."

Janice rubbed her tummy. "I hope they have a McDonald's there."

In Meteora they parked the car in a lot and were immediately besieged by street peddlers selling souvenirs, quilts, honey, and everything else they didn't need to be burdened with. They found a cab to take them to the foot of the cliffs, and a pedicab to take them a little higher. The monasteries were in view now, each set on its own impossibly high and narrow mountain.

"Where do we start?" Bethany whispered.

The guide overheard. "May I ask what you

are looking for in particular, miss?" he asked in articulate if heavily accented English.

"Which is the least accessible?" asked Fuentes.

"Sir, all of the monasteries of Meteora are accessible, but only with some difficulty."

Bethany looked up and down the road. The crowds were heavy, tourists in shorts and tank tops, oblivious to how their clothing would likely insult the monks.

"There are only seven," said Fuentes. "We can visit them all, I guess." He sounded distracted. Following his gaze, she saw another helicopter. And she knew that he was wondering, as she was, whether it was the same one.

Janice spoke up: "Is there a monastery where you can only go like one at a time?"

The guide turned toward her, confused. "Miss?"

"Where only one person can go in?"

"No, miss. They are accustomed to tourists."

But Janice was not ready to give up. "There! What's that one?"

They all followed her pointing finger. Off on a cliff at some distance from the others stood another monastery with a tiled roof and turrets.

"Miss, that is the Monastery of St. Theodore the Tyro. It does not receive tourists."

"You said they are all accessible," Bethany objected.

"Yes, miss. But you asked about Meteora. St. Theodore is not properly part of Meteora. The monks keep to themselves."

Fuentes had his binoculars. "And what's that?" Again they all looked. A gray blur was moving toward the mountaintop from a platform on an adjoining hill.

"Sir, that is the cable car. The monks of St. Theodore follow a very old rule. They open the gate only twice a year, March and September, for the equinoxes. If you wish to go any other time, you must take the cable car."

"How high is it?" asked Bethany.

"Miss, the monastery is four hundred meters up. About thirteen hundred feet." He chose his next words carefully, mistaking her inquisitiveness for fear. "Miss, the cable car is very safe. However, the monks do not always allow visitors. And the car will hold only one of you. They will not allow two."

"It's a one-person car?"

"Yes, miss. One person only. In earlier times, there was a device to allow the monks to open the bottom of the car while it was in motion, so that their enemies could not use it to gain entry. The government of course no longer allows such devices."

*Sed unus homo potest.* But only one man can do it.

*Et impium judicabit ceciderit.* And the wicked will fall.

They had found the *crypta.*

"They're in Meteora," says Kenny. "We have a confirmed sighting."

The Lord Protector nods. She and Melody are having tea, and it is to Melody that she directs her response. "Sometimes, my dear, you must let your prey lead you a bit. This involves the risk that they might escape, but the potential rewards are considerable."

"Do you think that's where the Pilate Stone is hidden?"

"They would certainly seem to think so."

They are seated on the veranda of an elegant whitewashed house near the edge of Katerini, a tycoon's hideaway borrowed for the occasion. Beyond the stone walls, the Aegean Sea is a crystalline blue. Most of the house staff has been furloughed, with pay, for the duration. Only two maids and the cook remain. Lillian Hartshorne's party numbers eight: herself and Melody and Kenny, a communications specialist, and four armed guards.

In case Findrake gets cute.

Kenny has withdrawn, and the two women are alone again.

"Why are we still sitting here?" Melody asks.

"Because we're having tea, my dear."

"Shouldn't we be going to Meteora?"

A rare smile tugs at the Lord Protector's papery lips. "You cannot do the work that we do without the proper degree of patience."

"Yes, but if they get away —"

"They won't get away. Findrake would never allow it."

Melody puts her cup down with a snap. "He's here?"

"Oh, no, my dear, no. I doubt that very much. The British practically have him under house arrest. But Findrake is clever. He'll have a hook into them somehow. Of that I'm certain."

"But —"

"Don't worry, my dear. We'll be on the way shortly. But, first, let's finish our tea like civilized people." She offers a silver tray. "Have another biscuit, dear. They're local, but they're quite tasty."

They were able to drive partway up the adjoining cliff, then got out and walked. The cable car terminated at a small stone building with a heavy iron door, locked. A bearded monk of indeterminate age peered at them through a grate. He and the guide conducted a swift, disagreeable conversation.

"Miss, he says that the monastery does not receive tourists."

"Please tell him that we are not tourists," Bethany said.

"Miss, he says you must go around by the gate and wait."

"The gate doesn't open again until September."

"Miss, he says you must wait."

The grate slammed shut.

"Let me talk to him," said Fuentes.

"No," Bethany said.

He saw her face. "You're not getting in that thing alone."

She pulled him to the side. "That's exactly what I'm doing. It will hold only one of us, and I know what I'm looking for, down to the last detail. You don't. Also, if something happens, you have to take care of Janice. Get her out of here safely. Back to the States."

"Bethany, come on. It's dangerous —"

"Don't go all macho on me. You know I'm right."

Janice was somehow beside them. Her dark eyes were wide and frightened. But her voice was strong. "She's right, Mr. Fuentes. She has to go alone."

Fuentes shook his head. He gestured toward the door. "Even if I agreed with you, he won't let you in."

"Yes, he will." She turned to the guide. "Please knock again."

"Miss, we should go."

"No. Not yet."

"I am sorry, miss. They will not receive you."

"Knock again."

"Miss —"

"Just do it, please."

The guide took one look at her face and hastily complied. The monk opened the grille and snarled something. Before the guide could translate, Bethany stepped up to the door.

The monk stared, scandalized, and was about to shut the cover again.

She said, quite loudly, *"Sed unus homo potest."*

The monk whispered something.

"Miss, he asks you to say those words again."

*"Sed unus homo potest."*

The monk turned to the guide, snapped

out a series of sharp sentences, and closed the grate.

"Miss, he says you may proceed. However, women are not permitted to wear trousers in the monastery. You must wear a long skirt."

"I didn't bring one."

But the guide was impervious to sarcasm. "Miss, as you can see, the cable car is departing. The brother will proceed to the monastery and bring suitable attire. A long skirt and also a long-sleeved top."

"Where am I supposed to change my clothes?"

"Miss, you are to put them on over what you are wearing now."

It was well more than an hour before the cable car returned. The helicopter passed overhead twice.

"You shouldn't wait for me," said Bethany. "You can't be on those roads after dark. Who knows what could happen?"

"I'm half-crazy to let you go over there by yourself," Fuentes said. "I won't go the rest of the way by deserting you."

"I'm thinking about Janice —"

"Me too," said Janice. "And Janice is staying here."

Bethany shook her head. "Cell phones

don't work up here. You won't be able to call for help."

Fuentes was firm. "And you can't call us if you get into trouble. There's no way we're leaving. And if you're not back here in a reasonable amount of time, I'm going to drive around to that gate and knock it down."

"Me too," said Janice.

The monk opened the door. He handed her the heavy wool skirt and sweater, watched without expression as she fixed them over her loose clothing, then studied the result critically.

He nodded.

Bethany turned to Fuentes. This time she did take his hand.

"You're a good man," she said. "Take care of her."

"And you take care of yourself."

"Miss, he says we must hurry," said the guide. "He will soon change his mind."

About to say something else, she changed her mind and kissed Fuentes on the cheek, then turned and hurried through the door. The monk showed her how to climb into the car and secured the safety panel.

He also had a parting word of advice.

The guide translated. "Miss, he says to stay on the bench or you may fall. He says do not address one of the brothers unless you are addressed first."

"Is that a special rule you have just for women?" she asked, but neither of the men heard because the guide had pulled a lever and the cable car, drawn by gravity, had begun its swaying journey.

As the car descended — to rise after the midpoint by a counterweight-added climb — she fought the urge to turn and look back at Fuentes and Janice. The car swayed. Instinct made her brace herself against the sides, although there was no real point. If the car fell, it fell. Better this way than how Annabelle died; or Grant Apple or Adrian Wisdom or Elliott St. John or any of the others.

Still, she didn't look down.

*If I were you, I'd keep searching for the Pilate Stone. It's the only insurance you're going to get. Just try not to get killed on the way.*

Advice from a hired killer.

And the man called Morgan was right. Finding the Stone was the only way to buy her long-term safety. And Janice's.

Now at last Bethany did turn to look. She couldn't help it. Even from this distance, she could see that Janice had her head buried against Fuentes's shoulder. He in turn had a strong arm around the girl, but

501

his eyes were on the cable car. He didn't wave. She didn't wave back.

The cables sang and sagged under the car's weight, and the gentlest of breezes made her rock so hard she worried about wind shear inverting her. But even while holding on for dear life, Bethany kept her eyes locked on her two remaining friends in the world until they vanished into the blue mist.

# FORTY-FIVE

Eight vertiginous minutes later, the car scraped through the portal and into the monastery of St. Theodore the Tyro, then shuddered to a halt. Bethany tried to work the door but was unable to figure it out. A monk who looked to be several years her junior manipulated the latches and held the door open. He wore the *riasa* and colorful *analavos* common to monks of the Great Schema.

"Don't send the car back," she said at once.

The young monk looked scandalized, and Bethany realized that she had been here only five seconds and had already broken the only rule the older monk at the other end had recited.

"The car is staying right where it is," he said rudely and with an American accent. "It stays there until you depart in it. Which I hope will be soon." He noticed her expression. "I'm from Queens."

The chamber they were in was small, consisting mainly of machinery and counterweights for the cable car. A narrow passageway led into the monastery proper, and she realized that the room had been designed to facilitate the warding off of attackers.

"What is it that you want here?" the monk asked.

"I would like to visit the *crypta*," she said.

"We have a number of crypts. The public is not allowed."

"This one houses a relic."

"We have a number of relics."

He was waiting, she realized. Waiting for her to come up with the proper words, as she had at the cable car terminus.

So she offered the only other Latin phrase she knew: *"Et impium judicabit ceciderit."*

The monk took a step back. His robe brushed the stone floor. "And you didn't fall. That doesn't prove you're not wicked." He slid his hands together in front of his chest, creating the illusion of a clean unbroken sleeve. "Where did you read those phrases?"

"A scroll from the fourteenth century."

"Why do you want to visit our crypt?"

Instinct told her not to dissemble.

504

"There's an ancient stone that a lot of people are looking for. Some people have died searching for it. A man named Adrian Wisdom says it's here. In one of your crypts."

The monk seemed amused. "That's his actual name? Wisdom?"

"Yes." She hesitated. "He died. I think it was to keep him from revealing where the Stone was hidden."

"Disclosing."

"I beg your pardon."

"Only God can reveal. Humans merely disclose." As she puzzled over this philological question, he continued, "If lots of people are looking, then this stone of yours is valuable."

"I'm told that it is."

"Is that why you're looking? For the money?"

"No."

"Are you a scholar?"

"No."

Perplexity. "Are you a religious searcher, then? Do you need to find this stone to confirm something about your faith? Because if your faith is built on the evidence of what man has created, it is a weak faith indeed."

His tone was matter-of-fact but the words

were like a blow. "I don't know why I'm still looking," she said at last, surprised to discover the truth of her own words. "I don't know what's driving me. I just know that I have to see it."

"Have to see it or else what?"

Bethany shook her head. "I don't know."

The young monk seemed more confused than ever. "Wait here, please."

He stepped through the passageway. It was guarded by a heavy iron gate, but the gate looked as if it had stood in an open position for years, perhaps centuries. According to the guide, the monastery had been completed around the middle of the thirteenth century. She wondered how long it had been since the monks actually had to worry about external attack.

She glanced back the way she had come. The wires hummed in the gusty wind. The cable car's far terminus was lost in the mist. She had no idea what had become of Fuentes and Janice, whether they were waiting for her return or driving up the hill toward the gate.

Bethany realized that she was ending her journey as she had begun it, so long ago in Virginia: alone.

The young monk was back.

"Please give me your cell phone. It will be returned before you leave." His pale palm was extended. She handed over the burner. "Come with me. And don't talk to any of the brothers."

"I won't."

"What is your name?"

She started to lie, then changed her mind. "Barclay. Bethany Barclay."

"Well, Bethany Barclay. Welcome to the Monastery of St. Theodore the Tyro. I am Brother Gabriel, and I am prepared to show you to our crypts. But you have only one hour."

"That may not be enough time."

"Then choose your requests wisely. We have vespers in an hour. You have to be back in the cable car by then."

He led the way through the passage into a wide lobby. Light came from high windows. A broad stair led downward. Fluorescent bulbs hung in dull brass fixtures, but there were none of the touristy accoutrements that were said to adorn some of the other monasteries — no gift shop, no postcards, no T-shirts — and the three or four monks who crossed the tiles carried themselves with a certain sense of order. All were walking purposefully. They were going somewhere.

"Why are you helping me?" she asked at one point.

"Helping you do what?" he answered.

A moment later the two of them were through the lobby and into the courtyard. Along the walkways the well-tended garden was a riot of color. Beyond a low fence date palms were surrounded by wildflowers. "There are three churches inside our walls," he said. "One is no longer in use due to damage over the centuries. One is under repair. There is also a small chapel, over there. And if you look to your left, you will see the road leading down to the main gate. The road runs for about two miles. In between is the farm."

"I imagine this place is self-sustaining."

"That is required by our rule, yes."

"I thought the Greek Orthodox didn't have separate orders."

"But we do not all live in the same way." They were descending a narrow circular stair. "St. Theodore the Tyro, according to tradition, was a soldier burned to death in a furnace during the fourth century for his insistence on praying to Jesus Christ rather than pagan gods. The monks of St. Theodore therefore lead strict lives. We attract adherents determined to live against the age." The walls were frescoed, many with images of Theodore, several showing him with a spear, others with the wreath traditional of martyrs. "You will imagine," he said as they reached the lower hall, "that there are not many brothers of my generation."

"I would imagine," she murmured, but if she was teasing, Gabriel seemed not to notice.

"We admit very few visitors. Some are necessary, in the course of business, for example. Some are seeking escape from the world for a time. A period of prayer and meditation, for example. Following vigorous examination, we will permit some to stay, but each must sign an agreement to abide by our rule when here."

"What if they change their minds?"

"They must wait until the gate opens. That, too, is a part of the written agreement."

"I wouldn't think such a promise would be enforceable," said her lawyerly half.

About to answer, Gabriel jerked his head upward. His eyes narrowed. A second later, she heard the sound that had drawn his attention.

A helicopter.

"We should hurry," she said.

Nothing to be concerned about, Bethany

told herself as they crossed the lower court. Tourists. Filmmakers. Routine police patrol. A wealthy investor headed to his castle. There were lots of possibilities apart from the most likely one.

They were standing in the entryway to the small chapel. Inside, two monks were praying.

"Please do not stare at them," said Gabriel, leading her along a side aisle. Alcoves held effigies. Although she was trying to walk softly, the sound of her feet on the brightly colored tiles seemed oddly loud. They reached an iron gate. Gabriel unlocked it with a key. The metal screamed as it scraped across the tiles.

"The crypts," he said.

They ducked beneath a low brick arch. The room beyond was very small and oddly quiet. Another gate stood open a few feet away. She saw a stairway leading down into darkness.

"What now?" she asked, because Gabriel was standing very still. His head was cocked. He was listening again. She heard nothing, but a monk who spent years in these silent halls would be alert to every peculiar sound. She tried again: "Did Adrian Wisdom make it this far?"

"I told you. I am not aware of that name."

"Do you get many visitors who ask to see the crypts?"

"No visitors are allowed in the crypts."

"Then what am I doing here?"

He stared at her. The intensity was unnerving, and the fear she had suppressed was rising to the surface. "Have you been expecting me?" Nothing. "Was Annabelle here, then? Annabelle Seaver? Or Grant Apple?"

"My superior instructed me to assist you," he said. "I know none of these people." He waved away her objection. "The crypts are very old, Bethany Barclay. Many of the rooms are not well buttressed. It is dangerous down there. Do you still wish to go?"

"I have to."

Gabriel nodded. "I cannot tell you whether you will find your stone or not. The collection is not well tended. There was a time, many hundreds of years ago, when the monks of St. Theodore the Tyro traveled many hundreds of miles to bring back scrolls and carvings from the time of Christ. The monastery in those days had the support of wealthy patrons. But the patrons are long gone, and so is the enthusiasm for the search. Our faith does not rest on dusty relics, Bethany Barclay. Neither should yours."

"I understand."

"You are deeply troubled, Bethany Barclay. Troubled in your heart. Troubled in your faith. Please be cautious in the crypts. Make no wrong turn. I hope you will find what you are looking for. And I hope that it sustains you."

"You're not coming with me?"

"My instructions are —"

Suddenly the pulsing beat of the helicopter was very loud. It had to be hovering directly over the chapel.

"Your people need to evacuate," she said. Still he didn't budge. "I don't think the people in the helicopter will harm you if you stay out of their way."

"The monastery has resisted invasion for eight hundred years."

"These invaders aren't barbarians with swords and spears."

He gestured toward the door at the far end. "You have forty-five minutes left. You must go."

"I think —"

"Forty-four minutes. At vespers the gate is locked. No one will enter the chapel until tomorrow. Take my flashlight."

"I think you should get moving."

"I shall be here when you return."

But somehow she doubted that.

# Forty-Six

Bethany descended the stairs. There were light fixtures near the entryway, but as soon as the stair made a single full turn she was forced to rely on the flashlight. By her estimate she descended two stories before reaching the ground. She was in a tunnel with bricked walls and a stone floor, and as the flashlight played over the leaks and cracks and crevices in the walls, the analytical part of her brain was trying to work out how many tons of mountain pressed down above her head.

She shivered but plunged ahead, ignoring the sounds whispering from the darkness. She ducked through an archway and her flashlight picked out a light switch. She turned the switch, and two bulbs in cages came on. Four others were burned out. She was in another chapel, complete with an altar, although by her estimation there was space for only half a dozen worshippers. The room looked not to have been cleaned in a hundred years. She supposed that the monks, if ever forced underground, could have held services here.

And wondered again who was in the helicopter.

On the far side of the chapel was another passageway. The air was cooler and there was a breeze, and as her flashlight pointed the way, she guessed there must be ventilation shafts. A thin stream of gray water trickled along the base of the wall. She heard a groaning rumble from somewhere, reminding her again of the weight of packed earth and aging stone above her.

She stumbled but didn't fall. Three steps down, and she was in another room. The ceiling was higher. The same unidentifiable sounds filled this room, but along the walls were flat stone boxes. Some were labeled with what appeared to be names and dates. Most were cracked, likely a consequence of the structure settling, and a few had crumbled with age, spilling their contents. It took her a moment to realize that the boxes were sarcophagi, and the piles of dusty debris were the remains of human skeletons.

A burial chamber.

The stones set in the wall, she realized,

gave names and dates of death but not of birth. The room was very long. The dates were all eighteenth century or later.

Plainly not all of the monks had been laid to rest here.

Another gate, and she was in an ossuary. No stones this time. Just rows of skulls on shelves, grinning in the beam of her flashlight.

Bethany swayed on her feet.

She should have brought Janice and Ray.

Then she talked herself down. They would never have been admitted. Only one can go. She was the one. The monks would have turned away a trio —

A scrape sounded in the passageway behind her. She spun, the skulls gleaming as she swung her light.

Silence. Nobody there.

She waited.

Nothing.

Something.

A footstep? The wind? She had no way to tell. She glanced at her watch and was appalled to see that eighteen minutes had passed. Less than half an hour left.

*At vespers the gate is locked.*

She would have to move faster.

Another ossuary. Another passage. Another

chapel. Then, all at once, the tunnel opened up into a wide room. The ceiling was supported by crumbling columns, and, for a terrifying moment, she was back in the crypt at St. Edmund, watching Grant Apple die.

"Stop it," she said aloud. "Concentrate."

There were three archways ahead, each with a stairway leading farther down, and she knew already there was time for her to explore only one. The silence did not fool her. She was not alone down here.

Three passageways, each identified by symbols carved into the keystone. The one on her far left was marked with three intertwined arcs or half circles. She remembered from one of her courses at Oxford that this design was known as the Triquetra, and symbolized the Trinity. The passageway in the middle bore the emblems of St. Theodore, the spear and the wreath. The one on the right displayed the image of a baptismal font.

*You must descend according to Tertullian.*

Now she wished she had pressed Ray Fuentes to say more about Tertullian this morning. She tried to remember his words. The Trinity. Theophilus was the first of the church fathers to espouse clearly the doctrine of the Trinity. The work of others arguably supported it, but Tertullian was un-equivocal.

The Trinity: the left-most passage.

She heard the steps behind her again and knew she had little time. Her cell phone was gone. She had to rely on memory. What else had Fuentes said about Tertullian? That he had argued that the seeds of the good are inside every soul from the moment of creation. Bethany racked her brain but could remember nothing else.

The Trinity was the most obvious clue, and its very obviousness left her suspicious. Adrian Wisdom had been terrified. He was writing the Pilate biography as a cover for his treasure hunt, and the clues he left behind were intended to mislead those who were on his tail.

She decided to discard the obvious. Not the Trinity. What else?

Bethany looked at the three tunnels and knew that if she delayed much longer, whoever was following would be upon her. She had to choose one, and choose it now.

The seeds of the good. The seeds of the good are planted in every soul. Satan works to obscure the seeds of the good, but according to Tertullian, they are liberated through —

*Through baptism.*

517

The image of the font.
Tunnel number three.
She started down.

"Ma'am, the guide says the monks never open the gate. There's a plowed field inside the walls. The pilot says he can land there."

"Fine, Kenny." As the helicopter banks, the Lord Protector studies the jagged landscape below. The monasteries are brown smudges atop the cliffs. She leans toward Melody, whispers loudly in her ear. "Are you frightened, my dear?"

"Yes."

"You'll be perfectly safe, you know. You'll stay outside. We'll be the ones enduring all the risks."

"Except for" — she glances around at the hard faces of the hired bravos — "taking care of . . . of WAKEFUL."

Lillian pats her hand. "It isn't an easy thing, I know. But you'll be surprised what you can get used to." She leans over, looks down toward the narrow cliff. "You're wondering why I don't just have Vassily's people take care of her. Or do it myself. Oh, yes, my dear. In my day I did a thing or two. By putting the matter in your hands, I'm doing you a favor. This is your chance to prove your loyalty." She turns back, a grim smile on her face. "Your only chance."

Bethany reached the bottom of the stair. The mountain seemed to groan and heave above her. She knew it was her imagination but she couldn't put the impression from her mind. The ceiling of the grotto was low — so low that she found herself wondering whether the Greeks themselves had been that much shorter a millennium and a half ago. Or maybe in their devotion they hadn't minded the stooped backs they must have earned from constant crouching. She had to scuttle along sideways, sliding her feet over the slippery rock, the water running over gray rock glimmering in the flashlight's beam. Ahead was only darkness and the same sounds she had heard before: the steady rush of water, and just at the threshold of hearing, the distant rumble. It occurred to her that if the rumble meant that the tunnel was about to collapse, she probably wouldn't even have time to scream.

"Stop it," she lectured herself aloud, almost jumping at the sound of her own voice.

Three rooms in, the monk had said.

At the arch, there was a little more headroom. A faded Greek inscription was chiseled into the keystone, but Bethany could make nothing of it. Peering closely she was able to make out another iron gate, standing open, probably for centuries, because it was covered in grime and some sort of lichenous plants.

Beside the gate the stone pillars had long ago started to crumble. She leaned close. The pillars in the other rooms were a mess, but these were on the verge of collapse. Somebody had propped them up with wood, but the wood was soft to the touch, meaning it was rotten at the core. Three or four good hard kicks would shatter the supports and bring down the roof.

She could be buried alive.

"Go," she said, then stepped through.

The next room had the same high ceiling and contained a crumbling stone monument that might have been an altar.

She had to crouch once more to enter the third room, and again she heard a footfall.

"Ray?" she called softly. "Janice?"

No answer. Of course not. Fuentes was resourceful, but he couldn't have broken down the massive gate.

More likely whoever was back there was whoever had arrived on the helicopter. She imagined legions of masked commandoes rappelling into the courtyard and taking over the place.

The sound again. She doused the flashlight and waited in the dank, dripping darkness. Nothing.

Something.

A skitter. A skree. A soft twitch across her ankle. She switched on the light, pointed the beam to the stone floor, and found herself surrounded by the largest rats she'd seen in her life.

Discipline held. She didn't shriek. But she did bolt, right into the next room, and suddenly there were no more rooms. This was the end.

A fresh breeze came from a dark hole in an upper corner. A ventilation shaft.

And three platforms like small altars. Bethany inched closer. One of them was empty. A second held a relic that had crumbled to dust. On the third lay a large stone fragment. The surface was covered with dust. Slowly, slowly, hoping she was doing no damage, Bethany brushed the dust away with her sleeve. Near the top, she was able to make out a few letters:

NTIUS PILATUS

RAEFECTUS IDUAE

In her mind, she filled in the missing letters: "Pontius Pilatus, Praefectus Iduaea."

*Pontius Pilate, Prefect of Judea*

And, a few lines down, in a sea of Latin

she couldn't have translated to save her life, one word leaped out:

IESUS

Bethany felt dizzy, and relieved, and disbelieving. She was in a dream.

She was looking at the Pilate Stone.

# FORTY-SEVEN

Bethany stared. The remainder of the inscription had been worn away by time and the elements. Only a few faint indentations remained. But from what Fabiana Cialdini had said, the letters could be raised again using the proper equipment.

The Pilate Stone.

The contemporary commentary of the governor of Judea on the life and ministry of Jesus Christ.

What Annabelle had died for. And Elliott St. John, and Adrian Wisdom, and Grant Apple, and Teddy Bratt, and Earl Hagopian, and Giuseppe Amendola, and countless others. Here it was, on the table in front of her.

The monks had allowed her down into the crypt without noticeable reluctance. Did they not know what they had? Was everything as it seemed? Or had they, as she suspected, reached some sort of accommodation with Adrian Wisdom? "I'll keep your secrets if you'll promise to open your doors to the one who brings the right words" — something like that?

The Pilate Stone.

Bethany wondered how much it weighed. She doubted that she could carry it, and dared not try: one slip and the entire tablet would likely be destroyed. She touched the surface again.

"What do you say?" she murmured, scarcely aware that she was speaking aloud, and to an inanimate object. "What did Pilate write?"

Fuentes, she remembered, had been skeptical. The expert he'd consulted in Virginia had pointed out that even if Christ's miracles were real, Pilate could hardly have admitted the fact. Therefore if the prefect wrote about Jesus at all, his purpose would be to make clear that He was neither Son of God nor King of the Jews.

But she wondered. Maybe this was why Professor Wisdom had quoted Deuteronomy: "The secret things belong unto the Lord our God."

Nobody could say what Pilate might have written or why. He could as easily have been confessing error and begging forgiveness. That alone would be reason enough for the Roman Empire to do its best to destroy all records that Pilate had ever existed.

No way to know until the scholars got their hands on it.

Less than ten minutes left. She had to go. Still, she lingered. Paramay had predicted conflicts, even wars, over the contents of this stone. Certainly if the brushfire war between the Garden and the Wilderness was any sort of —

Footfalls in the corridor. For sure this time.

Bethany looked around frantically for cover, but there was none. So she stood beside the Pilate Stone and waited. She wondered why her pursuer's progress was so slow.

And then she knew.

Even before the silver-haired woman stepped with difficulty into the chamber, she knew that she was about to come face-to-face with the Lord Protector of the Wilderness.

"Hello, my dear," said Lillian Hartshorne. "You did ever so nicely."

# FORTY-EIGHT

Bethany stood very still. Lillian leaned heavily on her cane. The effort of descending to the labyrinth had exhausted her. Beside her stood a slim thirtyish man holding a small gun, probably a Walther. Of course Lillian could have sent him ahead and waited upstairs, but she had wanted to see for herself.

"So this is it," said the Protector. "The Pilate Stone."

"I believe so."

The old woman shuffled toward the tablet. Bethany stepped aside. For a long moment Lillian stared down at the faded inscription as anguish and satisfaction warred on her face.

"Why didn't you stop searching?" she asked, not looking up. "Janice was free. Elliott wasn't around to pay you your millions. You had to know we'd follow you. You had to know Findrake would keep trying to kill you."

"Where's Janice now? Where's Fuentes?"

Lillian chuckled. "You're being evasive, my dear. Interestingly evasive, I might add. Your friends, I'm sure, are fine. I haven't seen them. But let's get back to you." She turned to face Bethany. "It's your faith that you're testing now, isn't it? Poor thing. You aren't content with evidence of things not seen, are you? You have to see in order to believe." The aged blue eyes searched Bethany's expression. "Tell me, my dear. Now that you've seen. Has it helped your unbelief?"

Again Bethany chose not to answer. "What happens now?"

"Now? Now we'll all go upstairs."

"And the Stone?"

"I have more people on the way. They'll know how to remove it safely."

"The monks —"

"The monks are not in a position to interfere. My people control the relevant parts of the monastery. There is no telephone, I'm told. No way for the monks to summon aid. The Council will take charge of the Pilate Stone. We will decipher the inscription, and then, most likely, make it public. Probably through a museum exhibition. We have academics who will vouch for its authenticity."

"Even after you've altered the inscription?"

The eyes flashed. "You know nothing of my responsibilities, dear. Don't presume to judge." She tilted her head. "Come, Kenny. We must be going."

"Ma'am, pardon me, but I need to search her."

"No, you don't. She's handy with a gun, but I don't think she's carrying one at this moment. Besides, she can't kill in cold blood. Only in self-defense. Am I right, my dear?" That chuckle again, sepulchral and cold. "Also, I'm her silly old Aunt Lillian. Edna Harrigan's best friend. Bethany would never do me any violence, would you, dear?"

They passed in silence along the passage and back through the chamber with the crumbling monument. When they reached the room where the faded Greek inscription emblazoned the single arch, the Lord Protector finally spoke.

"Don't worry, dear," said the Lord Protector. "We're not going to do you any harm. Are we, Kenny?"

The aide was walking behind them, his eyes locked on Bethany in case she tried something. "No, ma'am," he said.

"All these years," said Bethany suddenly. "All these years, you've been lying to Judge Harrigan. How could you do that? How can you look at yourself in the mirror?"

"Hear that, Kenny? Even now, her first thoughts are of others. A remarkable girl." To Bethany: "I wish we had gotten to know each other better before these unfortunate events. We could have worked well together."

"You're insane."

The words popped out. She hadn't meant to say them, not least because she was frightened about what the response might be. But the Lord Protector only nodded.

"I know it must seem that way to you, dear. Visionaries are never seen clearly by their contemporaries. Pursuit of a greater future will often put one at odds with one's time."

A greater future.

*Poor thing,* Lillian had said. *You aren't content with evidence of things not seen, are you?*

They were in the second ossuary, the one where the pillars were propped up with rotting wood.

"You're not some activist contributing to the right causes," said Bethany. "You kill people."

"So do you, my dear." She spoke with

529

simple complacency. "Every time one of your tax dollars pays for a bullet fired from a policeman's gun or a missile fired from a drone — Kenny, get her!"

But Bethany had dived into Kenny's knees, battering them hard with both forearms, the way Vivian taught. She was supposed to roll over and wind up on her feet, but Bethany had never managed it on the mats, and in the tunnel she did even worse. Even as the aide cried out and collapsed, his gun flying, she rolled against the wall, upside down, then onto her back.

With her feet against the wood.

Lillian saw what she was doing before Bethany realized it herself. "No! No, you cannot! You dare not!"

But she did. Kenny was shaking himself off. He turned her way. She kicked out as hard as she could. Not against Kenny. Against the rotten beams supporting the pillar.

Nothing.

He grabbed at her but she managed to dodge him and find her feet. She swung a heavy stone and caught him across the face. She swung it again but missed him and struck the wood.

It splintered.

The ceiling groaned.

She began attacking another pillar.

"Stop her!" the Lord Protector shouted. "No, no, don't worry about me, stop *her*!"

For an instant, Kenny hesitated, working through the options — get his boss out safely or try to prevent the collapse — and an instant was all Bethany needed. She kicked a third pillar, then put her shoulder into it. She shoved hard. The pillar shuddered, then went, and, with a roar, everything else went too.

# FORTY-NINE

Bethany spent a few days in a local hospital, but had no memory of the first two. On the fourth day, after two surgeries to stop internal bleeding, she was airlifted to Athens. Fuentes and Janice hardly left her bedside. They filled her in on the news. An entire wing of the monastery had collapsed. Age, said the experts. Poor maintenance. Nothing to be done. The ossuaries were gone, and with them all the precious relics the monks guarded.

"All?" asked Bethany.

"All," said Fuentes.

Janice squeezed her hand.

Lillian Hartshorne was at her chalet in the South of France. There was no record that she had been to Greece in years.

No trace of Lillian's hired guns had been found at the scene. But the body of a controversial American talk-show host named Melody Sunderland was one of five pulled from the rubble. Nobody knew what she was doing there. Nobody knew she was in Greece.

Melody's book sales went through the roof. Under her will, the proceeds would fund her favorite animal shelters.

A quiet man arrived from the American embassy, and from the looks he and Fuentes exchanged, Bethany understood his function.

She said she would see him alone.

"All of the charges against you have been dropped," he said. "I wouldn't be surprised if there was some compensation for the terrible ordeal you've been through."

"Paid for by whom?"

"A grateful government."

"Grateful for my silence?"

"Grateful to you for paths of investigation you've opened up."

"Investigations of what?"

"I apologize, Miss Barclay. I'm not permitted to say."

Later that day Felicia came.

"Paramay says —"

Bethany raised a hand. "Let me guess. He's going to pay me too."

Her eyebrows lifted comically. "What? Oh, no, no. He says to tell you, job well done. He's given to understatement."

"Is he angry? That he didn't get the Stone?"

"I think he understands why you did what you did."

"Do you understand?"

"Yes."

"I'm sure you do understand." Bethany eyed Felicia with curiosity. "Was it Fuentes you were in touch with?"

"I beg your pardon."

"Those times I caught you texting and you cleared the screen before I could see. That wasn't British intelligence. You had a secure phone for that. You were in touch with someone else." Felicia said nothing. "If not Fuentes, was it the other side? Findrake?"

"No."

"Then who?"

"My pastor."

Bethany had not thought herself capable of surprise. "You were in touch with your pastor? All that time in Berlin and Rome?"

"Yes."

"Why?"

She said the pastor's name: a big American activist, quite conservative. "A friend took me when he was here on a crusade a few years go. I went for laughs. I wound up converting."

Bethany was caught up short. "You?"

534

"I know. The last one you'd expect, right? But the Lord moves in mysterious ways."

"He does indeed." For a trembling moment she was back down in the crypt, kicking away the support, bringing the ceiling down on them all. "But, wait a minute. This pastor converted you. Okay, fine. That doesn't explain why you were in touch with him when we were undercover."

Felicia clasped her hands on her knee like a schoolgirl preparing to recite. "I work for British intelligence, Bethany. You know that. But two years after my conversion, this pastor told me about the Garden. He sits on — I guess you'd call it their board of directors. He's the one who got shot a few weeks ago. He's doing better." She turned and looked out the window. "He told me about the Garden," she repeated, addressing the white towers of the city and the bright blue water beyond. "He said they wouldn't want me to do anything against the interests of my government, but if I ever tired of intelligence work, they could use someone with my particular skills."

"So, that makes you — what? An agent of the Garden?"

"No. Nothing like that. They made me a job offer. They never asked me to do a single thing for them. That would have been wrong."

"Except for keeping an eye on me."

Felicia smiles shyly. "They didn't ask. How could they even know I'd be with you? No, Bethany. That's the point. I went to them."

"Why?"

"I wanted them to know you were safe. And I — well, the way you talked about Janice, I wanted to get the two of you back together. I didn't see any other way to manage it."

Bethany put her head back on the pillow. "How much does Paramay know?"

"He knows about the job offer, if that's what you mean. I may need it. He's furious that I let you leave Italy. I'm not in the field any more. I'm on a desk. I will shortly be confessing to him that I told the Garden where to find you. Frankly, he's probably figured it out already."

Bethany propped herself on an elbow. "Do you trust him?"

"Paramay? Of course."

"Is he sincere, though? About wanting to stop Findrake?"

"Lord Findrake hired him and mentored him. Paramay feels a great deal of affection for the old man. But Lord Findrake has gone too far. I know that Paramay has him watched now, which makes it hard for Findrake to call in his favors and send gunmen scurrying here and there. Unfortunately, Paramay doesn't have the legal ammunition to take him down, which is what he'd really like to do."

"I have to think about this." Bethany was on her back again, exhausted. She shut her eyes. "Can you give me a safe mailing address? Someplace where nobody will see the letter but you?"

"Of course. But can you tell me why?"

She remembered Fuentes's words. "Just in case."

It was another week and a half before she returned to the United States. Wendy Eisenman, the law school classmate who'd surprised her at Harrod's, negotiated the appropriate paperwork with the Justice Department and the attorneys general of Virginia, Ohio, Illinois, Pennsylvania, and the several other states where Bethany Barclay was alleged to have committed crimes. She couldn't bear to go back to her house, and she wasn't prepared to face Judge Harrigan. Not yet.

Instead she went to North Carolina to stay with Aunt Claudia.

She went alone. Janice Stafford, full of trepidation, returned to her well-to-do family in the Chicago suburbs and reported later, via Gchat, that all seemed to be well "for the moment."

Raymond Fuentes vanished to wherever he kept himself, but promised to check on her soon.

Aunt Claudia was wise enough to leave her niece mostly to herself. The farm was vast, and Bethany, as her strength returned, took to hiking for hours at a time. Now and then she spotted a shadow or two in the distance. Fuentes had explained that this was inevitable: for the next weeks or months or years, the government would keep tabs on her.

"Because they still think I'm a terrorist?"

"Because they're worried about what you know."

"What I know about what?"

"I'm not sure. That's what scares me."

Carl Carraway came to visit, and she was effusive in her gratitude. He was back with the Bureau, it seemed. His administrative hearing had been cancelled, and his superiors were behaving as if nothing had occurred.

"They're sweeping it under the rug, Bethany. The Wilderness, the Garden, the whole thing. It's too much to deal with."

"Or the tentacles reach too far in."

"That's possible, too," he said glumly.

From Edna Harrigan, no word.

A few days later, Harry Stean dropped by. The Church Builder was subdued and looked sick. He moved slowly, in obvious pain. Bethany tolerated him and struggled against the urge to sympathize. This was the man whose plan had cost Annabelle her life and set Bethany's own horror in motion.

"I won't ask your forgiveness," he said as they sat on the porch, watching the sunset. "I won't ask your understanding. I will ask you to consider one thing."

"What's that?"

"We were wrong in our method, yes, but our cause was just. The Wilderness is still out there. And it still has to be stopped."

"From what I can tell, they're all after each other now."

"That won't last. Yes, there will be a shakeout. I don't know how long Findrake and Hartshorne can co-exist. But sooner or later, one or the other will come out on top, and then it's back to the war. And make no mistake, Miss Barclay. Their side is winning."

She sat forward. "Why are you telling me this?"

"We have a vacancy on our own council."

"No. Absolutely not."

"We'll soon have another —"

"I said no."

He was sweating terribly as he battled the pain. "Don't let your feelings about me personally blind you to all that the Garden can still do. With new blood, new leadership —"

Trembling with rage, she ordered him off the property.

Aunt Claudia joined her at the window, watching him go.

"That's a man with a lot of burdens on his shoulders," she said.

Bethany didn't answer.

She was in North Carolina for two months. Janice visited and stayed for a week. Fuentes came three times, but never overnight. They spent time walking, deep in conversation or deep in silence, and it occurred to Bethany that in his clumsy way, Fuentes was probably courting her.

"He's a little sweet on you," said Aunt Claudia, who as usual missed nothing.

"It's never going to happen," said Bethany.

"Why not, honey?"

"We've been through too much together."

"Honey." Her stern aunt put a hand on her arm, but her eyes were soft. "That's a better foundation than the opposite."

The next day, Bethany borrowed her aunt's car. She drove into town and posted a letter to the address Felicia had given her. She despised the Garden and would never be a part of it, but there was another way to approach the problem.

Two weeks later she had a reply, also by post. Felicia's letter was brief and to the point. Bethany read it twice, then went downstairs to the parlor, where Aunt Claudia sat reading.

"It's time for me to go."

Her aunt put her Bible aside. "So soon?"

"It's been eight weeks."

"Where are you going?"

"Back to Virginia."

"Reopening your house?"

"No. I'm selling it. But there's somebody I have to see."

Claudia gave her niece a long look, then a long hug. "Go with God, honey."

Good idea, when you're off to see the Devil.

# FIFTY

They sat in the gazebo in the middle of the tulip garden, sipping iced tea as the August sun blazed down.

"It's so good of you to come visit an old woman," said Lillian Hartshorne. She was in a wheelchair. There was a cast on her lower leg. "You really are a very sweet girl."

"That's not a word that's usually applied to me."

"Because most people see only inessentials." She nibbled on a cucumber sandwich. "You heard about Edna, I suppose?"

"She moved to Charlottesville. Nearer her nephews."

"Those boys only care about getting their hands on her money. They'll be the death of her, mark my words."

"Unless you are."

The Lord Protector's eyes flashed. "There is no need for rudeness, my dear. I adore Edna. And you should repair your relationship with her. She misses you terribly. It hurt her to use you as she did. She is in pain, my dear. She needs your forgiveness."

"Does she know about you?"

"I suppose by now the Builder has told them all. That equalizes matters a bit. One of our greatest advantages in recent years has been our relative anonymity." She signaled to a steward, who hurried in from his post outside. "Charles, this ice is melting. Let's get some more."

"Right away, ma'am."

When they were alone again, she fixed Bethany with a clever stare. "Don't misunderstand me, my child. It makes no difference whether we are anonymous or not. The Garden can do nothing. It isn't as if they're going to hire hit men to strangle us in our beds."

"That's more your style."

"My dear, if you are going to persist in this belligerence, I shall ask you to leave. This is your meeting. I assume it has a purpose other than to insult my — ah! Fresh ice!"

The steward replaced their glasses, and a second servant brought a tray of scones and tarts.

"So, tell me, child. Tell me why you've come to visit the big, bad Lord Protector."

"I wanted to talk about what happens next."

"I shouldn't worry about that, Bethany dear." Lillian placed a thin hand against her breast. "I admire you. I truly do. We may not be active in the same cause, but we are hardly adversaries."

"You can't possibly be happy about what happened in Greece."

"I wasn't. Naturally. I was furious. I also broke my fibula and my tibia both." She tapped the cast. "At my age, mending takes a good while. If it happens at all. I'm told it may not." She smiled her pasty smile. "But I have no plans to do you any harm, my dear. There's no point. You did your job. I did mine. On this occasion, you simply did yours better."

The Lord Protector picked up an apple tart, examined it critically, then took a distracted bite. "So much work down the drain. So much planning. So much patience. Never mind. In the end, we'll get them. Thanks to you, we'll have to get them another way. Still. We will get them, my dear. Mark my words. You, however —"

Bethany tensed.

"Relax, my dear. You can do us no further harm. There is no story you can tell that anyone will believe. I'm a dotty old billionaire who gives away tens of millions a year. I have friends in most high places, and the rest of the high places I own. But you, my dear — well, your situation is different. I am delighted that you were cleared in the bombings, and I wish it had happened a good deal sooner. The FBI can be so *thick* sometimes, can't they? Still, my dear, we have more than enough evidence to make you out to be a madwoman. And, alas, in these degenerate days, the media requires very little evidence. Given half a reason, they will tear you to shreds. You must know that."

"I do know that."

"Excellent, my dear. Excellent. I ask only that you stay out of our way in the future. Stay out of our way, and we'll leave you be."

Bethany gently pushed her plate aside. "I'm afraid that might be a little bit of a problem."

"Oh?"

"There's still the matter of the missing half of the photograph."

"What photograph is that, dear?"

"The one that could lead British intelligence to the only American friend of Lord Findrake whom they never investigated. They didn't investigate you because they didn't know you and Findrake were acquainted. That missing half."

Lillian was spreading marmalade on a scone. "It's not missing, my dear. As you might remember, our man recovered it from Hagopian's place in Italy."

"That's what I thought at first too. Then I began to wonder. Why would Annabelle conflate the search for the photograph with the search for the Pilate Stone? She knew that your people would be relentless in the search for the first. Sooner or later, you'd be bound to discover Earl Hagopian's role. Annabelle would have known that."

The aged eyes narrowed. "Go on."

"I think that whatever was in Hagopian's drawer was intended to be found. It was a fake. A forgery. The original would be elsewhere."

"And you know where it is, do you? The original?"

"I do."

The animal within Lillian Hartshorne visibly awoke. Her gaze grew bright and sharp, and her voice hardened. "Is that why you're here, Bethany? Hoping to barter your knowledge against your life? The lives of those close to you?"

"There's no point in threatening me. It's too late."

"What do you mean? What have you done,

you stupid little girl?"

"The missing photograph never left Britain. Annabelle wanted you to blunder about, following her trail across the Continent, while the evidence you were desperate to find stayed right in Oxford."

Had the Lord Protector been capable of such an act, she would have leaped to her feet. The broken leg made this impossible. Still, the delicate hand flew across the table and snatched at Bethany's sweater.

"Tell me where it is."

"There's no point."

The grip tightened. "You know I can make you tell, girl."

"I told you, Lillian. It's too late." Using her first name was a rudeness, but she suspected that Aunt Claudia would understand. "Annabelle left it with an Oxford don called Gehringer. Nobody would have suspected him. I didn't even suspect him. He tried to tell me when I visited him. He kept asking where my letter of introduction was, or my token — he seemed to think I should have brought something along. He was waiting for me to show him the other half of the photograph. Then he'd have given me the half with your picture on it."

Lillian had already pressed her buzzer. Her aide Kenny and a guard were rushing toward the gazebo.

"It's too late, Lillian. Gehringer doesn't have it any more. I sent my half to British intelligence. I told them about Gehringer. They now have his half too. You're finished."

"You stupid, stupid girl. Simon Findrake *owns* British intelligence."

The words were out of Bethany's mouth before she realized she was speaking. "This is what your Council doesn't understand. There are people whose convictions aren't for sale. People who do the right thing because it's the right thing. And for most of them, it's their faith in God that gives them the strength." She was on her feet. "I don't like the Garden much more than you do, but there's a reason they call your side the Wilderness. Your world has technology in it. Wealth. But no belief. No spirit. It's empty at the core. That's why you're going to lose."

Lillian's restraining hand kept the guards outside. Her eyes blazed with hatred as she spoke. "Don't be so sure of yourself, little girl. You'd be surprised what's for sale at the right price."

"And you'd be surprised what isn't."

For a moment the anger vanished, and dear old Aunt Lillian was back. "Well, well. You've developed quite a bit of pluck. I suppose you've learned to believe without seeing, haven't you? You didn't need the Pilate Stone after all." The eyes clouded over once more. "Just don't run off to celebrate too soon. I have resources of which you know nothing."

But Bethany knew bluster when she saw it.

"I'll be looking for you on the evening news," she said sweetly. "Oh, and I forgot to mention. You'll probably be getting a call any minute to tell you that a bunch of your company's customer databases have been hacked. My understanding is that confidential account information has been stolen. Naturally, I don't approve of the groups that engage in that kind of activity. It's bad for customers, and it's terrible for business. Oh, and so destructive to the stock price."

Lillian glared, colored, and for once found no rejoinder.

"No need to bother your guards," said Bethany, smiling at last. "I can find my own way out."

Fuentes was waiting by the car.

"Well?" he asked as they drove off.

"I'm glad it's over. I think that was the hardest thing I've ever done." She looked at her watch. "Janice's flight arrives in three hours, doesn't it?"

"We'll be at the airport in an hour and a half."

"Good." Bethany shut her eyes. "Lillian is through. She knows it. The British will track her down, they'll share with the Americans — it's over."

"Don't underestimate her, Bethany. Lillian Hartshorne is a tough old bird."

"I know. I know. I'll sleep better when I read that she's been arrested."

They drove for a while in silence, each sunk in thought. They turned north toward the Interstate.

"The head of the Garden — Harry Stean — he wants me to join them. He's dying."

"What are you going to tell him?"

"I said no. But the truth is I haven't decided."

"Well, while you're working that out, there's another decision I think it's time we made."

"And what would that be?"

When he didn't answer, Bethany opened her eyes and looked at him. And it occurred to her that until this moment, she had never seen him smile.

"I think you know," he said.

# AUTHOR'S NOTE

For the sake of my story, I have made minor alterations in the geography of both Oxford and Rome. In addition, as the reader will have guessed, there is no monastery of St. Theodore of Tyro in Greece, still less among the seven monasteries of Meteora. A monastery of that name exists in Bulgaria, near Pravets, but is not the model for my fictitious abbey. The one-person cable car that I describe is not much like the one operated at St. Stephen Monastery at Meteora.

— S. L. C.

# ABOUT THE AUTHOR

**A. L. Shields** is a pseudonym for Stephen L. Carter, William Nelson Cromwell Professor of Law at Yale, where he has taught for thirty years. He is the author of seven acclaimed works of nonfiction and five bestselling novels, including *The Emperor of Ocean Park,* which spent eleven weeks on the *New York Times* bestseller list.